CALLSIGN, GHOST

THE HAUNTING SHOT

Written By: R.B. CARR

COPYRIGHT

Trient Press
3375 S Rainbow Blvd
#81710, SMB 13135
Las Vegas,NV 89180

Ordering Information:
Quantity sales. Special discounts are available on quantity purchases by corporations, associations, and others. For details, contact the publisher at the address above.
Orders by U.S. trade bookstores and wholesalers. Please contact Trient Press: Tel: (775) 996-3844; or visit www.trientpress.com. Printed in the United States of America

Publisher's Cataloging-in-Publication data
Carr, R.B.
Callsign Ghost: The Haunting Shot
ISBN Hard Cover 978-1-953975-48-5
    Paperback   978-1-953975-49-2
    E-book   978-1-953975-50-8

COPYRIGHT

Trient Press
3375 S Rainbow Blvd
#81710, SMB 13135
Las Vegas,NV 89180

Ordering Information:
Quantity sales. Special discounts are available on quantity purchases by corporations, associations, and others. For details, contact the publisher at the address above.
Orders by U.S. trade bookstores and wholesalers. Please contact Trient Press: Tel: (775) 996-3844; or visit www.trientpress.com. Printed in the United States of America

Publisher's Cataloging-in-Publication data
Carr, R.B.
Callsign Ghost: The Haunting Shot
ISBN Hard Cover 978-1-953975-48-5
    Paperback   978-1-953975-49-2
    E-book   978-1-953975-50-8

CHAPTER 1

Jack Kirby laid in the bed of an early 80's square body farm truck with a few dents and faded paint. The truck was traveling along a deserted country road in the dark of Southeastern Nebraska, a little above the posted speed limit, common for the area. The truck was as perfectly inconspicuous in the region as a Lincoln Town Car would have been in Manhattan, New York. Exactly as planned.

As the truck slowed for a four way stop at an empty intersection, Jack crawled over the passenger side truck bed. Maintaining as low a profile as possible to avoid being seen, he dropped to the ground; timing it to coincide perfectly with the truck's feigned rolling stop — no one in this country ever came to a complete stop. Jack landed with nary a sound, though there wasn't anyone likely to be out in the rural farming community at 1:45 am to hear or see him anyway. Jack, however was cautious. No need to draw undue attention, just in case there was someone out and about. In his life, Jack had seen what could happen to those who were careless based upon false assumptions.

As the truck pulled away leaving a fading glow of taillights, Jack was left in alone in the dark. However, he was in no way concerned with anything lurking in the dark. Jack understood the thing lurking in the dark that men should fear is him.

Before moving, Jack took a moment to embrace the darkness around him, allowing his eyes adjust while listening to the undisturbed rhythm of nature. Perfect cover for the night's work.

His tactical clothing blended into the surrounding vegetation perfectly. From the brown Danner Boots on his feet to his painted face and boonie cap on his head. Between the night and his attire, he was virtually invisible — a ghost.

With him he carried the tools required for the job. To put it simply Jack's job was killing. But he was not a murderous monster. Jack was an elite sniper, one of the best in the world. He killed only when called upon and only with purpose. His weapon of choice was a standard issue Remington 700 sniper rifle paired with a Mark 4 Leupold scope and bipod, was virtually the same set up as his M24 sniper system he used while in the Army, where he gained his credentials and notoriety as being one of the best. The rifle was a bolt action weapon that fires 308 Winchester rounds carrying a listed maximum effective range of 800 meters, though skilled shooters routinely hit targets exceeding 1,000 meters. In addition to the rifle, he also carried a fully loaded P226 9 mm sidearm, along with 2 reserves and a bench made knife, so sharp he could shave with it. In addition to his weapons, he also carried a 3 liter camelback full of water, a rolled up rubber mat, both slung over his back, and his state of the art communications gear.

Jack, a US Marshal and member of the US Marshal's SOG (Special Operation's Group) where he has served for the previous 4 years. SOG members perform a wide variety of tasks to include protecting dignitaries, providing court security for high profile cases, witness protection, dangerous prisoner transfers, asset seizures and fugitive apprehension, which was the Jack's current assignment. As the tactical sniper of the group Jack's mission was to get in a position to provide over-watch for the entry team.

From the drop point to his objective he had to cover 3 miles across unfamiliar terrain. This was nothing new to him. Jack was trained as a sniper by the US Army where he had served with distinction in the First Ranger Battalion. When in sniper school, one of his instructors, Sargent First Class (SFC) Bates, emphasized early on being a sniper required far more skills than sim-ply being able to hit a target. According to SFC Bates, there are plenty of people who could hit a target, but very few who could get into a position to do so consistently. SFC Bates gave the analogy of having a great three point shooter on a basketball team — if the shooter can never open to get off his shot he / she doesn't really do their team any good. Similarly, a sniper who can't get into position undetected is of no help to his team. It was a lesson Jack took to heart. He became a master at tactical movement. He became so good at moving undetected he earned the nickname "Ghost". The name remained his call sign.

Jack covered the 3 miles in a little less than an hour despite the dark and terrain to the target, a farm house where he set up an observation point. His observation point sat east of the objective; offering him a good view of the area. His chosen spot also offered him cover, concealment and a path of retreat. Moreover, as was Jack's preference because he was set to the East his spot would be further obscured by being directly in the rising son should anyone in the house be looking his way, though his expectation was to have the mission completed before the sun ever reached its zenith. Not only was he trained to look for these things his experience in the field made the decision second nature to Jack. Once he established the position he laid his mat in the desired position, set his rifle into to cover the target area and began his visual on the area. "Ghost Set."

CHAPTER 2

From his position, Jack could see the outline of a huge farm house but little detail was discernible in the dark. From the intelligence gathered before the mission, however, he knew the house was an ancient mansion. Nearly 4500 square feet, the home contained five bedrooms and multiple bathrooms, a rarity for the time it was built when most houses still utilized an out-door privy. The house had once been a grand home. At the height of its luxury it was a gleaming white but age, sun and lack of care had turned it a dingy grey. Despite the lack of maintenance, it nonetheless remained structurally solid do to how well it had been constructed.

To the right of the house from Jack's perspective, sat a huge ran down old barn; another relic of a time gone by, when the property was an active farm. Now, the owners reportedly used the barn as a garage and storage. The distance between the two structures showed a worn, unkempt yard which was partially visible from the illumination of an outdoor pole light between the structures. To the north of the barn, a tree lined driveway led to a main which intersected with another lesser used road to the West. The pair of roads created the border to the lawn. Along the yard's edge evergreen bushes were planted acting as a natural fence; though again the neglect showed as they had become overgrown and unruly.

The property was the owned by the Deen family. Befitting of the home, the family was once considered aristocracy. Now, the family was mostly considered to be bad apples by the locals. Currently, all those living in the house had spent time in the local jail for various charges and a few had even done some serious time in the Nebraska State Penitentiary in Lincoln. Their convictions included everything from minor violations such as public intoxication and possession of a controlled substance (marijuana) to more serious crimes including burglary and assault. The general consensus was the family were involved in many more criminal enterprises than those they had been found guilty of in a court of law. Thus, in Southeastern Nebraska the name Deen had a well deserved reputation for not being one to mess with.

The family patriarch, Michael Deen, inherited the farm from his grandfather years ago, being the man's only grandchild. His own father had joined the army as a lieutenant and went to fight in Korea when Michael was a mere baby. He died in the war, which crushed both his mother and grandfather.

He was raised in the mansion by his grieving grandfather and mother, who never remarried after his father's death. Neither instilled much, if any discipline, upon Michael; instead of correcting the young man the pair continuously made excuses for his unruly behavior. Thus, he never learned boundaries and grew up being mean and self centered; often bullying others at school and stealing or breaking stuff for his own perverse amusement.

As an adult, Michael became a mean drunk who spent time in and out of jail throughout his adult life including a majority of his own five children's formative years. Despite being almost 75 years old, he was still as cantankerous as ever. He would as soon slap someone as he was to speak to them. The old man figured the law was nothing more than a pain in his ass that was around to stop him from doing whatever he wanted. He believed a man should be able to have what he can hold, if others weren't able to hold their things so be it.

His current wife, Janey was of similar beliefs, she too having spent time in and out of prison for a variety of crimes. However, the majority of her crimes related to prostitution charges from when she was younger. In fact, that was how she met Michael Deen.

Janey was the mother of Deen's two youngest children, though she helped raise all five of the boys after Michael's first wife, Muriel had left him in the middle of the night while he was passed out drunk. Muriel married Micheal when they were both still very young. She fell in love with the tall good looking young man; feeling lucky to have married into such a wealthy family. It wasn't long however, before she realized much of the family fortune was tied up in the real estate holdings and their ability to produce wealth. Something Michael had no interest in pursuing. After his grandfather passed during their second year of marriage it went quickly down hill as he started drinking more and more. With the drinking inevitably came his hitting her. She finally left after receiving particularly brutal beating at the hands of Michael. While it certainly wasn't the first time he had beaten her she made up her mind it was going to be the last. Michael began punching her that night after she questioned him about Janey and his infidelity. It seemed the physical abuse Muriel could take but was unable to handle him sleeping around on her, especially with a much younger woman, made worse because she and everyone knew the younger woman was a whore.

Six years after she left, Muriel had been found brutally beaten to death. Her body was discovered in a ditch about 3 hours away from the Deen homestead just outside of St. Joseph Missouri along a deserted piece of country road. The body was so devastated from the assault and being exposed to the elements that police had to use finger prints to identify the victim. The suspicion was always that Michael had done it, though the authorities were never been able to find any physical evidence tying him to his ex-wife's death.

Of Michael's sons, four of the five boys followed the example of their father, each having been in and out of juvie as youths; jail as adults. However, Eric the eldest was the exception. As the oldest he remembered and was greatly influenced by his mother before she left. He remembered her telling him when he was a small boy not to be like his father. She reminded him the mansion in which they lived was built by men of vision and ambition and the same blood that built it still flowed within his veins. She told him as his ancestors had done, he should make his own place in the world.

After his mom left, Eric turned his focus to school and was a good student. He avoided getting involved in any of his father's schemes but kept his mouth shut about his father's transgressions to others knowing what his father's response would have been. Then the day he graduated from high school as an eighteen-year-old he joined the Army without telling his father or brothers. He left for basic training 3 weeks later. Since leaving, he had returned to his hometown on only one occasion: his mother's funeral. As expected neither his father nor his brothers attended the funeral. Eric did not bother to go see them afterwards. Instead he left town again before the hole was filled with dirt.

Of the other sons, John the fourth son, the oldest child of Janey, was by the far the worst of the bunch. John was a clone of his father in looks, tall and rugged. He also inherited his father's disdain for authority and sense of self over law and society. John was the reason for Jack's presence in the area. He recently escaped from prison as he awaited trial for three murders and a number of drug related crimes. Though John's current location was unknown a tip had come into the local police that he was in the area of his childhood home. The local police notified the state police who requested the assistance of the US Marshals in apprehending John.

The three men who John was charged for killing were former known associates of his. The four men together were suspected to be a part of a large multi-state crystal meth ring. The prevailing theory of the investigative team who originally apprehended John was he had people on his payroll inside the Missouri State Police departments and DEA informed him he had a snitch in his ranks. Instead of attempting to discover the trader, John simply killed all three to ensure he got the right one. All three murders were particularly brutal according to the file. The investigators believed John was not only taking out the trader but was also sending a message to any-one else who wanted to threaten his freedom.

According to the reports, the first victim was named Todd Love. Love was reportedly the manager of the drug ring's distribution network. Similar to John's family, Todd Love's family was full of carrier criminals, albeit with some connections to organized crime in the Midwest. It was through Love's family connections, the authorities believed the ring moved their product through distribution points in Kansas City, Omaha and St. Louis. From there the meth moved throughout the Midwest and beyond.

Love lived in a nice brick ranch style house out in the country with a big yard and tidy bushes along its porch. The home was in a very rural area of northwest Missouri between Kansas City and St Joseph. His nearest neighbor was over a mile away and property was surrounded by huge fields of the neighboring farms. Due to its remote nature the body had not been discovered immediately. Love's body was found by a neighbor who had driven onto the property looking for his lost dog. From his car, the neighbor saw the dog near the front stairs of Love's home chewing on a large bone. Getting out of his car to claim the dog, the neighbor threw up when he saw the bone the dog was chewing on was from partially decomposed body partially laying in the bushes along the front of the house. After throwing up, the man called the police to report what he found.

The coroner judged the body had been lying out in the elements for a few weeks before its discovery. Due to the exposure the job of determining the specifics details of the death had been difficult for the police. What they were able to ascertain however was Love had died from blunt force trauma. The body showed indications of being hit multiple times as there were multiple broken bones all over the body. In fact, the coroner suggested it looked as if it had been done in a very deliberate and methodical nature and there were enough signs for the investigators to come up with a theory of what had occurred. They believed that Love's killer had likely hidden in wait for him to come to home. When Love showed up the killer proceeded to sneak up behind him and hit him from behind with the blunt object, likely a baseball bat. Based on the multiple broken ribs, and scapula the investigators believed the killer had most likely came up behind the man on the left and hit him across the back with the barrel of the bat which struck the Love in the bottom of the shoulder blade and ribs. The blow likely sent him into the stairs leading to the porch of his home face first where he was hit again and again. While sprawled on the stairs, Love's legs were broken. The breaks indicating the man was being struck from behind. However, at some point the man either rolled over or was turned over by his killer. Love's forearms were shattered, characteristic of defensive wounds in what looked to be a last ditch defensive effort to protect his face. The investigators believed the killer continued his assault on the head and face long after the man had died. When the body was found his face and skull were crushed and caved in to the point the investigative team had to pick up the mess with a scoop shovel.

It wasn't long after the recovery of the first body the other bodies were discovered.

The second victim's death was even more gruesome. Thad Fischer was the suspected chemist manufacturing the meth. Fischer was a graduate from Missouri State in Springfield, Missouri where had earned a degree in chemistry. The investigation had discovered after graduation he went to work for Conagra where he worked developing fertilizers. However, he hadn't been employed by the corporate giant in the last two years according to the IRS. Instead, according to the IRS records, Fischer reported he was working as an independent contractor and farm consultant. Investigators discovered he was, in fact, working with some local farmers to ensure proper soil PH balances and fertilizer usage to be used for specific crops. According to the IRS, he had reported substantially more earnings as a consultant than he ever had as a corporate chemist. However, investigators were unable to substantiate the amount of money he reported earning from the farmers they had talked to. Investigators believed most of the money was likely from his earnings cooking meth. They were baffled as to why he reported it to the IRS however, but ultimately theorized he was more afraid of tax fraud than drug charges.

Fischer was found in his home by his mother. She went to his house 2 days after she had heard of Love's death. Knowing the two were friends she became concerned after she hadn't been able to get in touch with him as he wasn't answering either his cell phone or his home phone or even replying to her texts or emails. Out of her concern she drove to his house and let herself in the back door with the key Fischer had given her after he bought the home the year prior. The back door led into a small eat in kitchen where to her horror she found Fischer's body. He was sitting in a chair at the kitchen table with his arms zip tied to the arms of the chair. His torso was duct taped to the back of the chair and his feet had been permanently attached to the floor with lag bolts drilled straight through the top of the feet and into the floor boards. Directly in front of the body, the table top contained each of the man's ten fingers and toes which looked to have been cut off one by one with a pair of garden shears that laid in the sink. Joining the fingers and toes were Fischer's ears and tongue, though they appeared to have been cut off with a big knife which was also in the sink. Both of the eyes had also been burst leaving ghastly hollow sockets.

Because the body had been preserved in the air conditioned home investigators were more easily able to ascertain the events here. According to the autopsy the wounds appeared to have been endured over a few days. The fingers and toes had been cut off first, then likely the ears, tongue and eyes. Fischer had clearly been tortured by his killer, made to suffer a great deal before his death. Finally the killer either got bored or ran out of time and slit the poor man's throat ending his life.

The last victim, Joseph Ball was also discovered at his home, an ancient farm located within a few miles of the other two dead man's homes. Investigators believed the farm was of dual purpose to the men. First, the investigators discovered one of the older out buildings had a large cellar beneath it. Inside the cellar they found a very clean facility which was used to manufacture their crystal meth. Secondly, the farm was also believed to being used to launder much of the cash, as they were reporting higher crop yields and profits therefrom to cover some of the extra cash.

The investigators had all agreed despite the gruesome nature of Love and Fischer's death Ball's demise was still the worst thing they had ever seen happen to a man. His killer had somehow forced the man to get completely naked after which he was hog tied. Ball's hands were tied behind his back, with his ankles also bound together and then the bindings were Secured together forcing Ball into a position where his torso was arched backwards. Ball was then placed in a large corrugated steel tub farmers use for feeding and watering live stock in the barn yard. Around his neck was then placed a noose which was secured above the tub to the pulley above the barn's loft. The tub had been filled with water, but apparently not enough to drown the poor soul as his head was held above the water line with the noose. Around the metal tub was stacked trash, wood pallets and other scraps of lumber. The mound was then set a fire causing the water to heat up. Ball was subsequently left to decide whether to try and strangle himself or scald to death as the water eventually boiled. The body remained in the tub even after was the water had completely evaporated. The remaining skeleton was left clean in the middle as the man's skin and organs had cooked away and had charred to the bottom and sides of the pot once it had boiled dry. Similar to leaving a chicken in a pot to long. The forensic re - port indicated for the body to have been cooked as clean as it had been would have required whomever had started the fire to continuously refuel the blaze, despite the fact Ball would have been long dead before the pot had boiled dry.

The investigators had immediately focused in on Deen, as the primary suspect as they had in fact been working with an informant concerning the group's activities. However the informant was none of the 3 murder victims. The police had been receiving information from Evan Hawk, one of Todd Loves cousins. Hawk was one of the people used to transport the drugs around the Midwest from time to time. While Deen had insisted the mules know nothing of the group, Love had let a little to much slip to his cousin. On a run Hawk had been pulled over for speeding by a highway patrol officer outside of Kansas City. A user himself, Hawk was paranoid and appeared skittish to the officer who asked him if he had anything in the car that the officer should be aware of. That was all the prompting Hawk needed, immediately telling the officer of what hi cargo was and where it was going. The officer was stunned by the admission but immediately sensed an opportunity and alertly called in the state's drug task force division. The task force then turned Hawk into a full blown informant into the groups operation in exchange for his own freedom.

Before Hawk's traffic stop, the meth ring had been completely unknown to authorities. Since the murders, however Hawk begged for protection from the authorities. His paranoia had him fearing for his life; afraid Deen was around every corner waiting to kill him too. The task force arranged through the US Marshals to have Hawk placed under protection and the manhunt for Deen began in earnest. The authorities captured Deen two weeks later at the home of a woman who was a known associate of his. It was only three weeks after he had been taken into custody by police he had managed to escape. The investigation as to how it happened was ongoing.

CHAPTER 3

Jack diligently watched the house and the surrounding area for the entirety of the two hours he had been there. He had been trained to observe; not just to watch or look but to truly observe the details of his surroundings. One of the first days of sniper school the instructors had taken Jack and his classmates into a windowless room which was nearly empty minus a tarp sitting just off center. Each prospective sniper had with him a notebook and pencil. Their instructions were simple. They had 2 minutes to observe the room and then had another 8 minutes draw what they saw. Upon lifting the tarp the timer started. Jack immediately counted 15 items, including the tarp and pallet on which the random items were sitting. Amongst the other items Jack saw a compass, watch, an open notebook, fuel can, water can, ammo box, cot, sleeping bag, kevlar helmet, hammer, shovel and socket wrench.

At the end of the two minutes, Jack took the entirety of the allotted 8 minutes, accurately drawing each item. Jack was confident his sketch showed the items precisely as they had been in the room. Upon completion, each of the men stood in line and went into a separate room to turn in their pictures. In the room each sniper candidate would receive a pass / fail grade. Jack was fourth in line and was confident of success when he went in the room and turned the paper into his instructor, SFC Bates. Instructor Bates glanced at the paper. "Fail" he announced.

Dumbfounded, Jack asked what he had drawn incorrectly. Instructor Bates replied he had drawn every item and had placed all the items correctly. However, what Jack failed to note was the direction of the compass, the time on the watch, the lines and spirals in the notebook. He had also failed to depict what was written in the open note book, which had simply said, "Attention to Detail". Jack did not record the fact that the fuel can had a closed lid nor that the water can was open, its lid dangling from the spout by its strap. Jack further failed to "observe" the cot though folded was not strapped to army standard or that the sleeping bag was torn. Moreover Jack didn't recognize the kevlar belonged to a SSG Long from the 4th Infantry Division as was easily identified by the rank, name and insignia sewn to the cover of the helmet. Lastly, Jack failed to indicate the socket wrench had a 9/16 socket on it. Lesson learned.

From that point forward, Jack became obsessed with not only seeing, but truly observing his surroundings at all times. Now it was second nature for the man. His ability to focus on the details of his surroundings were second to none. Due to his training and experience Jack was thus confident when at the designated time he reported to the mission commander that all was quiet at the house. The mission chief, Sam Pearson, replied "Good copy".

Sam had been a member of SOG for nearly 20 years and like, Jack had also served as a Ranger in the Army. Sam was the elder statesman of the field unit and his men joked with him about needing to trade in his sidearm for a cane. While he was gruff, those under Sam's leader-ship knew he genuinely cared for them. Thus, the team was ready to run through walls for Sam, and more importantly trusted his judgment. Sam's experience taught him two things: the best intelligence is fresh intelligence and the best time to move on a target was early in the morning, getting into position in the cover of darkness and moving on the objective with the first hint of light on the horizon. The mission was no different.

The team, led by Sam, had arrived in town less than 24 hours earlier. After ensuring they had a warrant to search the property for Deen, the team had reviewed the available maps of the area, spoken to local authorities and a few locals about the layout of the objective. With the gathered information Sam and his team developed a plan of approach and apprehension. The plan broke the group into two teams: Alpha and Bravo. Each team assigned a specific role in the plan, with Jack served a dual role as advanced scout and over watch for the group. Now with dawn fast approaching and with the all clear from Jack he told the contact teams to move into position to enact the plan and breach the house.

On the signal and according to plan, Alpha team moved silently out of the darkness; moving hastily along the driveway. In their black tactical gear they were practically invisible, though Jack could depict their dark silhouettes against the slightly less dark sky behind them. The team moved directly into position along the side of the barn facing Jack. Alpha team was assigned to enter the front of the house.

On the same signal, Bravo team emerged from the shrubbery and moved through the dark to-wards the rear of the house, disappearing from Jack's view as they stacked on an old shed that was described as an old smoke house. Bravo team's assignment was to enter the rear of the home at the same time Alpha entered the front.

Jack, knowing the teams were moving into position, concerned himself with ensuring the house and surrounding area remained quiet. He knew if he allowed himself to watch the team's movement's he was endangering them. Jack understood their maneuver and trusted they would do what they needed to do while he continued his over watch, ready to take out any threats to the teams from his position. It was a job Jack had performed well since his very first mission. Similarly the teams felt safer in their movements because of Jacks' presence, trusting in his ability to spot any threats and taking out anyone should the need arise.

After moving to their respective positions, the team leaders for Alpha and Bravo teams each gave Sam the ready signal. A moment later, Sam gave the teams the order to proceed with the assault. Jack watched as Alpha Team exited the darkness from along the barn and move into the open towards the front porch and the front door, trying to take as direct approach as possible without exposing themselves to the light from the pole. Jack knew this was one of the most dangerous points in the operation as the team was exposed to possible hostile forces and am-bush. Jack also knew bravo team was moving simultaneously though their route wasn't as ex-posed.

Alpha Team made the porch and the door without incident. From seeing the drill literally thou-sands of time Jack knew as soon as the teams reached their positions they instantly stacked on the door in a text book fashion, ready to breech the compound. Both teams consisted of 4 men. The men were stacked tightly their legs interlocked as they stood shoulder to shoulder. In the stack, each man had his weapon covering a predetermined direction. As a whole the alternating weapons had with all exposed approaches covered. No sooner than had the men stacked the last man in the group bumped the man next to him to announce he was ready. That man then bumped forward into the next until it reached the man in front who pushed back until the tap was returned to the original sender. After receiving the return bump, the man announced over the radio, "Alpha Ready!" Almost simultaneously Bravo team echoed the call.

In response to the call, Sam, calm as ever, came on the radio saying to both teams "We go in 3, 2, 1".

Jack was too far away from the farm house and scanning the surrounding area for threats away from the house to actually see the teams breech the doors. But nonetheless he knew when they occurred as the moment Sam's countdown concluded he heard the distinct sounds of shotguns going off simultaneously. The guns were each loaded with breeching rounds shot into the simple locks of the two doors, allowing the teams access.

However the teams did not walk immediately in, instead each team threw in a flash bang grenade. Flash bangs are meant to shock the system of those caught in their wake as they make an incredible bright light combined with a piercing explosion that disrupts a person's equilibrium. The unexpected combination of blinding light and deafening noise disorientate anyone caught in their vicinity. Jack was certain those inside the home who had moments ago been asleep were now completely awake; though equally unaware of what was occurring, having been shocked awake by the shotguns and grenades.

As the teams performed their task within the house, Jack reminded himself to maintain visual surveillance of the surrounding area, looking for any possible dangers. This period was easily the most difficult part of the job for snipers, both the experienced and inexperienced. The curiosity of what the assault teams are doing inside the objective is often difficult to ignore; despite every sniper being told repeatedly the importance of vigilance and the need to trust the assault members to do their jobs as they trust the sniper to do theirs.

Jack recalled during the first few weeks of his first deployment he and his platoon had just re-turned to the FOB (forward operating base) after completing their mission. At the same time another platoon was also rolling in from a mission. The other platoon however had sustained multiple injuries, two of which were life threatening. After the men had received the necessary care it was explained the team's sniper and observer, a classmate of Jack's in sniper school, had gotten distracted listening to the radio and watching the door for the of the objective trying to see what the guys in the contact team had been doing instead of monitoring the perimeter. As such Jack's classmate had failed to see the movement an enemy combatant as he got into position across the street from the objective with an AK-47. As the breech team was exiting the building the shooter opened fire. It was something Jack vowed to never allow to happen. In the 12 years since he hadn't.

CHAPTER 4

Jack had marked the time on his watch as the team entered the house. His nerves began to jump after what seemed like an eternity though it was in reality less than 7 minutes since the teams entered, when the intercom in Jack's ear crackled "Alpha team. All up. All Clear."

"Bravo, all up. All clear." Jack felt a sense of relief. Not only were all his guys reported to be OK, but was further relieved there had been no shots fired.

"Give me a Sit-rep" replied Sam.

"The house is clear, target is not on the premises. Repeat target is not on the premises. We have five detainees however, repeat five prisoners. We are coming out"

Jack watched as the group exited the house by the front door through his field glasses. The group was led out by two of the officers, though with their tactical helmets and gear on, Jack was unable to specifically identify the pair. The two officers were followed out by a female Detainee, an officer, a male detainee, an officer and so forth until all 13 had cleared the house. The detainees all appeared distraught. Judging from their clothing, or lack there of, Jack sur - mised, the 5 detainees had not been expecting company when the teams hit the house. The group still seemed to be disoriented, trying to figure out what the hell had just happened to them. Or maybe more importantly, what was about to happen to them. As the group headed towards the open area in front of the barn Jack's earpiece chimed again. "Bring up the van."

Upon exiting the house the officers gathered the occupants from the home in front of the barn under the light. The pole light combined with the sun beginning to announce its arrival Jack was able to make out various details of the detainees. One of the men looked to be older than the others as did the woman. The other three appeared to be significantly younger. Even from the distance it was obvious they were all related. The officers grouped the prisoners into a tight circle keeping them covered with their own weapons despite the fact the detainees had each been shackled with zip cuffs.

The lights the of the first vehicle appeared in the driveway when a shot rang out. To his horror, Jack saw one of the detainees fall to the ground as the officers began diving for cover.

"Fuck!" Jack thought to himself. "What the hell were you doing!" he chided himself as he began searching for the shooter. As he searched another shot was heard and Jack's earpiece came to life. "He's shooting his own family damnit".

It was the third shot that allowed Jack to locate the shooter's position. The shooter was to the southeast of Jack's position, lying on the ground along a line of trees planted years before to serve as a wind break for the fields behind it. The shooter's position provided him some cover and thus it took Jack a moment to get a clean sightline.

Getting the shooter in his cross hairs Jack noted the man was using a bolt action hunting rifle of some variety with a scope. It also struck Jack the shooter was left handed and the rifle was a rare left-handed bolt action model. The shooter's position was approximately 200 meters from the group gathered in front of the barn. However, due to his position the shooter was almost 400 meters from Jack's observation point.

Jack preferred to have a center mass sight picture but since the target was laying on his stomach that was impossible. Instead, aiming a bit high to make up for the drop created by the distance he aimed for the center of the exposed man. As he acquired the sight picture he wanted he instinctively stopped his breathing halfway through his exhale as he had countless times on the range. The pad of Jack's index finger found the trigger but before he began his trigger squeeze he experienced a discernible moment of hesitation. During that moment, the man in the tree line fired a fourth shot refocusing Jack.

The GA Precision rifle's trigger pull was a feather light, two and a half pounds. Thus, the effort to squeeze the trigger was negligible. As was customary the crack of the rifle surprised Jack. Despite the surprise and the sound exploding in his ear, Jack knew the shot was true. Through his scope Jack saw the shooter's rifle fall from his arms and the man's head slack to the ground.

Despite the apparent hit, Jack worked the bolt of his own rifle ensuring another round was ready.

"Bogey Down, Bogey Down" Jack heard himself report, while experiencing, what felt to him like was an almost out of body experience, as he continued to processes all that had transpired in the last few moments. His preoccupation, with his guys in the house, his letting his guard down when they exited and the hesitation to pull the trigger on the shooter. Dumbfounded wasn't even the appropriate word to describe how he felt. The more he thought about it he felt his heart feel as if it were about to come through his chest and his breath becoming shallower.

He was snapped back to reality when his radio snapped with Sam saying, "I repeat, over-watch can you confirm the bogey has been eliminated?"

Jack refocused through his scope and replied "Negative, bogey remains down. Have yet to con-firm status beyond. Hold one, over-watch moving."

"Negative, over-watch stand fast, I will send Bravo team to ensure the bogey is down for the count."

Jack ignored Sam, taking the rifle and headed towards where the shooter laid, keeping his scope centered on the body. With the knowledge of all the errors he had just made Jack was determined to make sure the threat was eliminated to protect his team. As Jack silently moved to the down man he heard the call for ambulances in his headset. Despite his ignoring of the order and being angry with himself, Jack wasn't being completely haphazard in his actions.

Growing up Jack's father and uncles had taken him hunting every year. One of the lessons they had always emphasized to Jack was the most dangerous animal was an injured animal. Jack had discovered it was even more true when the wounded animal was a human. Sadly, in Iraq and Afghanistan, Jack had seen to many times the results when his fellow soldiers carelessly approached combatants they thought dead only to be injured or killed themselves when to late they discovered the person was not in fact dead.

Jack took a circuitous route towards where the shooter laid, moving swiftly yet utilizing as much cover as possible. Coming into the tree line about 50 yards from where the man laid, Jack weaved in and out of the sparse trees, his rifle held at the ready. The movements were to en-sure if the guy were paying possum there was no way he could get a shot at Jack without rolling over first and giving away any perceived advantage the person thought they may have. Covering the space Jack saw the body lying face down in a puddle mud. The mud, a result of the warm blood from the man's obvious wound mixing with the cold frosty ground's dirt. The blood on the ground came from a hole the size of Jack's fist had been punched through by the bullet between where the man's shoulder blade and spine would normally be. The bullet had entered just to the right of the man's neck, had expanded as it met the man's flesh and exited out the large hole. The concern over whether or not the man was still dead or alive was eliminated. Though the shot was a clean kill shot, Jack realized it was off about 2 inches from his aim point, another mistake he thought to himself. "Confirmed, Bogey eliminated," Jack reported back.

Jack stayed with body for a few minutes until the local authorities arrived to secure the scene. The body matched the description of John Deen, though Jack knew they would still need to get a positive identification at some point. Once the locals had taped off the area with their police tape Jack walked back to his observation point and secured his gear. He then slowly headed towards the barn where the team was gathered. He was still upset with himself for his mistakes and was nervous about facing the members of the assault team feeling he had let them down. As he walked he attempted to configure an apology to the team.

At the barnyard, the whole group appeared somber to Jack. He was prepared to tell the group how sorry he was but before Jack could speak Sam said, "Best we can tell the guy wasn't sleeping in the house. After the shots, his brother said there is another old smoke house on the property about 200 yards past the wood line built in the side of an overgrown dirt bank. He told us that no one outside of the family was aware of it. They said John had been staying down there. When we hit the house he must have heard the noise. Instead of running, he came back to get rid of more possible witnesses against him. The first shot hit his older brother in the center of his back. The guy probably died before he even hit the ground. The bastard's second shot injured his mom when it grazed her across the back but the paramedics said she will be fine. The last two shots didn't hit anything. The mom is on the way to the hospital and the other three are being held by the locals until we can talk to them. The youngest kid was already talking be - fore. You could tell he was in disbelief his own brother would shoot at them. Hell even the old man seemed shocked."

Before Jack could respond to the statement Jack's best friend on the unit, and alpha team leader Chris added "Thanks for nailing that son-of-a-bitch for us. Man if you hadn't gotten him we were sitting ducks out there in the open". The rest of the team nodded in agreement, though it didn't make Jack feel any better.

CHAPTER 5

ble to positively identify the man Jack
... been. They thanked the team for a job well
done. It was nearly 9 am when the team led to return home.
Despite the local's expressions of thanks and gratitude to the
Marshals the 5 hour drive from Nebraska to the team's
operations office in Kansas City was a somber one. No one
much felt like talking and personally Jack was happy for it. It
seemed the entirety of the group were satisfied being lost in
their own thoughts. Everyone except for Doug Levi, one of the
members of bravo team and the driver of the van which Jack
rode. The team had adopted an unwritten rule that whomever
was driving could pick the radio station. Doug had chosen a
Kansas City Sports Talk radio show and was adding his own
commentary to the know-it-all host's statements regarding
the Royals needs for the off season. Usually this was
something that would cause the entirety of the van to respond
with some sort of banter on a Friday afternoon, but not on this
day. Eventually, Doug took the hint and changed the station to
a classic rock station and the rest of the drive was mostly
conversation free.

The relative silence of the drive gave Jack time to reflect.
He had joined the Army specifically with the goal of becoming a
Ranger, thinking it sounded cool. Thus he went to the recruiter
and asked what was the best way to get there. The recruiter
explained the most direct path would be to join the Army as an
infantry man and then put in a request for Ranger School.
Which is exactly what he did and soon found himself at Ft.
Benning, Georgia, the home of the Infantry. It just so happened
while he was still in basic training a recruiter from the Ranger
battalion visited Jack's unit looking for anyone who was
interested in joining. Jack immediately volunteered.

After basic training, Jack attended Airborne School, followed immediately by Ranger Assessment and Selection Program or RASP. RASP is a grueling 8 week course made extreme physical and mental challenges designed to determined those who are and are not worthy to wear the Ranger Scroll on his sleeve. Not only was Jack able to complete the course but afterwards he had been selected to be a member of the First Ranger Battalion.

Once a Ranger, Jack quickly proved to be one of the best shooters in the entire unit. Because of his skill with a rifle he was selected to attend sniper school, where he quickly proved adept. Fol-lowing training, he remained in the Rangers for the next 8 years, which included multiple Deployments as a sniper. Jack had performed his duties in Afghanistan, Iraq, and lesser known conflicts around the world. During the entirety of his time overseas he never once felt a pang of guild or hesitancy about any mission or his duties therein. Looking back, Jack admitted to him-self as young man he thought he had the coolest job in the world. In fact, Jack enjoyed the rush of his job, taking out the bad guys. He literally bragged to people he was a Ranger.

He knew he carried the same mentality to his new job as a US Marshal. However, as he had gotten older the job had evolved from a rush to becoming a burden for Jack. The only thing that had kept him going was an axiom he picked up from the Louis L'Amour novels he had read dur-ing all of those deployments: As long as the world has bad guys willing to use guns and vio-lence, the world needs good guys who are willing to do the same.

While nothing had been said by the team or Sam, Jack remained bothered by his mistakes in Nebraska. Though Jack knew no mission was perfect, he held himself to a higher standard than he did anyone else. To Jack any misstep was unforgivable though none as much as the moments of distraction and the hesitation he felt before he pulled the trigger. Jack was simply unable to understand the why either had occurred in those moments, which seemed to be stuck on loop in Jacks memory. "It had never happened to before, why did it at that moment?" he asked himself.

While Jack was thankful the shooter's fourth shot was errant, "What if it hadn't been?" It was a thought Jack dwelled on for the duration of the ride to Kansas City. He felt it was those mis-takes, which allowed Deen to get off the four shots, killing one and injuring another. Despite the fact, Jack had taken more lives than he cared to admit before this morning, he still felt the guilt of the dead man who had died because of Jack's inaction in the moment. He knew if it had been a member of the SOG team, he's have felt even worse.

Jack acknowledged in the last couple of years he had questioned the moral effects of his duty he still understood his purpose as a member of the team. He was the groups security blanket and protector. As such, until that morning, his duty had always overrode the ever growing doubts in his mind. "But what now?" He asked himself, the thought making his stomach hurt and his heart beat accelerate.

CHAPTER 6

At the same time the SOG team was traveling home from Nebraska, three men were meeting in a field across the country. To anyone who could have observed the three, they couldn't have been more contrasting in their physical appearances. One man was huge, easily dwarfing the other two. The second man was of average size, yet was large in comparison to the third man who could almost be described as petite.

The large man was sitting on the dropped tailgate of his white pickup truck talking to the other two. "Dennis, is proving to be a problem," the man said hesitantly, feeling a sense of dread as he uttered the words he had been avoiding for to long. "He asked me to meet him somewhere to talk. I told him to meet me at the top of the stairs in the park to talk. I hope I don't need to ex-plain what needs to be done?"

The averaged sized man simply shook his head "no". The small man on the other hand, replied with an eager smile. "Consider that problem solved man".

As the two men rode away the big man wondered about the smaller man. Did he really enjoy all of this? While he had certainly shown himself as an adept tool for the job, the man almost seemed to enjoy it. The big man reminded himself to continue to watch man, who he decided was becoming to dangerous to have around. Much like a farm dog who had gotten accustomed to the taste of blood from the chickens, the man would need to be removed before he could destroy the entire farm.

CHAPTER 7

The US Marshall's tactical office was located in Southwest Kansas City, Missouri, near the Kansas and Missouri State line off Wornall Ave and 103rd street. The offices were in a very non-descript 6 story concrete and glass building holding a number of Federal Agencies ranging from the Department of Agriculture and Department of Interior offices to FBI and US Marshal offices. Despite being a federal building it was not open to the public, nor were there signs posted any-where to indicate the occupants. The Marshal's offices occupied the fourth floor, though both they and the FBI both had armories and tactical storage facilities in the building's basement.

Per standard operating procedure the SOG team went immediately into the conference room on to be debriefed after the mission, it was 2:45 when they were all seated. The conference room was typical of those in all the mid-tier government buildings, with a big shiny conference table of laminated press board surrounded by padded conference chairs. The windows allowed a spectacular view of the parking lot, another nondescript building containing private sector office space and the shared dumpsters. While some of the team seemed to enjoy gathering at the window before the various meetings started Jack avoided lingering in windows, in what my buddies have mockingly called professional paranoia. Jack didn't argue knowing more than once he had seen people taken out by snipers through windows, a few by his own hand.

Because snipers understood being directly in a window made them vulnerable they avoid set-ting up directly in a window. Instead, Jack and others like him are trained to examine angles that allow them to establish firing platforms further back inside a room where the shadows offered them protection against being spotted and becoming a target themselves.

After taking their seats the region's captain, James Dickson, began the debriefing. Captain Dickson was in his early fifties and while he used to be a US Marshall field agent, he no longer looked it. While the members of SOG are all in peak physical condition because they have to be to perform their jobs, Captain Dickson had been behind a desk for so many years he now resembled a bureaucrat with a paunch midsection and ill fitting suit more than the officer he had once been. The combination of his physique; the big framed glasses he wore on the end of his nose; his bald shiny and pointy head; and clearly bottle black goatee made Jim sometimes hard to take seriously for those who didn't know him.

His men knew and respected, however, that Jim did in fact know his job and ensured his teams had the best of everything available. Jim was also a leader who was quick to take the all the blame for any mishaps while heaping all the praise and accolades on those under him.

Yet he always seemed to be out of character after missions. During the mission debriefs Jim most often played devil's advocate to details and decisions made. Though Captain Dickson knew from his own experiences from being a police officer of some variety for nearly 30 years that no plan is perfect and the unexpected is expected; he always questioned an operative's actions, never once alluding to the fact that hind sight is 20/20. His purpose was two fold, one to ensure those involved could learn from the experiences and two so he would be able to provide an accurate report to his superiors about the various missions. The sessions became even more intense when shots are fired on any assignment. Despite this knowledge, Jack felt as if the debriefing was quickly becoming a personal attack on his actions.

"So Jack, you're saying you didn't see the cabin as you were going in to your position?"

"No, I came into my position from the other direction. The terrain wasn't bad so I went pretty much directly from the road to my firing point. It was 3 am, there wasn't much ambientlight out there and our intelligence said the point of focus was the third window on the second floor going left to right from my position. So once I was set my focus point was the window, the house and the barn in general during movement."

"And where was your focus once the fire teams were moving to assault position?"

" As the teams moved it was again, the house and the barn" Jack replied agitated. "The ground out there was flat and barren fields. And again the intelligence said the house and farm yard were the primary concerns for hostiles."

"So what were you doing upon the team's entry into the house?" Captain Dickson retorted.

"My job Captain! I was watching the windows to ensure nobody attempted to escape. I scanned the yard and barn as much as I could but I have only two eyes!"

"Calm down Jack," Sam said.

"I am calm, damnit. I just don't appreciate what is being alluded too," replied Jack.

"I'm not alluding to anything Jack," said Captain Dickson. "You know as well as I do how these things go. You also know, after this I am going to send you to Dr. Hartman for an evaluation. You will also be placed on administrative leave until the in house investigation is completed with the shooting. This isn't your first rodeo Jack. I'm just doing my job here. It's nothing personal."

Jack knew what Captain Dickson told him was completely right. But Jack felt he had still been overly aggressive with his line of questioning or was he just imagining things?

Jack continued to ponder the entirety of the situation for the remainder of the debrief as the Captain moved on to the other matters related to the situation with other members of the team

— particularly Sam. He addressed the handling of the scene, the gathering of the witness statements and the coordination of handing the case off to the local authorities and the FBI. Sam unlike Jack was calm cool and collected in response to the inquiries even though many of the questions posed by Captain Dickson were incredibly monotonous and repetitive.

An hour or so later as the meeting concluded, Captain Dickson asked Jack to remain for a second. "Jack, I need you to go out and see Dr. Hartman. You know the deal. She has to sign off before any officer involved in a shooting is allowed in the field again. We have arranged an appointment for you this afternoon at 5. She was willing to stay late to meet with you. I don't sup-pose you need directions"

"I know where the office is Captain, I have visited with her before." Jack replied stoically.

"I know. And Jack seriously don't take it personally. It was a good shoot and mission but we try to use these debriefs as learning moments so we can be better prepared for the next one. No-one has had anything but great things to say about you and your performance up there."

"Thanks Captain".

CHAPTER 8

As Jack was leaving the debriefing for his appointment with Dr. Hartman, West Virginia State Police Criminal Investigator, Catherine Elizabeth Greene was knocking on the door of Captain John Rodgers's office; having been summoned there. Detective Green was known as "CB" to her friends and co-workers. Her name had evolved over time; having been called Catherine Elizabeth as a toddler, which had been shortened to Cathy Beth as she got to elementary school and then shortened again to "CB" by the time she was in high school; befitting her tomboy demeanor. For those who never knew her as a child, the nickname seemed somewhat misplaced as the girl who had been a tomboy growing up; had become a truly beautiful woman.

Captain Rodgers was the long time commander for troop 3 of the West Virginia State Police, which covered a 10 county region of the state and headquartered in the town of Elkins. He was a man of average height with a hatchet face, his head covered by a severe high and tight haircut. His angular features were sharpened all the more because of his thin frame which he maintained by being an avid runner. A competent administrator, who had survived in the position for so long because of his ability navigate the political requirements of the job more than his ability to manage personnel. "Have a seat," he beckoned as she walked into the square office, its walls covered in medals and photographs from his running exploits.

CB sat in one of the two chairs sitting across from the man's desk and remained silent. While she had been under his command for two years she was never fully comfortable around the man; understanding first and foremost, he worked to please his superiors more than to support his subordinates.

After an uncomfortable moment, Rodgers said, "Detective Greene, I am dispatching you over to Audra to investigate the death of a man who was found shot this morning. I want to warn you however, the responding officers are reporting it looks as if the man could have possibly been killed by a rifle shot from long distance. As you know that matches the M-O on the four previous victims in the last couple of years."

"Sir, if you believe its connected to the previous killings, why are you sending me? I thought there was a special task force assigned to that?"

"The task force was disbanded after Kincaid was killed in custody" Captain Rodgers said, refer-ring to Anthony Kincaid the man who had been arrested after the task force had received an anonymous tip the man was involved in the drug ring and murders and subsequently killed while in jail, six months prior. "The powers that be have decided they want to start anew. Bring in a new set of eyes. I told them you were the best detective for the job."

Normally such a comment would have been flattering but given what she knew about the man she was skeptical of his sincerity. So instead of thanking him she asked, "Sir, you know, I knew Tony Kincaid? He was a friend of my Dad's."

"Detective Greene, Anthony Kincaid is dead." Rodgers said matter-of-factly. "Does his prior attachment to this case affect your ability to investigate this matter fair and impartially?"

"No sir, I had not seen him in probably 15 years.   I just felt I needed to disclose the matter".

"Duly noted, Detective but I don't believe there is a conflict here. Now there is a crime scene requiring your attention." Rodgers said before turning his attention to his computer.

Understanding the words were a dismissal, CB stood and opened the door to leave. Before she could however Rodgers added dryly "And detective if this dead man does turn out to be related to the previous murders there will be a number of eyes on you and this case".

Looking over her shoulder, CB gave a single nod and closed the door behind her. Walking away, she understood the last statement conveyed if she was unsuccessful it was her neck on the line.

*****

Audra State Park is a 365 acre recreational park in north central West Virginia on the border of Barbour and Upshur counties. The Middle Fork River is the park's primary feature, providing visitors fishing, swimming and rafting opportunities. The remainder of the park is heavily wooded featuring a campground and number of hiking trails along the river and the woods. It was along one of those wooded trails the gunshot victim was discovered. The body had been discovered by a pair of hikers who had come to enjoy an afternoon in the park looking at the fall foliage. Both had told police they had heard a single gun shot about 20 minutes before they found the body. Being in West Virginia, neither questioned hearing the sound of gunshots knowing hunting season was fast approaching and many people in the area were taking the time to ensure their guns were sited in. Though in reality, CB knew the sound of gunfire, wasn't uncommon in the area any time of the year.

CB entered the park from the South side entrance, crossed the bridge across the river and parked her Jeep Cherokee in the lower parking lot above the park's swimming area. As CB pulled in, she noted the parking lot was three quarters full. She also noticed there were vehicles from multiple law enforcement entities: county sheriffs from multiple counties, state cruisers and ever the State Department of Natural Resources, who had jurisdiction on park property. There was a large group of people gathered near one of the county sheriff's deputy cruisers near the trail head leading to the body.

Having grown up in the area, CB was familiar with the park as she had visited often as a youth. Because of her knowledge of the area, CB knew from the dispatcher's description pretty much exactly where the body lay. To get there, she would need to walk about a mile down the trail, there wasn't any way to get a vehicle in there. Getting out, she ensured her service weapon was secure, grabbed her back pack with her note book, camera and other investigative tools and went directly to the walking trail entrance.

She checked in with a county deputy who had been posted to keep people away. After being cleared she walked the trail to where the body lay. During the short hike, she declined 3 separate offers by various law enforcement men to carry her bag. CB, a very attractive woman, while accustomed to the attention of men and women alike; would rather be left alone — until she wasn't. She was 33-years-old with naturally blonde hair, high cheek bones, a rounded chin and blue eyes. While working however, she tried to downplay her looks wearing little makeup and maintaining a serious expression. She was 5'7" tall and weighed a solid 142 pounds she maintained with a combination of yoga, cross fit and muay thai training. She discovered her beauty remained both a detriment and benefit in her work. Detrimental because many of the men she encountered attempted to coddle her and thus slowed her down. Beneficial in that many people underestimated her; mistakenly thinking she somehow was given the position based on her looks; never considering she could have earned the position on merit.

Those who underestimated her were quickly shown the error of their ways, as the doubters soon found out CB was a great investigator, who once on a case overturned every stone until she found the truth.

She began her career as an agent for the ATF (Bureau of Alcohol, Tobacco, Firearms and Ex-plosives) working as both an investigator and undercover operative. Her attention to detail and ability to think on her feet had proven priceless. She was advancing in the ranks of the agency quickly because of her success. But 3 years prior her grandmother had died; essentially leaving her Dad alone in the area. She had unsuccessfully tried to find a transfer to the area within the federal service to come back to be nearer her father, who she was concerned for. That door closed she had applied for an open Detective position with the State Police. Since taking the job, she had one of the highest case closure rates in the entire state.

Despite returning to the area 2 years ago, she hadn't been back to the park. However, she fondly trail the trail and some of it's distinctive features from the trips of her youth. According to the dispatcher, the body of the man was laying face down in the middle of one of the trail's most prominent landmarks. From the parking lot she recalled, the trail took a long leisurely path from the top of the hill down along the river and back up again. At the point where the trail plays out near the river bank, the path turns sharply uphill to begin its ascent back to the top. Just past the sharp turn, the trail leads hikers up a set of 5 natural stone steps to a small landing made of the same stone. From the landing on the stairs, a hiker must go down two other stone steps, through a 30 feet long ravine ranging between 6 and 8 feet wide that traverses between large rock outcroppings on either side.

Her memory was good. The body was exactly where CB expected it to be based on the description of dispatch. After signing in with another deputy, who was securing the ravine; CB walked up the short embankment to the stairs and platform before stepping down the 2 rock steps into the tight space where the body lay, about 5 feet inside the ravine.

She walked around the body, careful not to disturb anything. CB didn't need an autopsy to tell her the cause of death was a gunshot wound; seeing an ugly black hole about the size of her thumb, leaving no doubt, a round had entered between the top of the man's shoulder blades. She assumed the round exited through the chest, though she couldn't see exactly where, as the man remained chest down and she didn't want to touch anything prior to the scene techs and medical examiner's arrival.

Normally a large caliber round would have exited the chest and left a large pool of blood around the body. Here however, there was little blood visible; a small amount of splatter on the surrounding stones but little on the sandy ground; which she knew could have absorbed any blood. Despite not being able to determine the size of the bullet, CB recognized the area was less populated making the possibility of witnesses remote, which was similar to the victims the task force had investigated previously from what she had overheard around the office and read in the local papers.

She wanted to assume the man had been ambushed as all four of the previous victims had; but she reminded herself to not jump to conclusions, as this could literally be a completely unrelated event or even an accident. Nonetheless, she also noted the man wore dirt stained jeans, heavy work boots, and a faded navy blue hooded sweatshirt, which suggested the man worked as some kind of laborer; which was consistent with the prior victims, who had all been employed by the area's various natural gas drilling companies.

The natural gas industry had exploded in West Virginia, particularly the North central part of the state in the early 2000s immediately after the wars in the Middle East ramped up after 9-11. With the boom, money flooded into the region, which had been in a prolonged recession that had followed the decline of the coal industry the decade prior. Much of the cash came in the form of wages to the men and women who worked the rigs. And what do people who have never had money do once they get some? They spend it.

As has been prevalent throughout history, the influx of money was immediately followed by the men and women looking to separate the money from those who earned it. The newcomers brought many temptations with them. Chief among them including drugs. The drug of choice for many became prescription pain killers. The four previous victims were all not only workers in the oil fields but she knew the investigations into their backgrounds revealing they each had rather nasty opioid addictions, which was why the DEA had been brought into the task force.

Based on the two vague similarities of his clothes and location the body was discovered, CB caught herself prejudging the man as another roughneck; which led to the assumption he too could have a history of opioid addiction. However, CB again reminded herself she was placing the cart before the horse and she needed to manage and process the crime scene completely and allow the evidence to carry her to the conclusion as opposed to trying to make the evidence fit a presumed outcome.

With that in mind she turned around, climbed the stairs to the small stone landing and began to scan along the area to see if she could discover where the shot had likely came from.

Looking it was easy for CB to recognize the trail she had walked up. The trail followed the natural contour of the hill through the trees before turning to her left along the river back towards the parking lot and disappeared into the trees and laurel bushes after about 50 yards. Because of the dense growth, she could not imagine a man with a rifle could have gotten in and out along this side of the river without being noticed by someone, as the park remained popular and had been busy judging by the number of cars she had seen in the parking lot. As such she felt there was to much traffic for the shooter have gone unnoticed with so much foot traffic in the immediate area of the body, and thus indicated it was likely another long shot with a rifle. Thus ignoring the trail, she turned her focus on a straight azimuth from where she currently stood. She used the body as the anchor and then focused between the stones on either side of her as a foresight and doing so realized a shooter could have easily remained hidden on the other side of the river.

Across the river was another wooded hillside, which was a steeper than the side she stood. Despite the trees, however there were gaps in the foliage that would allow a skilled shooter to ac-quire a target where she stood free of obstructions. Studying the hillside one particular spot stood out to her. A relative flat spot under a huge tree with a big rock sitting just behind it. Step-ping out to the officer guarding the area, CB asked "Do we know if anyone has looked at the area across the river to see if they can identify where the shooter was?"

"No ma'am" the man responded. "Really, I don't know if anyone has much looked at anything. We have been pretty busy just trying to secure the scene and trail and questioning witnesses. You want I can send Mike from up where you first came in across?"

"No, that's ok," CB replied. "We will get to it once forensics gets over here."

Returning to the top of the stairs, CB opened her backpack, pulled out her camera. The first picture she took captured the line from where she stood to the flat rock she suspected the shooter had laid and then she began to painstakingly take photos of the rest area and the body.

CB was a very talented photographer and honed in on the smallest details, which not only made her a good photographer, but a keen investigator as well. She took numerous shots of the scene from all angles and variety of zooms until she was satisfied she had captured every detail available. She knew the crime techs would also take their own pictures but she felt they often missed things, the finite details that helped in the investigation. In fact, she had noted a few items of particular interest as she had memorialized the scene.

As she was taking the pictures, she noticed a slight square outline in the dead man's back pocket. While she was hesitant to do anything to disturb the scene, she also knew identifying the man early would be paramount. Returning her back pack, she removed a pair of rubber surgical gloves and donned them. With her gloved hand she reached in with two fingers and removed a wallet careful not to touch anything else.

The wallet was a maroon nylon tri-fold type that was held shut with velcro. Even folded closed, it was thin. Tugging at the wallet's seam the velcro released, allowing CB to unfold it. In the center fold was a plastic window showing the man's driver's license, which identified him as Dennis Roberts. The address listed was for an apartment building near CB's office in Elkins. However, CB recognized the license had been issued years prior so the odds were that the address was no longer good; possible but unlikely. Nonetheless, she called in the information to dispatch to see what they had on the guy.

Dispatch told her they would get on it and have her some preliminary information within the hour.

After speaking with dispatch, CB returned her attention to the wallet. Other than the center section with the driver's license the wallet had two more sections. On either side of the driver's license one was slotted to hold credit cards and the other a panel with a small zipper pocket designed to hold a key or change. Finally, there was a pocket when the wallet open for holding cash. In the cash pocket the man had carried $117. One fifty dollar bill, three twenties, a five and two ones. Also in the compartment were a pair of carefully folded receipts. Looking closely they were pawn tickets from 2 separate stores. One was from a pawn broker in Elkins, the other was from a broker in Clarksburg WV, which was about an hour and fifteen minute drive from Elkins by highway though there were faster country road alternatives. CB knew the Elkins pawn shop had the reputation for being pretty relaxed on their standards for accepting items because it fell in the area she covered. The Clarksburg store she would have to look into but she guessed it had a similar reputation. She took a pair plastic bags from her backpack and placed the cash in one and the pawn tickets in the other. She wrote the names and transaction numbers of the pawn tickets in a notebook for follow up.

Money and receipts secured, CB turned her attention to the section of the wallet slotted for cred-it cards. The slots held a single debit card from a local bank along with a number of business cards. Counting the cards, CB found there were 13 total. Eight of the cards were from businesses clearly related to the gas wells and drilling. Two of the cards were for loan managers for local banks. There was 1 from another pawn shop. The last two cards were for strip clubs, one in Morgantown and the other in Huntington about as far away from each other as one could get inside the state; though CB knew the men who worked for the gas rigs worked all over; traveling not only throughout the state but all over the country. She placed the cards in another plastic bag from her backpack and wrote herself a note to check with the businesses under the pawn-shop note.

The remaining section of the wallet was the zippered pocket for change. Unzipping the pocket CB looked in and saw two white discs. She pinched the sides of the wallet and turned it over with one hand while holding the her other hand out. From the pocket fell two tiny pills into her hand. In the light the pair of pills weren't quite white instead more of cream color. Imprinted on the pills: 54 over 582. Unfortunately, CB had seen enough pills in the area to know without the need for reference these two particular pills were Roxycodone. While she supposed the man could have had them on a legitimate prescription, she highly doubted. She collected the pair and put them in a smaller zip-lock bag she also carried in her back pack.

As she was completing her inventory CB heard a racket behind her. Turning, she saw it was the medical examiner and forensics team with their gurney and bright orange bags of equipment. She got up and walked over to the man she knew to be in charge. His name was Josh Bennet. Bennet was tall and lean. He was a good looking man in his mid-forties with dark brown hair beginning to grey at the temples. He wore dark rimmed hipster glasses that went with the skinny jeans and plaid shirt he was sporting. CB though inwardly shook her head thinking the man was to old for such a look.

As Bennet approached she stated curtly, "According to his driver's license his name is Dennis Roberts. I didn't move the body any but I am sure there will be keys in his front pockets. Once you get your measurements and photos, I would like them".

"You're not staying?" asked Bennet.

"I'll be around, but right now I am going across the river to snoop around" CB stated before walking away, giving a few cursory nods to the others who had just arrived. No one was surprised at the briefness nor awkwardness of the exchange between the two; as all present knew Bennet and CB had dated briefly and it hadn't ended well; the rumors were many as to exactly why.

CB walked the trail back to her car. At the lot, she discovered most of the cars that had been there when she arrived were gone. All that remained were her Jeep, the van from the crime scene team, 3 police cars, the van to transport the body and 3 civilian cars. Walking over to the county deputy she had checked in with earlier, who was now sitting in his cruiser, she inquired if there had been any other witnesses or developments since she had first arrived. The deputy shook his head no and stated, "We took all their information down for you though. You want me to get it?"

"Yes, please," CB responded, wanting to add the information to what she had already gathered. Taking the information from the deputy she asked "Do we have anyone at the other parking lots too, particularly the one above on top of the hill?"

"Yes ma'am, but we didn't get anyone up there at first. We just put police tape across it until we had more officers on the scene."

"Were there any cars in the lot?"

"A few, but there were more down here. I don't know how many were up there. We talked to some other people once we got here but it's likely we missed a few too. You know a lot of kids come back in here to smoke pot and who knows what else. They avoid us like the plaque if they can."

"No worries, I am more interested in how the victim got here. Did you guys get a chance to figure out which vehicle is his?"

"No" said the officer shaking his head. "I haven't even been told the guy's name yet."

"Figures" CB thought cursing how inefficient communications went when multiple departments were involved on a case. "Ok no worries. Are any of these cars still unaccounted for then?" She asked.

"All of those still parked here are but you know we get hikers along these trails who go beyond the park down the river trail. It could be hours before they all come back."

CB nodded to convey her understanding and disappointment with the same movement. After the deputy gave her his list of compiled names CB added them to her own notebook and re-turned to her car. After climbing in she drove to the entrance to the parking lot. "Turn left to go to the upper lot and go talk to deputy there, or turn right to look for the spot the shooter set up?" she asked herself. After a brief second, she turned right.

CHAPTER 9

Dr. Lynette Hartman's office was located about 15 minutes from the US Marshal's office in a medical park off of I-435 and Roe Avenue in Leawood, Kansas, an affluent Kansas City suburb. Jack arrived ten minutes early and waited in his truck collecting his thoughts before he headed up to her office. Jack couldn't recall exactly how many times he had been here but he guessed at least a dozen.

He never found the experience especially fun as he didn't like being analyzed in general. Making matters worse, he was not a big fan of how Dr. Hartman always wanted to discuss how Jack didn't have much of a social life and how he needed to establish more of a work, life balance. It always frustrated Jack, she didn't appreciate how much he enjoyed work or that his identity was in part based upon what he did for a living. Today, however, he had even bigger concerns. Jack could not accept his "failure" in from that morning in Nebraska. As a perfectionist, who accepted perfection was unattainable for more than the briefest second; yet, he prided himself on for being as infallible as humanly possible when it came to his job. Which was why Jack could not fathom how he had let everyone down that morning. Even if those he let down didn't know it; nor was he sure he could admit it to them or anyone else. Nonetheless, at three minutes before the appointed time, he exited his truck and crossed the parking lot to Dr. Hartman's office.

Her office was on the second floor of the four-story brick building that housed numerous doctors offices of various specialties. Jack ignored the elevators and took the stairs to her office located on the second floor, as he always did. Taking a right from the stairs, he walked down the hall to Dr. Hartman's office, entering at exactly 2:00 by his watch. Though he was right on time, Jack felt a pang of guilt walking in; the Army had drilled into him being just on time was late and that being five minutes early was the expectation.

Dr. Hartman's waiting room was rather small with neutral colored walls. The walls held a few framed landscape prints depicting the Kansas Plains, which were used in an attempt to disguise there were no windows. In the space there were 6 empty chairs, a small glass coffee table, containing an assortment of dog eared magazines, with a coffee machine and small water cooler in the corner. The small waiting area faced the registration desk where the receptionist / secretary sat. Jack proceeded directly to the desk to check in.

Dr. Hartman's secretary was named Willow. She was a very attractive blonde woman with shoulder length hair, emerald green eyes, high cheekbones and a disarming smile. Jack estimated her being close to his own age of 35 but he would never offend her by saying it. She was very friendly but Jack's coworkers, who had all been there as part of their routine 2-year mental health check ups, told Jack she does not date cops of any variety before his first ever visit to the office. Thus, Jack always assumed any flirting the pair had participated in was only good natured on her part. Today however, he wasn't in the mood for flirting or even small talk when he approached the counter. Instead he simply gave Willow his name before sitting down and picking up one of the magazines.

Jack had not even made it through the opening ads of the magazine when Willow stated in a calm voice, "Jack, she is ready for you. Head on back."

Jack had visited Dr. Hartman on multiple occasions since joining the US Marshals, for his required mental health reviews and for clearance to return to duty after two previous instances where he had been involved in shootings. He never recalled being nervous at any of the prior visits. Nonetheless, Jack recognized a sense of unaccustomed pressure with this visit. Where-as his previous encounters he had been relaxed today he felt tight and on edge. Accordingly, the walk down the hall to the doctor's inner office seemed to take forever, though in reality, it was no more than 30 feet and a few seconds. Arriving to the door of her office, Jack took a deep breath and knocked politely. Secretly, he hoped she would not answer for some reason. To his disappointment however she replied "Come in Jack".

Walking into the office, it still struck Jack as odd that Dr. Hartman's office actually contained the stereotypical brown leather couch like he used to see on TV as a kid or in the Sunday morning comic strips depicting a psychiatrist's office. At the head of the couch sat a matching leather high-backed arm chair. Other than the couch, Jack considered her office was rather normal. There was a large wood desk sitting across from the couch behind which sat a nice overstuffed leather chair where the doctor sat. Facing the desk were two more comfortable leather bound arm chairs, that matched the chair and couch. The two inner walls were adorned with book-shelves filled with books that looked to be academic in nature, while the two outer walls featured large windows overlooking the manicured lawns of the building. As in his prior visits, the blinds had been pulled all the way up, allowing the natural sunlight to flood the room.

On his previous visits, Jack had never told Dr. Hartman about his dislike for the windows as he was afraid she would conclude he was paranoid. Instead, he would simply sit in the comfortable chair nearest the door, which naturally took him away form the window and placed the other chair between himself and the outside. In all his previous visits to the office, Jack had never even considered sitting on the couch. Today however he walked into the office and went directly to the couch and planted himself on it. The move wasn't missed by Dr. Hartman.

Though Dr. Hartman and Jack had discovered in his first visit the two shared the same birthday most people would have guessed she was much younger than he. Having grown up on a farm, deploying to the most extreme environments in the world and just generally spending a lot of time outdoors, Jack had a tanned weathered complexion. Dr. Hartman on the other hand appeared to Jack to have rarely if ever been exposed to the sun for to long and thus had perfect white skin that looked like a china doll. And unlike Jack who stood 6'1" and weighed in at a solid 200 pounds, Dr. Hartman was a very petite, 5'2" and 110 pounds, which also made her appear younger. She also featured raven colored hair that shown blue when the sun caught it just right which made her blue eyes all the more attractive.

Despite the demure china doll appearance however she was sharp and she was tough. "The couch Jack?"

"I know, but I think I may need it today."

"Oh now I am intrigued. Does this mean you actually want to let me in today?"

"Let you in how?" Jack replied.

"Come on now Jack, according to my records this is now the seventh time you have been here and never once in your previous visits have you revealed anything about yourself that I didn't already know from your service file. You refuse to discuss anything outside of work or acknowl-edge there is more to your life than work. So what I am asking is if today you are really ready to talk about something of substance instead of just going through the motions. Though they may not admit it, I have been able to help many of your co-workers who have confided in me."

Jack was surprised it had only been seven visits, thinking it more and in response Jack just nodded absentmindedly at first. Then he began to talk, slowly at first but picking up the pace as he went. In all, it took Jack nearly 45 minutes to unload his burden on Dr. Hartman. He explained the mission and how the shooter had gotten off his shots. He explained how he had hesitated and how it had bothered him ever since. He even told her about his frustration with himself and how it had caused him to blow up in Captain Dickson,though he knew it wasn't war - ranted as the man had a job to do. The entire time Jack was talking, Dr. Hartman stayed quiet and simply let him go at his own pace. She had asked to him to clarify a few of the details along the way but nothing Jack felt was intrusive or broke his train of thought. Jack also noticed she hadn't take any notes during his rant; instead she simply sat and appeared interested in what he had said.

After Jack finished they stared at one another a moment. Jack thought maybe she was trying to create an uncomfortable silence to keep him talking, but he felt he had said everything he need-ed to say and thus sat quietly, awaiting her response.

After the moment she simply asked one question, "Jack if you had to pull the trigger tomorrow on someone could you?"

The question took Jack by surprise. He sat for a long moment looking at her before he replied quietly, "I think so."

CHAPTER 10

As Jack was completing his visit with Dr. Hartman, CB was beginning her inspection of the site where she believed the shooter to have been waiting. It was high above the river bank on the steep hillside across the river from where the crevice in the rocks. There was no access for her Jeep to get back along the river that she knew of so she had left it parked where it was, instead choosing to cross the river jumping from rock to rock along a ford at the shallows not far from the crevice she had left where the medical examiner and his team were working. Once across the river, the climb had been so steep CB found herself jumping from tree to tree just to keep herself from falling back down the embankment.

Once she made it to the rocky ledge, she had tried to keep in her focus since leaving the body, she did not see any sign anyone had been there. She imagined there would have been obvious signs of some sort, yet something told her the shooter being on this side of the river was the only way the shot could have been taken without the shooter being seen.

Feeling as if she may have made a mistake she pulled out her camera to check the line of sight against where she stood to confirm she was in the correct place. She pulled up the image she had taken of the rock she now stood she taken from the other side. As she compared her sight line from the stone she was standing she realized that while she was in the spot she had taken the photo of it could no possibly be where the shot had been taken. There was no way a shot could have hit the man between the shoulder blades from where she stood. Where she was currently standing was to flat a line, while she could see the tops of the stairs, even through the zoom lens of her camera she couldn't make out the ravine itself and could barely see the tops of the heads of the men working in the crevice even using the zoom lens. The angle was completely wrong. As she recalled the picture again, it struck her: when she had looked for where the shots could have been from and subsequently taken her photo, she had been atop the three steps leading into the ravine, not in the ravine itself; thus, the angle was all wrong. The shooter had to have been higher up on the hillside. "Way to go Detective Greene," CB said to herself sarcastically, upset having made such a glaring error.

Looking around CB saw a few spots on the hill above her that she considered possibilities for a shooter to set up on for a shot in the gap of the rocks. The most obvious, a shelf of protruding rock about 25 yards from where she was currently standing. Normally 25 yards wasn't a big deal but the hillside here was incredibly steep. After a deep breath to steady her resolve, CB again began using the trees to help her climb reaching low branches to help her climb. She had almost gotten to her target spot when the limb she grabbed snapped causing her to fall and slide ten yards down the embankment before she was caught by another tree which she crashed into hard enough to knock the wind from herself. If she could have breathed she would have cussed instead she just remained against the tree. Taking a moment, she composed her-self, while at the same time chastising herself for not telling anyone what she was up to really, wondering how long it would take someone to find her if she really got hurt. Though she knew her independent nature was part of her strength in as much as it was a weakness; though she refused to ever admit to having weaknesses to anyone she worked with; as she never wanted it said she needed help getting where she was.

Refocused, she climbed to the rock shelf again, this time making it. Taking a moment to look around she knew she was in the correct spot. Though the rock itself was relatively clean she could see a few random smudges on the rocks surface that were likely made from a pair of boots. More importantly looking over the edge of the rock it provided a perfect view into the crevice where the body lay; even with her naked eye, she could even make out movement despite the distance and the trees with their foliage. She again checked the line with the zoom her camera and could make out even more detail; she figured with a scoped rifle it would be an even better view. Yet, she also knew that whomever the shooter was, he or she was obviously talented, as she estimated that the distance was all of 200 yards at a very steep angle. She knew shooting down hill was a tricky and required a shooter to compensate by holding low on the target. Yet the reports from all those in the vicinity was only one shot had been fired.

Camera still in her hand, CB took pictures of the suspected shot line and the surrounding area. As she took the pictures she saw what looked like a faint trail leading up the remaining hillside. She figured the trail was likely the way the shooter traveled to get to the stone where she now stood. After taking pictures of what she believed to be the line of travel. She climbed the suspected path up the slope and found it a much easier line of travel than she experienced since crossing the river. Along the whisper of path, she was able to ascertain some more distinctive indentations along the route. Again she took photos. While she was certainly no expert, she judged by the impressions that the person she was following was likely short as the strides were very closely spaced.

CB suddenly lost the path just short of the summit of the hill. She kept climbing hoping to pick it up again; unexpectedly, she came upon an obviously old gas well road near the top of the hill, near a tank. In all her visits to the park, she never explored this side of the river, and from the looks of the area and road she doubted few others had either though obviously the shooter had. She began to walk down the road thinking it would take her back to the main road and her car. She hadn't gone far when she saw both old and fresh tire tracks. A closer study revealed a vehicle had obviously and recently made a three point turn leaving tracks in the gravel of the road and in the grass on either side. Having grown up in the country, she could easily see the tracks were made from a large tires with aggressive pattern consistent with an off road tire. Again she took pictures hoping they would be able to match the tire to a specific vehicle.

Continuing her study the tire tracks, she saw a boot track as it emerged from the woods. She found two things very interesting about the track. First, the track was small; slightly smaller than her own woman's size 7. CB took a few pictures of the track by itself and then to get an accurate portrayal if its size took her own shoe off and sat beside the track and took another photo. The second item of note was the boot track appeared to have emerged from the passenger side of the vehicle. While she understood theshooter could have driven in and turned the truck around before walking in, her gut told her this wasn't the case. She couldn't prove it but she was certain there had to have been a getaway driver waiting on the road for the shooter. She found this odd because all the profiles said serial killers tended to be isolationists who work alone; if this murder in fact turned out to be related to the previous cases.

She continued to take pictures of the area, until she was satisfied she had captured everything. Finally deciding to return to her car she decided she didn't want to navigate the steep hillside again instead opting to walk down the gas well road, curious where it emerged. It took her almost 20 minutes of walking but the road did eventually come out on a road, just not where she expected. Instead of the main road, she came out on a side road about a mile northwest of where her car was. As she walked to her vehicle she saw a few houses and mobile homes set back from the road. At one of the homes she saw a pair of young kids playing in the front yard while a young mother stood watch. On a whim, CB stopped and after showing the woman her badge asked if she had noticed heard any gunshots or seen anything or anyone on the old well road. The woman told her she hadn't heard any shots, but she had seen some gas well trucks in the area the past few days, though that wasn't uncommon.

Finally, arriving back to her Jeep, she placed her bag in the back seat and got behind the wheel. Before closing the door she took a quick mental inventory of what she had just seen, wanting to get her thoughts straight before she was distracted by driving and the hectic environment of her office. However, her thoughts were interrupted as she heard the medical team emerging from the woods. Looking up she saw 4 men, including Bennet, carrying a gurney with a black body bag on top of it. She watched as the men made the asphalt of the lot they released the legs and wheels of the gurney to push the body to the awaiting van. Understandably she also noted the four men took a noticeable sigh of relief as their burden was eased. Getting out she met the men at the van. "Anything I should know?" she asked Bennet.

"Nothing, I am sure you don't already know. Looks to have been shot with a high powered rifle in the back from some distance. Other than that nothing definitive until we do an autopsy. I'll call you when we have it"

"Ok thanks," CB said still uncomfortable talking to the man. "Can I take one last look?"

"Be my guest," Bennett said unzipping the bag.

Stepping closer, CB noted the man was pale but otherwise matched the driver's license photo from earlier. She also noted the front the sweatshirt was covered in blood making the navy blue look more purple than blue, as the blood had drained from the exit wound as he laid facedown. She also thought she could see a semblance of some kind of logo on the shirt, though the blood made it nearly impossible to make out. She took one last photograph and nodded to Bennet and returned to her Jeep, with the intent of getting out ahead of the coroners van, not wanting to follow it all the way to the highway on the curvy roads.

CHAPTE R 11

After talking with Dr. Hartman, Jack went to his apartment, in nearby Overland Park, Kansas another Kansas City suburb. Walking through his door, he went directly to the fridge and opened a beer, a Boulevard Tank 7. He took a big satisfying pull of the dark amber liquid. His throat thirst quenched, he tried find something to occupy his mind, afraid of where his mind would wander left unattended. Living alone in a one bedroom apartment, his options were limited. His first instinct was to read, though looking at his bookcase filled with an assortment of novels by Micheal Connelly, Lee Child, Vince Flynn and others, nothing seemed appropriate considering the circumstances. He considered going to the gym but admitted truthfully the beer simply tasted to good to leave his home.

Finishing the first beer, Jack took a long hot shower; letting the water beat on him for 20 minutes as trying unsuccessfully to scrub the dirty feeling of self-doubt from his skin. Getting out and drying off Jack changed into a pair of old grey sweat pants, and a blue Royals t-shirt before opening a second beer.

Taking a drink, he looked around the apartment and decided it needed cleaning, even though he kept it neat and clean to begin with. Instead of simply tidying up however, he went full blown Army GI party on the space. He cleaned every nook and cranny of every corner of the apartment along with every item in it. He cleaned the coffee maker, microwave, stove, toilet, shower, television screen, and windows; dusted the book shelves and ceiling fans; vacuumed the floors and furniture, swept and finally mopped. The chore took him nearly 8 hours, two bottles of cleaner, an entire roll of paper towels, 6 beers and a few shots of Crown Royal after the beer was gone, but in the end Jack felt a person could eat off any surface in the entirety of the space without fear.

Satisfied the place was sufficiently clean, Jack looked at the clock and realized it was 2 am, he was a little drunk and a little light headed from the cleaners and went to bed and proceeded to have visions of blood haunt his dreams.

The next morning Jack awoke to the sun light streaming through his window, a rarity for him. With his first movement he discovered he felt like shit. In hindsight he decided the whiskey had probably been a bad idea though there was not much he could do about it now. Getting up he made his way to the into the kitchen and saw the clock on the microwave said 10:22 AM. As he made coffee, he pondered when was the last time he had slept in this late. He honestly could not remember, as he had been getting up before the sun for almost as long as he could remem-ber. Between having grown up on a small farm and the years in the military it was simply en-grained in Jack's DNA to get up early. Even after finishing long night missions, he had barely been able to sleep whilst the sun was up afterwards.

Sitting down with his coffee, Jack turned on the tv looking for something to occupy his mind but the search proved fruitless. His normal go to television channels were ESPN, the History Channel and the Military Channel but none of the three held his attention; nor did any of the other channels on his cable package; having rounded the dial twice by the time he finished the cup.

The coffee helped some but still feeling like crap, Jack decided the best therapy for him was a good long run, which he had always found therapeutic. He checked the temperature on his phone which said it was in the mid fifties. Returning to the bedroom he changed into a pair of shorts, a hoodie and grabbed his New Balances. After getting dressed, Jack laced his shoes, left the apartment and headed directly for the Johnson County recreation trail which was accessible behind his apartment complex. He put his ear buds in, chose a playlist

from his phone featuring 90's alternative music and began to jog.

Jack started slow, feeling his head pound with every stride for the first mile. While he enjoyed a beer now and again, Jack rarely if ever drank to excess. The bottle of Crown Royal had been in his apartment since the Christmas before last when a girl he had been dating had given it to him as a gift. Prior to the previous night's binge, the bottle had less than 5 shots taken from it. As he began to sweat the headache began to subside though the smell of alcohol also started coming through his pores. Jack kept running nonetheless.

Jack ran for an hour and a half, covering 12 miles. Through the entirety of the run, all he could do was replay the scene in Nebraska over and over in his head. Repeatedly asking himself, What the hell happened? Why had he hesitated and allowed that fourth shot to occur? He had the shooter in his sights, he had stopped breathing, had his finger on the trigger; yet in that one split second his head had said stop. Why? And almost as bad, why was Deen's death riding on him so hard when Deen was such a bad guy himself — likely as bad or worse than any person he had killed previously based on the reports.

Returning home exhausted, Jack took the time to drink a bottle of water before having another cup of coffee. Feeling somewhat better, he took a long hot shower, attempting to wash the smells of sweat and liquor off his body, as well as the shame once again. He let the water pour over him until it started to get cold. Getting out of the shower he toweled off, dressed and began to pace once again.

Inside the small space the thoughts of what the hell happened continued to invade Jack's inner thoughts. To distract himself, he made a sandwich and sat down at the little breakfast bar separating his kitchen from the living room. Yet before he could eat, he began to feel the walls closing in. He felt short of breath. His heart raced. He saw nothing of the apartment around him just the image of the shooter in a Nebraska corn field pulling the trigger as Jack watched powerlessly. Soon the scenario got worse as the shooter's shots began finding targets, Jack friends were falling under a barrage of bullets, while Jack did nothing, frozen in horror!

Despite knowing these thoughts were all just in his head, Jack could not help but feeling guilt for it. He sat at his small bar hovering over the uneaten sandwich for over an hour paralyzed; unable to eat his sandwich, feeling sick to his stomach, riddled with guilt.

Just as he was feeling on the verge of vomiting, Jack's phone rang, snapping him back to reality. Looking around he found his phone plugged in on the coffee table. Checking the caller ID he saw it was Chris. Needing the reprieve from his own confinement he quickly answered.

"What's up?"

"Hey man was just checking to see how it went with Dr. Hartman yesterday?"

"Oh you know, same stuff as the last time. Asked me how I was doing after Nebraska and all that."

"Cool. After you left Dickson told me that all the guys were scheduled to see her next week be-cause of how close in proximity we all were to the bullets. I tried to tell him we were all fine but he insisted."

"You know he is just playing C-Y-A. Covering his ass with the boys in Washington should some-thing ever happen. I wouldn't worry about it."

"Yeah I'm not but just wanted to see if she had said anything to you about it."

"Nah we didn't talk about it at all. She was pretty much focused on me. You have been through these things before you know how it is."

"Yeah, cool. Anyhow I was also wondering what you were up to this evening? Me and some of the guys are going to head down to Shooters and play some pool around 7 if you wanna go and grab a beer or 2 and hangout?"

"Sure man sounds good. I will probably pass on the beer though. I had one to many last night and still recovering."

"Cool man see you there" said Duke laughing as he hung up.

Ending the call, Jack felt like a big weight had been lifted from his shoulders, if only because he would be able to get out of the house for a bit. Checking the clock again, however Jack realized he had a few hours before he was supposed to meet the guys. He again looked at the sandwich but decided against it. Instead, he thought he would try and grab a quick nap. He went to the bedroom climbed into the sheets and somehow found sleep quickly, though the dreams of dead men returned.

Awakening, Jack found himself wet with sweat again. His heart felt like it was about to jump from his chest. 'Seriously Jack what the fuck?', he said to himself. After taking a few deep breathes, Jack got up and realized he had slept longer than he had intended and was going to be late meeting up with the guys.

Despite that Jack was determined to go and get out of his apartment. He grabbed another quick shower, dressed in a pair of jeans, hiking boots and a West Virginia University hoodie. After dressing, he snatched up his wallet, keys and phone, went downstairs, jumped in his truck and headed out towards the pool hall. Jack hadn't gotten a few miles down the road when he realized he hadn't eaten all day and stopped at local Quik Trip on the way and grabbed a sandwich, bottle of water and an energy drink and slammed them down.

CHAPTER 12

As Jack was heading to the pool hall, CB was leaving her office. She had been there since 7:30 am and had spent the next 13 hours going through the files of the five unsolved murders which had been placed on her desk while she was at the crime scene the day prior. A review of the records showed that they were very sloppy and haphazardly put together. She could clearly see the records were being compiled by multiple people, all of whom were seemingly working the case from different approaches or agendas. She also noted the work appeared to have been completely abandon after the anonymous tip came in regarding Tony Kincaid. The file wasn't clear on the tip but it appeared the tipster called in and said Kincaid was operating a pill ring for someone and he had just had a large shipment of pills delivered to him. The tip had been enough for a friendly judge to issue a search warrant for his property. Once executed, the task force had discovered boxes of opioid pain pills in generic brown prescription bottles sitting in the man's spare bedroom, who had never bothered to hide the stash while he had been at work on a gas rig in Pennsylvania at the time the warrant was executed. The estimated street value of the pills was estimated at over 1.5 million dollars. After the discovery the task force apprehend-ed Kincaid and placed him under arrest. The man was in custody for less than 24 hours before he was found stabbed to death in his cell. The man had not even had time to contact a lawyer yet, though he reportedly had been issued his Miranda Rights. Reading, the account for the first time, CB understood why the task force was disbanded as no group would want to be associated with losing the key witness into such a large drug operation and multiple murders. By dis-banding it allowed all the associated agencies to pass the blame elsewhere, at least to a degree; harkening back to the political games that those such as Captain Rodgers were so adept at playing.

She gave the records a bit of a pass because having worked on multiple task forces and joint operations in her time with the ATF she knew the investigation likely was controlled by the Fed-eral Agency involved, in this case the DEA. The files she was looking at were most likely the individual notes of different individual investigators for the joint operation and not a copy of the collaboration, which she would request but knew the Feds would be hesitant to relinquish. She wrote herself a reminder to ask Captain Rodgers about seeing if she could talk to someone from the task force to help shed some more light on the investigation.

Nonetheless undeterred, CB went through all the notes and crime scene photos making connections between the 5 individual cases; paying particular attention to how the new information collected on Roberts fit with the older cases. As she had theorized on the scene, she confirmed Roberts had worked as a roughneck on the rigs, similar to the other four victims. He worked for a company called Marshall's Drilling and Troubleshooting Services, the same company both Tony Kincaid and her father worked for.

She also knew the company was owned by a man named Jeremy Marshall, with whom she had known or known of since high school though she was younger. She knew since school he had made a fortune through a number of business ventures in the area, including the natural gas rigs and servicing thereof. It was also suspected by many in the police force and the community itself that not all of his money had been earned in honest business practices. In fact, he suspected of more than shady dealings, though Marshall had never actually been caught doing anything. Most of these rumors stemmed from not just the fact that he had money alone, but like many of his other employees, her father included, most of those he employed had serious criminal records. Moreover, she surmised the money for all those pills had to come from some-where and Marshall was the closest source of such wealth to Kincaid.

A quick search of Roberts revealed he too had a criminal record, mostly for theft and minor drug possession offenses. He had served time too, though in total less than 3 years and nothing with-in the past 4 years that she could find. He was only the second victim to have an arrest record; though the other victim with a record, named Harp only had a DUI on his record from a decade earlier.

After confirming his record, CB cross referenced Roberts with the other four victims. The preliminary findings were he had likely never known any of the other men. In fact, the previous investigation by the task force revealed that none of the men ever had worked together, despite the fact, that similar to most of the men in the drilling business, they had all bounced around to various companies in the area.

Moreover, the task force had found that none of the men were close associates of any kind. The closest any of the foursome had to a relationship was victim 1, Micah Low age 37 and victim 3, Charles Harp age 35. The pair had certainly known each other, having played high school football together and being only 2 years apart in age. However, there was nothing in either man's recent past that showed that they had kept in touch. Just to be sure, CB accessed both men's Facebook information and found that they had only 24 mutual friends between them and they weren't "friends" themselves.

There were a few other loose connections. Harp was also known to have frequented the same bar as victim number 2, Allen Gumm who was by far the youngest of the victims at 25 years old. Again their possible connection seemed to have ended there. As one waitress put it, according to interview notes from the task force: "The pair likely knew of each other but they didn't appear to know each other". The same waitress also said the two men never seemed to associate with each other when they were in the place at the same time, which was a rare occurrence accord - ing to the witness. Victim 4, Joseph Ramirez was the eldest of the group at age 44 and there was no known association between either he and Harp nor any of the other 3. However, Ramirez and Roberts had attended the same high school though were to far apart in age to have gone at the same time.

After cross checking the men against each other she searched to see if any of the crime scenes themselves could be related. A quick search of the task force investigation showed all the victims had been killed from ambush near gas wells, similar to how Roberts had been. The task force had noted the different owners of the wells.

CB's own review of property records took some time but she was finally able to ascertain the old service road she had found across the river belonged to well owned by Hawker Inc., a medium sized natural gas company from the area. The name was familiar to her because she had seen previously that Hawker also controlled another of the wells where on of the victims had been killed.

On a whim, she then combed the files looking for the contact information of the companies. Thinking she would see cross reference the well owners to the men who had been killed. But when she found the listing she was looking for that contained the name Hawker, she saw the task force had already cross referenced the wells to the men. Dead end. The wells, much like the men seemed random, with no connection amongst them other than the industry itself.

Nonetheless, she still knew Marshall remained connected to all the victims, since Roberts worked for the man. Another inference to be made from the information was Kincaid's death did not break the continuity to Marshall. But looking at the case files, she found virtually no notes on Marshall. Of course, until the anonymous tip, there had virtually no notes on Kincaid either, at least in the limited case files she had access too. In an effort to get the remaining files CB sent an email to Captain Rodgers asking if he would inquire on getting the outstanding files.

In the mean time, CB knew of one person she could call whom she had been reluctant to use in the past: her father. Thomas Greene, like many of the men in the area had worked for the drilling companies for years, and now worked for Marshall. He had worked through the prosperous times as well as the low times. Additionally, he had also developed an opioid addiction. Due to his substance problems he had been in jail a few times for theft and possession but never anything felonious, though she knew that was really a technicality since he had pled out of felony charges twice. But since the last arrest he had sworn to her he had been clean and sober. She believed him based on his appearance and improved behaviors. Nonetheless, CB knew, even if she would never say it aloud and certainly never to her father, that he knew a great deal about the inner workings of the local drug trade. He was especially in tune to the trade around the drilling rigs.

She had overheard to many bits and pieces of phone call and conversations around her dad as a youth and since. While she knew his history, she had always willingly looked the other direc-tion when any little thing she saw or heard made her police instincts scream in his presence. She never wanted to strain their relationship, as he was the one man in her life she felt she could always depend on. However, now there were to many dead bodies for her not to make every effort, no matter how uncomfortable, to use every resource she had available to capture the killer. She thought maybe her dad would be would be willing to help her out since he and Roberts worked together, or at least for the same company.

She reminded herself to tread lightly though because of his association with Marshall she would have to play it just right or else she could be endangering the most important man in her life. And she knew the danger could literally be life threatening.

CHAPTER 13

The pool hall was located in a strip mall in Olathe, Kansas, yet another large Kansas City suburb southwest of the city. The homes in Olathe are more affordable than in some the more affluent suburbs. It is also remains a manageable commute to the US Marshall office, thus many of the married SOG members with kids chose to live there, given their limited government salaries. Jack considered the pool hall out of his way but since all his colleagues lived in the area he went regularly with his coworkers whom he typically socialized with.

Being ex-military, one of Jack's biggest pet peeves was being late for anything. Because he had overslept, Jack was irritated when he arrived to meet his friends, almost 30 minutes late. Pulling into the parking lot, the pool hall was already packed, despite it being relatively early for a Saturday night. Instead of wasting further time driving around looking for a closer parking spot, Jack pulled into the first open spot available near the back of the lot.

After parking, Jack climbed out of his truck, pushed the lock button and began walking across the large lot to the entrance. As he walked Jack noticed three guys hanging around a 70's model Chevy truck drinking beers under one of the parking lot lights. Having visited this establishment before Jack didn't blame them for pre-gaming, given the over inflated drink prices inside.

The 3 men were all large. As Jack walked by he gauged each of the 3 men stood a few inches over his own 6 feet. The men were more than just tall however, as Jack estimated the smallest of the trio was a plump 250 pounds with the other two easily pushing 300 plus. All three men wore jeans and work boots. The small one had on a red Kansas Jayhawks hoodie, while the other two wore Carhartt style jackets; one with a Jayhawks baseball cap and the other a

Jay-hawks beanie. Jack nodded to the three men as he passed by as the men were throwing their beer cans into the bed of the truck and followed him inside.

Entering the pool hall, Jack walked through a set of double doors into an eight feet squared room where two benches sat along either side and then through a second set of double doors to the main room, where there was another square space where two bouncers sat. Having visited the establishment previously, the inside was familiar to Jack. The inside of the room was a large rectangle with pool tables distributed evenly throughout, in two long rows. To the left of the doors, a bar ran the length of the room, serving beer in bottles, fountain sodas and bar snacks such as popcorn, nachos and hot dogs. To the right was an area with bar height tables and the restrooms.

Entering the main room, Jack stepped to his left giving the 3 men behind him an opportunity to pass, as he allowed his eyes time to adjust to the dim lighting. As Jack was searching for his friends, he heard someone say, "You need to take that shirt off".

Not realizing the remarks were directed at him, Jack continued to scan the crowded room trying to locate Chris and the others.

"Hey West Virginia, I said take that damn shirt off! This is a Jayhawk bar," the raised voice garnering the attention of the entire room.

This time Jack was acutely aware the statement was directed at him. Peering to his left, he saw the trio from the parking lot. "Take that bullshit off. This is a KU establishment," the smallest man growled.

"Yeah, I don't think so pal," Jack replied his voice dripping with contempt.

"Oh you're going to take it off, or I am going to take it off you," the man sneered.

Any other day, under similar circumstances Jack would have attempted to avoid the confrontation. Today however he didn't feel passive and stated matter of factly, "I'd like to see you try fat boy. I'll break your damn arm before you can lay a fat finger on this shirt".

"You and what army you fuckin punk!" raged the small man stepping towards Jack cocking his right arm.

"Trust me guy you don't want none of me, back the fuck up" Jack said in an even tone stepping forward with malice intent.

Before the pair of men could come together however, the two bouncers stepped between them. "Hey Jimmie! Cut that shit out. I told y'all last time we don't do that shit here." One of the two intervening men said, "This is your warning, one more and I call the cops and ban y'all from ever coming back.

"C'mon man" the one with the beanie said as the two larger men hurried Jimmie away, "no need to waste your time on this guy".

Though not before Jimmie could spout off, "You're lucky West Virginia."

Jack watched the trio walk away. When he turned back to the room, Chris and another member of his team, Tom Ball, were standing there. "What was that all about?" Tom asked.

"No idea, some idiot with liquid courage and no common sense apparently," Jack replied.

"Damn," Tom said. "I thought I was going to get to see you tear into somebody other than us," referencing that Jack, in addition to his sniper duties, was also the regional hand to hand com-bat instructor for the US Marshal Office.

Chris chuckled at Tom's remark before adding "C'mon man we're over here".

Jack and his friends occupied a pair of tables near the restrooms. For an hour, Jack and his fellow Marshals shot pool and told stories of better times. Tom and John Pearson, who was the breach man for alpha squad, were easily the two best pool players of the group though Chris was able to give them both an occasional run for their money. In total there were seven men from unit present.

Jack recognized it took him a moment to wind down from the earlier confrontation yet it was very nice to just relax with his friends, letting go of his worries. While the other six team mem-bers were nursing beers, Jack chose to sip Diet Cokes after waking hung over. After the third soda, nature called and he needed to use the restroom.

The men's restroom was typical of public restrooms. Inside the door there was a short area walled on both sides leading to a big trough sink on the left. Beyond the sink were a row of three urinals and a single stall in the rear of the room. After stepping from the dim lights of the main room, the bright florescent lights of the restroom were very harsh, showing the fading green and cream colored tile. Walking into the tight space, Jack stepped around a guy washing his hands sink. He relieved himself in the second urinal.

As he zipped up and turned to wash his own hands, the door opened and the three fat guys from the parking lot entered led by Jimmie. Once all three were inside, the guy with the base-ball cap locked the door behind.

"I told you to take that fucking shirt off asshole, now I am going to take it off for you," Jimmie sneered.

Jack had always been taught and believed there is a time for words and there is a time for ac-tions Jack knew Jimmie and his buddies probably thought that since they locked the door and out numbered him he would be scared. They probably thought he would try to talk his way out of the confrontation or would look to retreat. They were mistaken.

As Jimmie finished speaking, he brought his right hand back to swing the same haymaker he wanted to unleash earlier before being stopped by the two bouncers. Instead of backing up Jack stepped forward on his left foot then simply used the ball of his left foot as a pivot point, kicking with his right foot from where it stood, a much more efficient movement. The kick landed solidly on the outside of Jimmie's left knee. The sound of the impact was a sickening crack in the en-closed space. The knee buckled in a manner it was never intended to go naturally. Jimmie went down in a heap, as an ugly scream escaped his lips.

Taking advantage of the momentary confusion of the two fat guys, who were slow in processing what had just happened to their friend, Jack instantly sprung over the fallen body of Jimmie into the guy with the beanie on his head. Using the momentum of the jump, Jack got inside the guy's arms and smashed his head into the bottom of the man's chin. Instantly the big man's head ripped back, staggering him. With his arms flailing as he tried to catch his balance, his midsec-tion was left open. Jack drove both of his fists into the big man's exposed diaphragm, knocking the wind from his massive frame and sending him further back on his heels. The action sent the man into his partner with the baseball cap, who tried to catch him but was overwhelmed by the man's size. The momentum carried both men into the locked door where they hit hard, before sliding down to the floor. At the end of the crash the man with the baseball cap was pinned on the ground under his friend, unable to get his arms free.

Jack took the opportunity to place his knee in the front man's chest effectively immobilizing the pair. "Next time your dumb asses decide to pick a fight. Don't" Jack yelled. Driving his point home he swung a viscous backhand across the face to than man on top, smashing his lips into his teeth, bursting them instantaneously. Jack raised his hand again and the man raised his hands across his face to ward off another blow. The guy beneath him had lost the baseball cap and began to cry, trying to hide his face behind his friends head and shoulders as his arms remained stuck beneath his friend. "We good?" Jack yelled. Both man began nodding furiously. "We good?" Jack yelled again. Again they nodded. "Say it, 'we good'?" Jack yelled again.

"Yes, we're good," they responded in unison.

"Louder."

"We're good!" they yelled.

"Good, now I am going to get off you and you're going to get up and open the door. You are go-ing to walk out and sit down at one of the tables outside and we are going to call an ambulance for your friend over there and wait around for the cops to make a statement. And if either of you try anything stupid I am going to hurt you. Do you understand?"

Before they could answer, there was a pounding at the door. "Jack, everything all right in there?"

Looking at the pair Jack said, "Understand?"

"Yes," they mumbled.

"Good." Jack arose and stepped back, kicking back into Jimmie to ensure he didn't do anything stupid. The pair of fat guys got up slowly and carefully. The guy on the bottom upon rising turned, unlocked and opened the door.

"Now go sit your fat asses down. I will be out in a second."

As the pair treaded away Jack turned and looked at Jimmie laying on the ground still holding his knee. "Ambulance will be here in a minute, do you have any weapons or anything on you?"

"Man fuck you, you busted my goddamn knee!"

"Whatever asshole, you're lucky I didn't bust your damn skull. Now you got anything on you be-fore the ambulance gets here. Because if one of the cops or paramedics get hurt helping your ass I will do more than hurt you."

"I ain't got nothin man. You busted my leg, how am I supposed to work like this?" he sobbed.

"Honestly I don't care asshole. Maybe you will think twice before you try that shit again with someone." Jack said as he pulled out his phone and dialed 9-1-1.

The police and paramedics showed up within 10 minutes, as Jack was explaining what had happened to Chris and the pool hall's owner. Jack's rendition was confirmed with an occasional nod from the two bigger guys, who were brothers named Tom and Tony Rollins. The two men were Jimmie's cousins. Upon arrival the police took Jack's statement along with the brothers who were arrested for assault and disturbing the peace. Jimmie was also ordered under arrest but was taken away by the paramedics. One of the paramedics was overheard telling Jimmie he would likely have to undergo reconstructive surgery on the knee.

Upon finishing with the police and paramedics, Jack's mood again turned sullen. He tried to re-main engaged with his friends but he got more and more uncomfortable as time went on. He began feeling like everyone in the bar was staring at him, talking about what had happened. By 10 pm he had enough and told the guys he was heading home. His drive home took what seemed an eternity as he felt tightness in his chest as his hands shook the entire commute.

CHAPTER 14

CB called her dad and the two agreed to meet for breakfast Sunday morning. They met at a place called Maggie's Diner which is a small diner near French Creek, on route 20, near the state ran Game Farm, which exhibited native West Virginia wildlife for people to view. More importantly, it was near CB's childhood home where Thomas still lived and a place she and her father had frequented when she was but a girl. She had suggested the place, knowing its location and nostalgia would be to much for her father to resist.

CB arrived first despite having to drive 20 minutes to get there. Pulling into the parking lot, she could not help but recall fond memories of the place; mostly of her dad bringing her here regularly as a little girl. While she hadn't been back since high school, the place looked virtually the same. The outside was a white sided long low building with a slant roof. There were two big windows on either side of the red door that was perfectly centered, with a quaint sign featuring the restaurant's hours, yet was so sun faded it was nearly illegible.

Walking through the door, CB realized the interior had also seemingly remained untouched by time. It was a long narrow room. Along one side was a white laminate lunch counter, stained a dull yellow from years of coffee rings and cigarette smoke; from before the smoking ordinances banned smoking indoors. Along the walls, on either side of the door, were similar laminate topped tables with tall ladder backed wooden chairs. Even the greasy spoon smells were the same: bacon grease and coffee.

The fact she recognized the smell, reminded her about something she had read in college: a person's sense of smell is strongly tied to memories, similar to music. And just like a song coming on the radio can take a person back to a moment in time certain smells can do the same.

CB was broken from her trance when one of the waitresses at the bar said, "Seat yourself honey, we'll be with you in a minute".

As a kid, CB recalled, she and her dad had always sat side-by-side at the counter on the traditional round barstools. She fondly remembered the bar stools. As a small girl, her feet didn't reach the floor and her legs would stick to the red vinyl material when she wore shorts. She liked the funny sound it made when she peeled them away and how much she enjoyed spinning round and round as they awaited their meals.

Today however, despite there being space at the counter CB chose an unoccupied table tucked away in the corner of the room, wanting a little more privacy away from the other customers and the staff. She took the seat placing her back against the wall, allowing her to see entirety of the room and the front door.

After she was settled in her seat, an older waitress came over and asked CB if she needed a menu. CB asked for two and ordered coffee, telling the woman she would order food after her father arrived. The waitress quickly brought a tall heavy mug full of black liquid and a small bowl containing single servers of creamer to the table. CB added two of the half and half cups to the cup, along with two sugars, stirring it in with a spoon from the napkin roll.

Drinking her coffee, a flood of memories from her childhood came pouring in, inspired by the sights and smells. Her mom had left her and her Dad when CB was 10-years-old. Since she left, CB had talked to her on only two occasions:

her high school graduation, when she had called out of the blue, and again at her aunt's funeral five years ago. Alas Thomas Greene had raised CB himself during her formative years. While working in the gas fields had made it difficult for him to be there all the time; he was a loving and supporting father. When he was home he made it a point to take her fishing, on motorcycle rides, or to this diner as much as he could. Thus, CB and her father were really close growing up. They remained close even through high school when she was involved in a number of extracurricular activities and became more interested in boys. Thomas, she recalled with a grin was very supportive of the extracurricular, the boys not so much.

While he was a good father, he nonetheless, often reminded CB it takes a village to raise a child. The reminder typically meant she was going to be staying with someone while he worked. Most often, she spent her days with her grandparents when Thomas was working. She spent many days with her grandmother in the garden or on the porch snapping green beans or shelling peas. When not with her grandma she would be with her grandfather in the garage, working on old cars. However as their health deteriorated as they got older, Thomas would call on the neighbors of the surrounding community when she was in high school asking everyone to keep an eye on her, since she was often home alone. Thus, even when Thomas wasn't avail-able to do it himself there was always a grandparent or neighbor to get her to practice, help with homework, or even talk about boys and the pressures of life as a teenage girl in a small town. She acknowledged that even though she hated it at the time, she wouldn't change a thing about it.

She acknowledged she took a small piece from all those who helped raise her but she was still very much her father's daughter. He taught her the value of hard work and that she could accomplish anything when she put her mind to it. She even appreciated how leaving her alone so often while he worked, helped to mold her into the strong and independent woman she was to-day.

It wasn't until CB had left for college that Thomas had gotten into trouble with opioids and the law. One day as he was standing on the platform of the drilling rig platform when a drive chain snapped behind him. Thomas turned towards the ugly sound, to see what was wrong. His turn took him straight into the path of the chain which was whipping across the platform. He tried to jump — to late. The heavy steel caught Thomas shin high on both legs, snapping the bones. Worse yet, the blow swept him completely off the platform, where he fell 8 feet before landing flat on his back.

He was rushed to the hospital via ambulance. Doctors determined he would need hardware in his right leg to help the bones heal. After surgery he had been prescribed opioids for his pain. The pills were continued to be fed to him for the next 6 months of rehab like they were candy while Thomas recovered and learned to walk again. However, when the worker's compensation people determined he had reached full medical improvement, the medications stopped.

From CB's perspective it seemed, the doctors and pharmacists apparently never considered they had created an addict. Without the medications, Thomas struggled. He wasn't in pain physically be needed the medications to feel normal. Because of his need, it didn't take Thomas long to find a supplier for the pills his body craved. In the beginning he bought enough to take the edge off. But soon he was needing more and more pills. As the need for pills grew so did the price; but, because he was making good money at the time, he could afford it. With the aid of the pills he continued to be functional at work, but was becoming more and more withdrawn at home. But because he had even earned promotions while using, moving from roughneck to tool pusher, the man essentially in charge of any drilling site; Thomas didn't think he had a problem at all.

But then six years after the accident and constant pill consumption there was a market correction and the drilling stopped essentially everywhere. Thomas was laid off from work and the paychecks stopped coming. It wasn't long after, he was arrested — for petty theft. For the next 3 years Thomas was in and out of jail for a series of crimes, all related to his addiction. Finally he was caught with a substantial amount of pills. He was charged him with felony possession and intent to deliver. Luckily, he was still new enough in the system, the prosecutor agreed to a plea of felony possession but was willing to drop the intent to deliver charge. He served nine months after good behavior in the State facility. After his release, he swore to CB he had remained clean.

Clean, he was also able to return to work in the oil fields. His friend, Tony Kincaid had gotten Thomas a job working for Jeremy Marshall, where Kincaid also worked. At first he works on a crew under Tommy who had been Marshall's right hand man. However he was quickly promoted to run his own crew after proving himself to Marshall. Now he worked as Marshall's head trouble shooter going from site to site along with an engineer, examining drill sites and equipment when trouble arose and Marshall's company was asked to consult.

In addition to the consulting, he also ran a specialty crew for really difficult jobs that required more than a consult. The position often required him to essentially live on the drilling sights 24/7 for weeks at a time. On job sights, his role was one of project manager, technical expert and motivator. Once he and his crew arrived, Thomas assumed command of the entire operation. It was a job that not only required an understanding of drilling but also a man who could handle a crew of rough necks and keep them on task. On the site his word was law and anyone who broke the law was dealt with accordingly.

CB was under no illusions when it came to her dad. While he had always been kind and loving to her, she also knew he had a reputation for being a man not to mess with. As a big man, 6'4" tall, weighing every bit of 260 pounds he was a man who could certainly bring violence into play if he needed. CB knew, in fact, he had at times.

CB had just finished her coffee, when through the window she saw her father pull into the parking lot. He was driving his pride and joy, a 1977 Pontiac Trans Am which he had restored to match the car from Smokey and the Bandit exactly. CB had watched the movie with him so many times growing up she thought she could probably still quote it beginning to end. Her dad though had always loved the car. Shortly after her mom had left he had found and bought a junked out version of it, saying he was going to restore it. The car had remained sitting in the garage for years and years just collecting dust thereafter. Even in his hard times, the two things Thomas would sell were the car or his property, though CB knew he had been offered money for both. Finally in the last few years, Thomas held true to his word and got the car finished. CB admitted the car looked good, T-tops and all.

Her thoughts were interrupted when the bell over the door clanged lightly as Thomas walked in. As he came in CB though thought he looked well, all things considered. Though, she thought to herself, he could stand to trim his scraggly beard and get a haircut. Standing she said, "Over here Dad".

At her call, Thomas turned and saw his daughter. He walked across the room, gave her a big bear hug and sat down. Despite being 56-years-old the man was still strong as a bull. "It's good to see you baby girl. We don't get a chance to do this often enough".

"I know Dad, I'm sorry."

"No worries baby girl we both gotta work. I know you got big things to do, chasing all those bad guys" Thomas said with a grin, sitting down opposite her.

No sooner had he sat down than the waitress reappeared with a mug and a cravat of coffee having recognized Thomas. Thomas poured himself a cup of the coffee while the waitress con-firmed he wanted his usual big breakfast, which consisted of 3 eggs, 2 slices of bacon, a sausage patty, hash browns, 2 pancakes and a bowl of grits. Thomas smiled at the girl saying yes to the order. The waitress turned to CB who asked for yogurt and fresh fruit. The waitress wrote down the orders and left.

As the waitress walked away, CB refilled her mug with coffee. Taking a breath she the said, "Funny you should mention work Dad, because honestly that is why I am here." No sooner had the words left her mouth than CB could immediately perceive a change in Thomas posture and the look on his face immediately went from smiles to a hard frown. The look reminded her to be very careful in how she approached this and to not let him know her suspicions about Marshall and what she was really looking for.

"Look honey I don't know what you have heard but I haven't done anything, I swear. I go to work, sometimes for weeks without a break and come back to the house to sleep and that's it."

"No, no Dad, nothing like that. What I need is information," she said quickly, trying to get to more comfortable ground.

"Information about what?" he asked still obviously suspicious.

"Dad you heard about the man was killed out Audra Park this last weekend?"

"Yeah I guess I heard something about it since we work the same place. Come on now baby what do you really want to know?" he asked her matter-of-factly.

She chided herself at the question and for trying to be to covert. Choosing to be more direct she said, "Dad I am the lead investigator on the case."

"Oh wow!" Thomas responded, truly shocked by the statement and the accompanying realization he didn't really know what his daughter did as a State Policeman. Taking a moment he finally responded "But what do you want from me? I mean I kinda knew the guy from around the shop but I mean he didn't work on my crew or anything."

"Dad to be honest you I am looking for any information. Anything you can tell me about Roberts would be great. I talked to his parents who are clearly distraught. They said he didn't have a girl friend or any significant others in his life. Said he was friends with someone named Tim but they didn't know any last name," she said now feeling like she was on more comfortable ground.

"Honestly, baby girl I barely knew the man. We worked for the same company, but he had never been on one of my crews. Like I said he was more one of one of those guys I would see around the shop on occasion, but that's about it. From what I hear, he was a decent enough guy but I heard he may have been caught up in some stuff, but that's really just rig talk. You'd have to ask the boss for anything specific."

"What kind of stuff?"

"I don't know drugs and stuff I guess. I mean he if he's working with us, you know he has a record too. But I promise baby girl, I've been clean since I got out of jail. It is pretty well known amongst the crews I am clean and don't want that shit anywhere near my rigs, so people don't exactly confide that kind of information to me. If you know what I mean."

"I know all that Dad. But what if I told you I think this could have been related to the stuff Tony got caught up in. It just all five of the dead guys are like you in that they are all are or were roughnecks on the rigs with addictions to pain killers".

"Honey there are a lot of guys on the rigs who are prescribed pain killers."

"Come on Dad, don't bullshit me. You and I both know that isn't what we are talking about here. These guys were addicts. Like you are an addict. They were getting their drugs somewhere and I am looking for a name or a direction. I have never asked you for anything like this before and never will again but someone needs to find this guy before more people get hurt. Hell Dad be-fore you get hurt" she said more forcefully than she wanted, and noticed a few heads both the other patrons turned her way.

Thomas just sat there and stared at his daughter with his mouth agape. Never before had his daughter spoken to him like that and frankly it shocked him into reality. Not only was his baby girl all grown up but she had a job to do. And for the first time in years she was asking for his help; something she hadn't done since she was ten years old when her mother left leaving just the two of them. It showed how desperate for help she was. After a moment he responded "Baby girl, you're looking for a needle in a haystack. There are a ton of guys who can get pills on the rigs".

"I am sure there are dad but these guys all live within a small area. The area I am responsible for. And every single one of them were using low dosage Roxycodone, the same stuff they found Tony with. There can't be that many guys who are dealing that kind of stuff around here."

"Look I might be able to help you out honey. But you have to be careful. These people don't fuck around. They will hurt you. They will hurt everyone."

"Dad, I am investigating a murder for sure and quite likely five murders. I think I am more familiar with what they can do than you."

"Ok, ok, look honey I can't give you a name right now. I really have been clean and sober since I was released the last time. Besides you already know Tony was who used to hook me up. But let me put out a feeler or two and I will let you know what I find out."

Hearing her dad refer to Tony for the first time made CB think. CB remembered a fun loving man who used to hang out at her house with her dad when she was a little girl. She remembered how shocked she was when he was picked up for distribution and even more shocked when she found out he had been killed in the regional jail; found stabbed to death with an improvised chiv made from a broken toothbrush handle honed to a sharp point. He had been in custody less than 24 hours, hand even spoken yet to a lawyer or offered a bail hearing. The murder had never been solved. The belief was he was killed because someone was afraid he was going to turn a deal with the police. The thought made CB look away and reply simply and softly, "Be careful Dad, please."

"Always baby girl," the big man replied reaching across the table to turn her chin towards him and to give her his standard cocksure grin that always reassured her that the man was unbreakable.

"Thanks Dad. Just a name, nothing else," she said.

Thomas nodded and a moment later their food arrived. The pair then enjoyed their meal together catching up and reminiscing, the awkwardness of the conversation now behind them.

CHAPTER 15

Sunday, Jack was up at 5 am, which was his norm. As his thoughts began to focus on another day alone, he braced himself for another day of self pity. He couldn't or wouldn't, he was unsure, explain it to Dr. Hartman, but Jack felt he was trapped in his own head. All morning he tried to keep himself occupied but despite his best efforts, his thoughts kept returning to what had happened in Nebraska. Why it was different from any of the other missions he had ever been on in his life? Why could he not drop the guy who was clearly a danger to the assault team? Not to mention the man's own family.

Worse still, the further he analyzed his actions he recognized he felt guilt over ending the cold blooded killer's life; though he knew in reality killing the man was similar to killing a rabid dog. While he never wanted to be the judge, jury and executioner for any man, he knew Deen's death was likely a favor to society, likely saving lives and tax dollars. Thinking about it further, he thought if anything, he should feel more for some of the enemy combatants he had killed in Iraq or Afghanistan. At least some of those men, he knew, were acting out of coercion. With them he recognized feeling somewhat empathetic but not the overriding guilt he was currently experiencing.

When he was able to thwart the thoughts of the men he had unceremoniously killed, he spent time wondering if there was anything he could have differently at the pool hall. He admitted to himself he likely could have stopped the trio without putting the guy in the hospital but at the same time the 3 men had forced the fight.

Having been as introspective as he could stand, Jack decided he had to get out of his apartment. In an effort to clear his mind Jack went to the gym, hoping the physical exertion would help. At the gym, he put in his earbuds and put on his workout music playlist. For the next three hours he jammed out to Rage Against the Machine, Pantera, Metalica, Linkin Park and others while he worked out. He pushed every weight and used every machine he could find. By the time he was done, he was as exhausted physically as he felt mentally.

After showering at the gym, he still didn't feel ready to go home and be alone. Instead, he went to a nearby book store, trying to find something to occupy his mind. His efforts took him all over the store's aisles. After what felt like an eternity of aimless wandering, Jack found himself facing the self-help section, looking over books about managing anxiety and depression. He picked a few up off the shelf, but the thought of buying any of those titles scared Jack nearly as much as his hesitation in Nebraska had. Just looking at the covers and the photos of the authors, all wearing fake smiles, triggered another cold sweat and rapidly raising heart beat. Leaving the self help section, Jack remained steadfast about finding something. Finally, frustrated by not finding anything new by one of his favorite authors, and not willing to pay the cover price for anyone he hadn't yet read, Jack bought a pair of books off the discount table.

Leaving the bookstore, Jack realized he was starving. He made a quick stop at a Chipotle near his apartment for a burrito. Once home, he sat down to eat and read. He finished the burrito in a few bites but found neither of the books were able to get hold his attention. A new search of the television proved fruitless once again. Still feeling the need to do something to avoid his own thoughts, Jack spent the remainder of the day stripping and cleaning his weapons while he flipped back and forth between football games he had absolutely no interest in.

Finally at 8 pm he took a shower and tried to force himself to go to bed. He spent the night tossing and turning.

CHAPTER 16

The next morning, Jack was up at 4 am having gotten almost no sleep. What sleep he did get was again interrupted with dreams from Iraq, and Afghanistan. The dreams were so vivid Jack felt the heat of the desert sun and the iciness of the mountain sides at night. Disturbingly, Jack thought this was probably the first time he ever really considered what had occurred over there. Deciding he would rather be tired than relive those experiences again, Jack went into the kitchen, made a pot of coffee and watched the local news until it was time to get ready for work.

Jack finished off the last cup of coffee in the truck on his way to the office. Arriving at the office, he immediately headed to the conference room for another cup. Still tired from the night before, though he wasn't quite sure if he was more tired from the lack of sleep or the emotional drain the dreams had brought.

To start each week, the SOG team met in the conference room to review the upcoming training schedules and task assignments. When Jack arrived there were already a few people there, including Chris and Kevin. As Jack filled his coffee cup Chris said "Hey man, Dickson wants you in his office first thing"

"Dickson? Why?"

"I don't know I assume he is going to ask you about Dr. Hartman since the rest of us have to go see her today."

"Oh, yeah, forgot about that, I'll head down and see him in second."

Jack took a sip of my coffee and went to Captain Dickson's office, on the opposite side of the building from the conference room. As he walked, Jack noticed many of the people he met along the way avoided eye contact, which made him feel somewhat on edge.

Captain Dickson's door it was standing open. Dickson was sitting at his desk looking at the screen of his laptop perched in front of him. Instead of overlooking the dumpsters his view was of the main street leading to the building, some trees and another office building across the street which had a fountain out front. Every time Jack entered Captain Dickson's office he could not help but wonder why corporate executives and others brag of the view from their office's and yet have their desks turned to face the hall as opposed to the view they are so proud of. Jack knocked firmly on the door frame and Dickson looked up for whatever he was looking at and said, "Oh hey Jack. Come on in and close the door".

The request caused to close the door added to Jack's unease. Never once in the time Jack had been under Dickson's command had the Captain asked him to close the door. For that matter, Jack couldn't recall having ever seen the door closed at all. After the momentary delay to process the unexpected request Jack closed the door. As the door audibly clicked closed "Jack you may want to sit down".

'Damn,' Jack thought, 'close the door and sit down, this can't be good'. Jack sat in the chair to the left of the desk, closest to the door he just closed; realizing he may want to leave the room in a hurry.

"Jack, I don't know how to say this so I am going to be straight with you. After your little incident this weekend at the pool hall I sent an email of the incident to Dr. Hartman yesterday as a matter of protocol since you have not been cleared by her yet after the thing that happened in Nebraska last week. Jack she called me last night and recommended you be placed on 30 days of administration leave. I tried to tell her it wasn't necessary but she insisted. I need you to go over to her office at 10 am this morning after we complete the paperwork here. But until she gives you clearance you are officially on leave."

"Leave? What the hell are you talking about? For what?"

"Honestly Jack I have no idea and Dr. Hartman wasn't willing to tell me why she recommended the action but she did. We can see about getting you to another shrink for an evaluation but honestly that would take longer than the 30 days will."

"I know that, I just don't get it. All because I got into a fight with a few guys who attacked me? It doesn't make any sense!"

"I know, I don't get it either. Look man go talk to doc at 10 and see what she says. If you can change her mind get back in here tomorrow. If not, all I can say is enjoy your vacation because it's out of my hands."

After signing a few papers and leaving the office, Jack didn't know what to do. He wasn't sure whether it was appropriate to be disappointed, pissed off or somewhere in between. Strangely though, he admitted feeling some relief. While signing the administrative leave papers, Captain Dickson advised Jack not to say anything to the guys, again reiterating the need to go see Dr. Hartman. Following Dickson's advice left the building and walked straight to his truck. Getting in and turning the key, however Jack realized it was still only 8:20 am and Hartman office didn't open wasn't until 10, though Jack had had earlier appointments with her previously. He drove to her office anyway stopping for another cup of coffee on the way.

****

The first thing you have to learn in the Army is patience. There is a reason "hurry up and wait" is something of an unofficial motto for the US Army as soldiers experience the phenomenon routinely. It begins the first day of basic training and continues until the day a soldier is handed his DD 214 (discharge papers). However, the patience required of the common soldier is nothing compared to the patience required of a sniper. Snipers literally have to be able to lay motionless, in the same position, for hours on end, awaiting on one specific circumstance to occur before they can do their job.

To emphasize this point, in sniper school, SFC Bates told Jack's class he had sat watch on one widow for 18 hours a day for 22 straight days on a mission. Jack openly admitted he never approached that threshold, though he had spent multiple shifts lasting 12 or more hours scanning an assigned area without break in every imaginable condition: desert heat, falling rain, mountain cold and sand storms to name but a few. Thus, his wait in the parking of less than an hour for Dr. Hartman's arrival was nothing to endure as he enjoyed his coffee and listened to the radio.

Dr. Hartman arrived at 9:30 sharp, though Jack noticed Willow, the receptionist, had been there for 32 minutes more, having arrived at 8:58. Jack however did not immediately follow Dr. Hart-man in. Instead he remained sitting in the parking lot, still unsure of what, if anything, he should discuss with her. He knew he was supposed to ask about the suspension but in hi mind he was more concerned with if he would ever be "normal" again.

At 9:50 he climbed out of the truck and proceeded directly to her office. He found the front door unlocked despite the office not being officially opened. As he walked in Willow said completely unsurprised by his presence, "Head on back Jack. She is waiting for you."

Similar to his prior visit, Jack again contemplated how the hallway from the receptionist's desk to Dr. Hartman's office seemed much further away in perception than in reality. Covering the distance seemed to take an eternity. Arriving at the her office door, which was open Jack remained standing at the threshold unspeaking and unwilling to knock to announce his presence. Jack asked himself once again "what am I doing" as he watched Dr. Hartman typing something at her desk. As he watched, without saying a word she raised her right hand and waived him in as she continued to type with the left. Somewhat taken back by the unanticipated movement Jack entered the room and eyed the couch again; thought better of it and instead sat in the chair across the desk from the doctor, remaining silent while she finished typing.

After a moment Dr. Hartman completed her typing, closed the laptop and finally looked across the desk at Jack. The pair sat and stared at one another for over 2 minutes before she finally spoke. "So Jack, you don't seem upset that I recommended you be placed on admin leave?"

"What is there to be upset about? You're the expert. You don't tell me how to do my job and I am not going to tell you how to do yours," Jack replied evenly.

"So you are ok with taking leave?" she asked.

"Look Doc, I am going to be straight with you. I don't know what is going on upstairs right now. I can't get the other day out of my head. I feel guilty and I don't know why I hesitated. I don't know that if I am in the same situation again if I will hesitate again. I got lucky last time the guy missed. I can't take that risk again. If you think sometime off is going to help then so be it." He responded quickly, afraid if he didn't say it now he never would.

"Time off. I would not call it time off. I want you to use this time to clear your head. I want you to get a way from it all. I want you to reflect. I want you to take the next 3 weeks and simply go away and find something to do that is as far away from work as you can get. Then after three weeks I want you to come in here everyday for a week and talk to me about what you have learned. Afterwards we'll make another determination."

"That's it? What am I supposed to reflect on?   What am I supposed to tell you in 3 weeks?"

"I don't know, Jack. But in three weeks I think you might," she said in an assuring manner, putting Jack at ease.

The two talked for a few minutes more before Dr. Hartman gave Jack a note pad, asking that he write down a few thoughts every day. When he asked her what thoughts, Dr. Hartman asked that he write his feelings regarding his life's path and how it has affected him and whether he has balance inches life. Then she emphasized she wanted nothing negative written down with-out 2 positive attributes to offset it. Finally Dr. Hartman reiterated she thought it was important he get away. She said getting away from work, his friends from work and finding a place where he could leave it all behind for a bit would help him reflect.

Before Jack left Dr. Hartman added she would like for him to check in with the office once a week before his appointment, just so she knew he was all right. Jack told her he would. Walking out, Jack stopped by Willow's desk, scheduled the appointment and left.

*****

Returning to his apartment, Jack looked the place over. The reality of the small space, making three weeks leave sound like a really good idea. However, as a career government employee, first in the Army and now in the US Marshall service Jack didn't have the money to just pack up and go to the Caribbean or Europe for a three week hiatus. Nor did he honestly have much of a desire to leave American soil once again; having toured much of the world in the Army, just not the places you see on the post cards. Instead he saw what he would describe as the real world. Jack admitted the US was not without its flaws too, but understood there is always something to be said for home. Thus he decided "home" was exactly where he was going to go: West Virginia. Where he had been born and raised; where his parents, two siblings and a few friends still lived.

Walking to his bedroom, Jack grabbed an old ruck sack from the closet. He quickly packed some clothes, then went to the bathroom and threw his shaving kit. His clothing and hygiene needs taken care of, Jack returned to the bedroom and pulled the slide out from beneath the bed. While it looked like a big drawer, or what one female acquaintance had described as a trundle, the big box was actually a gun safe. Opening it, Jack pulled out his own Remington 700 sniper rifle was an exact copy of his service weapon. It had cost Jack damn near 2 months salary with all the upgrades and accessories but it was worth it in his mind. Despite Dr. Hart-man's advice to get away from work and relax, Jack admitted he was most relaxed on the range shooting. He knew other people relaxed by playing golf or fishing or in a number of other ways but Jack always felt most comfortable at the weapons range and he planned on firing some rounds at his parent's farm over the next few weeks.

Jack threw the ruck sack over his shoulder, picked up the rifle and a few boxes of ammunition for each his weapons and went to his truck. Jack owned a black crew cab F-150. Like most four door pickups the back seat is designed to fold to allow for cargo space inside the cab. In his, Jack had a custom box built that fit perfectly in the space underneath the rear seat, similar to the weapons box under his bed. The box was padded and sectioned off specifically to hold firearms. Inside the lockbox Jack placed his rifle and the boxes along of ammunition.

After securing the lock, Jack locked the truck and returned to the apartment to check the fridge. He dumped the last bit of milk he had down the drain, made a ham and cheese sandwich for the road and then put the remaining bread, meat and cheese in the trash. Fairly certain there was nothing remaining in the place that would go bad, Jack locked the apartment, took the trash to the dumpster, hopped in the truck and headed for I-70 E. His planned line of travel was I-70 E to I-64 E in St. Louis to I-79 N in Charleston WV to his child hood home, Buckhannon.

CHAPTER 17

The drive from Kansas City to Buckhannon, took 12 hours with 2 stops for fuel, food and bath-room breaks. Jack had always enjoyed road trips, even when by himself, which he had done many during his time in the military. He found there is something about the open road that just helped his mind decompress; and admitted if there was ever a time for decompression this was it.

As he drove he called his parents to tell them he was coming for a visit and spent the rest of the journey listening to Outlaw Country on the XM radio. No better way to take the mind off his problems than listening to Willie Nelson, Johnny Cash, Waylon Jennings and company sing songs about the problems of their day.

While their songs regularly referenced the coal mines and coal miners of West Virginia, Jack was reminded how times had changed. Beginning at the State line separating Kentucky and West Virginia, Jack was saw few signs of coal mines, but instead saw natural gas derricks lit up all over the state. Despite the hour and darkness, the tower lights from the drilling platforms marked their presence. The economy of the area was no longer driven by coal, but instead an-other of the state's natural resources, natural gas. It seemed half the people Jack knew from his youth now worked the rigs, including his brother Bob. As kid, Jack remembered having a small gas well on his family's farm along with a few neighbors having wells, though they seemed rare enough. Today, however, the drillers were placing the wells everywhere and the state was liter-ally pock marked with wells and tiny gravel roads to service them.

By the time Jack exited US 33 at his hometown exit it was almost 11 pm. Other than being stiff from the drive, Jack was actually feeling rather relaxed. At the light at the bottom of the exit ramp Jack decided to make one last pitstop to use the restroom and fill his tank before driving the remaining 20 minutes to his parents house. Jack pulled up to the pump, got out and stretched.

As he stretched, Jack realized he hadn't been in his hometown in almost three years and hadn't lived there in almost 20. Nonetheless, his initial glimpse told him the place looked relatively the same as it always had. The Walmart was still behind the gas station with an adjoining strip mall and a few small stores beyond. Looking in the other direction, Jack saw The Donut Shop, a lo-cal landmark, still stood looking as it always had.

He debated going through the drive through to get a pepperoni roll. A pepperoni roll is a West Virginia tradition in which the bakers bake yeast rolls stuffed with pepperoni and various cheeses, similar to a calzone — but different. In Jack's mind the Donut Shop made the best pepperoni rolls in the state. He decided against stopping tonight but made a mental note to have a few while he was in town.

The kinks worked free, Jack headed inside to use the restroom and to prepay for the fuel. Walking across the parking lot, Jack noted there were 3 cars parked in front of the store. One a beat up Subaru, appearing to be held together by an assortment of bumper-stickers on its backend; a newer model GMC pickup truck with the logo of a drilling company along its flank and a Jeep Cherokee. Opening the door, he heard the bell chime, notifying the clerks of his arrival.

Inside the door, Jack stopped momentarily to allow his eyes adjust to the florescent lit environment. As his eyes adjusted he took a moment to look at the big mirrors mounted around the store, which were used by the clerks to keep an eye out for shoplifting. He saw there were more people inside than the amount of cars indicated. There were 2 clerks working the register and food area. Both appeared to be younger guys, in their early twenties, who Jack guessed were likely students from the local college working part time jobs based upon their general frat boy looks. He figured the Subaru likely belonged to one of the pair. There were 3 males dressed in jeans, sweatshirts and work boots who looked like they were getting ready to go to work on the rigs and likely belonged to the oil truck. There was also a very pretty woman in the store dressed in yoga pants and pull over who looked like she had just finished workout. Jack figured the Jeep was likely hers. Lastly, there were two other males inside who looked to be half strung out and very unkempt, wearing dirty jeans, over sized sweatshirts and beanies. Despite the similar attire to the drillers, it was obvious the pair weren't of the same cloth.

Jack saw and catalogued all of these observations in less than 3 seconds by habit before making his way to the restroom. After washing his hands, Jack left the restroom, nearly running into the two dirty guys who had gathered near the restrooms staring into the beer cooler. "Excuse me guys" he said as he walked by the pair towards the register, where he gave one of the two college kids two 20 dollar bills, asking him to put it on pump 4. He left the store, walked back to his truck, removed the nozzle and began to fill the tank.

After the nozzle audibly clicked and kicked off indicating the $40 had been dispensed, Jack re-moved the nozzle from the tank to return it to the pump. In doing so he turned and saw the two little dirty men from inside creeping towards him with their hands carried deep in their pockets. "Damn you movin up in this world ain't ya," the man on the left said.

Confused, Jack asked if they were talking to him.

"Who else would we be talking to asshole" the other responded as he slapped the tailgate of the truck and continued his approach towards Jack between the pumps and the truck. At the same time in his peripheral vision Jack noticed the other man walking around the other side of the truck. Jack realized the man in front of him was attempting to distract him while his partner moved behind him to box him into an enclosed space. After what had just happened with the at the pool hall the other night, Jack thought to himself he really didn't really need this right now.

"I think you have me confused with someone friend," Jack said, stepping to his left and back, around the fuel pumps into the open.

"Oh we know exactly who you are and you are going to give us the money you owe the boss".

Still confused Jack replied, "Look fellas I don't know who your boss is but I know for certain I don't owe anyone around here any money"

"Look pretty boy, don't think you are going to talk you away out of this," the man said as he pulled a fixed blade knife from his sweat shirt pocket.

"That's right motherfucker" said the other, slipping what Jack assumed to be brass knuckles on his hands.

Reaching to his hip, Jack reached under his own sweatshirt and pulled out his service weapon. He then very deliberately aimed it right at the guy with knife. Unsure why but with a snicker Jack quoted Sean Connery from the Untouchables, "Leave it to a Dago to bring a knife to a gun fight".

Seeing the gun the guy with the knife stopped dead in his tracks, the guy with the knuckles however continued his approach getting nearly within arms reach. Aware of his approach Jack said calmly, "I would advise you two to drop whatever it is you're carrying and get the hell out of here. Looks like the kid at the counter is calling the cops."

At Jack's words the man with the knuckles turned his head to look into the store window. The man's attention adverted, Jack swung the butt of the pistol right into the side of his head. He was out cold before his face bounced off the pavement. The man with knife stayed frozen in place his mouth agape having seen what happened to his partner.

"Like I said y'all got me confused with someone else. I don't know what this shit was about, nor do I care but if I see you two again I am going to feel threatened and I promise you that isn't something you want. It will end badly for you. Now drop the knife"

The man still staring at the gun and his friend laying flat on the ground quickly complied, letting the knife fall to the ground. "Now take five steps back and sit down," Jack ordered.

The man complied again.

Kneeling to keep the sitting man in his sights, his weapon in his left hand, Jack used his right to remove the brass knuckles from the man on the ground. He then retrieved the knife. "Now drag your friend to whatever hole you two crawled out of and get the hell out of here. Like I said next time I wont be so nice."

Jack watched as the little man grabbed his friend who was starting to moan back towards the store. As he watched the pair he walked over to the storm drain in the parking lot and dropped both the knife and knuckles down it as the man who had had the knife watched intently. Jack then very calmly walked back over to his truck, climbed in, and drove off to complete his journey to his parent's house.

CHAPTER 18

CB was completing her daily workout when her dad called and asked if they could meet some-where, explains he was near town, having had to run into the shop to get something for his crew at the drill site. CB told him she was just finishing up at the gym and she would meet him at the gas station in front of the Walmart in 20 minutes. Her father agreed.

CB pulled into the station at the same time as a pickup truck with one of the local drilling company logos on its side arrived from the opposite direction. At first she thought maybe it was her dad, who drove a similar truck, but as she got closer she realized she was mistaken. She parked two stalls down from the truck and watched three big men climb out, still appearing half asleep, walk toward the store entrance. From their appearance CB figured the trio were just heading out to work night shift. She followed the men inside as one of the men held the door for her. As she thanked him she saw another pair of headlights, belonging to another truck, pulling into the parking lot. However, as the truck pulled under the lighted canopy she saw it was black. Obviously not her father's she continued inside.

Inside the store she saw two of the local college kids working the register, Eric and John. Both said hello to her as she came in having seen her regularly after her evening workouts. As she walked towards the back corner of the store, where the fridge with the protein drinks was located, she saw two smaller men in dirty clothes huddled in front of a freezer talking in low tones.

Curious, she paused for a moment to see what the pair were doing when she realized she recognized the men: Jeff Neemer and Scott Viles.

She had known the pair in high school. Back then they were mischievous, as most of the boys were, CB recalled. They had smoked a little pot, though seemingly the entire school did, and had been known to skip class from time to time but they were essentially harmless. However, the two locals were now known addicts and trouble makers.

She had been back in the area long enough now to know the inner workings of he territory, as all good cops do. She knew the pair had both been arrested multiple times for possession, public intoxication, possession of stolen goods and a few other misdemeanors. She also knew the city, county and State police all suspected them for more than the petty crimes the pair had been previously convicted of; yet, had been unable to catch them.

As she studied the pair, they noticed her. They stopped talking and stared for a moment before nodding a greeting and slowly walking around the corner away from her. She continued to watch the pair as they wondered off curious.

As she watched, the bell toned on the door announcing the arrival or departure of another per-son. Turning slightly to see which, CB saw a taller good looking man with an athletic build walk in. She surmised he likely owned the black truck parked next to the gas pump outside. She continued watching as he stopped inside the door for a few seconds. In that moment, she was unable to identify the man yet she felt she recognized him, though was couldn't say from where. She continued to watch as he walked down the aisle towards the beer coolers and restrooms, finally entering the men's room.

When the door to the restroom closed, CB preceded to the appropriate refrigerator to get her drink. Unfortunately, when she went to get her preferred drink the slot was empty.

She momentarily considered another flavor but then decided to ask one of the guys up front if they had any more in the back since she was awaiting her father's arrival anyhow. At her request, Eric told her would gladly look for her and to just give him a second. He came from behind the counter and entered the freezer to search.

While she waited, she noticed the man from the black truck go to the register, pay for gas and leave. She also saw Jeff and Scott whisper for a moment near the door before they followed the man out. Her cop senses tingling and curious to see what the two were up, she walked to the door to see what the pair were doing. She watched as the two approached the man, each pulling something from their pockets. CB was sure Scott had a knife but was unable to tell what Jeff had.

In that moment she realized her service pistol was in her Jeep. Feeling helpless, she told the clerk to call 9-1-1. She continued watching as the two men split up in an obvious attempt to box the man in from two sides between the truck and fuel pumps. What she saw next however was completely unexpected. The man nonchalantly stepped out and away from the enclosed space, forcing Jeff and Scott to come out together in front of him. Nonetheless her eyes remained transfixed on the ne'er-do-wells, knowing they were both carrying some sort of weapons. With her eyes fixed on Jeff and Scott however she didn't see the man pull a gun on the pair but she did see Scott stop at the sight of the gun, while Jeff continued to move toward the man. She then saw Jeff turn his head and look back towards her. No sooner had he looked and the man with the gun stepped in and cracked him upside the jaw with his gun hand. Jeff fell to the ground in a heap. She then watched as the man said something and Scott dropped the knife and step away. She wished she could have heard what was being said between the 3 as she was afraid she was about to see the two trouble makers die in front of her.

Instead she was surprised by the stage man once again. She saw him bend down, pick up whatever it was Jeff had in his hand and then the knife and walk to the storm drain before drop-ping both items down it. Thereafter he calmly walked to his truck, got in and drove away.

"CB, it's the dispatcher. What should I tell her?", the clerk asked snapping her out of the moment.

"Um, tell'em they can send over a city cop, and maybe an ambulance but no need to rush"

The clerk relayed the message over the phone.

Her protein drink forgotten, CB went outside herself. First, she went into her Jeep and grabbed her weapon. She then approached Jeff and Scott, who had returned to the storefront to sit on the curb. Scott had developed a very visible knot on his head from where he had gotten hit. "What the hell was that?" she asked the pair holding her badge and service weapon.

Seeing the gun and badge the pair swallowed hard in unison but remained silent. Finally Jeff replied, "I don't know. That guy in the truck just attacked us."

"Bullshit, I just watched the whole thing. What were you going to do? Rob the guy?" CB asked.

"Man we didn't do nothing, he attacked us," Jeff insisted.

"You know there are cameras in the parking lot right? I am sure they will tell the story."

"This such bullshit. He attacked us," Jeff replied again. His protest was soon joined by Scott who seemed to finally realize what was going on. The pair continued to insist they were attacked and the man in the truck was the one who needed arrested. They spoke of how the cops did nothin but harass them. All stuff CB had heard plenty of times before. Though at one point the two even told CB she should let them go because they knew each other in school.

After arguing with the two for seemingly forever, though in reality it was less than 4 minutes a city police car with its lights on pulled into the parking lot followed by white 4 wheel drive pickup with a blue decal on the side which read, "Marshall's Drilling and Troubleshooting Services". At the sight of the police car the pair started to protest all the more. The Police car and truck both pulled up near the trio along the sidewalk. The officer got out of his car and out of the truck stepped CB's dad. Walking around the truck he said, "Whatcha doing baby girl?"

"Nothing Dad, go in the store and I will be with you in a minute."

At the sight of the police officer, Scott and Jeff suddenly became quiet. CB then explained to the officer, a career small town cop named Keith Rowe what had happened as the now sudden-ly quiet pair stared sullenly at the ground. As she covered the pair, Officer Rowe frisked them both. Neither had a weapon, nor to CB's surprise any drugs or paraphernalia on them. Though each had over $300 in cash on them. "Where did you get the money from?" She asked.

"A job" Scott said simply.

"A job, doing what? You two don't work" she said very matter-of-factly, knowing the men's histories.

The pair remained silent. She helped officer Rowe place the pair in the car and watched as they drove off. Even upon doing so she knew they were unlikely to stay in jail long since neither the city nor county prosecutor would likely do much without the man pressing charges.

*****

Inside the store, CB caught up with her dad who again asked what all the excitement in the parking lot was about. She briefly recapped the story, telling her dad the two had bitten off more than they could chew and how some guy had gotten the best of them.

"Who was the guy?" Thomas asked.

"I don't know Dad, though he looked vaguely familiar. What I can tell you is that when he was pulling away he had out of state tags. So maybe he was just passing through."

"Yeah and maybe those two dumbasses will learn their lesson about who they should and shouldn't pick on then," Thomas responded, his disdain for the two men coming through plainly by his tone.

"I doubt it Dad. I don't know if the two of them even have a working brain cell left between them to be honest," CB said matching his contempt.

Thomas snickered before replying "It happens baby girl. If not for guys like them how would all these drug dealers stay in business."

CB shook her head in disgust at the incredibly simple accuracy of the statement.

"Speaking of which baby girl we have something we need to talk about, but not here. Lets go out to my truck".

CB agreed but told him she would meet him outside; explaining she still needed to get some-thing first. The two parted ways. Thomas made his way to the door and CB returned to the cooler, finding her preferred protein shake which had been restocked.

*****

Thomas was sitting in his truck tapping his hands on the steering wheel to a tune only he could hear when CB climbed into the passenger seat. She was going to give her dad a hard time about his drumming skills until she opened the door and had seen the floor boards littered with empty coffee cups and fast food wrappers. "Dad you know you can't be eating this stuff all the time" she said for what seemed to be the thousandth time regarding his diet.

"I know honey, but it isn't like I have a kitchen on the job. Hell I am lucky to have the mini fridge and microwave and even those don't work until we get the generators hooked in. So I do what I have to do to get by. Now we didn't meet to talk about my diet again." Thomas continued before CB had a chance to respond, "So I have been quietly asking around with some of the boys.

They all told me the same thing essentially. They could get me pills, but they wouldn't or couldn't tell me from who. Baby girl, there aren't many secrets out on the rigs but I will say this; if those boys are all being tight lipped about whoever it is there is a reason. My guess is they are all to scared to say anything."

"Dad, I guess five deaths would kind of have that affect on people"

"You want me to keep asking?"

"No Dad, I knew it was a long shot anyhow but thanks for asking."

Thomas chuckled "You said long shot, seems appropriate given what you have said about how these guys have died".

"Dad, that's horrible!" CB snapped at his joke before adding, "That was just a figure of speech. I certainly didn't mean it that way"

"I know baby girl, I'm sorry. Your old man just has a dark sense of humor I guess," he responded still trying to suppress a smile.

Despite herself CB smiled at him.

Quickly changing the subject, Thomas asked, "Did you ever get a hold of Jeremy or anyone else at the shop about Dennis?"

"Yeah, I went over and talked to one of the secretaries. She gave me the personnel file but said Jeremy Marshall told her that was all they would give me without a subpoena. I tried to talk to a few of the other around but you know they don't much like cops. I asked to speak to Marshall himself but the secretary said he was out, which was bullshit since I saw him through the window in back. I thought about bringing him in and asking a few questions, but honestly I don't have enough to do that. Plus he would demand a lawyer if I did. Not to mention all the political connections he has. So as of now that's it, I got his file. All it has in it are his last known ad-dress and copies of his pay stubs. Hell there isn't even a job application in there. When I asked about that, the secretary said he was hired solely on the recommendation of one of the other guys. I asked her which one and she said she thought maybe it was Troy Stevenson but then I think she realized she spoke out of school and said I'd have to ask Mr. Marshall himself be-cause he handled all of the hiring and firing," she said, her frustration plain in her voice.

"I can tell you that for sure, the Boss does do all his own hiring and firing. And he does take re-

ferrals from us all on people. I'll tell you though Troy works with me and I don't know that I have

ever heard him even say he even knew Dennis, though I suppose its possible." Thomas replied.

"Thanks Dad, for everything"

"Sorry I wasn't much help baby girl"

"Oh no Dad, you've helped a ton" she added quickly trying to brighten the mood, though neither seemed to buy it. The two spoke for a few more minutes and then CB got out of the truck and got into her Jeep and drove away. Thomas sat for a moment longer and stared after his little girl deep in thought before he too put his truck in gear and pressed the accelerator.

CHAPTER 19

The next morning, Jack felt strange awakening in the room he had spent the majority of his youth in. Something just felt different; not just his posters were gone and the walls were painted. The feeling wasn't the physical differences, however. Studying closer he saw the view out the window remained virtually the same; overlooking the pasture and woods beyond. Then it hit him; it was daylight! He couldn't remember when he had last slept past dawn. Even nights fol-lowing grueling missions he would get up early, even if for only a few hours before going back to bed.

Getting up, Jack did some light stretching to get the kinks out and proceeded to the kitchen for coffee. His parents were sitting at the table as he walked in. Glancing at the clock on the microwave, Jack saw it was nearly 9:00 am. Doing the math he realized he had slept for nearly 9 hours, unheard of for him. After pulling a mug from the cabinet and filling a cup, he sat down and stared sheepishly at his father. Jack felt a pang of guilt having slept so long. He couldn't recall either of his parents sleeping in past 6 am, let alone 9.

As expected the first question from his mother, Dorothy, was how Jack had slept. The first question from his father, Woody was what did he want for breakfast. Jack openly smirked at his Dad's question, knowing Woody was hoping he would request something not approved on his diet so he could get some too. Amused, Jack told his mom he had slept fine and then told his Dad an apple and oatmeal would be fine, to Woody's obvious disappointment. Jack was pretty sure he saw his mom grin, however.

While his mom heated water on the stove for the oatmeal

the three chitchatted for a bit. Trying his best to avoid the inevitable question about his unexpected vacation, Jack shared what had a happened at the gas station the night before.

Hearing the story, Woody sat silent a moment before saying seriously "Jack, this isn't the same place you left behind after high school. It's full of drugs, junkies and drug dealers in some form or fashion. Hell even the news talks about nothing but the drug epidemic in West Virginia.

Sounds like you ran into a couple of guys who either thought you were an easy target because they didn't know you or they really did mistake you for someone else who owed them money. Either way if your in town you need to watch yourself."

"Watch myself? What the hell are the police doing about it if it's so bad?" Jack asked clearly incensed.

"Hell boy I bet they are in on it too. Whole damn place is dirty. We'd move ourselves if not for your brother and sister and the grandkids." Woody retorted, completely serious.

Somewhat taken back, Jack looked from his father to his mother, who just nodded in agreement with her husband.

After a few moments of unsettling silence, Dorothy caught Jack up on his younger siblings. His youngest sister, Jill was still working at a local lumbar yard doing something with orders, Dorothy explained clearly unsure of what that meant.

As to Jack's brother, Robert "Bob" Dorothy said he still working on the gas rigs, something she had never cared for. While Jack and Bob were only 13 months apart, Jack acknowledged, they were not particularly close, nor did they stay in touch, like they probably should. After high school Jack went straight into the Army. Bob, on the other hand, went to college for a year after high school, where he admittedly spent more time partying and chasing girls than in class. After his year "to find himself" as Bob called it he went to work for one of the local drilling companies. He had remained in the industry since.

Bob had traveled up and down the East coast with his job, while Uncle Sam assured Jack got to see all the lovely spots the world has to offer:Korea, Bolivia, Iraq, and Afghanistan to name a few. Jill on the other hand simply never left and the truth was the 3 had grown apart. They would still talk a few times a year on the phone and see each other on during the holidays if they could, but that was it. Otherwise the only news about one another was passed via Woody and Dorothy, whom the boys tried to call at least once a week, while Jill and Dorothy talked nearly on a daily basis.

CHAPTER 20

CB had been correct. At 4:30 pm the day following their arrest, Scott Neemer and Jeff Viles were released from the city jail without any charges being filed. The DA was not willing to bring charges without the statement from the man in the truck, despite the statement of CB and the surveillance footage from the store's parking lot.

The two men collected their personal belongs and told the city jailer "bye" as they walked out of the holding area with smug grins on their faces. The exit door of the jail opened to an alley just a block off of main street. Having already discussed it, the two men turned right and began to walk the half mile back to the gas station where they had been detained the night before.

Upon arriving at the gas station they each bought a twelve pack of the cheapest beer they could find, a big bag of chips and a couple of pre-wrapped sandwiches. After making their purchases, they crossed the street, went over the train tracks, past some old railroad service buildings and to the river that ran there. In a secluded spot along its banks they had intended to visit the previous night they cracked the first of their beers.

As it got dark the two men built a small fire with some drift wood and fallen limbs from nearby; in a rock ringed fire pit where many fires had been built before. Fire going, they returned to their beers, each having already consumed more than 6. Between the fire and the beers neither man noticed as headlights momentarily passed over their hangout.

The two were telling tales regarding their conquests of

some of the local girls when they heard a deep voice say, "Where is my money." Both shot upright, recognizing the voice.

Both strained to find the speaker but were unable to see anything in the dark after having stared into the flames for so long.

"I paid you to do a job last night. You didn't do it. Now where is my money" the voice sounded again as a big man priced the halo of light given off by the fire.

"We were in jail man, we couldn't do the job," the pair said nearly in unison.

"You were in jail because you are stupid," the man responded cooly.

"No man. Some guy… uhhh he just came at us and we uhhh" the two stuttered.

"Shut up! You two dumbasses tried to rob some guy when you should have been doing my job. Now give me my money back."

Both men reached into their pockets and handed him their money. He counted a combined $572. "Where is the rest?"

"We spent it," said Scott.

"But we just figured we would do the job tonight or tomorrow. We were just waiting on you to tell us" added Jeff quickly.

"You fuck stick, you can't do it tonight because your drunk. And by tomorrow it will be to late. When I give you a job I expect it to be done do you understand me?"

Both men nodded, fear showing on their faces. Their fear realized when the big man stepped forward and punched Scott solidly in the solar plexus, knocking the breath from his lungs. Scott reflexively bent forward, only to be caught by the big man's hands which used the momentum to push Scott's head into his a rising knee. Scott went down to the ground instantly, out cold. Nonetheless, the big man proceeded to kick him repeatedly.

Seeing his friend being pummeled, Jeff turned to run but before he took a step he immediately stopped realizing that another man had been behind them. The man was holding a gun and smiling. "Where ya goin Jeff?" the man asked menacingly.

While the man was smaller than Jeff, the gun loomed huge in his hand as Jeff was aware that the man was more than willing to use it. However that was the last computed thought that ran through his head as something hit him hard from behind and he too fell in a heap.

As the two men returned to the truck, the big man asked rhetorically, "Why is it so hard to get good help these days?"

The smaller man shrugged. A moment later they drove away leaving the crumpled bodies of the pair by their fire.

CHAPTER 21

Jack spent the next three days at his parent's house, helping them with a few projects that needed doing but the pair no longer should be doing, at least in Jack's mind. The first day he cut firewood, cleaned the gutters, and caulked the exterior of the house against the upcoming winter. The second and third days he mended a section of fence, fixed the barn door, chopped some more wood and mowed the lawn. Jack found the physical labor therapeutic. In addition to the work, he also found time to get in a light run everyday in addition to spending time with his parents.

After three days, Jack became restless and ready to get out for a little bit. Friday came and he made plans to see his sister Jill and her daughter in the afternoon as Jill had the day off. Jack had wanted to see his brother, Bob too, but he was currently on work a schedule that had him in New York for 12 days and home for 3. Bob wasn't due back home until Wednesday according to his mother. In the alternative, Jack was able to get in contact with his best friend from child-hood: Jeremy Marshall.

Jeremy and Jack were the same age and had grown up three houses down and just under 1 mile from one another — neighbors by country standards. The pair met on the school bus the first day of kindergarten and were nearly inseparable from that point on until graduation. As a pair, they were always into some kind of mischief, be it chasing the girls in elementary school, pulling pranks in middle school or throwing parties in high school. Reminiscing about his friend Jack couldn't remember it clearly but he suspected he likely had his first beer, smoked his first cigarette and any number of other things with the guy. After graduation, while Jack had left after joining the Army, Jeremy had stayed behind to attend the local college.

The pair had only been reacquainted through social media in the last few years and Jack was looking forward to catching up with his old friend. The two had made arrangements to meet at a local grill and bar at 7.

Leaving his parent's home to go to his sister's Jack drove past the property where Jeremy had grown up. To Jack's surprise, the double wide trailer Jeremy had lived in was gone, in its place stood a large two-story brick home with a wide wrap around porch and 3 stall garage. He wondered who owned it.

The visit with his sister was pleasant and Jack laughed as his 8-year-old niece made it a point to introduce Jack to her cat, Puddles, along with each and every one of her baby dolls. When not speaking with the dolls, Jack and Jill spent the afternoon catching up. Their conversation started out a bit forced as the pair talked about work and family, as two strangers sometimes do. But as the pair became more comfortable their talk lightened and became easier. Relaxed they shared some laughs and genuinely had a good time reminiscing about their childhoods and how the world had changed, even in small town America.

It wasn't until Jack was getting ready to leave for town that he told Jill of what had happened at the gas station on his first night back in town. Suddenly, Jill got real serious and told Jack he needed to be careful around town.

"This isn't the same friendly place you knew as a kid. The addicts would steal from you as easily as look at you and the drug dealers are even worse." She warned.

"That's pretty much the same thing Mom and Dad said," Jack responded.

"Its true big brother. Don't trust anyone, not even the people you think you know and definitely not the ones you don't. And whatever you do, don't trust the police, those guys are bought and paid for by the drug dealers themselves. Hell the damn magistrate is the sheriff's son. How is there really any justice when that's supposed to be the checks and balances you know"

"Is it really that bad?"

"Look Jack, if they aren't family assume the worst.   Better safe than sorry" she said.

Warning received, Jack left his sister's house and drove to town.

CHAPTER 22

To get to the restaurant, Jack had to drive past the same gas station where he had encountered the two men and then take a left on main street. Driving down main street, Jack could see a lot of changes had occurred over the years. Changes, he knew many of the residents, wouldn't appreciate as much as he since the likely had occurred over time. Most, if not all, of the store fronts had changed. Gone were the small businesses he remembered. In their place were a collection of restaurants and antique stores; a bank, a T-shirt printing shop, and even a bicycle shop. Jack also noticed along the street there were now only two working street lights, though there were five during his youth. With the completion of Route 33, 20 years previously, the through traffic no longer drove downtown of the small town instead going around it on the speedy route; a real life example of Radiator Springs from the movie "Cars".

Nonetheless, as the sun descended the street looked as if it came straight from a magazine ex-emplifying Americana. Framed in the imaginary were the old brick county courthouse, the small shops and businesses, with their colorful signs and people casually walking the side walked looking as if they didn't have a care in the world. The highlight of the scene was the neon lights to one of the few remaining walkup Dairy Queens left in the country, which Jack knew would soon close for winter, yet on this night had a line three people deep at its window.

Despite the picturesque scene, Jack reminded himself looks can often be deceiving and rarely is everything as it appears. Even with the cynicism, Jack acknowledged the street remained close to his heart and without the experiences and people he had encountered here growing up, he would not be the man he was today. On the other hand, he also knew he could have never become the man he was had he not left either and despite the events of the last week, Jack was rather happy with the man he had become. Looking around, he knew wouldn't have stayed for anything.

Having traveled across main street and memory lane, Jack arrived at his destination; the Whistle Stop Bar and Grill. While, main street had changed, much of the surrounding community remained the same; including the restaurant. The place had always been busy around dinner time, even more so on Friday and Saturday. Tonight was certainly no different, as Jack pulled into the crowded parking lot and began looking for an unoccupied space. While looking for a space, he couldn't help but notice there was one new truck taking up two spaces; parked diagonally across the two spaces done in such a manner the driver had done so intentionally to en-sure no one could park directly next to it.

The truck was a white F-150, similar to Jack's own, albeit a few model years newer. While Jack had left his truck essentially stock, other than adding a spray in bed liner and new subdued black steel wheels and tires, after the original tires had worn out; this truck appeared to have every aftermarket accessory one could buy on it. New bumpers, brush guard, winches, lift kit, rocker panels, rims, tires, roll bar, light bar and light covers to help emphasize the gleaming white pain with heavy metal flake, clearly not original. Judging by the truck, Jack figured the owner had to be an asshole who was making up for something.

Jack finally found an unoccupied space near the rear of the building and parked. Walking up to the door, Jack was able to study the exterior of the building more closely. He noticed the place has been well maintained, looking exactly as he remembered it; a big square building with natural wood lap siding that looked as fresh as the day it was built. The front of the building featured a big porch with a green metal roof.

Under the roof were porch swings mounted to the ex-posed rafters on either side of the front door along with benches and old advertisement signage from times gone by. Both the swings and the benches were occupied by people awaiting a table.

Jack wondered if the inside had remained unchanged too and walked in to add his name to the waiting list. However, as Jack got in the door and paused a moment to allow his eyes to adjust to the building's interior, he heard a familiar voice call "There's my man, come on in." Jack recognized the voice instantly as his friend Jeremy, though it came from a man who looked different from the man he remembered.

Jack was surprised by the appearance of his friend. While most judged Jack to be 5 to 8 years younger than his true age due to his baby-face and his physical shape, Jack guessed most would say Jeremy looked 10 years older than their actual age. Gone was the thick brown hair from high school, instead Jeremy sported a shiny bald head. While he clearly shaved his dome Jack could tell it was because he had lost his hair. Jeremy also had a full thick beard that was beginning to show grey streaks through the brown. In addition, the man before him wore thick black big rimmed glasses, dark brown corduroy pants, a navy blue cardigan over a red shirt, and brown clunky shoes. Jack assumed the man was trying to look hipster but it failed and looked more like an old college professor. Moreover the look did not fit his friend's personality, as he remembered it; nor did Jack think it looked appropriate on a man of Jeremy's stature. Jeremy had always been big, standing at least 6'5" tall and thickly muscled. Though now he looked a bit softer and needing to lose 25 to 30 pounds. Jack extended his hand to shake Jeremy's hand.

Ignoring his outstretched hand, Jeremy enveloped Jack into a massive bear hug, revealing under the pudgy exterior, the powerful frame reminiscent of his defensive lineman days from high school remained, as the man effortlessly lifted Jack from the floor. Jack fought the urge to head butt his friend in the face to free himself and after a second Jeremy sat him back down.

Laughing at the expression on Jack's face, Jeremy told Jack to follow him, turned and walked away.

Feeling a bit embarrassed, Jack followed, walkingpast the hostess station and the groups of people who continued to await an open table.

As Jack followed, he studied the room. Similar to the exterior, it had remained largely unchanged by time. Continuing the same theme, the large wood-paneled room were adorned with porcelain advertising signs from days gone by. Most from companies that no longer existed.

Jeremy led the pair got to a booth in the most remote corner of the dining room, far away from the hottest station, restrooms and kitchen. Jeremy took the seat that placed his back in the corner facing the room, leaving Jack to sit across from him; thus exposing Jack's back to the room. Jack rarely sat in such a position, as it made him incredibly uncomfortable, though with the nostalgia of the place he didn't feel as threatened by it as he usually did. However he still took the time to identify the exits and possible threats scrupulously before taking a seat.

CHAPTER 23

Friday morning CB was able to get some much needed extra sleep because she was working out of the State Police office in Buckhannon near her home, saving her the 45 minute commute to her regular office. She had been called into Captain Rodgers office the evening before and told until further notice she would be working out of the Buckhannon office with Detective John Ashcroft from the point forward on the investigation. When she asked why she was being as-signed a partner, Rodgers explained Ashcroft had previously been a member of the prior task force that had investigated the murders and the Kincaid case. He elaborated that ballistics had just confirmed to him the round that had killed Roberts indeed matched the weapon that had been used in the previous murders and thus he had coordinated with his superiors to bring in Ashcroft to help fill in the gaps missing from the work files she had been given from the task force.

While thankful for the help, CB was not happy Rodgers had made the move without asking her opinion, nor was she happy he had been informed about the ballistics match before her. In-stead of addressing those concerns however, she asked Captain Rodgers why Ashcroft had been chosen to assist her.

Rodgers explained Detective Ashcroft had been one of the first members to the disbanded task force, so he would be able to provide a big picture assessment of the previous investigation. He was all the most vocally upset member when the group was disbanded, letting anyone and everyone know the murder of Kincaid only proved they were on the right track. While there were many who agreed with the man, few would back him on it, for fear of the stench attached to the task force would find itself on them too. Thus Captain Rodgers was able to get Ashcroft reassigned without issue. Before she left Captain Rodgers office he added, Ashcroft was reput-ed to be more than just a competent investigator; he was known as man who got things done and bad guys off the streets.

She wasn't sure if he was implying anything by the statement or not, however it made her curious about the man. Returning to her desk she did her own research on the man. She discovered he began his career in the State Police in the narcotics unit. He had gone straight from the academy directly into undercover work, which he had proven adept. However, after years as an undercover agent, he was reassigned to be an investigator after there were some within the State police had suspicions he had turned. However, he soon proved those doubters wrong by developing more contacts and informants through the years leading to the convictions of more drug dealers than any other detective in the history of the state.

When the pair had met that morning, Ashcroft's appearance was not what she had expected. The picture in his official file had been the man's academy graduation photograph from 20 years earlier and for some reason she had imagined he had stayed in shape with the same full head of hair. Instead, Detective Ashcroft was a bald man of medium height whose once plain features had deteriorated by too many cigarettes and to few meals. Though the man was close to her father's age, in his early fifties, if CB had to have guessed she would have estimated the man to be 10 years older.

Because Ashcroft's home base was District 1, in Shinnston; it was decided the pair would set up the meeting in the more centralized Buckhannon office. When they had met, CB had been apologetic about his being assigned to help her but Ashcroft quickly put her at ease when he informed her he had in fact volunteered for the assignment, feeling he still had unfinished business regarding the ordeal.

CB couldn't help to be impressed with the man's dedication. But also could not help but ask what had happened previously with the task force.

Ashcroft told her the task force had been made up of FBI, DEA, State and local authorities. He said even though they were all supposed to be working together there remained obvious factions in the unit had led to infighting and distrust. When the anonymous tip came in through the joint hot line and Tony Kincaid was finally arrested, each individual group was again positioning themselves to take the credit. But then when Kincaid had been killed unexpectedly while in custody each group then could wait to wash their hands of the whole ordeal. Shortly thereafter, their best lead dead, the task force was disbanded.

CB and Ashcroft spent the remainder of the day comparing notes, with Ashcroft filling in the gaps as best he could to the files she had been given. Early in their session, CB had shared her suspicions with Ashcroft regarding Marshall. Ashcroft confirmed the task force had looked pretty hard at Marshall too once Kincaid had been arrested because of their association but they were never really able to gather anything concrete on him; just the conjecture of many based upon his money and the men he associated with, neither of which was a crime he had joked.

CB asked how hard they had looked into Marshall given the timing of it all after Kincaid's death. He told her frankly he was unsure because by that point it was obvious to everyone the group wasn't working together effectively and was destined to be broken up. He also informed her he hadn't been privy to that angle because the FBI had been the group tasked with that part and they were probably the worst of the group to share information.

After more than 8 hours the two detectives decided to take a break for dinner.

*****

CB and Ashcroft stood in the corner near the hostess station, waiting to be seated among a throng of others, when the door opened behind them. Instinctively, CB turned to see the new arrival. She immediately recognized the man walking in as the same man she had witnessed disarm the Jeff and Scott at the gas station earlier in the week. She was again struck by the feeling she somehow knew the man, though she wasn't sure.

She continued to study the familiar figure, trying to place him as he walked to the server's station. He appeared about to say something when he was greeted by Jeremy Marshall and em-braced in a huge hug.

Unlike the new man, CB would recognize Marshall anywhere. It wasn't just the sheer distinctive size of the man, as he had been big since high school, but his picture was in the paper seemingly on a weekly basis for something. She admitted it chided her but CB knew because of all the articles featuring his exploits and philanthropy in the local paper, Marshall was considered as close to aristocracy as one could be within the small town. His standing was maintained be-cause of the mint of money Marshall had made in the last decade and persisted despite the rumors some of his money was tainted.

The sight of the man upset her more than she cared to admit and certainly more than she want-ed to show Ashcroft during their first day working together. Her anger wasn't because of his lo-cal celebrity however, instead because that just days before he avoided her questions by having his secretary run interference and say he wasn't in his office. Making it worse, she saw him through the window behind her looking right at her without a care in the world.

CB thought it interesting the new guy in town, whom could obviously handle himself would be greeted in such a manner by Jeremy Marshall. She made a mental note to inquire further, preferably while she was confronting Marshall about Roberts.

CHAPTER 24

After Jack took his seat in the booth, a young waitress appeared quickly, asking the pair if they were ready to order. Both men ordered large beers, Jack, a Guinness while Jeremy opted for a Bud Light and a plate of fried pickles for the table. Jeremy then politely asked for another moment to look over the menu. Moments later the beers arrived in large frosty mugs. The two friends spent the next 20 minutes sipping their drinks and reminiscing.

It did not take long for the two men to revert to their customary roles. Jeremy dominated the conversation, while Jack sat back and listened, adding in a few words from time to time to keep the conversation moving. During the course of the conversation, Jeremy informed Jack he had done well for himself.

Starting off he had bought his own dump truck, joining his dad's business hauling rock and gravel to the gas well roads. Shortly thereafter, against his father's wishes, Marshall bought four additional gravel trucks and negotiated two exclusive hauling service deals with two of the drilling companies in the area, effectively becoming their exclusive gravel haulers. Within an-other year he expanded his services by operating the water trucks for them too.

He explained while he was making a dent living in the trucking services he figured out the real money was in the drilling rigs themselves. He bought his own small rig and started bidding for those contracts too. Jeremy explained however, "I lost my ass on drilling for the first few years because the only contracts I was landing was the contracts for sights none of the experienced contractors wanted because

they were difficult sites to drill. That too turned out to be a
blessing because my crews got really efficient at those difficult

jobs. After a time, demand grew as the difficult jobs became more and more common with everyone trying to drill everywhere. It helped my guys earned a reputation for being good at it and I was able to charge a premium price be - cause of it. Then the really big companies started asking me if I could consult on some of their projects, so I started an offshoot company where I have a couple crews worth of guys who don't do anything but trouble shoot for the big boys." Marshall finished by describing himself as an entrepreneur who had many business interests around town.

"Impressive," Jack said, congratulating him on his success, before asking if people held his success against him.

Jeremy responded, "Some do, for sure. They don't like my success or how I do business. Its nothing personal but people take it personally." Warming to the subject, Jeremy further told Jack how through his business interests he had been able to keep up with many of the locals. As Marshall spoke Jack would occasionally ask about certain people and Jeremy would tell him what he knew, including the details regarding the skeletons people tried to keep hidden in their closets. Jack noticed Jeremy seemed to know a little about everyone but some responses were more elaborate than others; especially the less flattering ones, though he kept the opinion to himself.

CHAPTER 25

CB and Ashcroft were finally seated after about a 20 minute wait. They were taken toward the back of the room and sat at a table near the rear corner. Seeing their table was only a few tables from where the new man and Jeremy Marshall were sitting, CB ensured she took the chair allowing her the ability keep an eye on the pair.

After sitting, Ashcroft ordered himself a beer, while CB opted for a diet soda. As the pair waited for their waitress to return with their drinks, Ashcroft tried to make small talk but CB was to busy studying the pair of men to participate in the conversation. She watched as the Marshall and the stranger drank their beers while talking and laughing; or at least Marshall was talking and laughing as the stranger's back was toward her.

Finally Ashcroft asked what had her so preoccupied. CB tried to explain without pointing or drawing Marshall's attention. After a few awkward gestures with her head and eyes, Ashcroft finally looked over his shoulder to see the pair of men. "Oh, I see," he mouthed to her.

*****

Jack was finishing his beer when he looked over his shoulder in an attempt to locate a waitress to get another round. He saw a waitress taking the order of a couple just over his left shoulder. The woman was quite pretty and was sitting with what appeared to be an older guy. "Lucky guy" Jeremy thought to himself. Finally, the waitress finished with their order and Jack said, "Excuse me miss" in the waitress's direction.

As the waitress turned towards Jack, her movement allowed a clear line of sight to the front of the restaurant. In that second, Jack could not help but notice a police officer speaking with the hostess who was pointing in Jack's general direction. Jack saw the policeman confirm the location, by pointing with his right hand, which the hostess nodded to in response. Jack then watched as the officer used the same hand to key his shoulder mounted radio. Curious Jack continued to watch as the officer walked straight toward their table. Instinctively, Jack sized the young officer up; he was of average height, with a slim build but looked to be in decent shape. Studying more closely, Jack noted the guy's service belt and the way the officer carried his equipment.

He continued to watch until the man stopped within two feet of his table, behind the waitress who had stepped over at Jack's request. "Two more beers," Jack heard Jeremy say as he looked at the officer, who stared at him.

*****

After giving the waitress their orders, CB watched as the young girl stepped towards the table with the Marshal and the new guy. Following right behind the waitress was a young city police officer, named Jake Poles who was also walking towards the new guy and Marshall.

CB knew the young officer had been in uniform for less than 2 years. She had met him on few occasions and he had acted professional and courteous towards her, which wasn't always the case for her, as some of the locals resented the State Police generally, and women detectives even more so. She had heard Poles was generally a pretty good officer overall who genuinely tried to follow the book, but it was known he could also be a bit of a hot head and lose his temper from time to time.

*****

As the waitress stepped away, the young officer cleared his throat as Jack continued to look at him. The officer took another step towards the table and looked down on Jack. Jack thought the kid was trying his best to look intimidating, which Jack felt he was doing in an effort to hide his nervousness. "Excuse me sir," the officer addressed Jack directly, moving his hands to rest on his service belt, near both his baton and pistol. Jack wasn't sure if the posture was an attempt to look intimidating or simply to reassure himself. "Is that your black F-150 out front with the Kansas tags?"

"It is," Jack answered directly.

"Sir I need you to stand up and come with me."

"Excuse me?"

"I said you need to get up and come with me," the young officer stated more loudly, though a bit shakier.

"You're going to have to explain that before I go anywhere," Jack replied a bit agitated.

"Jake, what is this all about?" asked Jeremy, obviously knowing the younger man.

"This man and his truck match the description from an occurrence from in front of Sheetz the other night, in which he reportedly brandished a gun and pointed it at two men" said the officer calmly to Jeremy, seemingly much more relaxed addressing someone with whom he was familiar.

"Are you kidding me!" Jack said. "You mean the two jackasses who pulled the knife and brass knuckles out on me?"

"I don't know about that sir but those same two men are now in the hospital having been beaten within an inch of their lives. You are a person of interest in that occurrence. Sir, you need to come with me peacefully or else" said the young officer in an awkwardly formal manner, trying to exhibit control of the situation.

However, Jack could sense just how unsure of himself he really was. He wondered why the young cop was doing this on his own without back up. "Or else?" Jack asked cryptically letting the phrase hang adding to the man's nervousness.

"Yes sir, or else," said the officer again, sliding his hands further towards his weapons.

"Let me tell you something," Jack said matter of factly. "At the moment you're trying to detain a person of interest who based upon what you have already said, you should suspect is armed and you're here without backup. You're standing here with your hands resting on your belt, yet the thong of your holster is still covering your service weapon so if you should need it you can't get to it quickly. And your baton is positioned in completely the wrong place on your left side where you would either have to draw across yourself to get it or draw it with your non-dominant left hand. And I bet the reason it is there is because you don't like having to take it out every time you sit in your patrol car because it gets caught on the center console and instead rides in the gap between the seat and the car door. Buddy, don't let laziness get you hurt. You might want to learn your damn job before your start throwing your weight around because simple mis-takes like those can and will get you hurt if you plan to be a police officer for long."

The young officer just stood staring for a moment, confused by what he had just heard.

Jack's intent with his little speech had been to settle the man's nerves and to get him to think about his actions. Unfortunately, to late, Jack realized he went too far. Instead of calming the situation, he had embarrassed the young cop making him mad.

CHAPTER 26

CB watched the situation develop from her table overhearing nearly the entirety of the conversation. Hell, she thought, the entire restaurant had seemingly quieted and heard the new man's speech. However, the words from the new man gave her pause; realizing every word was true. Each critique was textbook and something any officer would know, though even she admitted she missed the baton. In acknowledging the validity of the man's words, CB also realized Poles was hopelessly in over his head. CB considered helping him but the thought came to late.

"What? Don't tell me how to do my job asshole!" Poles screamed as he reached for Jack across the table intending to pull him from his seat.

From Jack's position in the booth, the officer was on Jack's left hand side. As the young officer leaned forward, he extended his right arm to grab Jack. Anticipating the move, Jack rolled ever so slightly onto his left hip from his seated position while at the same time bringing his own right arm across his body. In the blink of an eye, Jack caught the wrist of the young cop's incoming hand with his own right hand and pulled while rolling his hips back from left to right. The unexpected movement combined with the officer's own forward momentum threw him off balance and further over the table than he intended. In an attempt to keep from smashing his face Poles attempted to catch himself with his left arm against the table. However before he could brace himself Jack stood up and slammed his own chest across the man's back, collapsing the man's left arm beneath him while simultaneously reversing his right arm which still had the man's wrist, bringing the officer's right arm behind him, driving it back towards his shoulder blade. The move was done with blinding quickness and efficiency.

Afterward the young officer was left effectively pinned to the table with his left arm pinned beneath him, his right arm controlled from behind by Jack and his feet dangling off the floor with Jack's weight on top of him to prevent any roll out. In jiu jitsu terms Jack had gained the back and perfect side control.

*****

CB was stunned by the speed and efficiency of the man's movements, watching him move from sitting calmly in a chair to on top of an aggressor in the blink of an eye. She noticed Marshall was just as awe struck, noting how he stood shakily, a few shades whiter than he had appeared moments ago. She was snapped out of the moment however as she saw Ashcroft in her peripheral vision stand and reach behind him for his holstered weapon. CB followed suit.

*****

As officer Poles struggled against the pressure Jack had on his arm and the body weight on top of him, his uniform was getting soaked from a puddle of beer that had spilled from Jeremy's mug. As Jack reached behind his back with his free left hand a look of pure panic showed on Poles face, which Jack assumed was from fear that Jack was reaching for a weapon. But be-fore Jack could get to what he was reaching for he heard a male voice say, "Hold it mister".

Turning his head, Jack saw two people, the couple he had seen at the nearby table earlier, both holding pistols, pointed in his general direction. Jack replied evenly, "Stand down you two. Be-fore someone here gets hurt for real".

"I don't think you understand sir. I am State Police Detective Ashcroft and this is my partner Detective Greene. You are under arrest for assaulting a police officer. Now release him and step back".

"I wasn't assailing anyone. I was simply telling junior here the error of his ways and showing him what could happen when he doesn't do things correctly."

"I don't care what you think you were doing, what I saw was you assault the man" stated Ashcroft.

"The last I checked assault is defined as to cause someone to experience fear by an action or a threat of an action that victim felt could be enacted upon their person. The young officer certainly wasn't afraid, simply misguided. Now if your partner there would be so kind as to reach into my front right pocket and pull out my wallet, I think we can save people a bunch paperwork and embarrassment."

Ashcroft was about to protest when CB stepped forward towards Jack who rotated his feet and hips to grant her access to his pocket. His movement also exposed a pistol holstered in the small of his back. She removed the pistol with her left hand without protest and then carefully reached into the right hip pocket and pulled out the wallet.

"Open it." Jack said.

Opening the wallet and peering inside CB simply said, "Oh shit."

"What?" asked Ashcroft to which CB responded by showing him the badge inside.

"Are you fuckin kidding me" Ashcroft mumbled.

Still in the dark Jeremy asked "What is it?"

CB looked at Jack who just nodded towards the table. CB placed the wallet down so as to show both officer Poles and Marshall exactly what was inside.

"Holy shit your a cop!" Marshall exclaimed, "I thought you were in the military"

"No man, I am a US Marshal. I have been for a few years now" Jack replied.

"I'll be damned, you never said."

"You never asked" Jack retorted.

Looking down at the guy on the table, Jack asked him if they were good. Poles nodded and Jack let him up. As Jack straightened it became plainly obvious everyone in the place was still staring. Looking around the room at the stunned faces, none of whom really seemed familiar to Jack, he said, "Maybe we can discuss all of this outside."

Ashcroft and CB both nodded and turned to leave with Poles in tow.

Turning back to his friend, Jack apologized and said he needed to go out and talk to the trio. Marshall said he understood. As Jack was getting money out to pay for the drinks, Marshall told him not to worry about it, he would cover it. Before Jack left, Jeremy added he and a few of his friends from work were going to go out the holler the next morning to shoot and Jack should come. "The holler" as it was known locally was simply an old strip mine where local people had been muddin, shooting and drinking beer for years as Jack recalled. He and his friends had spent many an evening and weekend up there during school. Jack asked him for the time and told him he would think about it.

*****

Outside the trio of officers waited for Jack. Ashcroft again asked Jack for his credentials saying he wanted to make sure they were legitimate. Jack handed the man his wallet again. Ashcroft looked at it a moment and passed it on to CB who also looked at it more thoroughly. For the first time she saw the name: Jack Kirby. Recognized the name she asked, "Are you the same Jack Kirby that played football and baseball at Buckhannon-Upshur?"

Looking at her somewhat puzzled Jack said, "I am."

"I thought, I recognized you" she said. "I am Cathy Greene, I was a freshman when you were a senior. I'm sure you don't remember me but I remember you."

After thinking a moment Jack responded, "Cheerleader right? You have grown up."

"We all have," she said, looking embarrassed.

Poles interrupted, "So you two know each other?"

"Not really, we were in high school at the same time. Jack here was a senior and part of the popular crowd, along with Mr. Marshall in there. I was just another freshman." CB answered.

Once the pleasantries were concluded, Jack spoke with the three officers for about twenty min-utes. He explained he was currently on vacation for a few weeks of R&R and he had returned to visit family and friends. Jack then went through the events of his first night in town which CB confirmed. Since that night he informed them he had remained at his parents house and they had been home the entire time and thus would provide an alibi if needed.

After listening to his explanation Ashcroft informed Jack if an alibi was needed they would certainly inquire; and followed up the statement asking Jack about his association with Jeremy Marshall.

The question seemed odd to Jack but he knew it was a common integration technique to ask unexpected questions. Undeterred he explained they had been friends since elementary school and had decided to get together for a beer since they hadn't seen one another in 20 years. While the officers seemed pacified by his response, Jack nonetheless found it telling the three asked about Jeremy; reinforcing that things had indeed changed since he had left all those years ago.

Finally, officer Poler left, though it was obvious he was still not happy with what had happened to him inside the restaurant. As Poler climbed into his car, Ashcroft told CB he was going back inside to get their food packed up and to pay for the check.

Left alone in the parking lot, CB said, "Hell of a way to be welcomed back to town."

"Yeah reminds me of why I left," Jack joked.

"Tell me about it" CB retorted "I told myself I would never come back when I left for college but here I am trying to fight the good fight and save the place from itself"

"Good luck, with that," Jack told her self conscious the statement sounded more sarcastic than sincere.

"Thank you," CB responded reflexively.

The two then just sat and looked at one another for a few awkward moments, before Jack offered CB his phone number "just in case".

She put his number in her phone and then hit the call button causing his phone to ring. "There now you have mine too. If you should need anything while your in town, let me know."

"I will, thanks" Jack said before returning to his truck, once again shaking his head at the over accessorized truck taking up two spots.

CHAPTER 27

Returning to his parent's home, Woody was already in bed while Dorothy was watching one of the Friday night cop shows on television. With nothing better to do, Jack sat down and watched with her. During the show's climax there was a hostage situation requiring a SWAT and sniper team called in to assist the detectives. The show portrayed the sniper setting up on top of a building requiring the man to lean far over the side; creating an impossible angle to the target. Once the sniper was set the show depicted the swat team using a battering ram to enter the building. Curios, Dorothy asked Jack if was an accurate portrayal.

Laughing Jack told her no. He explained in such a situation he would have either been on the street for a direct line of shot or would have tried to procure a window in one of the first floors in the building across the street. He then began to point out the other blatant mistakes of the scene, such as the breech team not checking the door for booby traps, failing to cover the rear doors and other exits, and allowing the detectives to enter the building with the swat team. The explanation took longer than the duration of the show and Jack looked over to the couch and realized his mom was grinning once he was done with it. "What?" he asked, responding to the expression on Dorothy's face.

"You really do love that stuff don't you," she said stifling a giggle.

Jack laughed with her. A big full belly laugh, which caused Dorothy to laugh all the harder. Jack laughed so hard he had tears in his eyes and it felt great, for the first time in a long time. That night Jack slept like a baby, something he had not done in a long time.

*****

Jack awoke the next morning refreshed, having slept the night through without the haunting images plaguing him since Nebraska. After coffee, he went for a long run in an attempt to get his thoughts in order, wanting to write something down for Dr. Hartman. As he ran, he considered all that had happened, looking for some sense of clarity. In his heart, Jack knew that the world still needed good guys who were willing to stand up to the violence in order to protect those who were unable or unwilling to do so. He also knew he was still ready to protect those who could not protect themselves, as it was engrained in his nature. What he didn't know was could he do it without his head getting in the way, causing him to hesitate and endanger others again.

His run complete he called Dr. Hartman's office with the excuse of looking for guidance on the writing assignment though in reality he just felt the need to talk out what he had just hashed out in his head. His call was answered by an answering service who stated Dr. Hartman was not yet in her office. The operator said if it were an emergency she could direct his call to an on call doctor otherwise he could leave a message for Dr. Hartman who would return it within 24 hours. Jack left a message.

After showering, Jack dressed in a pair of brown canvas pants, a grey wicking t-shirt, and then a light weight fleece navy blue pullover. After putting on his Danner boots, he filled his coffee cup and jumped in his truck and headed to the holler, the abandoned strip mine Jack and his class mates went to frequently during his high school days. Jack thought of often in the years since. The memories of the place and the people he had met and befriended there had always helped him get through the harder times he faced when he was over seas questioning why he did what he did. But it always came back to the same answer: it was guys like him who ensured the next generations would get to experience their own carefree youths. Secretly Jack liked having that responsibility.

Tho hollor wao looatcd in Hodgesville which was a small community about 8 miles outside of Buckhannon. Like many small towns in West Virginia, Hodgesville started as a mining town. The employees of the local mines would be provided homes and company cash for the local store(s) as their wages. The miners would then be totally beholden to their employers since the company script would be no good any place other than their own controlled stores, bars and restaurants. While the practice was eventually outlawed, many of the established towns re - mained. While some of those old company towns were abandoned and fell to ruin after the local mines closed, some like Hodgesville continued to be a stable community, with many of those living there having jobs related to the natural gas industry.

To get to Hodgesville from Buckhannon you simply travel north on WV Route 20. During high school, Jack and his friends had a competition to see who could cover the 8 mile distance the fastest. Typical of teenagers, yet older now Jack admitted he and his friends were incredibly naive to have never considered the danger of the contest; ignoring the fact the road is one of the most dangerous in the country. The road features many rolling hill and turns which are often misjudged even by more experienced drivers. Seemingly every curve of the road between the two communities features a roadside memorial. The most infamous of which was known throughout the region as "decapitation curve"; named for two high school girls who lost control of their car, going through a guard rail and over the road bank. When they were found they both had been beheaded.

In addition to the twists and turns, the road was also heavily traveled, despite its rural nature because it was the main thoroughfare between the two communities. The traffic consisted of not only the typical passenger cars and pickups;

but also had many commercial gas, coal and log trucks. Nonetheless, Jack and his class mates drove the road as fast as their cars and traffic would allow. They had some ground rules, the most prominent of which was the time had to be witnessed by two individuals other than the driver, so no one could cheat the record books.

Jack recalled being a passenger in the car when the fastest time was set amongst his friends. His friend Wren was driving with Troy, Jeremy and himself along for the ride in Wren's mom's Toyota Celica. Wren made the drive in less than 8 minutes, averaging better than 60 mph. Jack satin the back seat along side Troy, both of whom were to busy looking for something to hold onto to talk. Jeremy sat in thepassenger seat, to large to fit in the back, encouraging Wren the entire way. Marshall always having had the ability to talk Wren into doing anything, no matter how crazy.

Now older and somewhat wiser, he hoped, Jack was driving within 5 mph of the speed limit be-tween the two towns. About half way, Jack looked in his review mirror and noticed a red speck behind him along one of the few straight aways allowing a full view behind him. A moment later, checking the mirror again, the red speck had become a big 80's model Chevy truck, which continued gaining on him fast. Glancing down at his speedometer, Jack saw his speed was be - tween 45 and 50 mph. He guesstimated that for the truck to have gained on him that quickly it had to have been traveling more than 70 mph.

As Jack approached a sweeping right hand turn, the big truck had made it to jack's rear bumper. No sooner had Jack began to negotiate the turn when the old truck pulled out and accelerated around him, the big 4 barrel carburetor opening up making a huge rumble drowning out the ra-dio in Jack's truck. Because of the turn, the truck's driver was unable to see an approaching car. Jack did however, slamming his brakes to avoid the crash! The on coming car did the same. The tires from both Jack's truck and the oncoming car squealed as smoke arose from the rubber burned on the asphalt trying to stop the momentum of both vehicles. As the pair screeched to a halt, the red truck quickly switched back into the right hand lane and accelerated along as if nothing has happened.

When Jack and the on coming car both came to a stop they were practically door to door. Looking into the other car, Jack saw the driver was a young woman, who could not have been more than 22 or 23, was white as a ghost. As Jack watched, the young woman looked over her shoulder. Jack's eyes followed the motion of the woman's head and saw there was a young kid in a car seat in the backseat, who was obviously scared from the experience. The woman held her hand to the child in an effort to ensure he or she was ok and then looked back at Jack waived politely and accelerated away. Jack followed suit.

The remaining few miles to Hodgesville Jack was seething at the idiot driver in the red truck. He had to remind himself repeatedly no one got hurt, fighting the urge to see if he could catch the guy. He told himself he was out here to relax and enjoy himself with an old friend and being up-set simply because of one asshole was not going to do him any good. Especially, Jack reflect-ed, not with everything else going on in his head at the moment.

CHAPTER 28

Upon arriving in Hodgesville, Jack turned east onto Teeter's Creek Road and traveled about two and a half miles before turning left onto a graveled lane. On the road ahead of him he saw there were at least five cars heading in the same general direction, though with the dust cloud it was difficult to get an exact count. Because there were only four houses along the lane before the gate leading to the old mine, Jack assumed they were going into the holler. Passing the last house, Jack applied the brakes, recalling the road got rougher beyond as the county was not responsible for maintenance of the road beyond the homes. However, instead of finding a road in disrepair, Jack noticed the road actually improved, having recently been graveled and grated. In addition to the improved road, he also noted there were shiny new florescent signs posted on new fence posts along either side of the road that read "Posted, No Trespassing".

About 300 yards past the last house, Jack crossed over an old cattle guard, he remembered, and went through a freshly painted open gate made of 3 inch steel tubing he didn't recall. The gate appeared relatively new and was attached to a pair 8 inch steel pipes Jack guessed were full of concrete, making them nearly impossible to move. Jack admitted he could be have mis-remembered about the gate, while also acknowledging things change a lot over a decade.

Continuing his drive, Jack turned off the radio, rolled the windows down and started to listen for any shooting as the old strip mine was quite large and Jeremy hadn't really elaborated as to where they would be shooting. He continued slowly along the newly graveled road which fol-lowed the base of what Jack had been told was a large mountain before the mining company cut its top off to extract the buried coal before Jack was even born. The remaining area looked like a mesa from the southwestern desert. About a quarter way around the base the road began its ascent. Emerging onto the plateau, Jack spotted a new model white Jeep Grand Cherokee with darkly tinted windows sitting just off the road. On its side was a blue decal that read "Marshall's Drilling and Troubleshooting Services". As Jack approached, the tinted window of the Jeep came down, revealing Jeremy in the drivers seat. Recognizing his friend, Jack pulled along side.

"Hey man glad you could make it. We are setting up about another half mile straight down the trail just on the other side of that stand of trees" Jeremy said, pointing to some trees Jack did not recall. Seeing the expression, Jeremy explained the trees and grasses had been planted after Jack had left for the Army as part of the EPA's order to coal companies to reclamate the messes they had made with the strip mines. Then added, "I am waiting on a few more cars of people and I will be down".

"A few more cars? I thought you said there were just a few friends from work coming?" Jack asked.

"To a point" Jeremy said. "I invite all my employees out here from time to time to do some shooting and maybe do some grilling and have a few beers. It's good for morale"

"Damn man how many employees have you got?"

"Full time I employ about 50 I guess, but I also have crews who I subcontract with pretty regularly too."

"And the owner of this place don't mind you coming up here? That is a lot of traffic and I re-member having the sheriff called on us more than once for playing back up here"

With a laugh Jeremy explained "Man I bought the place about three years ago from the coal company who used to run it when they were getting ready to file for bankruptcy. I own the entire mountain side. We come out here to blow off steam. Just stay on the road and head on back there you will see everyone. There are a few people down there already. You will know Troy, Wren, and Jaime for sure. They are supposed to be out setting the targets" Jermey added.

Jack nodded and drove on.   He smiled thinking it would be good to see his old friends again.

Troy Stevenson and Wren Tyler had been inseparable in high school and ran in the same circles

Jack had. Jaime Miller was another member of their clique with Jeremy rounding out the group.

Jack had known Wren since kindergarten, who had been in the same class as he and Jeremy. Although Wren had gotten held back at some point in elementary school, he has nonetheless always remained close with Jack's classmates. It was no surprise to Jack that Wren was driving as he recalled Wren was always bit of a daredevil and considered himself the greatest driver around. To give him credit, Wren was talented though reckless. Jack had seen the kid take cars to their limits over a wide variety of roads and terrains. In doing so Wren typically had tried to do his best to scare his whomever was riding with him on any given night. Jack was never sure if he was doing it to show off or because he was simply a passive aggressive asshole. Jack remembered on more than one occasion being in a car with Wren and one of the passengers threatening to beat the shit out of Wren if he didn't cut the stunt man shit out. The threats typically worked as Wren had always been a small guy; short, thin and very slightly built

Jack had met Troy in the fourth grade after two of the elementary schools had merged to form another school. Troy was always a bigger kid, and at some point along the line, in the years following elementary school, had somehow became Wren's unofficial protector. Though the two often argued between themselves, like brothers, no one messed with Wren without drawing the ire of Troy. Jack remembered one instance in high school there was a kid named Jeff who was picking on Wren in art class, throwing paper wads and making fun of his hair every time the teacher would turn his back. Jeff wasn't much bigger than Wren was and was kind of a little nerdy kid. Jack remembered thinking at the time Wren could have stuck up for himself. Instead, however as Jeff continued to harass Wren, it was Troy, a defensive end on the football team, a wrestler and power lifter, who told the Jeff to back off. Shortly after the warning, for seemingly no reason the teacher left the room. Unfortunately for Jeff, he failed to adhere to the warning and wadded up another sheet of paper, stood up and threw it directly in the back of Wren's head and laughed. Troy, whom was sitting caddy corner to the pair calmly stood, walked behind Jeff, squatted down, wrapped his arms around Jeff and the chair he was sitting in and suplexed the kid directly into the table behind him. Jeff's head bounced off the corner of the table and split wide open. As Jeff held his head and bled Troy reiterated he had been warned as Wren laughed. Jeff ended up going to the hospital for stitches. To his credit he kept his mouth shut as to how he busted his head; telling the teacher he was leaning back in his chair and the legs slipped. The rest of the class also stayed quiet.

Jaime, the third member of the group, Jack had met in the 6th grade shortly after he had moved to the area. Jaime had always been the quiet one, and of the three the one Jack knew the least as he didn't share much though was a cool guy. He was the type who often sat away from the group and observed. The unknowing often thought he was day dreaming but Jack had figured out over the years, Jaime was always watching and listening. Even back then nothing ever went on near Jaime, which he wasn't aware of. The other trait Jaime possessed that was often mis-construed, Jack knew, was he always followed his own sort of code. Jaime simply did what he thought was right, even in the face of opposition. Peer pressure never worked on the guy, even in high school and Jack had always respected that about him. But the moment that always stood out the most Jack recalled was a particular occasion in high school when he, Jeremy, Troy, Wren and a pair of girls were sitting together at a table in the lunchroom. As they were eating and conversing among themselves a big guy named Larry came over to their table leaned down and told Wren that after school he was going to kick his ass, taking a moment to stare Wren down, trying to intimidate him. Jack did not recall why Larry was wanting to fight Wren though he assumed Wren had probably done or said something to the guy. However, what Jack did remember clearly was what Jaime did. Jamie had been sitting at the table across from the group by himself just listening to the group talk as he often did, which put Larry between Jamie and group. After hearing the threat towards his friend Jaime calmly stood up from his seat and picked up his lunch tray. Upon standing he pivoted and swung the tray with two hands towards Larry. Larry turned just in time to take the full brunt of the tray across the face. The blow knocked Larry to the floor instantly where Jamie added a few kicks for good measure before turning and walking directly into the principal's office without one teacher even having time to ask, leaving the entirety of the lunch room in shock and Larry with a bloody face and bruised ribs.

Jack was aware both Jaime and Troy had also joined the military after high school, though Jack had not stayed in touch with them. Apparently the pair had returned to the area and reunited or at least reacquainted themselves with Wren. The sentimentality that childhood friends could re-unite and be inseparable once again, while comforting, also made Jack feel lonely.

Driving around a stand of trees, Jack saw seven vehicles parked together. Three of the trucks were newer model Chevy 3500 work trucks featuring the same "Marshall's Drilling and Troubleshooting Services" decal. Near the vehicles, a group of 15 to18 people were standing around, all dressed similarly in jeans, boots, hoodies and most also wore baseball caps. Looking closer he noticed that a few of the group were women, dressed in the same manner as the men. For some reason, Jack felt self conscious being dressed just a bit differently than the others, causing him to wonder if he should have come at all. Nonetheless, he knew it was to late to turn around and parked along side of the other trucks.

Taking a moment before getting out, Jack took a deep breath. Sitting there he couldn't help but notice the amount of fire power on the property. Not only were most of the group already hold-ing a variety of rifles; he saw there were more guns laying out on the hoods of the trucks. He assumed more guns were hidden away in the vehicles and most of the group carried pistols hidden away under their sweatshirts. If he wasn't already apprehensive the realization certainly didn't help, yet he still turned off the key and got out, checking to ensure his 9 mm was within easy grasp — just in case.

Out of the truck, Jack paused to familiarize himself with his surroundings; areas of approach, possible ambush points, and any other possible lurking dangers. He did this as a matter of habit, so ingrained in his nature it would have been physically impossible for him not to do so. While making his examination, away from the main group Jack saw a pair of guys setting up targets at varying intervals, which Jack roughly measured in his minds eye at 150 to 350 meters from where he sat, though had no idea where they would be firing from. As he watched as the two men, a red truck emerged from an imperceptible dip. The two who had been placing the targets climbed aboard, one in the cab with whomever was driving and one in the bed. Once inside the truck turned around and headed back towards the group. As the truck neared Jack realized it was the same red Chevy that damn near crashed into the girl and her mother. Recognizing the truck, Jack felt his anger return with a vengeance.

Jack watched as three men climbed out of the truck a small blond man from the driver's seat, a stocky barrel chested man near Jack's height from the passenger door and another man near Jack's height but probably 25 pounds lighter jumped from the back. Jack immediately recog-nized the men as his old friends despite having not seen any of the three in over a decade: Wren, Troy and Jamie.

Wren stood maybe 5'7" tall and couldn't have been more than 135 pounds. His blonde hair which he wore long in high school was pulled back in a ponytail under a red bandana. He was wearing a pair of tattered Levis, a red flannel shirt and a pair of heavy workbooks. After reaching the ground he turned around and removed a bolt action rifle from behind the seat.

Troy still appeared to be bull strong, the baggy sweatshirt he was wearing featuring Marshall's logo doing nothing to disguise the muscle beneath. He too removed a rifle from behind the seat of the truck.

Seeing the pair just reinforced, Jack's anger. Walking around the truck he saw the entirety of the group's gaze upon him. He ignored the stares and walked right up to Wren, getting close enough to emphasize the size difference he had on the smaller man. Wren met his gaze with a smirk reminding Jack to keep an eye on Troy.

"Jack? Jack Kirby?" a male voice asked from the group.

Jack neither confirmed nor denied his identity. Instead he asked "That your rig?" Jack asked, pointing over Wren's shoulder at the truck while at the same time marking Troy's location.

"It is" Wren said still smiling, "Pretty fuckin sweet, ain't she?"

"You drive it up here this morning?"

"Man you should know don't nobody drive my truck but me"

"You still drive like a fucking idiot I see. You know you damn near ran me and some woman with a little kid off the road about 15 minutes ago?" Jack stated bluntly.

"Ah man I wasn't even close to y'all" he chuckled, continuing to look at Jack with a devil may care grin.

"The hell you weren't, I locked up my brakes so your stupid ass had room!" Jack growled step-ping even nearer the smaller man. But before Jack got to close Troy and Jaimie stepped be-tween the pair.

"C'mon Jack calm down. We are all out here to have a good time and shoot some stuff. There's no need to fight. I'm sure Wren is sorry, ain't that right?" Jaime said, firmly backhanding the Wren in the chest.

"Yeah, Jack I'm sorry. I was just having some fun. No one got hurt". Wren said with a smirk belying the words.

Looking at his former friends standing in front of him, Jack took a deep breath to calm himself instead of pressing the issue. Once composed, Jack turned and walked back to his truck.

Once Jack was out of ear shot Wren said to Troy and Jaimie "Ah man, why did y'all step in there, I didn't need no help with ole Jack. Would have been fun to knock him down a peg or two, he always was a cocky son of a bitch".

Before Troy could reply Jaime laughed. "Jack would kick your ass without even breaking a sweat".

"Oh bullshit, you think just because he is a little bigger than me I couldn't take that guy? I'd fuck that goddamn pig up good."

"Not even on your best day Wren. You may not have noticed but that ain't the same kid from high school you remember. Take a closer look. That right there is a man who you don't fuck with without help and if your smart not even then. Not unless you have a death wish" Jaimie said bluntly before walking off himself.

CHAPTER 29

Returning to his truck, Jack opened the rear door and raised the seat, still upset with Wren whom he considered a friend, though the dead look in the man's eyes a moment prior made him wonder. As he pondered the brief interaction, he unlocked the locker box and removed the sniper rifle. Out of habit he ensured it was unloaded — though he had checked it before he had stored it at home and again before he put it in the truck. After ensuring the weapon was clear he sprayed the bolt with a small spritz of oil from a can he kept in the gun box and worked the action. Satisfied the bolt was working smoothly Jack returned the weapon to its cushioned bed. He then removed the 4 magazines and loaded them each with 3 rounds, the standard shot group loading. Jack knew of people who kept their magazines loaded at all times but he had seen to many malfunction from worn out springs as a result of the constant load. Even the 9 mm he carried he regularly rotated the magazines to help ensure they functioned properly when needed.

After loading the last of the magazines Jack placed them in his rear pocket, and sat the remain-der of the box of bullets on the bed of the truck. He then removed the rifle once again from its case. He closed and locked the case, returned the seat to the down position, closed the door and locked his truck. Only then did he turn to walk back to the group rifle and spare ammo in hand.

As Jack returned to the group 3 more vehicles were arriving; Jeremy's Jeep, a beat up 70's model CJ Jeep with a hard top and another white pickup truck with Marshall's logo its door. Jack watched the three park and its passengers exit; Jeremy from the new Jeep, two younger kids from the CJ and an older guy, who was nearly as big as Jeremy himself, from the truck.

The two young kids, each carried AR-15s and the older man pulled out what appeared to be a vintage M1 Garand, which was essentially an early predecessor to Jack's own rifle. Between the newcomers and the group already there, Jack estimated there were at least 30 weapons but still felt sure there were more hidden away.

Jeremy saw Jack approaching and stopped putting out his hand. Jack shook it. "Damn man, thats some grip you got there." Jeremy said appreciatively. "Its good of you to come out and play with your old buddy. Let me introduce you to the group. You may remember a few of the guys but probably not most."

Before Jack could say anything Jeremy yelled "Hey everyone this is my oldest buddy Jack." Unaware of what had just happened between Jack and Wren, Jeremy didn't recognize the looks on the groups' faces as he continued. "Jack here is an old army vet and he came out to shoot some with us. Lets show him how we do it. And one more thing before we start remember tonight is the service for Robbie and I would appreciate it if all of y'all were there."

Jack remained back watching various people begin to head off various points. As the group passed by some nodded and others said, "Hi". Jack thought he recognized a few of the people, though there were only 1 or 2 whose names he knew beyond his old friends. He also noticed how most every person in the group made sure to say hello to Jeremy, whom they all called "Boss".

As the group thinned out the late arriving big man with the M1 walked up. "Wow, that's a nice rifle. I bet that cost a pretty penny" he said indicating Jack's weapon.

"It wasn't cheap" Jack replied matter of factly, while he studied the man's own rifle. "Your M1 an original or reproduction?"

Obviously appreciating of the recognition of the rifle, the man said, "Real thing. My Grandpa carried this old gun in Nazi occupied France and brought it home with him. He gave it to me when he passed on and its still the best shooting gun I have ever had."

"Yeah they still used those bad boys in Vietnam as sniper rifles. A lot of old soldiers I have talked with over the years swear by them."

The bigger man smiled and introduced himself, "Thomas Greene. I work with most of these ya - hoos. Been telling them for years I can shoot as well as any of them. Finally have a few days off so figured I would come on out and show em a thing or two."

"Jack Kirby." Jack responded while reaching out his hand "I went to school with Jeremy and a few others. In town visiting and they invited me out."

Thomas took the hand in a firm grip and gave a single pump up and down. "Good to make your acquaintance Jack. Lets go see if we can't show these boys a thing or two."

"You too, good luck." Jack said, as Thomas moved towards the line of people that had formed facing down range.

As the line cleared Jack looked towards Marshall once more and asked "Who is Robbie?"

"He was one of my employees, Dennis Roberts. He died last week and they are having his funeral tonight before he is cremated."

"Oh man, I am sorry to hear that" Jack said as sincerely as he could "were you guys close?"

"Nah man, I barely knew the man but if you work for me your family you know?"

Jack nodded at the sentiment, he had served with many men during his time and had lost a few guys from his units while in Iraq and Afghanistan. Though he had never been particularly close to any of them he still felt the sting of their loss and still experienced the survivors guilt when he thought to much about it.

A few moments later, Jeremy wished him luck with the targets and went to an unoccupied lane to join the others on the firing line. Jack however remained standing and watched as the others began to fire down range.

The targets were orange spheres attached to heavy blackened cardboard with were tacked to wooden posts. The circles ranged from 8 inches round to the size of a quarter. From where the shooting line was located there were multiple targets set up between 50 and 200 meters. Jack remained standing and watched through binoculars as the other shooters began firing down range.

After watching for about 15 or 20 minutes, it became abundantly clear to Jack while everyone in the group were competent marksman, Jeremy and Wren were the best of the bunch. Jeremy was shooting a bolt action Winchester 30-06 with a Bosch scope and Wren was using a semi automatic Remington .270 with Nikon Prostaff optics. Both were easily tagging the 2 inch tar-gets on the 200 meter circle with fairly consistent shot groups.

Moving on from them Jack also watched Thomas Greene, fire his M1. Despite the open sites Jack watched as he too was able to consistently hit the target at the furthest range, albeit with-out as tight of shot grouping of Jeremy and Wren.

After about 45 minutes, some of the shooters on the line began to stand up and take a break. One of those taking a breather was Jaimie, who Jack noticed had been shooting an old 30-30 lever action and had stuck to shooting the nearer targets, though was pretty efficient in doing so. "Hey Jack, are you going to just stand there and watch or are you going to shoot something with that fancy rifle."

Grinning Jack told him he was getting ready to do just that. Walking to the patch of grass Jaimie had just vacated, Jack laid down in the prone. Taking aim at one of the unblemished 200 meter targets away, Jack felt the familiar ping of excitement he still got every time he took target practice. Once comfortable with his position, Jack took a breath and slowly let it half out. As he acquired the site picture he wanted, he slowly applied pressure to the trigger. Most people miss their target because of the jerk caused when they "pull the trigger". To cure this common mistake, Jack found it is better to think of the movement as a squeeze of the hand as opposed to a pull of the finger. As Jack squeezed off his shot the rifle jumped slightly. Before firing off his second round Jack examined the target. There was a hole in the smallest quarter sized circle, though it was slightly off center. Frowning at the slight imperfection, Jack worked the bolt action on the rifle. He took aim and shot again and again. After the three shots were fired the quarter sized target had three holes in it all three of which could be covered by his thumbnail though still slightly right and below center of the perfect center. Satisfied with his shot group Jack loaded his second three round mag and adjusted his aim ever so slightly to account for the consistent drift of the round. He fired the next three rounds seeing they were more centered. Satisfied with the adjustment, he loaded and fired the next two magazines. Jack fired the 6 rounds in less than a minute. At the end of the last magazine, the center of the circle was gone.

From behind, Jack heard a whistle. Jack turned and saw Jaime looking down range through a pair of binoculars. "Damn dude you can shoot".

"Yeah that's not bad, though to be fair I usually practice on targets further away"   Jack replied.

"How far away?" Jaime inquired with a serious look.

"With this thing," Jack said patting the rifle "I consistently hit targets twice as far as this and then some"

At the statement Jaime began looking around with a curious look on his face. "Hold on a second, I got me an idea".

Jack watched as Jaime went over and began talking to Jeremy, Wren and a couple others. After a short conversation, Jaime and Troy grabbed another pair of targets, wooden stakes and a stapler. They jumped into the old Jeep and took off down the service road.

As they drove away Jeremy and Wren approached Jack. "Jaime said you think you can hit a target double the distance" Jeremy said.

Jack nodded and said simply "I can".

"Bullshit"   Wren said contempt dripping from his voice.

"Care to bet" Jack asked, still annoyed with Wren from earlier.

"Sure pig, I will bet you. I got a thousand bucks says your full of shit."

"Pig? Really?"

"That's what you are. Jeremy said you some federal cop, fucking pigs. We're gonna see if you can back it up pig. See if you can do it when it counts" Wren sneered.

"Whatever, Wren. I've done it when the target can shoot back. Have you?" Jack asked rhetorically.

Before the smaller man could reply Jeremy boomed "Shut up Wren. Why don't you get the range finder and see if they got the distance right." Wren looked at the much larger man for a moment, seemingly about to say something else for a moment before thinking better of it and walking away.

"Sorry about that. Wren spent a couple years in the pen a few years after we graduated. You know he was never a big fan of authority, but since he was released he really hates anyone who has a badge. Blames them for the time he lost in prison."

"What was he convicted of?" Jack inquired.

"He was caught by the game warden spot lighting deer. When they searched his truck they also found drugs and the gun he had been using had been stolen. It didn't help his cause any he was 21 years-old at the time and he had a 17-year-old high school girl with him, who just happened to be the mayor's daughter. They pretty much threw the book at him for it.

From what I gather his time in the pen wasn't to nice. You know he always had a big mouth and thought himself a tough guy but they did something in there to him that changed him. The easy going Wren is gone man. Now he is just on edge all the time and has a deep hatred for anyone carrying a badge, lawyers, judges and politicians essentially. Thinks we all need to rise up against the tyranny as he calls it."

"That's rough man, but I don't suppose he ever considered breaking the law may have had something to do with it?"

Jeremy laughed "Nah man, he probably doesn't."

The two men remained standing together, watching as Jaimie and Troy set the target. As the others gathered around binoculars and scopes in hand to watch, Jack loaded 5 rounds into 2 different magazines as the others whispered amongst themselves. Once set, the targets appeared as nothing more than dark spots with the tiniest of orange flecks against them with the naked eye. Jack heard someone ask how far away they were and he heard Wren say, "522 yards".

Doing the math in his head, Jack knew 522 yards was about 475 meters. Despite the distance, it was still a relatively easy shot as he routinely practiced shots up to 800 meters with significantly more wind on his practice ranges in Missouri and Kansas.

When Jaime and Troy returned, Jack took his rifle and laid down in the prone again. He adjust-ed the sights on his scope to account for the distance and the minimal wind. He placed a magazine into the weapon and again felt the flicker of excitement. In his head, he heard his former instructor, SFC Bates say this was what he was born to do. The brief thought was interrupted by the sound of an approaching vehicle. Out of habit, Jack looked and saw a newer model Jeep coming up the trail from the bottom. Seeing no -one else in the group appeared surprised or up-set by the arrival, Jack returned his attention to the rifle and target.

He heard a door slam as he settled in but as he took aim he blocked out everything around him. Working the bolt, he chambered a round and then found his mark along the stock for his cheek before looking through the scope. Satisfied with the sight picture he took a microsecond to relax his body and mind through the process of taking a full breath, releasing half of it and only then did he begin taking up the slack of the trigger. The weapon jumped with a loud crack. Looking through the scope Jack saw the round had hit the orange just outside the innermost circle, to the left and above. He took the same aim point and fired again. Again the round hit just outside the circle, but on the opposite side of the circle than the first round, below and to the right. While still an impressive shot at the distance Jack wasn't happy with the distance between the impact points between the first two rounds. He again took aim at the same center point and fired. The third round again hit outside the inner circle, closer to the first round than the second. Jack then fired the two remaining rounds which completed the grouping with the first and third entry points. Satisfied, Jack dropped the empty magazine and loaded the second.

This time Jack took aim at the second target and adjusted the aim point ever so slightly to compensate for the small deviation he had discovered on the first target. Jack then fired the five rounds rapidly, working the bolt action in a blur for those watching. Each of the rounds hit the target. Despite the distance and the speed with which he shot all 5 of the rounds were within the 4 inch circle.

When he was done Jack heard a long whistle. Standing up, Jack turned and heard Jaime say to Wren "I think you just lost your title as the best shooter in town".

"Whatever, I could do the same thing. Plus its easy with that rifle, damn thing practically aims itself."

"Has nothing to do with the rifle. That's world class shooting right there" Jaimie said.

"Bullshit, I aint seen none of his graveyards."

Jaime just grinned and walked away to retrieve the targets saying, "Wren just stop and admit the guy is good."

Wren stood for a second watching Jaime before he stalked off towards his truck.

Jack watched feeling something more than hurt pride had just transpired between himself and his former friend. "Nice shooting" Jack heard a female voice say snapping him from the thought. Looking he saw CB Greene standing there. He gave her a quizzical look.

"I just pulled up. My dad said he was coming up here to shoot with some guys from work. I told him I would meet him here and we would go grab lunch"

"Your dad?" Jack asked.

"Thomas Greene, you probably don't know him but he is here. Jeremy invites most of employ-ees"

"The big guy with the M1" Jack finished her sentence as CB grinned.   "We just met" he finished.

"Do you know where he is now?" she asked.

"He was right here a minute ago" Jack responded, turning to scan the area. It took him a moment but he eventually spotted the man standing alongside Jeremy, Wren and Troy away from the crowd behind Wren's truck. The quartet seemed to be having a pretty intense conversation based upon the mannerisms of Wren, although they were beyond earshot to be heard. "He is over there." Jack pointed in the direction of the group.

CB saw them.   "Thanks" she said looking concerned.

Noticing the change of expression on her face Jack asked, "What is it?"

"Huh?" CB responded as she continued to watch the four men.

"You don't seem thrilled to see your dad talking to those guys"

Turning to look at Jack she said, "I'm not."

"Why?"

"Look Jack you have been gone a really long time. There somethings you probably don't know about Buckhannon ok."

"Ok, so explain it to me."

"This is not the time nor the place for that."

"Ok so name the time and place," he said.

CB hesitated and stared at him. She knew the man carried a badge but she also knew these guys all used to be his friends. Did he know anything about what was suspected of Jeremy? Did he know Wren and most of the others in the group had all done time in prison? Would he care? She turned away from Jack and looked back towards her father, watching as the four appeared to come to some sort of an agreement and break up. Jeremy and her Dad walked to-wards her and Jack while Wren and Troy climbed into the big red truck.

Watching them she said, "Do you really want to know Jack?"

"I asked didn't I?"

"Ok I will tell you what, meet me tomorrow at noon at Sam's pizza and we will talk. Do you re-member where that is?"

"Sure" Jack said.

Jack stayed around for a little longer and watched as most of the people there began to pack up their things and drive off. Having no real reason to linger himself, he went to his truck and put his stuff away. While doing so he noticed, CB and Thomas drive out, the Jeep following the big work truck. He wondered what she wanted to tell him tomorrow.

His thoughts were broken by Jeremy's voice, "You outta here too?"

Turning to see his long time friend approaching Jack said "Yeah man, I got some things to do"

"Well man, glad you got to come out. You damn sure can shoot. I didn't remember that."

Jack simply nodded in response.

"Anyhow don't be a stranger. Hit me up before you head back and we will finish that drink from last night"

"Sounds good." Jack said noncommittally before climbing into his truck and drove off.

CHAPTER 30

On his drive home, it suddenly dawned on Jack he was going to have lunch with a woman the next day. A very attractive woman he corrected himself. He could not remember the last time he had actually been on a "date". The closest thing he had was drinks a few times with women whom guys at work had tried to set him up with.

The first girl, Duke had set him up with. Her name was Jessica and she very attractive and well spoken. They met at a bar called Johnnies she had chosen. Things started off well and each had ordered a second drink. However any prospects of a second date ended quickly thereafter when she began telling him her political views. While Jack considered himself fairly moderate it became painfully obvious she was a leftist extremist. Though she gave him her number he dis-carded it immediately after leaving the bar and then scolded Duke for the suggestion the two meet. Duke laughed it off and confessed it was Carrol, his wife's, idea and he thought the prospect of Jack and the girl going out would be funny.

The second girl he was set up with was actually Captain Dickson's cousin and the sister-in-law to Sam. Her name was Heather, she was very nice and Jack felt a strong connection with her. Jack had spoken with her multiple times on the phone and had many more text conversations before they had agreed to meet. She was hesitant because she didn't like seeing what her sis - ter went through everyday when Sam left for work and the inherent risk their jobs required. As luck would have it the pair had just sat down when Jack's phone rang and he was called out to work. She never returned his calls thereafter. Instead she simply sent a text a week later "Sorry Jack, I can't."

Truth be told Jack was aware due to his time in the military and his current job, he had never had a real relationship. The closest he had come was with Nan, a friend with benefits from work a few years prior, whom he had grown very comfortable with. But she had been offered a pro-motion requiring she transfer from Kansas City to Denver. The pair had said they would keep in touch and had actually met once about 4 months after she had left in Ft Hays Kansas for a weekend. During the visit while they both enjoyed themselves it became readily apparent to them both it would be the last time.

Despite, his history and everything currently going on in his life, Jack was excited to have lunch with CB the next day. He was preoccupied with the idea the rest of the evening and into the night.

CHAPTER 31

CB followed Thomas back to town, where they stopped for lunch the Donut Shop, each ordering 2 pepperoni rolls with hot cheese. They sat in one of the small booths near the front window overlooking the small parking lot.

CB had just taken a bite when Thomas said, "I saw you talking to that cop friend of Mr. Marshall's. Did you two know each other?"

"No, not really. I mean I knew who he was in school, but he's older than me and I doubt he knew me. I hadn't seen him until the other night. Why?"

"Oh nothing. I tell you what though that guy can shoot. He put on a show for sure."

"You have no idea."   CB responded under her breath.

"Whats that baby girl?"

CB then explained what she had seen the man do on the previous occasions she had encountered him in the last week. As she explained, she became very animated and excited.

"Sounds like an impressive fellow." Thomas said. "The boss said that he was some kind of Federal Cop though. I am sure you know a bunch of guys like that from you ATF days baby girl."

"No Dad, I don't. Most officers can't do anything like that, and certainly not all three. I even reached out to one of my old friends about him yesterday to see what they could tell me and that was before I saw him put on the show at the range this morning." CB answered.

"Sounds like he made quite an impression. I like him better than that Bennet asshole already." Thomas said smiling.

"Whatever Dad." CB laughed somewhat embarrassed.

*****

After lunch, CB went back to the office to get back to work. Walking in she was surprised to see both Captain Rodgers and Ashcroft already in the conference room they had been given to use. Hearing her walk in both men looked up from Ashcroft's laptop.

"Glad to see you can join us" Captain Rodgers said sardonically.

"Did I miss something? I didn't know we were all meeting here today?" CB asked.

"I sent you an email about 10:30 last night. Did you not get it?" asked Rodgers.

"I haven't checked my email yet. I was just getting ready to." CB   responded half heartedly.

"We just got started about an hour ago. Ashcroft was just giving me a summary of the evidence from the 5 cases and where you guys are currently. Frankly, I was hoping for more progress."

CB ignored the barb. She knew Rodgers was a career administrator and had little idea of what an investigation actually entailed - another reason she didn't trust the man. Feeling he was only concerned about how quickly the investigation was completed in how it would reflect on him, certain he would be at the front of the line when the brass was passing out praise for a job well done.

"Anyway, we were just finishing up here." Rodgers continued. "From here moving forward I would like a progress report nightly via email and want you both in my office Wednesday morning for a face to face. Now carry on."

As he was leaving the room, he turned and added "And Detective Greene. Moving forward I expect you will be working this matter at all times. No more coming in after noon. Understand?"

Looking at him CB nodded and the man left.

"What an asshole," Ashcroft said. "He always like that?"

"Pretty much. He only cares about the numbers. And he will throw us under the bus if he thinks it's going sideways." CB warned.

"I know the type, remember I was on the first task force that went sideways. These damn bureaucrats care more about public perception than they do their own people or the work we do. Its why I have turned down opportunities to go into management. Fuck those guys."

"Amen," CB said still mad before opening her own laptop to check her emails and get back to work. Checking her in box she had only 6 unread messages. One was the aforementioned message from Captain Rodgers, telling her he had procured overtime for the case and he would meet them at noon. The message just reinforced her dislike of the man. 'like he can't call or text' she told herself.

The second and third messages were from the state medical examiners offices and just con-firmed what they already suspected. The toxicology screen showed Roberts had opioids in his system; consistent with the previous victims. The fourth and fifth messages were simply administrative messages about the overtime being permitted and another saying she was required to do her annual weapons qualification at the range within the 30 days.

But it was the sixth message that grabbed her attention. The night prior after she and Ashcroft had witnessed Jack incapacitate officer Poles and spoke with his she had sent an email to one of her old friends with the ATF to see if he could find out anything on the man. What she read was completely unexpected.

CHAPTER 32

The next day, Jack was awakened hearing the television in the next room. He went to the kitchen to see his parents sitting at the bar having coffee and watching television, both dressed nicely. Before he could ask why they were dressed up, his mother asked if he wanted to go to church with them. Jack thought about how to respond but before he could answer his dad said, "Go get dressed boy there are some people there who will be excited to see you."

Not wanting to be rude and thinking it would be nice to visit his childhood church Jack left the room, grabbed some clothes and headed towards the shower. On the way to the bathroom, he told his parents they should go ahead and leave for Sunday school and he would meet them at the church for the main service. He explained he had plans to meet someone after church for lunch and thus he would take his own truck. What he didn't explain was he hated being tied to someone else's schedule when he did not drive.

Jack arrived to the church as bible school was ending, before the main services were set to be - gin. The church was now in a new building, built for the ever growing congregation, across the road and nearer the highway than the building Jack sat in during his youth. Jack found a spot towards the back of the 3/4 full parking lot. As he was walking up the stairs to the main doors he heard a horn blow. Looking up, he saw the same overdone F-150 he had seen the night he and Jeremy had drinks. As he continued to watch, the window came down and Jeremy stuck his head out "Hey man, hold on a second". Dumbfounded, Jack watched as he parked, once again angling the obnoxious truck to occupy 2 spaces.

As Jeremy approached Jack said "I thought you drove a Jeep"

"I have a Jeep too, but KC Jones there is my baby. I drive her around town. The Jeep is for when I am going off the road. I also have a Cadillac Escalade I use for business and a 1970 Chevelle with a 572 big block I cruise around in once in a while to impress the ladies."

"Must be nice" Jack responded.

"I've done well here" Jeremy said. "I am single, no kids and no pets. I put my money in the house and into my toys. You know we cant take it with us"

"Indeed we can't. So did you really just call that truck 'KC Jones" as in the Grateful Dead? As in "Drivin that train, high on cocaine, KC Jones you better watch your speed!"

Jeremy laughed, "Like I said put my money into my toys. We all have our vices Jack."

Jack shook his head.

"What brings you out to services this morning Jack?"

"My parents still go here and asked me to come"

"That's right, I see them here most every week, though they tend to sit further in the back than I do."

"So you're a regular here now?   I don't remember you being the church going type"

"Been coming here since college, after Dad passed away. Hell Gary has become like a second father to me. Good people here my friend."

"Never doubted it for a second." Jack replied "the people here have always been good to me and my family".

As the pair walked into the main auditorium, Jack saw his parents and nodded to Jeremy as he made his way to an unoccupied chair next to Woody. As he made himself comfortable he watched Jeremy walk towards the front stopping here and there to shake a hand or say hi seemingly at every aisle.

"Funny isn't it"   he heard his Dad say.

"Whats that pop?"

"How a snake can change it's skin for an hour each week on Sunday Morning"

Before Jack could reply, the music worship leader asked the congregation to rise and join them in song. When Jack was a kid, the band consisted of one guitar, an organ player and a few singers who led the congregation in the singing of a few tradition hymns. However, on the stage today Jack saw a full band, with drums, a bass, keyboard and three guitarists. There were also three singers standing in the center of the stage. The band went through a set of four songs that were much nearer to rock and roll tunes, none of which Jack knew, than any of the hymns he remembered. The experience reminded him he needed to get into church more often. After the songs the music leader led the congregation in an opening prayer and introduced the pasture for the weekly message.

The pastor of the church was a man named Gary Davis, who had been in the position since Jack was a kid. He was a small bald headed man with a quiet scholarly face. Jack remembered him as being a friendly and mild mannered guy when speaking with him one on one.

However on Sunday mornings during his sermons his voice became firm, his actions became animated and his messages always seemed powerful.

He opened "Forgiveness. What does it mean to forgive or to be forgiven? How does the lord forgive us? Acts 3:19 says, 'repent then and turn to God, so that your sins may be wiped out, that times of refreshing may come from the lord' or as John 1:9 states 'If we confess our sins, he is faithful and just and will forgive us our sins and purify us from all unrighteousness.'"

As Jerry continued Jack became lost in his own thoughts. He understood the principle Gary was discussing but wasn't sure if what he was feeling guilty about was entirely wrong. He understood the Bible said though shall not kill, but he also understood King David and Paul had both killed people and yet were celebrated for their services to God. Was his service to God?

Jack was unsure. He told himself he was serving to protect others but were those he was protecting the innocents who needed protection or was he just a blind tool being used by the hand of the unjust? Could that be forgiven? How much blame does a person take if he or she is deceived by others to sin if when they act they do so thinking they are serving a better good?

So lost in these thoughts, Jack didn't even realize the week's sermon was over until the people around him stood and the band began to play again. He stood noticing he was wet from perspiration and his heart was pounding. He was breathing fast and shallow and his fists were clinched tight. Shaking his head, as the others sang along Jack closed his eyes and forced himself to take a deep breath and then another. He opened his hands and flexed his fingers across his thighs and tried to force the muscles in his neck and shoulders to relax. After a moment he reopened his eyes to reorient himself. A moment later, the band completed their song and announced the congregation was dismissed.

Jack mindlessly merged in to the aisle with the others exiting. He walked the short distance to the door where Gary, Jeremy and some of the other church elders were shaking hands with those leaving. As Jack got to the door Gary grabbed his hand and pumped it firmly while he clasped Jack on the shoulder with his left. "Its good to see you Jack. Your mom said you were in town. I'm glad you were able to come"

"It was good to come" Jack said, then added "Hey Gary do you think that I could talk to you sometime this week?"

"Of course. I'm here everyday from about 9 o'clock till 4 or 5 and then come back later when we have evening activities. Stop by anytime."

"Thank you, I will".

Outside, Jack told his parents he would be home later and spoke to a few other former acquaintances as he made his way to his car. He still had some time to kill before his lunch with CB so he wasn't in a big hurry. On his way he passed by Jeremy's "KC Jones" occupying two spaces and shook his head. 'Fuckin ridiculous' he thought to himself.

Looking past the truck, towards his own, he saw someone standing next to it, wearing khaki slacks and a light blue button down shirt. It took Jack a moment to recognize the man as Jaimie Miller, who was without a baseball cap and had his hair combed back neatly. Not only had it been years since he had seen the man prior to the shooting range yesterday, it was the first time he could recall seeing him in anything other than jeans.

Getting closer Jack said "Hey Jaime, I didn't expect to see you here"

Smiling Jaimie said "I could say the same for you"

"Mom and Dad come here. Have been members since for as long as I can remember and they made us come as kids. They asked me to come this morning, said it would be good for me. It was".

"Yeah man, been coming here a while now myself. A couple years anyway since I got back to town. Once I came back from Afghanistan the second time and got out of the service I was lost for a bit inside my own head. I came here one Sunday morning for no real reason really and comin back ever since when I can. I like it."

"Yeah Gary is one of those preachers who always seems to be speaking directly to you. Always has been. Hell even as a kid, he would preach about stuff I didn't understand but I'd've sworn he was talking only to me at the time."

"You feel that way this morning still?"

"Shit man, more than you know."

With a laugh Jaimie said, "I think I understand man. Trust me I do."

After a long second, Jaime continued, "Hey man, I am actually glad I saw you in there today. I think you should know that you need to be careful. Our little town ain't the same place we left back in the day. I know it may look the same but the people are different."

"I've heard," Jack said.

"You heard right. I don't know how long your in town or anything but seriously man keep your head on a swivel. You embarrassed Wren yesterday whether you meant to or not and he is pissed. He isn't one to take that very well"

"Ah hell, someone just needed to tell him to stop driving like an asshole. He is lucky I didn't do more than embarrass him. I wanted to kick his sorry little ass for that stunt."

Shaking his head Jaimie said, "Man it wasn't the driving beef that you got him on. It was the shooting. He always bragged he is the best shooter in this State and here you come home and make him look bad knocking him off his high horse."

Jack shrugged nonchalantly, thinking to himself Wren would just have to get over it.

"Anyhow man, it was good seeing you again. But seriously be careful and go back to Kansas or wherever your from now in one piece. Don't get caught up in the drama here. It's no good for anybody." Warning delivered, Jaime walked away and got into a brown Dodge Ram pickup which was a few model years old. He started it up, waved and joined the line of cars exiting the parking lot. Jack watched the man leave and then climbed into his own truck and followed the crowd of cars out of the parking lot.

CHAPTER 33

Despite lingering after church and driving slowly in pretty heavy traffic by small town standards, as the two largest churches in town completed services, Jack still arrived at the pizza shop 30 minutes early. The store was on the corner of a strip mall giving it access to the main road. It was across the street, from one of the town's largest employers, a food distribution company, and just down the street from both the local middle school. Jack decided instead of waiting in-side by himself he remain in his truck. Not wanting to draw to much attention to himself, he backed into a parking spot towards the back the strip mall away from the restaurant, which still allowed Jack a view of the traffic approaching from the main road as well as the parking lot to the distribution center across the street.

As he waited, Jack replayed the morning's sermon in his head while he absentmindedly watched the passing cars drive by, wondering could he be forgiven? Could he continue down his path with a clear conscious?

The train of thought was broken when first heard and then saw a beautifully restored Trans Am pull into the parking lot taking an unoccupied spot in front of the restaurant. He watched a big man emerge from the car and go inside. Jack who had been trained to never forget a face, rec-ognized the man as Thomas Greene, CB's father. He wondered if it was a coincidence he was also at the restaurant and considered going inside. He reconsidered however, after peering at the dash clock, seeing he still had 20 minutes before he was supposed to meet CB. Jack decid-ed to remain in the truck rather than go in and talk with a man he had only just met.

After a moment, his thoughts returned to the sermon. Jack again found himself asking where was the line between serving others and serving God. He knew men were selfish by nature and he knew serving others was supposed to be showing service to God. But how was serving the selfish and helping ensure their safety, a selfless act that serves God? Especially when his ser-vice to others involved taking the lives of other men who also proclaimed to be in the service of Allah.

The circular thoughts made him both sweat and heart race. He even found himself gripping the steering wheel until his knuckles were white. 'Seriously Jack,' he thought to himself 'you have got to pull your shit together'.

Finally, after what seemed to take forever, Jack saw CB's Jeep pull into the lot. Leaving his truck parked in where it was, Jack got out and walked quickly, meeting CB at the door. Opening it for her, he heard the door chime ring to alert the employees of their arrival. "Thank you" she said simply as she passed, slightly blushing at the kind gesture of which she was unaccustomed.

Jack nodded to acknowledge the response and the two walked in together and across the small alcove to the register which was directly across from the entry doors. The register was located behind a large pass through window, which also revealed the kitchen beyond. From where Jack and CB stood at the counter, to their right was a hallway leading to the restaurant's restrooms, to their left the dining room.

After standing at the window for a brief moment, the pair were greeted by a college aged kid wearing a white t-shirt and a red named tag reading Jon, who took their order. Each ordered the buffet and sodas. Jack quickly handed the man his debit card telling him he would cover both. The young man took his card and filled large hard red plastic cups with their drinks, placing them on a brown tray along with silverware rolled in white paper napkins, while he waited for Jack's card to process. Jack signed the receipt after adding a generous tip, took the tray and thanked the young man at the counter.

"After you" he said to CB, who smiled and led him into the dining room to find a table.

The room was a large slightly rectangular space filled with square faux wood tables, surrounded by four padded chairs and 4 large booths along the far wall. To the immediate right of the room's entrance, along the near wall was the long buffet line, which allowed the workers from the kitchen to monitor the line and keep it stocked with a variety of pizza, pastas and salads.

Jack noted Thomas Green was sitting at a pair of tables that pulled together almost directly in front of the room's entrance near a large window that gave view into the parking lot.

"Are we sitting with your dad?" Jack asked.

"No, I didn't realize he was going to be here until I saw his car when I pulled in. But I need to say hi real quick."

"Of course." Jack said, before choosing a table corner table towards the back of the room from opposite from where Thomas was sitting. Jack placed the tray on the table and went to the bar. At the bar, Jack picked up a "new plate" as the sign said, filling it with 2 slices of pepperoni and jalapeño thin crust pizza and a small salad. Returning to the table he chose the chair in the corner giving him a complete view of the room, including the windows allowing him to see the street and parking lot.

He was looking out the window, eating his salad when he saw Wren's red truck drive past through the lot. A few moment's later he heard the door chime, indicating a new customer or customers had arrived.

Jack was watching the entry to the dining room and finishing his salad when CB sat down; her plate filled with bread sticks and 2 slices meat lovers. Noticing his glance at her plate she said, "Cheat day, and I'm a carb girl. I'll pay for it in the gym later."

As she spoke Jack saw over her shoulder, Wren and Troy enter the room and sit with Thomas.

Ignoring the pair and stifling a giggle at her statement Jack said, "I understand. My weakness is sweets. I have to watch myself around bakeries. I am the stereotypical cop, who loves coffee and donuts."

Holding her own chuckle, CB responded "Your anything but stereotypical Jack. I was actually going to ask you about something later but since your brought it up."

"Hold on" Jack said. His focus returning to the entry of the dining room seeing Jaime, now wearing his customary jeans, work boots and a long sleeve t-shirt, take his own tray to Thomas Greene's table. The three newcomers then headed to the bar to fill their plates. If Wren or Troy noticed Jack, neither gave any indication while Jaime gave an inconspicuous nod in acknowledgement, which Jack returned.

Following his gaze, CB turned and saw the trio. "They're meeting dad and Jeremy. Tomorrow morning they are going out to a rig to work on a new well that is apparently giving the guys trouble. Dad said it's a new big deal for the company and they are scheduled to be there for the next 10 days pulling 12 hour shifts. They're all meeting here to figure out the game plan for the site."

"Oh I guess I didn't realize they all work together, though I guess I knew they all work for Jere-my."

"Jack everyone in this town works for the rigs who can even. Jeremy is one of the few who will hire the guys who have records" CB said. "Its where the money is."

"I guess so, even the convicted felons". Jack stated, more harshly than he intended, in reference to Wren.

CB however, misconstruing the comment to be aimed about her father responded defensively, "They need to work too and your friend Marshall gives many of the guys a second chance at working again, though he pays them less the going rate because of their records. A lot of people hate him for both."

"What do you mean?" Jack asked confused by the comment.

"Look Jack half the population doesn't think a felon deserves to ever work again and are upset Marshall hires them. Then there are also the rumors that he hires cons for other purposes. Then many of the guys who work for him, while they appreciate the jobs at first, they soon grow resentful because he pays cut rate wages. Or at least that's the story," she said.

"And what do you think? I mean your Dad works for him and yet you seem to have no love for Jeremy either?" Jack asked.

"I honestly don't know. I mean my dad works for him like you said so I am probably biased. And I wouldn't say I don't like the guy but I mean, really Jack there is always the guilt by association stigma whether we admit it or not," she stated.

Jack contemplated the statement but didn't respond. The guilt by association line triggering thoughts about Nebraska and how the eldest Deen brother must have felt judged simply be - cause of his last family and how it had ultimately forced him to leave the town and abandon his family. As it turns out it saved him from being his brother's target, Jack thought.

Thinking she had somehow offended Jack, CB sat silently for a few moments as they ate their pizza. Jack, finished his plate and returned to the buffet without a word, making her feel worse.

Returning to the buffet line for a new plate, Jack picked up another two slices of pizza along with some cinnamon bread sticks smothered in frosting. As he sat, he saw CB studying his plate. Smiling he told her he had forgotten how much he had missed the place.

Sensing the perceived tension from earlier had passed, CB spoke again to change the subject. "So Jack going back to your being the prototypical cop comment. You don't know this but I spent a few years in the ATF myself as a field agent. And I still have a few contacts with the feds. So Friday after I spoke with you at the restaurant and saw your credentials I asked one of my friends to look you up when he had a chance."

"So you ran a background check on me?" Jack asked, again a little firmer than he intended.

"No, no nothing like that. I was simply curious after seeing you disarm two men without breaking a sweat and then 4 days later give a cop a lesson in arrest procedure. It made me wonder what your deal really was. Like I told you I was a fed too for a while and most of the officers at the local, state or federal levels I have worked with and met wouldn't have been able to manage either situation as you did as well as you did, let alone both. I was curious." CB replied a bit defensively.

"So what did you find out?" Jack asked, unsure how to perceive her response but wanting to give her the chance to explain.

"I certainly didn't expect to get an answer back in less than 24 hours. That in and of itself was telling in a way. But then my friend tells me you're a member of the special ops for the Marshals. He said you're both an expert in hand-to-hand combat and a sniper. My guy went on to say people who know such things, say you're probably one of the best snipers on the planet and not just your ability to pull a trigger, which you showed yesterday. But rumor has it from a tactical standpoint you're just as good if not better."

Jack sat silently looking at her, unsure of how to respond for a moment before asking "Is that all it said?" Worried she knew he was on administrative leave for his mental state.

"Yeah, I mean for the most part. I mean it said you had been recruited for the position from the Army and you were stationed at the Kansas City field office." Before he could say anything she continued, "Jack, you know I am a state police officer, what you probably don't know is I am a detective and special investigator. I don't know how much you have kept up with the news from back here but this area has a huge drug problem. And lately the both the addicts and the dealers have gotten more aggressive and violent. Currently me and Ashcroft, my partner that you met the other night, are investigating multiple murders that have happened over the last couple of years which are all drug related."

"So what does that have to do with me?" Jack asked, while kicking himself for hoping CB had asked him to meet was more of a personal nature as opposed to business.

CB explained, "Jack, the killer has been laying in wait for the victims and killing them with a rifle. The records show he shot a couple of the victims from some pretty impressive distances."

"OK, but again whats does that have to do with me? You cant think I had anything to do with that. Hell I haven't been in town but a week. You can have your buddies check my damn work record and clear that in less than 2 minutes" Jack said a little louder than intended, drawing the attention of Wren and Jaime, who both looked in his general direction.

"Oh no, no, no. I'm sorry Jack. I wasn't trying to imply that you did it. What I was trying to say was; or ask you rather; is if you would be willing to take a look at the crime scenes with me and give me a feel for anything you see? I was hoping maybe your expertise would help us see something we are missing."

Jack sat and looked at her for a moment confused by the turn of events. Again chiding himself for hoping the invitation had been more than a professional interest. Finally, after what was be-ginning to become an uncomfortable silence he said, "Sure I can look over them for you. I want you to know though this isn't in any official capacity and I am no detective or investigator. I don't know what you think I will see that you and your people didn't."

"Thank you Jack. I don't know if you will see anything either but at this point any help is greatly appreciated."

Jack nodded and the pair agreed to meet Tuesday morning at 9 am at the state police barracks to go visit the scenes. Thereafter they each finished their lunches with a few awkward attempts at small talk, though neither was really engaged lost in their own thoughts. Their meal complete, they were getting up and placing tips on the table, when the door chimed again, causing Jack to pause in his tracks. A moment later, Jeremy Marshall walked into the restaurant, still wearing his church clothes. Following him were two other men dressed in work clothes similar to those worn by Thomas, Troy, Wren and Jaime. Unsure if it was his policeman's instinct or the power of suggestion, but he thought the pair each looked like they had served time at some point. Jack watched as his friend walked straight to the table where the others awaited and sat down oblivious to Jack and CB's presence. "Morning Boss" the four men said nearly in unison.

After waiving their greeting off Jack overheard Jeremy say, "Sorry, I'm late gents. I had to go get Johnny and EJ here from another job to fill out your crew. We can't screw this job up."

"Glad to have you" Thomas said. "Whyntcha boys sit down and lets talk through the game plan". The two men sat down at the table each taking a seat on either side of Jeremy. None of the trio apparently going to eat.

For reasons he couldn't quite explain to himself Jack decided to sneak out without saying any-thing to his friend. Walking to the parking lot Jack escorted CB to her car, and confirmed their meeting time for Tuesday. He watched her drive away, before walking to his own truck and left to return home to his parents house.

CHAPTER 34

The next morning Jack awoke shivering cold. The clock read 8 am. The time was late for him, though not totally unsurprising after another night of fitful sleep, nightmares and racing thoughts. Climbing from the bed, which was damp from sweat, he went into the kitchen for coffee. On the counter by the coffee pot was a note from his Mom saying Woody had a doctor's appointment at the VA and the two of them would be gone most of the day. The note also informed Jack where the extra key was hidden and asked that if he should leave to please lock the door. It was a stark reminder of how much his childhood home had changed as Jack could not recall ever locking the doors growing up.

Having read the note, Jack poured himself a cup of coffee in an attempt to wake up. He drank two cups while absentmindedly cruising the television for anything of interest. Despite the cof-fee, Jack still felt the morning haze on his mind and body. To shake the fog off he decided to get in a workout.

After putting on shorts and a t-shirt, Jack went to the barn and filled an old burlap bag his dad kept on hand with a mixture of sawdust and sand. Picking it up he estimated it weighed some-where near a 100 pounds before hanging the bag from the rafters using a chain. He wrapped his feet and ankles with sports tape and then slipped on a pair of 4 ounce MMA gloves. He spent the next hour working on punches; knee and elbow strikes; and kicks. Once finished with the bag work Jack was drenched in sweat but still felt restless. After removing the gloves and wraps, he put on socks and running shoes.

Jack ran 8 miles along a deserted country road, four miles out and four miles back. He covered the distance in just under 50 minutes but was frustrated with himself for missing his goal of 48 minutes. Afterwards, he was physically spent, which was of little consequence. Jack was more concerned that the effort hadn't cleared his mind as intended. Despite his best efforts Jack could think of nothing but Nebraska, Gary's sermon and the non-date with CB. Each of the three trains of thought seemingly touching a nerve somewhere in deep. Jack hated the feeling.

Jack continued to dwell on the thoughts as he took a shower and got dressed for the day. Once finished it was nearly 11 am. Due to the difference in time zones Jack decided it was to early to check in with Dr. Hartman, whose office had just opened. Yet feeling he needed to talk to someone, if only for the distraction, he locked the house, jumped in his truck and left.

Jack took the most indirect way he possibly could, traveling amongst the lesser used back roads to town. He told himself he was taking the roundabout way to reminisce, though he knew he was simply stalling; knowing where he was going. At 11:45 having wandered as much as he could, Jack pulled into the church parking lot.

Looking around there were more cars in the lot than Jack expected, which made him pause momentarily, nervous about who might see him. Ultimately, though, after looking in the mirror he told himself, he had to do something, talk to someone and get out of his own head. Deter-mined, he got out and walked to the front door, where he had entered just the day before and numerous times as a youth. Though the distance between his truck and the front door was less than

100 feet, it felt like it took forever to cover the distance, eerily like Dr. Hartman's hallway. It reminded him of crossing alleys in Iraq during a mission without an ounce of cover. You just couldn't help but feeling exposed.

At the door he took a brief breath and pulled on the handle. Locked. He tried the other door. Locked as well. "Seriously," he said to himself. Then he read the bottom of the welcome sign mounted on the wall: "M-F 8-5 please use the side door next to the daycare. Thank you." Jack couldn't help but laugh at himself. Still grinning in spite of himself, he walked to the side door.

Jack entered the door, which led into a small foyer where there was a bar style desk to the left of a long hallway. There was no one at the desk but there was a hand bell. Jack tapped the bell which chimed with a ping. Behind the bar, a single door opened and a small older woman with white hair came out. She wore gray slacks, an orange blouse and a blue sweater over her shoulders. The woman's glasses dangled on an old chain around her neck. "May I help you?" she asked.

"Yes, please. I am here to see Gary. He told me to stop by anytime this week."

"Name?"

"Jack, Jack Kirby"

"Jack Kirby. As I live and breathe, I haven't see you in 20 years. I remember when you were a bashful, cute, little boy," the woman said.

"I have been gone quite a while" Jack said trying to be polite, not recognizing the woman.

"You don't know who I am" the woman said pointedly. "I am Margret Callahan. You were in my second grade class"

Looking closely, Jack could see it. When he was in her class Mrs. Callahan had seemed old, though he supposed she was likely in her late fifties or early sixties, at the time which meant she was likely pushing 80 now. She seemed smaller now, though he knew that was from his having grown up, but the face seemed right. "Oh hi Mrs. Callahan. I am so sorry, I didn't recognize you."

"That is quite all right Jack, I didn't know who you were either. What brings you home?"

"Just visiting friends and family, I was at service yesterday and Gary said to come by."

"Of course.   Have a seat and I'll let him know your here."

Jack didn't bother sitting, preferring to look at the announcements on the community board on the wall. The listings ranged from lawn and home repair services to self defense classes and substance abuse rehabilitation. Jack assumed the services listed were probably provided by members of the church for other members of the church. He was disturbed by the substance abuse counseling announcement and the self defense classes, however. Obviously feeling everyone should have the ability to defend themselves, but upset that the local demand was likely directly attached to the substance abuse problems in the area.

His thoughts were interrupted when he heard from behind "Jack, I wasn't expecting you to be in so soon after you mentioned coming by yesterday."

Turning towards the voice Jack saw Gary standing near the hallway and asked "I hope that's ok?"

"Of course. Gives me an excuse to take a break. Come on back to the office." Gary motioned with his head.

Jack followed the pastor down the hall to a good sized office. The space featured bookshelves filled to the brim with books along the wall to either side of the door, to the wall to Jack's right as he entered. To the left, sat a nice desk. Behind the desk sat a comfortable looking chair and old fashioned filing cabinets. In front of the desk were two wooden arm chairs with floral patterned padded seats. Directly across from the door and to the left of anyone sitting behind the desk was a huge picture window offering a view of the main road and an old cemetery beyond. Gary saw Jack admiring the view and stated, "Its never bad to have a reminder of why I come to work each day".

Jack contemplated the statement before nodding unsure of how to respond.

Sensing his discomfort Gary let him off the hook "So Jack what is it that you wanted to talk about?"

Taking the statement as an invitation, Jack sat down in the open chair furthest from the window and began to talk. He gave Gary a brief history of his time in the Army as a sniper, the awards, medals and accolades; his job at US Marshall's office; the events in Nebraska leading to his "vacation"; his new concerns related to the morality of it all and the need for forgives and repent based on the previous day's sermon.

"Jack what exactly do you feel you need to be forgiven for?"

"Gary, I have killed a bunch of people. More than I care to admit. I know it was my job. I know I was sent there because the government thought it was necessary for us to be there. They obviously say it's for National Security but was it? Did anything I did over there matter? Would my failing to pull the trigger on any of those guys have really affected the United States and the people I care about here?"

"Jack, you know no one can answer that definitively. But I have talked to a ton of vets the last 15 years, and one recurring theme I have heard from them is that once over there the reason isn't why are you there but its to get you and your buddies home. Let me ask you this. If you hadn't been there would your friends made it home?"

"I don't know. I mean it's not as if I weren't there the army wouldn't have had someone else in my place"

"But from what you said Jack, you're better than most. Could anyone else have done everything the way you had? Would whomever had been there instead of you have had your skill or judgment?"

Jack remained silent. Unsure of how to respond.

Sensing his frustration Gary added, "Jack, you're dealing with a ton. More than I can ever un-derstand. But let me ask you this. Have you ever killed anyone out of malice or cruelty?"

"No, not exactly, but there was a time when I enjoyed my job. I took pride in it. I was happy to for the chance to show off my skills. Surely that can't be right?"

"Jack being a soldier is not a sin. Consider the story of the soldiers who visited John the Baptist on the river who had similar misgivings. They asked John what it was they should do. John did not tell them to flee the Army, though that may have been the answer the men sought. Instead he told them, do not take money by force or false accusations and be content with your pay."

"But that passage isn't about killing people"

"Ok then, do you remember the Apostle Paul?"

"I do"

"And you remember he was called Saul and was a great persecutor of the early Christians be-fore he became an Apostle?"

"I know. But he never killed anyone despite the label."

"Ok probably not the best example though Paul did stand idly by as Saint Steven was stoned to death. Yet God forgave and used Paul despite his past. And what about Samson and King David or even Joshua. They were all soldiers. They all killed in battle. Yet God did not forsake them."

"I know but they were all doing God's will. Was I? I was there because I essentially volunteered to do so. I didn't do it as an honorable undertaking to serve my country or my fellow man, I did it because I enjoyed it. Maybe not the actual killing, but certainly the Army and certainly showing off my abilities."

"I understand that Jack. But you are not a soldier anymore. Why did you go into the Marshal service when you got out?"

"I was recruited because of what I did in the Army."

"But did you think about why you left the Army and actually went? You are obviously a smart guy Jack you could have done anything at the time. Why that?"

"It just seemed the right thing to do."

"And do you still think it's the right thing to do?"

Jack paused, pulling his badge from his pocket. Showing Gary he said, "Like it says, 'Justice, Integrity, Service' I believe in them all, as cheesy as it sounds. So no, I have no regrets."

Gary nodded and smiled knowingly. "Jack I think that's half the battle right there."

"Half the battle?" Jack asked unsure of his meaning.

"Yes, you just implied you believe in what you're doing right? That seems to be more than what you were saying when you first came in. I would say that is progress right?"

Jack considered the idea before acknowledging its validity with a slight bow of his head.

The two men spoke for a few minutes more and Jack thanked him for his time and asked if he may come back again before he left town. Gary assured him he was welcome anytime. Jack remained confused but feeling better walking to his truck, still carrying the badge in his hand, rubbing his thumb across the motto.

CHAPTER 35

As Jack leaving the church, CB was heading into a meeting with Ashcroft. Her day had begun with a face-to-face meeting with Josh Bennet, the local medical examiner and her ex-boyfriend at his insistence. Bennet had confirmed the victim had high level of opioids in his system just like the other victims. He also confirmed the ballistics indicated the same rifle had also been used. The evidence was material to her case; however, CB told him she had already received the state reports. Thereafter the real purpose for his insistence upon meeting her in person came to the forefront when Bennet asked her who she was having lunch with the previous day.

CB asked him how he knew she was having lunch with someone and Bennet replied a little birdie had told him.

Angered by his flippant respond CB retorted, "Tell your little birdie that what I do or who I do it with is really none of his or your business."

Bennet stood. He remained standing over her silently for a moment before saying, "Tell that guy, whomever he is good luck. He is going to need it to put up with your ass. Sweet as it may look".

"Fuck you. We are done. Next time you call me or you email me and stay out of my business. Oh and if you must know the guy I was meeting with just happens to be an expert sniper who is going to help on this case. So shove that up your jealous ass while your at it!" CB shouted, and walked out of the office back to her car.

She remained upset for the entirety of the drive back to the office. Bennet was one of the big-gest mistakes she ever made. Sure he was good looking and smart but also a controlling ass-hole who cared more how CB looked good on his arm than anything else. 'What a prick,' she thought.

She was also upset with herself for saying Jack was just meeting with her to talk about the case, knowing she screwed that up. She had been hopeful the lunch could have sparked something else down the road, but then she got the correspondence from her friend describing his back ground. She didn't mean to imply that she wanted to talk with Jack just as a professional courtesy, though she understood how it came off. Still upset with herself, she walked into the conference room with Ashcroft.

"So what did Bennet tell you" Ashcroft asked before she even had time to sit down.

"Just confirmed what we already knew, the guy was full of opioids when he died."

"That couldn't have been done with a phone call?" Ashcroft asked.

"He was using it as an excuse to see me. I knew betterbut whatever.   What did you find out?"

"I had asked one of my friends to do some digging on the tread pattern of tire you had taken a picture of from on top of the hill. The good news is he was able to determine it was made by a BF Goodrich. Bad news is it is one of the most popular all terrain tires on the market. Worse yet, another buddy of mine who owns a tire shop, told me that most of the gas company trucks running around have these same tires on them because BF Goodrich is one of the fleet vendors the gas companies use."

"Damn. Not that it was anything conclusive anyhow but would have helped." CB muttered.

"Anything else that we have learned since we last spoke?" Ashcroft asked.

"Actually there is one thing. Do you remember the guy from the restaurant who took down the young police officer at the dinner table?"

"Sure, the US Marshal guy right? Kirby or something like that?"

"Yes, Jack Kirby. So I asked one of my old contacts to look into the guy for me. Out of curiosity more than anything."

"Curiosity huh?" Ashcroft joked with a smirk on his face insinuating more.

"Shut up," CB cut him off before he could go any further. "Anyhow it turns out Kirby is an expert sniper for the US Marshal's office and is considered by many to be one of the best shooters on the planet"

"You don't seriously think he is our shooter CB?" Ashcroft asked failing to see her point.

"No, no of course not. He hasn't even been in West Virginia for a few years. But I did run into him again Saturday morning with my dad, where interestingly enough he was shooting with some other guys. He is really good. Anyhow he and I got to talking and I asked if he wouldn't mind looking over the scenes to see if he can see something that had been missed since he is pretty much an expert. I figured it can't hurt."

"Is he going to do it?"

"Yeah, he's supposed to be here tomorrow morning at 9 so we can take him around."

"No, not we CB, you take him around. I'm going to talk to another contact of mine who said he may have some information about pills coming through the area."

"Oh, no big deal. I don't think we really need all three of us running over the same ground all over again. Or did you want me to tag along to talk to your guy?"

"No, this CI is kinda finicky anyway. Hard enough to get him to talk to me alone. He'd freak if I brought someone else along."

"Okay. Cool."

"I don't suppose you cleared this little tour with Rodgers or anyone else did you. Those federal guys don't typically play nice with we lowly state cops you know? Especially with everything that's happened with this case."

"No, but this isn't anything official. Just want to pick the guys brain a bit. Besides he is here on vacation. Kind of feel bad for dragging him out."

CHAPTER 36

A few hours later, in a small metal room that was built off a much larger piece of machinery, three men stood. The room was filled with a variety of tools and equipment, along with a work-table that doubled as a makeshift desk. The big man had summoned the two others inside to discuss new developments he was not happy to have been told. Even with the door closed, the room was filled with mechanical noises from equipment running nearby. Thus, the big man spoke loudly to the pair, "My little birdie told me that the cops are going to be out looking around tomorrow. This time they are going to be out with that new fed who they think may be able to help them see something they are missing. I want to know what exactly they are looking at".

"Okay. How do we do this boss?" asked the one of the men.

"We know where they are going, I want each of you to choose one of the sites and sit on it. Wait until they show up and watch them but make damn sure no one sees you, especially the cops. When they get there I want to know what they are doing. What they are looking at?" the man responded.

"Why?" asked the other man with an undertone of contempt in his voice.

"Because I said so" the big man retorted in a tone leaving no doubt that he wasn't in the mood for being questioned as stepped towards the other two to emphasize his point.

"You got it boss" replied the first man as he guided the second man from the room, opening the door to the outside where the noise was even louder. As the two closed the door the big man stared after them asking himself what was he going to do with them.

CHAPTER 37

Tuesday morning, Jack pulled up to the State Police barracks at 8:55 am. He had debated finding an excuse to text CB and call off but ultimately decided he couldn't live with himself if he had. He admitted, part of his apprehension was because his feelings were still hurt over his misperception regarding their lunch "date". Yet he told himself he couldn't let someone else get hurt on account of his hurt feelings.

More concerning, Jack also recognized his anxiety bubbling just below the surface about what they were about to do. He wondered how he would react to being in the field again — even if in only an advisory capacity. In the end, unable to overlook Gary reminder that he had committed to protect and serve. Especially knowing the public he served in this particular case involved his childhood home, his family and friends. Knowing should anything happen to any of them, he'd never be able to look at himself in the mirror again.

He was unsure if he was supposed to go inside or if CB was going to come out and meet him. Nonetheless, he climbed out of his truck and opened the back door to grab his Camelback, a backpack with an internal bladder that held water that fed a hose the person wearing the pack wore over his shoulder for easy access for drinking. In addition to the water, he also packed a light jacket, a lighter and tinder; a few protein bars, a compass, a range finder and binoculars combination, a Benchmade fixed blade tactical knife, and three loaded magazines for his 9 mm. He seriously doubted he would need any of it, but he'd rather have it and not need it; as op-posed to needing it and not having it.

He was also dressed for work, wearing a pair of khaki Blackhawk tactical pants, his Danner boots and a form fitting drifit navy colored long sleeve shirt with a US Marshall insignia on the chest. The shirt was tucked into his pants and gave him easy access to his pistol he carried on his belt along with an extra magazine. He also wore his favorite sun faded baseball cap he had gotten years ago at a Kansas City Royals game. Topping off the look was a pair of tactical Oak-ley sunglasses. He looked just what he was, a country boy turned soldier. Satisfied he had everything he could possibly need for the trip, Jack took a deep breath still debating the sense of it all, locked the truck doors and turned to go find CB.

Just prior to Jack's arrival, CB and Ashcroft had completed a conversation with Captain Rodgers via telephone, providing the man another update. They explained Sunday afternoon and Mon-day they had contacted the names of interest identified by the task force and asked to speak with them again to help clarify the record. CB went on to state her goal for the day after they finished their update was to visit all the prior crime scenes to see if anything was missed while Ashcroft told the man he was meeting with an informant who may have some knowledge about the case. Rodgers again tried to impress the need for the two new partners to solve this case quickly, causing CB to roll her eyes, while Ashcroft mockingly gave the speaker phone the middle finger. Upon hanging up they simultaneously muttered "asshole" causing them each to smile.

After the phone call they moved to the break room and were standing near the window of the break room, providing them a view of the parking lot. The pair were having one last cup of coffee before they went their separate ways, idly attempting to chit chat though both were seemingly lost in their own thoughts more than the conversation.

Staring out the window, CB saw Jack's truck pull into the lot and park. She continued watching as Jack climbed out, opened the back door and picked up what looked like a backpack. As she watched she couldn't help but appreciate the man's physique and mentally chided herself again for the mishandling lunch with the man on Sunday. After a moment, she ceased her visual, in-tending to meet him outside so he wouldn't have to come in the building, as the meeting was still technically unauthorized as she did not ask Captain Rodgers permission to bring Jack along. However, when she turned to leave she saw Ashcroft looking at her with a goofy grin on his face. "What?" she asked defensively knowing she looked like the cat who was caught with the canary.

"Nothing, you two kids have fun on your field trip and don't do anything I wouldn't do," Ashcroft chuckled.

CB rolled her eyes and walked past him to the parking lot.

CB met Jack just outside the entrance to the building. They said hello to one another in an awkwardly formal manner before they made their way to CB's Jeep after she offered to drive since she had planned the route. She had decided earlier to take the journey in the most convenient line of travel as opposed to doing in chronological order. She plotted a circuitous route she hoped would make the most efficient use of the limited time she had with Jack, still feeling guilt over taking his vacation time to try to help her. The route was also designed to allow the last stop of the tour to be the site of the most recent killing and nearest her office. While she hoped to be done before dark settled in, she secretly hoped it would still be late enough that maybe she and Jack could have dinner.

Driving to the first site CB's original plan was to try to get to know her passenger better though her attempts at beginning conversation had been awkward for both. The ill attempts at conversation she noted made Jack appear as uncomfortable as she herself felt. In an attempt to make them both feel more at ease she decided to give him more background on the case and discuss what her investigation had thus far revealed since she had taken over, little as it might be.

To start, she told Jack to grab a big three ring binder from the back seat explaining it was her investigation book, which contained notes and photos. For the remainder of the drive she walked Jack through the investigation. CB explained to Jack at first all the victims appeared to be random, the only connections being they all worked for the local drilling companies, had an opioid addiction and had been killed from long distance by the same .270 rifle according to the ballistics. She further explained neither the oil field connection nor the opioid addiction were something rare enough to make them of any special interest or a distinguishable connection. She then told him about the arrest of Tony Kincaid, leaving out that she knew the man, and how she came to be assigned the matter after the most recent killing. As she spoke, she got more comfortable speaking to the man, liking that he was engaged in the conversation, asking smart and pointed questions about many of the nuanced details she had taken for granted in her own mind. Before she knew it they had covered the 90 minute commute to the first crime scene.

The first stop on their tour, was where victim number 3 Charles Harp had died. It was the most remote of the five, located in Tucker County, West Virginia between the towns of Parsons and St. George. The terrain was a stark reminder to Jack of why West Virginia was known as the mountain state. The area was full of steep wooded hillsides and low river valleys where the lo-cal farmers grew crops and raised cattle. The roads had to follow the terrain, so even though the location of the body was only 20 miles as the crow flies off of route 33, the main highway; it was nearly twice that in road miles.

The body was discovered behind a summer camp for kids known as Camp Kidd and Holly Meadows Golf course near the river. Alongside the river was a fair-sized field that played itself out near the base of the mountain where there laid a series of flood water ponds, filled with cat-tails and surrounded by high grasses. Harp had brought his truck down the main road past the golf course and onto a dirt path that accessed the ponds and the field beyond.

The body had been discovered by a pair of teenagers who had called it in. The two boys made the call anonymously but there happened to be an officer in the area who had intercepted the pair walking down the lane as he was responding to the call. The boys told the investigators they were in the area looking for golf balls, though the intercepting officer told the detectives he knew the pair and suspected they had likely been in the area smoking weed.

CB drove down the gravel lane and pulled into a wide clearing near where Harp's truck had been. Getting out, CB and Jack used the crime scene photos to confirm they were in fact in the right spot, by referencing the points in the photos with those they saw on the ground. And while the landscape appeared different due to the change in season it still allowed the pair to get a feel for what had happened here.

Harp had died from two bullets that had struck him in the upper chest. His body was found about 100 feet from his truck laying in the mud near one of the ponds. It was estimated he had been there a couple of days before he was found, the body partially eaten by scavenging birds. CB told Jack when she first read the file she had been surprised the body hadn't been drug off by a mountain lion or bear until she saw a note in the file that the golf course paid a pair of hunters to keep the animals away from the property — apparently quite successfully.

After confirming they were in the right place, Jack studied the photos of the body and crime scene. Though the body had been scavenged he could see the two wounds in the upper right center of the chest. He noticed one wound was larger than the other. From experience he knew one was an entry wound, the second an exit wound. The entry wound had entered just below the collar bone. The exit wound was centered about 6 inches below and two inches to the left. Though not a medical examiner Jack was quickly able to deduct what happened.

"So let me guess," he said, "the higher entry wound was first and it exited low down near the waist line. The shot likely knocked the guy down and as he tried to crawl away he was shot in the back. That's why the second wound appears to have been flatter."

Stunned by the accuracy and succinctness of the statement, CB told him without having to look at the report she held in her hand, "That's what the file said almost to the letter. The theory is the shooter was elevated. But how did you figure that out so quickly?"

"You don't do what I do for a living and not figure out what bullets do to people or what people's natural reactions are. I once had an instructor named Bates say the best guys aren't just the guys who can pull the triggers but the ones who can see beyond the target, anticipate the ef-fects and can plan accordingly. I always tried to be one of the best."

CB nodded absentmindedly, surprised by the statement. While her inquiry had said the man be-fore her was one of the best snipers in the world, it wasn't until then she realized she had not considered what it truly meant.

Returning to his study of the body Jack then began to double check the location for more information and details. He understood she had asked him out here to help her determine the actions of the shooter, so he put himself in the shooters shoes. Asking himself if he were going to set the ambush how would he do it?

As he contemplated, Jack saw the immediate area was wide open with little cover for anyone. The victim had no where to go outside of jumping in the pond or trying to get back to the truck which CB had said was 100" from the body. Jack then turned to face the same direction the body had been laying. To his 6 o'clock was the golf course where it was incredibly unlikely the shooter would have been. At 9 o'clock was a huge field. Checking the crime scene report and photos he saw the field was nearly 35 acres and at the time had been planted with potatoes which allowed for little cover. To his 3 o'clock was the access road. "Does the file say if they were able to ascertain if the body had been moved far after he was shot? I mean did the ani-mals that had started in on the carcass move it any?" he asked.

Checking the file to ensure she hadn't missed anything CB answered, "Not that we could tell but since it had been a few days its possible it could have moved some, but the scavengers were mostly birds so it wouldn't have been far."

"So where do you think the shooter was?" Jack asked, testing his own theory.

"This is one of two sites that task force were unable to get a definitive location on. They assume it had to have been from across this pond up on the hillside up there," CB said pointing to a steep hillside across the way which was covered in trees and laurel bushes.

Nodding, as her answer was in line with his own theory Jack asked, "How would the shooter get up there?"

"There is a gas well and service road back up there he likely came down," she said pointing again along the top of the ridge.

"Can we go up there?"

"Yeah we can go up and look around. The file says we have had guys all over that hillside and no one was able to determine with any amount of certainty where the shooter had actually been."

Jack handed the photos back to CB and the pair climbed back into CB's Jeep. Retracing their path she drove up the hill, past the golf course and camp. Returning to the main road, CB turned left. After a quarter mile CB turned left again into what looked like a gravel driveway. The gravel traveled past a small white square home with a green metal roof then veered right to-wards a cluster of trees, which proved to be a gas well service road.

At the trees, the road took another turn to the left maintaining a rough course almost parallel to the main road back towards the area the body had been discovered, though significantly higher in elevation. Jack thought the well wasn't to old from the how the road appeared to still be in really good shape, as gas well companies were notorious for letting the service roads fall in dis-repair once the wells were placed. His theory proved correct. After a short but bumpy drive, they came to a clearing where a completed gas well stood. The platform and drill gone, the sight now simply appeared to be a series of red pipes leaving the ground running into a large red tank, the paint still new enough it was vibrant instead of the sun faded pink it would become with time.

After looking over the area, Jack said, "Pretty smart. Gave himself an escape route away from his target, though climbing that hill doesn't look easy. I'm guessing whomever was at the house was asked if they had seen anything that day"

"Yeah an elderly woman and her son live there. The guy works over at the charcoal plant we passed on the way here and wasn't home during the day and the woman is in her eighties. She said she doesn't remember anything unusual though she thought that she had seen one of the gas men drive down sometime that week. But admittedly that isn't unusual since they come to check on the tanks fairly regularly. We also asked how many people knew of the road since it took us a while to even figure out its existence, after all it looks like their driveway from the road. But they said almost all of the locals know about it. The son even told the investigators they have had to call the cops a few times with local high school kids coming back here to drink beer or smoke weed."

Jack took a moment and retrieved his backpack from the truck and put it on. He then proceeded to walk around the clearing along the wood line to see if there was a trail leading towards the pond, where the man had been killed. There wasn't an obvious path leading that way so Jack simply walked in the general direction through the woods along what felt the path of least resistance to him. He had walked about 150 yards from the clearing before the slope of the hill got incredibly steep. To get down a person would have to use the surrounding vegetation as hand holds in order to keep from falling. Operationally Jack wouldn't have went down the embankment because it would have effectively cut him off from his escape route and concluded the shooter had likely thought the same. He continued to walk along the small ridge line but be-tween the heavy brush and the steep slope there just wasn't anywhere Jack felt was right for the killer to have set up to get the shots. After crisscrossing the area for nearly 30 minutes he climbed the hill back to the clearing along the same line he descended, emerging from the wood line between the Jeep and the big tank.

"Find anything" CB asked.

""Nothing"

"We didn't either. Like I said the team had been all over the side of this place looking but never could pinpoint anything."

As she spoke Jack was facing the giant red collection tank. For the first time he truly studied it. Jack judged it to be about 15 feet tall and another 10 feet across. "Can I see those pictures again?" Jack asked.

CB went back into the truck and returned with the photos. Jack skimmed them quickly bypassing the photos of the body and field, choosing to focus on the photos of the hillside. Looking closely at two of them he realized near the top of the pictures was a flash of red, that had to be the holding tank.

The pictures reminded him of his first instructor, SFC Bates, in sniper school telling Jack and his classmates, "You're only as good as the platform you're firing from." At fist, Jack had no clue what the guy meant but learned quickly a shooter who is able to relax his body allowing him to place all of his focus on target acquisition, breathing and trigger squeeze, is incredibly more effective than a shooter who is also worried about balancing, falling or leaning. Thus, for any and every mission Jack went on thereafter, be it in the Army or with the Marshals, he was always very choosy about where he chose to set up — looking for the most stable position available given the parameters of any given mission.

With the thought in mind he paused and thought about it again. He decided if he were ambushing someone the way the killer had, he would have chosen the tank as a platform. It was perfect. It was flat on top and allowed the shooter the ability to get comfortable unlike the steep hill-side he just traversed. He walked around the tank, finding a steel ladder giving access to the top. He climbed it. On top there was an access hole in the center, though covered with a domed steel lid. Otherwise the surface was flat steel. Jack climbed onto it and walked to the edge over-looking the hillside. From here he could clearly see the golf course and camp. Looking down he was also able to see the pond and the access road where they had been.

More convinced he was onto something, Jack laid down in the prone to look at the situation. His feet hit the domed lid behind him, making it somewhat awkward, but not incredibly so. Studying it, Jack knew from here he could have made the shot, though it certainly wouldn't be an easy shot for the average shooter. Taking his range finder from his bag Jack, marked the approximate spot the body had been found. 420 yards or 385 meters. With the steep angle of the hillside making it more complicated again. If there had been any wind it would have been even more difficult though a skilled shooter could still have hit his target at a fairly high percentage. Another factor Jack calculated was as a result the angle from the platform to the target, a bipod or other shooting platform would have been useless. Such an apparatus wouldn't have allowed the shooter to get the needed downward angle. In order to get the correct angle the shooter would have either been standing or like Jack laying prone with his weapon on the rim of the tank using for a rest. Doubting the man was standing and firing freehand, Jack slid further forward on his belly to the very edge of the tank and began looking left and then right.

"I found where your shooter's nest was" he shouted down to CB. "The guy was laying right here and shot down towards the guy. I can see where the paint on the corner of the tank was rubbed off and rust is starting show. It could have been from something else but I am guessing its was rubbed raw from where the guy was resting his weapon to help stabilize the shot. Laying here you can see the sightline of the shot. Even in the spring and summer with leaves on the sight line would have been relatively clear from here. Pretty impressive. The guy is either really good or got really lucky".

CB climbed up to see what Jack was pointing at. "Damn, I bet we never came this far back to look. The other shots weren't nearly from this kind of distance."

"Told you the guy was either lucky or good. I tend to think he is really good."

"That's scary"

"Take it from someone who knows, snipers are the scariest thing in the world. Drives people crazy with always having thinking in the back of their head they are always vulnerable, never safe and without warning a bullet could strike from seemingly nowhere"

Mesmerized by the man's words and unsure of how to react, CB simply grabbed her camera and began taking photos of the rubbed off paint and the sightline to the clearing where the man had been found. After taking her pictures, the pair the headed back into her Jeep to head to the next crime scene.

As they got in the truck Jack inquired, "Why was the victim out here anyhow? It isn't like this is a place people would just come to."

"The task force was pretty sure he was led out here. They believed all the victims were killed in predetermined locations. Unfortunately, we don't know how they were led to the various locations. The group cross referenced phone logs, emails and even Facebook and Snapchat mes-sages, but have not been able to find anything specific of why or how they all came to be where they were found."

"Hmmm" Jack muttered in response.

CHAPTER 38

The two drove a few miles further along in silence when CB asked "May I ask you a question? I mean you don't have to answer but out of curiosity, why a sniper? You don't seem the type to me somehow."

Jack chuckled. "I don't know that we have a type really. I have served and trained with a bunch of snipers and they have been every personality type you can imagine. Some guys are super intense and others laid back and mellow. Some are loud and really boisterous, others very soft-spoken and quiet. We come from all walks of life without rhyme or reason. Kids from the ghettos, kids like me from the country and kids from the suburbs. It doesn't matter when it comes down to it. They either have the skills to do it or they don't. But I will tell you one thing, it's a job you can either do or you cant. And all the training in the world can't give you whatever 'it' is to do the job."

"I can see that" CB said. "But why did you volunteer for it? I assume you volunteered?"

"I did, but it kind of happened by accident. When I was a kid, I grew up shooting and hunting like every other kid we went to school with. I think dad gave me and Bob our first BB gun when I was like 4 and our first .22 by 7 and we used to shoot a ton.

I knew even in high school I was going to join the Army as soon as I graduated. I even tried to join the delayed entry program after my junior year in high school but I was to young even with my parents signature so I waited until after graduation. So my senior year while all my friends were preparing to take their ACT's and touring schools I was running, doing tons of push-ups and pull-ups and even did some ruck marches to be in shape for the basic training. 2 weeks after graduation, I was in the MEPS station in Pittsburgh took the ASVAB test and was picking a job. I scored high enough on the test to have essentially any MOS or job they had. But I knew what I wanted to be was a ranger, so when they were showing me all of the available jobs I could choose from I straight up asked the recruiter what was the easiest path to ranger school. The guy told me anything in the 11 series, or infantry. So I signed up on the spot to be an 11 bang bang, an infantryman. As a bonus I was able to get a guaranteed airborne slot to go with it.

Three weeks later I was at Ft. Benning, Georgia for basic training. Believe it or not the first time out at the range in basic I was pretty bad. Partially because of nerves and partially from bad habits. But one of the Drill Sergeants gave me a few pointers about my sight picture on the steel sights and keeping the same cheek to stock each and every time. After that I was consistently one of the best in my platoon and class overall. Come qualifying day I fired expert with the M16 hitting 39 out of the 40 targets. Thereafter, I fired high marks on the other weapon systems we got to try.

Not long after we finished qualifying with weapons a Ranger recruiter came in and gave my platoon a presentation about the Rangers and asked if anyone was willing to sign a new contract to try to join the Rangers. I volunteered immediately along with about 8 or so others in my platoon.

After we finished basic we all went straight to Airborne school, made our 5 successful jumps and then straight to Ranger school. After we completed Ranger School, I was one of the lucky ones who was chosen to be an actual Ranger and placed in the First Ranger Battalion. While there I impressed a few people with my ability to shoot and as luck would have it my company was granted 3 sniper school slots, one for each combat platoon in the company. They asked if I had any interest in going and I said yes, thinking it sounded fun. It turns out I thrived in at the school and from there the rest is history."

He went on to tell her about how much he had enjoyed his time in the Army, but ultimately decided he needed to get out. His decision based on the changing of the attitudes of the new soldiers, leadership and political climates, not to mention having become tired of the constant deployments each filled with more and more regulations and restrictions, putting soldiers in more dangerous positions with fewer options for dealing with it.

Finally he told she already know he had been recruited into the US Marshal Service. But he added, he really liked his new job and how comforting it was to have the ability to be in his own bed regularly. As Jack finished speaking the two arrived at the second crime scene.

CHAPTER 39

Victim number two, Allen Gum was killed at his home near Philippi, West Virginia off route 57. Route 57 is a windy thoroughfare that is the most direct line of travel for those in the small town to the interstate system and larger towns of the area. Pulling into the driveway, CB told Jack she was going to tell the parents they were here looking over the scene.

While CB walked to the house, Jack got out and stretched his legs. He watched as CB climbed the stairs to the house's door and knocked, feeling a pang of guilt for admiring CB's back side in the snug khakis. A moment later the door opened and a woman who looked maybe 50 ap-peared in the door. Jack was to far away to hear any of the words spoken, but he could tell the woman was upset just by her body language. He watched as the woman became more and more animated at the door. Just as he considered walking up there himself the woman stepped back and slammed the door in CB's face.

CB turned and walked back down the stairs towards Jack. "Everything ok?" he asked.

"Yeah its good, Mrs. Gumm is just upset we haven't been able to arrest anyone yet. It is completely understandable. We are the fifth or sixth different cops who have been out here. So from her perspective I am sure it looks like we are spinning our wheels," CB replied.

Jack nodded understandingly before changing the subject, "So lay it out for me".

CB explained that Gumm was the only victim who hadn't appeared to have been lured to the location of his death. Gumm was the youngest of the victims and still lived in his parents home. He was found shot dead walking between the front door of the house and his truck as he was getting ready to go to work. He had been killed at 6:20 am, shot dead as he was leaving to go to work.

Having seen the mother's reaction to CB at her door, Jack asked, "Did the mom discover the body?"

"Afraid so, the file said she and her husband were having coffee at the kitchen table when they heard a single shot. At first they weren't really sure what it was but they decided to look outside just in case. When they looked out the window they saw him laying in the yard and rushed out-side to see half of his head was blown away."

"Did they see anything else? I mean did they see car or anything?" Jack asked.

CB shook her head, pointing across the yard to a line of tall thick bushes. "The shooter was over there under the bushes. There is a gas well service road hidden behind the bushes." To rein-force her point, CB produced a set of photographs, laying them out on the hood of the Jeep. As they went through the pictures she pointed to the areas that corresponded with the photos.

Jack listened to her explain how the man was shot through the head at the moment he was al-most exactly halfway between the porch stairs and his truck. The fact the shooter awaited the moment from which the victim was the furthest away from cover on either side as a smart tacti-cal decision. However he thought the shooting in the head wasn't. While it's an almost full proof kill shot, its also an unnecessary risk to take as its easier and nearly as effective to aim center mass which allows some room for error.

"So did they pin down precisely where the shooter was?"

"Yeah this one was easy" said CB as she pointed to a row of evergreen hedges and trees less than 100 meters from where the pair stood "He was right there under the hedges and waited for him to leave his house."

Looking at the area Jack could tell the hedges were planted to specifically separate the yard from what was beyond. He could also tell they were still relatively young plants and in another few years would be so thick they would be out of control if they weren't pruned regularly. Young as they were though they were still thick enough that even in full daylight Jack was unable to tell what was behind the brushy bushes. He suspected they also would help deaden any sound from the opposite side. Curious he asked, "What else is over there? How did he get in and out?"

"Same as our last place, there is a gas well road on the other side of the hedges. Sadly, the road serves a well located on the parent's property. The file says Gumm was just getting out of high school when the well was being put in and its what made him interested in going to work on the rigs," she said.

"Lets go have a look," he said, adding a slight bow and sweep of the arm indicating she should lead the way.

Shaking her head and grinning slightly at the gesture, CB gathered up the photos and placed them back in the file and carried it with her as they walked across the yard. As they walked CB pointed out the forensics group had confirmed the shooter had been lying in the prone and fired from beneath a cluster of the evergreen bushes about two-thirds down the line.

CB led Jack directly to the place she had pointed to but there was really nothing to see beyond a few smudges of orange paint that had been used to mark the area but had mostly worn away. Kneeling down, Jack looked to where the shooter was supposed to have been but didn't really like the view from this side and preferred to see what the shooter would have seen. "Can we go to the other side?" he asked.

"Sure," CB replied, turning and walking down the line of bushes. Jack followed. The bushes were thicker than Jack had originally thought and were practically impassable, which forced them to walk down to a break in the bushes, where a gate granted access to the road beyond. Once through the gate, they reversed course, walking back towards where the shooter had laid in wait.

As they walked around to the point of attack, Jack appreciated the shooter had once again chosen a good place for his ambush. In addition to the ability to shoot, the most practiced skill snipers trained for was the use of cover and concealment, as they were truly a matter of life and death. The first lesson snipers were taught was the two are very different. Cover is something to protect the shooter from harms way. Concealment is something that hides the shooter. So while bulletproof glass is cover; it doesn't provide much in the way of concealment. And while the infamous ghille suit is great for concealment in vegetation it isn't cover as it does little to stop a bullet. Thus, snipers want to find a shooting platform offering the best cover and concealment possible for any given mission. However, there is a balancing act to consider depending on the mission and often times the sniper has to choose one over the other. For example in a hostage situation it is often beneficial to display a show of force allowing a suspect to see the presence of a sniper, so giving up a bit of the concealment is acceptable. Then in a tactical situation in a battle field there are times to get the right angle for taking down a target the sniper must abandon some cover yet stay concealed.

Before even looking at the sight line for the shot, Jack again saw the shooter had chosen his location wisely. The bushes provided excellent concealment for the shooter's actions, not only did the bushes hide the shooter himself but also his movements into and away from the location allowing him or her to get away quickly. The fact it was most likely dark when the shooter had set up would have made it all the more effective. While the bushes did not offer much in the way of cover, Jack realized for the objective at hand that was of little to no concern as there was little threat of return fire.

Finally, CB stopped walking and said, "This is it".

In response Jack simply laid down on his stomach and crawled into the in the firing position. Once in position between the scuffs of orange paint, Jack turned his focus to the line of sight. It was perfect operationally speaking, having zero obstructions between where the end of the rifle barrel would have been and the target's position.

Furthermore, with the amount of space between the house and the vehicle as it was described by CB and crime scene photos, the shooter would have been able to get off multiple shots be-fore the target would have been able to find cover if he'd missed the first one.

The only thing Jack didn't give the guy credit for was the amateur move of taking the head-shot. The instructors in sniper school repeatedly drilled it in Jack's and his classmate's heads the importance of aiming center mass on a potential target. Not only is the head a smaller target it is also more likely to move unexpectedly than the rest of the body is. Nonetheless, in the field Jack had seen reports from real world missions where a sniper had missed a target because they had going for an unnecessary head shot. More often than not a sniper is only given one good shot ; because once missed a target not only moves but begins to hunt cover as soon as possible.

The thought of a miss, gave Jack a quick shiver and he felt his heart begin to flutter as his head took him back into the field in Nebraska. "No damn it" he said aloud, talking to himself.

"No, what?" he heard CB ask, breaking the train of thought.

Not wanting to sound like a complete idiot Jack climbed out of the bushes and looked down to see he had left a mark in gravel with his feet. Quickly he said, "I just thought of something. Let me see the pictures of the scene."

From the file, CB handed the pictures to Jack. As Jack looked through the photos CB explained to him the photos of this scene were actually some of the better crime scene photos taken. Be-cause the parents inside the house had heard the shot the local sheriff had arrived immediately thereafter, preserving the scene and getting photos taken that were still very fresh, before the scene had been disturbed by to many people or weather. From the pictures she explained it was obvious from the markings on the ground the shooter had crawled under the bushes and laid in wait to kill the youngster.

Looking closely, to appear to be looking for something in the photo to save face, Jack actually did notice something. The pictures indicated whomever had been laying there had moved around quite a bit. The leaves and pine needles had been kicked around and moved leaving a near perfect indentation in the foliage of the shooters positioning. Comparing the photos to the ground in front of him Jack said matter-of-factly, "The guy isn't very big."

"How do you know that?" CB asked excitedly as the statement aligned with her own theory after having tracked the man previously.

Pointing to the bushes, Jack pointed out that the bushes themselves were not but a few feet wide and were carefully trimmed by the property owners. Secondly, the photos showed the gravel on the road was disturbed only a short distance from the base of the bush, which Jack explained was most likely from the shooters foot. To emphasize the point he handed the photo-graph back to CB and then got down on his own belly again at the same point the shooter had been. Repeating what he had just done, Jack crawled forward to the front edge of the shrubbery and mimicked a shooters stance. Satisfied with the position he sawed his right foot back and forth in the gravel of the road marking a line; while doing so he explained to CB he could go no further without giving up his cover and thus the killer would have likely done the same. Finished with the explanation, he carefully crawled out so not to disturb the line he had just created.

As he dusted himself off, Jack pointed at the line he had just made in the dirt and gravel with his foot and asked CB to compare that line to the markings from the crime scene photo. CB looked at the photograph. "You see how the dirt and gravel are disturbed in the picture?" Jack asked.

"Now look at the lines I made. The way the road lays there are at least a good 6 inches between the two and that was with me moving as far into the bushes as I could without exposing myself on the other side. Like I told you, I assume the shooter would want to stay hidden. Even though his weapon would have been exposed, even that would be sensible since it was dark and clearing the bushes with the rifle barrel would eliminate any chance of the bullet catching a wayward branch or anything else in flight to knock it off its intended course."

CB admitted she was impressed by the man's reasoning, though she wasn't sure it added any-thing to the profile, as she was already certain the man wasn't very tall. Nonetheless, she took a few photos of the line for the file, as much to show Jack she appreciated his efforts as to add something else to the files.

As CB was taking her photos, Jack took time to study the area some more. His study continued to emphasize the man had chosen a tactically smart post. The position offered the shooter many advantages: a direct firing line to the target with a predictable time and place, access to an easy escape path and concealment. Not only did the bushes provide hide the shooter himself but also his truck allowing him or her to get away quickly.

Once CB had taken all the pictures she wanted she asked Jack if had spotted anything else of note as they walked towards the truck. He reiterated the shooter had chosen the spot wisely and the layout indicated the guy had scouted the area beforehand as it was to perfect to have been spur of the moment. Beyond those few observations there was nothing else Jack could offer CB at the scene that she and the task force investigators hadn't already determined.

As the pair drove away, Jack took one more look at the gas well road. He told himself this service road wasn't as new as the one they had seen at the previous sight, but still appeared newer than most in the area based upon how the gravel was still relatively level and there weren't any huge pot holes or grass grown up like the older wells. Jack wasn't sure why but he filed the observation away in his head as they traveled to the third site.

CHAPTER 40

As she drove to the third crime scene, Jack turned the tables on CB asking her why she had become a cop. She pondered the question for a moment and debated how much to share with him. Taking a moment, she decided to give him the cliff notes version.

"So unlike you, in high school I never had any idea of what I wanted to do but always pictured myself going to college. I made good grades and scored well on the ACTs, got a few scholar-ships and grants, and attended WVU, though Dad wanted me to stay closer to home. Obviously being far from rich, I had to get job to help supplement my income and through the school I got a job working security for the dorms, which essentially meant I wore a uniform while I sat at the front desk of the different dorms with another student guard and did my homework.

The first year I did well in the basic classes but still didn't know what I wanted to. When I was signing up for classes that summer there was really a limited selection available for someone who had no major, but it just so happened one of the girls I worked with told me I should sign up for the Muay Tai seminar, which was 2 credit hours. The course was primarily for criminal justice majors but could taken as an elective regardless. Because it fit my schedule and I liked the girl I signed up.

When the class started it became readily apparent I was the only person in the class who had neither no martial arts experience and was not a criminal justice major. The first few classes were rough and I even ended up with a black eye and busted nose at one point. I was considering dropping out until one of the instructors in the class took me under her wing and worked with me before and after the class. With her help I got better. The better I got the more I enjoyed it. The more I enjoyed it, the more I began to interact with my classmates. By the end of the summer I was hanging out with many of them regularly and even though the formal class had ended they still let me come practice with them.

The instructor who had helped me was named Jennifer Robinson and in addition to the Muay Tai class also taught an intro to criminal justice and I signed up for it that fall. The class fascinated me, though not from the police work angle as much as the legal perspective. That spring I declared my major as prelaw, with a minor in criminal justice. Because I continued to work the security job, my grades stayed up. Because I continued to stay active in the gym with the Muay Tai, I was also in really good shape, even better than in high school when I was a cheer leader.

Then in the fall of my junior year, I took the LSAT and scored really well. Between that and my grades not only was I assured I could get into WV Law School but honestly could have been accepted into most any school I wanted. I was even accepted into both Georgetown and Virginia but in the end I stayed here and attended WV Law. While in school, I still continued the same routine I had in undergrad, working the security desk to do my homework and going to the gym with the criminal justice majors.

Then the fall of my second year in law school I was looking at the applications for internships for the following summer, when Professor Robinson saw me and handed me a pamphlet about summer internships available for some of Federal Law Enforcement Agencies, the FBI, DEA, and ATF amongst them. While I wasn't necessarily interested in working for any of them Professor Robinson reminded me such an internship would look really good on the applications. Deciding she was right I applied, though I wasn't really hopeful of being selected.

To my surprise a month later I received an email from the ATF that I had been chosen for an interview and physical fitness assessment for their internship. So early one Saturday morning I went to Pittsburgh and did an interview, took a physical and did some exercises for them. Two weeks later I got a phone call saying I had been chosen for the internship for the summer.

When I first reported I was still really unsure of what I was doing, but was determined to do well so I could get a good referral. I worked harder that summer than I probably had ever worked in my life. But something funny happened while I was working, it didn't feel like work at all be-cause I really liked it. I was again fascinated by the entire process the gathering of evidence, getting the warrants and they even let me go to a raid. It was great. At the end of the summer the Agent who had been in charge of the summer program, Agent Elrod, pulled me and another of the interns, a kid named Jon Flowers, aside and gave us letters of recommendation, we had worked so hard for.

I was happy to get the letter, but Flowers was crazy excited, jumping up and down and screaming "Thank you Jesus" and hugged Agent Elrod. Agent Elrond finally got him to calm down shook our hands and said congratulations. Not quite understanding the reaction from Flowers I finally looked at the recommendation. It wasn't simply a recommendation, it was a job offer con-tingent upon graduation next summer. I was floored. I had no idea that was even a thing but there it was I had my letter.

Returning to school that fall, I talked to many of my classmates who talked about their miserable experiences working for some of the large firms. Working 70 hours a week researching the most mundane of legal topics, being paid pennies on the dollar in comparison to the associate attor-neys at the same firms. Hearing them talk and reflecting on the summer I had with the ATF it was no contest. I took the job. From there the rest is history," she said as she pulled the Jeep off the highway and near the day's third destination.

CHAPTER 41

Site three on their tour was actually where victim number one, Micah Lowe had died. The shooting took place outside of Fairmont WV, just off the I-79, Picket's Fort exit in the Park and Ride parking lot, which were parking lots set off the highway to allow commuters to park their cars and catch public transit to go into cities. The locations had also become popular locations for the roughnecks to meet and car pool together to and from their work sites because they were convenient near the highways.

Exiting the highway, CB explained to Jack Lowe's investigation had originally been handled by the Marion County Sheriff's Department and the State Police office in nearby Morgantown. It wasn't until after victim number three had been killed that it was established that all the victims were related and the task force was formed.

As CB turned her Jeep into the parking lot, Jack counted 14 cars, leaving another thirty some-thing unoccupied spaces.

Noticing his counting CB mentioned, "This lot used to be packed every day from what they tell me, but the killing here put a damper on it and it has really never recovered," CB said as she eased into an unoccupied spot near the back of the lot.

"I bet. But with so many cars in the lot, surely someone saw something?" Jack inquired.

"Somebody was here and saw something because they called 9-1-1 from the pay phone on the other side of the highway at the gas station. The shooting occurred later in the evening but given the time of year there would still have been plenty of light. At the same time traffic would have been light that time of day on the adjoining road and the highway," CB read from the file.

She then pointed out, "But just looking now, a passing driver on the highway would have been very unlikely to have seen anything anyhow." Returning to the file she read "The police got here eight minutes after the 9-1-1 call came in. But by the time the officers arrived to the scene there were no witnesses remaining and the hillside was empty. The officers recorded all the plates of the cars remaining in the parking lot but the owners all had alibis that put them else-where when the killing occurred."

After she finished summarizing the file Jack looked around a moment before asking, "Don't these lots have cameras or something?"

"No, the lots are park at your own risk. There has been complaints of drug deals and other stuff going down in them for years. The local cops all try to patrol them regularly but there has never been room in the budgets to add cameras."

Jack nodded knowingly at the statement, having seen many places where camera's would have been a helpful deterrent but were fiscally impractical according to the powers that be, thus he let the subject drop. Instead he remained in his seat and studied the crime photos, commenting the photos weren't as clear or as in depth as the previous scenes.

CB explained like any job some people do a better job than others and the crime scene tech who worked this particular scene had been particularly poor. She then added most of the techs in the area failed to do a satisfactory job at all in her opinion, missing details that are often times critical for a case. She stated when she first began working with the State

Police, she would ask the crime scene techs to take more photos but the techs would always act as if she was asking them for something unreasonable. Then even when they did produce more photographs, they would essentially be more of their standard crap. Thus, she began to carry her own equipment, taking her own shots to supplement the files. She added because of it, she now does photography as a hobby even outside of work, enjoying the search for the "perfect shot".

Jack liked the explanation and then added he'd like to see her other photos sometime too.

CB feeling a bit embarrassed at the prospect, felt her cheeks turning red and quickly changed the subject back to the crime scene at hand.

Lowe's murder was unlike any of those that followed. Lowe was killed while sitting in his truck, whereas all the others were caught in the open. He died in the drivers seat of his F-150, very similar to Jack's own. The shooter, as Jack referred to him, unable to use the term killer even to himself, put 7 bullets through the windshield of the truck. Lowe was struck three times. Two of the three would have been kill shots according to the medical examiner. The medical report showed Lowe had been hit in the left forearm, which while painful would not have killed the man. He was also hit in the upper chest about two inches below the right collar bone which sent the bullet through the lung before hitting the shoulder blade and ricocheting down towards the man's kidney, a kill shot on its own in all likelihood but for the third round. The third shot struck Lowe in the upper abdomen just below the breast plate and slightly left of center. The bullet ripped through the man's stomach and liver. Jack understood piercing the liver almost guaranteed death, but it was far from a clean kill, meaning the person struck would suffer a bit before succumbing to the wound.

Jack appreciated how difficult it is to shoot through tempered glass. Windshields in modern cars are solid, tilted and concave. When the rounded bullet strikes the tempered glass, the bullet deflects downward — the greater the angle, the greater the deflection variance. Based on a few observations, Jack assumed the shooter was unaware of this. First and foremost this was the man's first victim and only one killed inside a car, thereafter the shooter made sure to get the targets out into the open. Secondly, if the killer knew the bullets would be deflected by the glass he'd have also likely known that the larger caliber the bullet the less effected it is in comparison to smaller bullets. Because the killer was firing a .270 round, which is small, the likelihood again indicated that the shooter was unaware of the effect or else didn't have access to a larger caliber weapon.

As he was about to open the door Jack asked, "Is this the spot where the victim parked?"

CB looked at the file a moment and then visibly began pointing and counting the parking spots before answering, "No he was parked over there, three spots to our right."

"Ok" Jack said climbing from the Jeep before walking to where the victim had parked. He positioned himself the parking spot approximately where Lowe would have been sitting when the shooter opened fire and began to study the area around him. As he looked around he felt a pang in the back of his mind that something wasn't quite right; ignoring it, Jack forced himself to look at everything but the hillside where the shooter would have logically been.

First, he turned his attention back towards the highway from where they had just exited. He at-tempted to examine the traffic but from the ground it was impossible to see anything but the roofs of the of the passing cars over the concrete sides of the overpass bridge. While he watched he noted the traffic exiting the highway from both the north and southbound lanes turned in the opposite direction of the lot where he stood, towards town, seemingly indicating the odds of any random passersby of seeing anything was slim.

Turning his study away from the highway, again ignoring the hillside, he observed the immediate area around the lot with a critical eye. He saw nothing but typical West Virginia hillsides covered in trees, hay fields and scrub brush. In fact he had to look much further south before he could see the roof lines of some buildings and homes. Anyone who lived or worked there would have been to far away to have seen or heard anything. Closer still, directly across the road from the parking lot where he stood, there were mature trees and a field that still had large round hay bales sitting haphazardly across the landscape. Jack knew in the spring and summer the field would likely have been tall with the grass making up the bales. Jack noted, if he had been set-ting up an operation for this parking lot, he'd have preferred the field because the shot would have been far easier, though he acknowledged the shooter likely had other factors to consider in choosing his ambush point, specifically his get away.

Satisfied he had a strong picture of the area, Jack turned towards the hill side where the shooter had been. From where Jack stood in the parking lot a steep hill arose directly to his front with the highway immediately to his rear. The bottom of the hill was covered in brush with more ma-ture trees showing themselves toward the top of the slope, which indicated the bottom of the hill had been cleared of the natural growth at some point in the recent past, likely when the parking lot had been built. To the South, the slope of the hillside was less steep and Jack could see a discernible grayish colored line that differed from the shades of brown of the vegetation. Jack knew from experience the line likely indicated a pathway or road. He followed the line along the contour of the hill towards the North. From his point of view he could barley make out, near the top around the other side of the hill, the top of a round, navy blue, slightly doomed shaped tow-er, indicating yet another gas well. Similar to the first sight they had visited, he noted the well was either relatively new or it had recently been repainted.

Taking a few more seconds to look things over Jack again had the feeling he was missing something. It was a feeling he did not like. Unable to pinpoint exactly what it was he asked. "So where was the shooter exactly?"

CB pointed to the hillside and swept her hand along the grey line Jack noted. "Up there," she said, "about 150 yards from here between that large maple tree and the point of rock". The two landmarks she noted appeared to be no more than 10-15 feet apart from where Jack stood.

"Let me guess, on a gas well road?" Jack responded.

"How'd you know?" CB asked.

"Lucky guess." Jack said smartly before adding, "Do me a favor and park your Jeep in the spot where the guy's truck was and then we will go up".

"Ok, but climbing that hill side is a little rough. It is easier to drive down that way and catch the gas well road and come back up."

"How far away is the entrance to the gas well road?"

"Almost a mile, apparently it was the only place the gas company was able to get a suitable right of way for it," CB answered.

Jack pondered her statement for a moment before replying "I'll climb the hill. I want to see what the shooter saw.

Or at least close to what he saw. I'd rather have the car in the spot"

"Ok but if you're climbing up then I am going too." CB replied in a manner leaving no room for debate.

CB moved her Jeep into the correct parking spot and rejoined Jack. Together, they headed through the grass to the base of the steep bank and began their ascent. The hillside was mostly grass and scrub brush but the ascent was so steep they each needed to use their hands and feet to climb. Their efforts reminded Jack of the "bear crawl" exercises he did so many of in basic training. Jack had initially wondered about whether CB would be able to keep up, but his concern was quickly forgotten as he found himself trailing her on the climb. He also had to again remind himself they had a job to do and stop admiring her ass as she pulled ahead of him.

By the time they made the road they were both winded from the climb. Taking a moment to catch his breath, Jack began anew his study of the area, taking his time. Looking down from the gas well road to CB's Jeep reinforced how steep a climb it was. Similar to the first scene they visited, it indicated that the shooter had some skill. The windshield miscalculation not-withstanding, Jack still recognized the skill it took to hit a target from the extreme downward angle he currently saw.

The sight also reminded Jack of another lesson from sniper school. Instructor Bates told Jack and his classmates the power of the sniper on the battle field doesn't lay in his ability to take a life — any infantry soldier can do that. The sniper however is key to psychological warfare and is the reason the enemy cannot sleep at night. The looming threat of a possible sniper who can kill without the target even knowing of his existence means there is never a moment's piece for the enemy. They have to account for the fact that lurking in the shadows - in any shadow could lie a man to take life as he chooses.

At the time it was first told him Jack felt it was just some cool propaganda the instructors fed the recruits to keep them motivated in the hard hours of monotony the course required. But his real life experiences told him different. Not only had he seen the fear on the enemy, but he had also been in many a base camp taking sniper fire. He discovered that the ever present knowledge that an attack was always possible wore a person down. Hyper-vigilance becoming so en-grained in you its impossible to let go, even when you got home.

His self-examination was interrupted when he noticed a flash of light in his peripheral vision coming from above him to his right. At the flash, he immediately dove to the ground, pulled his weapon and began to scan the area for threats. He first looked to the area he saw the flash then to the left, right, and behind.

As he scanned he also realized there was scant cover upon the ridge where he and CB were other then the rock and tree marking the point where the original shooter had waited in ambush. Concerned over the lack of cover, he felt his heart start to pound, his breath quicken and beads of sweat arising on his back and forehead.

"What is it?" CB asked scared at his sudden movement, herself squatted down with her hand over her own weapon.

After a moment, Jack shook his head side to side and said, "Nothing, I saw a flash of light, like off a scope but it must have been off one of the windshields from one of the cars in the south-bound lane". He got up and dusted himself off while trying to nonchalantly get between CB and where the flash of light had come from.

CB could tell he was unconvinced of his own words from the look of concern remaining on his face and the fact he had yet to put his weapon away. She also noted how he was moving be-tween her and where he perceived the danger to be. She was flattered by the move though couldn't help but think of how some of the feminists she had trained with would have been of-fended by the maneuver. She continued to watch him as he continued to scan for dangers until he finally seemed to let out a breath and relax a bit.

"Are you sure you're ok? You seemed weird there for a second, like you were a world away or something," she asked. She immediately regretted the last sentence remembering his back ground.

"Yeah, I am good. I just got a weird feeling about this place now." Jack answered still scanning the area.

"What kind of feeling?" she asked.

"I'm not sure but lets go back to the truck. Nothing really to see here anyway. Sorry I made you climb up here with me" he responded almost robotically in short clipped sentences. Before CB could answer Jack took her by the elbow and led their descent down the hill continuing to keep himself between her and where he had seen the flash, his weapon drawn the whole time.

CHAPTER 42

Jack's instincts were right, they were being watched by a man on the gas tower using binocu-lars. As the two began their trek back down the hill the watcher was on the phone. "They are here boss. What do you want me to do?"

"Did they see you?"

"No, I am at the tank watching them through binoculars. They haven't even came out this way. You want me to try take them out now or something?"

"No man, right now I just need to you to lay low and keep watching. Killing two cops, especially a fed would bring in heat we don't want or need."

"Ok boss but I still don't like them poking around. Even though I know you have personal con-nections," The man said trying not to sound accusatory.

"They're cops, that's what they do. As for my personal connections, don't you worry about it. Remember I was the one who arranged things for Tony and he was like a brother to me. This ain't any different, you understand me? Now tell me what the fuck were those two doing?"

"Nothing really," the man answered nervously. "They parked down in the lot. Jack got out and looked around a bit. Then they climbed up the hill and looked around a few more minutes. Now they are walking back down towards her car." He intentionally left out the part about Jack hitting the ground and pulling his weapon, which had spooked him so bad he damn near had dropped his binoculars. He hadn't bothered to put them back to his eyes; instead keeping his visual with his own eyes. It was like the man had a sixth sense of his presence or something. The watcher also knew it would also spook his boss and he most assuredly didn't want to get on his bad side the man admitted to himself, the big man was one of the few who scared him. He always had.

"They haven't found anything yet and they wont. After they clear out of there give them a head start and then get outta there yourself. I'll see you up here tonight" The big man on the other end said to the watcher.

"Sure thing boss, see ya tonight," the watcher said, before hitting the end button on the phone. He remained in place until the two cops climbed in their car and drove away. He then climbed into his own truck and started the engine. Before leaving, he sent a text, "The Boss will do whats got to be done."

As he was driving down the gas road, his phone chimed indicating a text. He looked and saw the response to the message he had just sent: a smiley face emoji.

CHAPTER 43

Leaving the scene of victim one, the pair traveled south along to I-79, beginning their closure of their circular route. As they rode, Jack attempted to study the victim's files, feeling somewhat embarrassed by what had occurred on the side of the hill. In his mind, he was trying to deter-mine if he had experienced another anxiety attack or in the alternative whether his reaction was warranted due to the possible threat? After all, he was on the side of a hill with little cover against a possible hostile whose weapon of choice is a rifle, while he had only a pistol. Either way he was less than thrilled.

As she drove, sensing something wasn't quite right with Jack, CB tried to think of a way to en-gage him in some small talk to make him more comfortable. She acknowledged her interest wasn't simply to ease his burden as she was truly intrigued by the man. As she was looking for the right words she suddenly remembered something from the report her friend had sent. "Jack, I have to ask you, in my friend's report he said that people call you 'the ghost'. I hope that's not because you bed women and disappear the next morning?" she joked.

Shocked by the statement, missing the jocular nature, Jack looked up from the file to see CB smiling broadly, seeing she was in fact joking with him. He couldn't help but chuckle at the barb. Feeling a bit better he asked, "Do you really wanna know?"

"I do," she responded sincerely.

Jack explained the name originated from his days in sniper school. He told her how one night at 2100 hours he and his classmates were informed that the following day they would be partici-pating in an exercise. The objective of the exercise was to move across a small wooded area and then across an open field to an objective, a large open sided tent, without being detected. For the next hour the class was then briefed on the specific criteria of what was expected of them. They were shown a map and overhead photographs of the area to be negotiated. To get to their goal the men would have to navigate approximately 800 to 900 meters of ground cov-ered in woods and open field. The map showed the wooded area was roughly 250-300 meters across depending on any particular entrance point and from the photographs it looked to be rather dense with growth, making movement within it pretty safe for the participants. The field, on the other hand appeared to be long and open for about 450 to 600 meters. The only con-cealment available appeared to be waist high grasses and some gently rolling hills that could be used to the advantage of the candidates.

The catch was there would a group of sentries monitoring the forest and field on foot and with trucks. Making it more difficult is the men acting as sentries were both expecting them and had been trained to spot the participants, a real world worst case scenario the instructors empha-sized.

The candidates would be taken to the point of entry in the early morning hours before dark. Once on site, the instructors told the participants they would be given approximately one hour to prepare and ensure they were fully camouflaged. Because it would be dark they were also re-minded light discipline was to be exercised and anyone caught using a white light or other unau-thorized light source would automatically be disqualified and sent to the commandant for an in-tegrity violation, which would result in an immediate expulsion. After the command to move out was given they would be have 8 hours to make the objective.

Jack recalled some of his classmates essentially gave up before the task even began, believing that it couldn't be done based on the information provided. The more confident members of the class scoffed at the notion it would take 8 hours to cover the total distance of less than a half mile.

At 0300 the next morning the candidates were awoken and told movement would occur 30 min-utes later. At 0330 the men were loaded into the back of a 5-ton troop carrier. In the back of the truck the guys got as comfortable as possible on the wooden slat benches and metal floor, un-sure of how long the drive would take them; as it was not a part of their briefing and they had all failed to ask. Turns out they drove for nearly an hour. Some of the candidates used the time to go over their gear one last time, some studied the maps they had each been issued while others simply slept. Upon arrival at their destination, the men in the back of the truck were dropped off one-by-one at separate points, ranging between 200 and 250 meters apart.

During the preparation period using only his red lensed flashlight and feel of hand, Jack took painstaking care to prepare his ghillie suit and his weapon. Given the operation's brief he was more concerned about remaining concealed crossing the field than while amongst the trees and covered his suit with as much long straw colored grasses as he could find near the prep area. He wasn't quite finished when the command to go was given, 15 minutes early. He debated re-maining in his prep area to finish the suit but reconsidered, thinking the early start was a ploy to catch them flat footed. He deduced the soldiers tasked with searching for them would likely be canvassing the area shortly. Mind made up, Jack shot an azimuth on his compass to ensure his line of march, took a deep breath and moved into the woods towards the objective.

As he and his classmates had practiced again and again in the weeks leading up to the exer-cise, Jack moved through the small wooded area without a sound. Nonetheless, he moved quickly through the wooded area wanting to utilize the lack of light for as long as possible. De-spite the swiftness of his movements, he left nary a trace of his existence, remaining conscious of leaving a trail that could be followed by one of the hunters if he were careless.

Just as the sun was beginning to rise, Jack found himself near the edge of the field. Remaining back in the shadows of the trees he reshot his azimuth to confirming he was still on course. Sat-isfied he was still aligned with the objective, he studied the general line of travel he must take; understanding that while maps and overhead photographs are great tools, there is nothing like getting a view of an area with one's own eye. He looked the field over thoroughly for a line of travel across the expanse providing the optimum concealment for his movements.

As he studied, Jack recalled deer hunting as a child with his grandfather, who told him the key to hunting was watching for movement. His grandfather explained that the deer's coloring allow them to blend in with their background almost perfectly and even the most practiced eye has difficulty differentiating the deer from the surroundings because of their god given camouflage. However, the best hunters are successful because their eyes have been conditioned to be very good at picking up movements. Ultimately it is the deer running, walking or even the less obvi-ous bob of the head or flick of a tail the hunter will detect. With that in mind he picked the line that offered the greatest concealment for covering his movements, though it wasn't the easiest or most direct path to his targeted destination.

Satisfied with his planned line of travel, he moved nearer the edge of the field, bellied down into the grass and began the pain staking journey across the expanse. He crawled on his belly mea-suring his progress in inches. He was cognizant of the wind and the bent grasses around him and moved with them, trying to ensure he left no sign of his presence an observer could follow.

As he moved he periodically detected his classmates moving far ahead of him. He also ob-served the sentries moving directly towards his overzealous classmates, tapping them on the shoulder, confirming they had been identified and thus eliminated. Most of the class were spot-ted with in the first two hours, captured within 150 meters of the objective by the roving guards. The guards had set a perimeter around the tent at approximately 100 meters and simply walked back and forth, waiting for the men they knew were coming. Along with the perimeter of men there was also a Humvee driving in a circle around the area, checking on the sentries and carry-ing those "captured" back to the gathering point.

It took Jack nearly 5 hours to cover the distance to the perimeter, moving painstakingly slow to ensure he wasn't spotted. As he moved he continued to study his approach to the finish line, looking for a hole in the watcher's perimeter to allow him to make it through. Finally, he detect-ed a pattern of weakness with one particular sentry. While covering his area the sentry would take the time to smoke and talk with the pair of soldiers in the Humvee as it came by every other time. With that in mind Jack continued his crawl forward getting as close as he dared before set-tling in to await the truck's return.

As he waited, "the smoker," as Jack had labeled the man in his head, had walked within 20 feet of Jack twice without detection. Both times Jack forced himself to look away afraid the man would feel Jack's stare. After having laid in the same spot for what seemed an eternity Jack heard the Humvee approach and then stop. Jack watched the smoker walk to the big vehicle and saw the driver and passenger step out. Each man lit a cigarette and began talking idly to one another. Jack took the opportunity to do something he hadn't done in the six hours since the test began. Arising from the ground, he made a quick rush across the inner perimeter marked by the rough line in the grass the truck made in its circuitous rounds that morning. Once across, he bellied down once again and silently proceeded forward.

Inside the perimeter Jack kept low, focusing on his objective. He continued to refuse to look at any of the sentries for to long for fear one would sense his gaze upon them. Before making the tent he avoided 3 more soldiers walking around, one who came within 12 feet of Jack as the man took the time to relieve himself on a nearby bush Jack had just left. Finally, he traversed the remaining distance and stopped just short of the tent where he remained hidden in a patch of tall grass.

From his spot in the grass, Jack was able to get a good look inside the tent where the other 11 candidates were all seated at tables in the shade. He watched as they played cards and joked around with one another. Jack was also able to see and hear most of the range cadre in the other corner of the tent discussing amongst themselves whether Jack could have possibly got-ten lost somehow. The idea made Jack smile and he was forced to stifled a laugh.

From his hiding spot Jack also couldn't help but notice Instructor Bates remained isolated from the others, sitting in a chair at the other side of the canopy, a cup of coffee in his hand and a slightly bemused look on his face. After what seemed to have been forever laying there unmov - ing, Jack saw the cadre in charge of the exercise look at his watch and say time. He directed a young E-4, assigned to the group, to blow the air horn signifying it was time to muster at the tent. Jack further heard the man in charge say to the other cadre "I hope we don't have to go looking for that kid".

In response to the statement, Bates laughed aloud announcing "You wont. He has been 20 feet from here watching us for the last 40 minutes. Get in here Kirby".

At the word Jack stood. To the others he seemed to materialize out of nowhere, candidates and cadre alike. As he revealed himself, Jack heard a few of those present speak. Amongst the phrases uttered were "Bullshit," "I'll be damned," and "Are you fucking kidding me."

After the shock of his presence was revealed the class was debriefed on the exercise. Follow-ing the debriefing, as they were awaiting the arrival of the transport truck, Jack overheard some of the instructors talking again.

"Have you ever seen that?" one asked.

"Hell no, I cant even remember the last time anyone got to the inside of the perimeter, let alone right next to the tent" said another.

Then Bates said as understated as ever "I told y'all the kid is good, he's a god damned ghost".

Jack then told CB as they arrived at the scene of the 4th victim, "From there forward I was called the ghost for the rest of sniper school. Then when I was given the outstanding soldier award at course graduation, the commandant announced the award to Specialist Jack Kirby, AKA The Ghost. The name then followed me back to the unit and stuck."

CHAPTER 44

Joseph Ramirez, the fourth victim, died near a small farming community known as Johnstown. Traveling from Fairmont CB drove south on I-79 to the Lost Creek exit where she followed the main road through the little town until it turned into Johnstown Road. They traveled the well maintained road back into the hills until they reached a small side road called Peel Tree Run, which they traveled beyond where the blacktop ended, evolving into a gravel covered lane. They had not gone far off the blacktop before they came upon a gas well tucked just off the track.

Upon arriving, CB pulled off the road onto a graveled covered square placed there for the well's service trucks to park. As she parked she asked Jack to check the file to ensure she was in the same location Ramirez's truck had been found, not wanting move the vehicle again as she had at their last stop.

Jack confirmed the location and began to look the area over from the passenger seat. The well again appeared to be newer, though he decided that wasn't such a strange phenomenon given the amount of drilling going on the state. Satisfied he had seen all he was able to see from in-side the vehicle, Jack opened the door.

As they stepped out of the SUV, a car came down the road, causing both to turn. They watched as the car passed by, continuing along the lane to points beyond. "Where does this road go?" Jack asked watching the car round the turn and continue out of sight.

Checking a map in the file CB answered, "If you keep following it around you will loop back out to Route 20 but the record says its gets rougher as you go. Not to many people live out this way but the local farmers bring their trucks and tractors through here apparently."

"In other words, our shooter had another way in and out again if he didn't want to travel the way we did."

"That's the size of it," CB replied.

This time Jack led the way to where the body was found, as the file contained very thorough notes and an assortment of photos, which marked the scene so obviously anyone could have located where the body was found, even so many months later. The body had been discovered at the base of the holding tank near the well's service box, about 30 feet away from where the man had parked his truck.

As they were walking to where the body had been CB explained, "When I told you earlier that there were two scenes that the task force were unable to specifically locate the shooters posi-tion, the place up in Tucker County being the first. This is the second. In fact, this is the one murder, that they weren't even positive the shooter was hidden and waiting for the victim to come through." CB explained.

"What do you mean? What other possibility is there?" Jack asked.

Pointing to the wooded area across the road from where they parked CB said, "The forensics say the shot came from that direction. Yet that thicket over there is so dense the investigators were never able to find a way for the shooter to get into it. They reportedly had all kinds of peo-ple out here looking at it from every angle, and no one could find a way to get to a point near enough the road to have gotten an unobstructed line of sight. There certainly wasn't any evi-dence the shooter had gotten in there. They never found any broken branches or cuttings. In the end they just couldn't see a way for the shooter to lay in ambush."

"Okay, so what's the alternative theory?" Jack asked.

"The theory was the shooter simply performed a drive by and shot Rodriquez from a car as he drove by."

"He didn't" Jack interrupted bluntly.

"Why would you say that?" CB asked, though the statement matched her own thoughts.

"A few things, the first being the pictures clearly showed that the guy was shot in the back. Just like when we got out of your car, out here when you hear a car coming, its instinct to turn and look. Secondly, the reports matched the bullet as being the same .270 that had killed the other victims. You aren't going to stand still and watch someone point a rifle out the window and shoot you in the back. More than that, it's simply impractical someone would be able to drive, put the
rifle out the driver's window, aim and score two clean hits the way the report said, since it also said there were no other wayward rounds listed in the report. Even if he were going the other direction and had the gun rested in the passenger window and firing as he drove by it would be virtually impossible. I can count the number of people in the world on one hand who could maybe hit a target from a moving platform without missing at all. So no I would definitely say your guy stuck with his normal pattern. We just need to see how."

CB smiled at the explanation and was seriously impressed at how quickly he had deciphered the evidence and the improbability of the alternate theory in such a convincing way.

The drive by theory dismissed in his own mind, Jack studied the scene to see exactly how it was done. There wasn't much left to see, though it didn't take long for Jack to confirm to his own satisfaction that the set up was consistent with the previous pattern. The shooter had once again managed to either draw the victim out to a specific location or had known where the per - son was going be. The shooter had simply just arrived first and waited for the victims to show up and then shot them down, seemingly without hesitation or remorse; very cold and very dan-gerous in Jack's opinion.

No sooner had Jack made up his mind CB told him the file reported Rodriguez was a well ten-der whose job was to do safety checks on wells. A check of his dispatch log showed he had been sent to this well because someone had reported the place smelled strongly of eggs, a tell-tale sign of a gas leak. A cross reference to the gas company's database showed the service request had been made the same morning as the shooting from an unknown number and who-ever had made the compliant had said enough on the call to require the gas company to imme-diately dispatch the man. The task force team was also able to determine whoever made the call likely choose to complain about this particular well because it is one specifically assigned to Rodriquez. Another indication the killer has some inside knowledge to the industry.

It definitely fit the pattern, showing the shooter had an overall plan that worked for him, though each individual murder required some specific planning and patience on the shooters part. But how patient was he Jack wondered? What did the man do as he waited? The second site they visited had shown the shooter had scuffed the ground quite a bit moving around and the first place he had rubbed the paint off the tower with his gun from repetitive movements, indicating the shooter was undisciplined while he waited.

In sniper school and thereafter in both training and in the real world the most difficult lesson for Jack and many others to learn was how to wait. Being a sniper required the shooter to remain patient at all times while on a mission, with the ability to stay laser focused for hours and some-times days on end for the chance that something could happen, a designated target may present itself. The unofficial Army motto is 'hurry up and wait'; but the mantra takes on an en-tirely new meaning for its snipers. The sniper must learn how to be prepared to move at mo-ments notice yet remain perfectly still while awaiting that moment of action.

Having grown up hunting with others and then joining the army thereafter, Jack knew there were very few men whowere truly able to sit still and wait. As often as not people would fidget around at least a bit; some more than others, ultimately leaving a sign of their presence, and thus evidence. However, Jack reflected, the record showed the investigators here were unable to pinpoint the exact location of where the shooter had been, hence the alternate theory. But Jack didn't buy the theory, the investigators were wrong.

Looking carefully, the opposite side of the road where the shooter would have to have waited in the underbrush was made up of thick native mountain laurel. Mountain laurel is a plant of thin woody vines and long, narrow waxy evergreen leaves. The plants would have provided the shooter ideal concealment from both the victim and any chance passerby from the road. But as the file stated the plant is incredibly difficult to penetrate.

Jack asked CB for the file again. He read the investigators considered bringing in chainsaws to cut the foliage back to see if they could find the exact position. But ultimately it was decided against based on the cost and the fact it was likely the men with the saws would have destroyed any evidence to be found. The decision not to invest the resources was made even easier when the alternate theory of the drive by was introduced. Thus ultimately, the forensics team simply took measurements of the distances and angles from the bullet's path, tagged the branches of the laurel with ribbons and took a ton of pictures to depict the scene.

Handing the file back to CB, Jack walked across the road and studied the area. Even though many of the area's trees had begun to lose their leaves, the laurel is an evergreen plant, thus the thicket remained thickly covered. Moving some of the leaves around he was able to find the weather faded ribbons. Jack spent ten minutes studying the area and just couldn't see how anyone could have gotten into the area from where he stood.

Nonetheless, convinced the shooter had been in the thicket, Jack began walking down the road searching for an access point. CB followed curiously. Rounding the apex of the corner the pass-ing car had previously disappeared around, a wide point off the shoulder of the road became visible on the opposite side of the road about 200 feet further.

"That is where the task force theorized the shooter's get away vehicle wold have been parked while they were under the working theory that he waited in ambush" CB stated following Jack's eye.

Nodding, Jack continued to walk until he was nearly abreast of the wide point and paused.

"What is it"? CB asked.

"Don't you see it?" Jack responded.

"See what?"

"The game trail," Jack said pointing toward the brush.

CB studied the area but saw noting but a wall of thick brush. Then Jack stepped off the road and suddenly ducked into the growth, disappearing. She listened trying to determine which way he was moving but couldn't hear anything. Just a minute ago she would have told anyone it was impossible for anyone to get into, let alone to do so silently. It was kinda unnerving.

Jack walked about 30 feet into the bush before the little game trail turned back towards the well. He continued along, ducking and dodging the wayward branches until the trail for all practical purposes played out. Still feeling it was how the shooter had gained access to the ambush point, Jack began to closely examine the position. Through the thick foliage he was able to make out the red of the tank. Using he tank as a guide of direction, he was able to find a place he could belly down and crawl forward. Despite being very adept at low crawling it took Jack several minutes to get through the tangled mess. To his practiced ear he felt he was making a ton of noise along his way, though he knew the bushes would dampen much of it to anyone who wasn't really close. Finally, he was finally able to get to a point in the mire of sticks and leaves where he remained concealed but would have been able to get a limited sight picture of where the man was killed. In Jack's mind it was less than tactically ideal but it had obviously worked.

Lying in place, Jack also contemplated how much more difficult it would have been to navigate the mess carrying a weapon. Then he remembered, the killer was likely much smaller than himself. Not only would the shooter have had an easier time in the brush, Jack noted a smaller man would likely have been able to get closer, improving the sight lines. Satisfied it could be done, he retraced his steps to meet CB.

After standing a moment bewildered at Jack's ability to disappear into the thicket the investiga-tion team had declared impenetrable, CB took a photos to mark its location. Once she was sat-isfied she had captured the spot completely she realized Jack had been gone for a while. After a few minutes, she was getting restless, feeling somehow vulnerable standing along the road alone. Not liking the feeling, she began to wonder if Jack had gotten lost or stuck inside the thicket. She was wondering how much longer to give him before she should call his phone, when as if by magic he reappeared from behind the same limbs he disappeared behind. Re-lieved, she asked, "Did you find anything?"

Jack explained, "I bet this is how the shooter got in. It's thick but possible, especially for a smaller person. I got to a point where I was within 25 feet of the road across from that tank and saw where someone probably could have gotten closer, though the shooter would have likely made noise getting in and out of the position doing so, especially carrying weapon."

He was going to continue to tell her how he thought the shooter could have probably even pulled the same trick as Philippi crime scene where the rifle barrel was outside the thicket yet allowed the shooter to remain in cover but before he could do so he thought he heard some-thing. Jack paused to listen closer.

Noting the expression on his face and the sudden stop in the conversation, CB was about to ask Jack "what was wrong" but he put a hand up as she was about to talk. And then she heard it too, a car approaching from the same direction he and CB had come from. Turning towards the sound, the pair watched for a few moments as the sound grew louder and louder until finally an old beater of a car emerged on the road. Stepping back and in front of CB, Jack instinctually nodded to the passerby who waved back, which was customary for the area.

The entire transaction struck something with in Jack. "CB what time of day did the medical ex-aminer estimate the death to be here?" he asked.

Checking her folder to ensure she answered the question accurately CB responded, "Between 11am and 1 pm, around lunch time. Why?"

"That car got me thinking. We haven't been here but about 30 minutes, and we have already seen two cars. How did the shooter go unnoticed out here by some random passersby?" Jack asked.

"What do you mean?" CB asked, "he was hidden in the bushes"

"Maybe but people would have still seen the guy's car or truck sitting here. I know I have been gone a while but wouldn't people question a random car pulled off the road in the middle of no where? Or did I miss something in the notes?"

"You didn't miss it. Honestly, I don't think it is addressed. I mean they did put the public service announcements out about if anyone had any information they should contact a hotline but noth-ing came of it," she admitted.

Jack paused and mentally retraced his steps. While he had been giving the guy credit for his ability to pick spots and allow himself a back door of escape, he now reconsidered and realized the shooter actually consistently made a mistake — the same mistake. Yes, the shooter consis-tently gave himself a backdoor of travel to and from the general area of the ambush points. However the shooter never placed himself in a firing position allowing for a hasty retreat, negat-ing the escape routes. The first site they looked at the top of the tank was certainly not easily or quickly escaped from should he get caught. It was the same under the brush beyond the yard, on the side of the mountain over looking the parking lot or here under the brush along the road. In all of them the shooter had taken a huge chance in that his line of retreat could easily be thwarted if discovered. If caught in any of them he would be forced to fight his way out without the ability to avoid the fight. As a sniper it was something to consider. Especially if you're oper-ating without support something Jack was taught was a cardinal sin for operating. 'Unless,' he thought, 'what it the shooter hadn't been working alone?'

"CB what if there is another explanation to why no one noticed a random car sitting here?" Jack asked.

"What do you mean?" CB responded.

"I think that you need to reconsider something, what if the shooter isn't working alone?"

"What do you mean?" CB repeated.

"Look around. There is no way our guy just left his vehicle parked along this road and no one noticed. We haven't been here that long and have already seen 2 cars ourselves. The killer wouldn't have known exactly when the victim was going to arrive and would have been in there for a while. A car or truck just sitting there would have been remembered by someone out here. Hell the farmers who go up and down the road routinely would have assuredly found it odd be-cause you know they all know every vehicle in the area by heart most likely. To have a random vehicle sitting out here by itself. That means, that the shooter had either been dropped off by someone and picked up later. The alternative would be the getaway car didn't look out of place sitting here. Same thing with the other sites for that matter."

"Go on" CB said, liking how the man was thinking.

"I'm saying, I think your guy has an accomplice. I maybe didn't learn much in the Army but one thing I did learn is that a sniper never works alone and always has a means of support. I think this guy does too. I don't know if that helps you or not but to me it's the only thing that makes sense given all we've seen. I think the shooter or his accomplice has some connection to the gas well industry too. I mean no one has ever seen anyone who doesn't belong at any of the sites or at least no one has questioned their presence at any of the sites. And you can tell that the sites had all been scouted. They were all to perfect. If that makes sense?"

"It does. And it's something Ashcroft and I have considered but it doesn't help us since we haven't got anymore evidence on the shooter than we do. They have been very good at cover-ing their tracks. While we know the guy is using a .270 rifle and is likely a smaller guy, that de-scribes literally hundreds of people" CB said.

"I know" Jack acknowledged "but what about the gas well connections? I mean doesn't that at least narrow it down some?"

"We've looked. But there isn't a connection we have found there either. The gas wells are owed and serviced by four different companies. And the five men, while they all worked the rigs we haven't even been able to establish they were connected or even knew one another. Hell we can't even find that they knew some of the same people other than a few loose connections here and there.

And forget about connecting them through the drugs. Running down the drug angle is next to impossible. The entire state is in the middle of an epidemic and we have been hit as hard or harder than the rest of the State. The damn pharmaceutical companies and the doctors who push their products on patients have caused an entire populace to be hooked on pills. And now the whole charade is being exposed and its now politically incorrect for the doctors to keep pre-scribing the medications, the people remain addicts. Of course those guys in their suits and ties who caused the fucking mess seem unwilling to address it but the black market has certainly stepped into fill the void. The people we've busted either know nothing or are willing to go jail rather than turn against their suppliers. Hell Ashcroft has been working in the narcotics task force for years and hasn't been able to get a sniff of this thing.

I mean honestly I am at my whits end with it. I know I am missing something, but I'll be damned if I know what the hell it is," CB said obviously angry.

For the first time, really Jack understood how truly frustrating this must have been for her. It made him appreciate how truly personally she took her job, which is likely what made her good at it. He knew that was the case for him. Unlike some people, Jack knew "good enough" was never "good enough" and sensed that CB felt the same. Trying to encourage her he simply said, "You will figure it out. You're the best, that's why they gave you the case".

CB nodded and thanked him, though the sentiment actually made her feel worse. The two spent another few moments looking the place over before climbing back into her Jeep.

CHAPTER 45

They drove to the five miles to route 20 virtually in silence, each trapped in their own thoughts. As they approached RT 119, the quickest way to get to Audra Park and the last crime scene CB asked Jack if he minded if they went back to the office, apologizing to him for having kept him out all day and not wanting to take up any more of his vacation.

Jack told her it was no problem and volunteered to look over the last crime scene later in the week if she had time, adding he would take her to get something to eat afterwards if she want-ed.

The suggestion made her smile. She asked if they could do so Thursday morning and go to lunch or something after, as her schedule was otherwise looking full the rest of the week. Jack agreed.

Arriving back to the station CB saw Ashcroft outside talking to Josh Bennett causing her to cuss under her breath.

Overhearing her Jack asked "what's wrong?"

"Nothing," CB responded watching as Bennett walked towards he car. "Just someone, I'd rather not deal with at the moment."

"Anything I can do?" Jack asked.

"No thanks. You have been great all day. I can't take up any more of your time. But I will text you later about Thursday," she said, hurriedly exiting the car.

"Sounds good" Jack said as she closed the door.

Jack watched CB meet the tall man who had walked across the parking lot towards her. He continued his visual as reached into the backseat and grabbed his backpack. As he watched, Jack saw the man point towards him as he himself got out. As Jack emerged from the Jeep Bennet commanded "Stay right there. I want to talk to you".

"Goddamnit Josh, I told you what I do and who I do it with is none of your business! Now get out of here!"

"It's ok honey, me and your new friend over there are going to have a talk. I'm just going to tell him he should stay away from you if he knows what's good for him is all" Bennett said loudly while continuing to try to stare down Jack.

As Jack was opening his mouth to respond CB grabbed Bennet by both shoulders with either hand and jumped off the ground driving her right knee into the man's groin. The force of the blow causing the larger man to immediately bend over, clutch his midsection with his right hand while grabbing the fender of the Jeep with his left to keep from falling over.

CB walked away without a backwards glance into the building while Bennet puked all over the parking lot.

The move made Jack like the woman all the more. Amused Jack walked around the Jeep to-ward his own truck, pausing along the way to tell the still bent over man, "Dude I think maybe you're the one who should probably stay away from her. I mean if you ever want to have kids or anything that is."

At the comment Bennet attempted to stand but fell back against the Jeep for support giving. He nonetheless gave Jack the middle finger. The sight caused Jack to laugh aloud before he climbed into his own truck and left.

*****

Walking into the office, CB walked straight to the conference room and got herself a cup of cof-fee attempting to calm herself. Coffee in hand she looked out the window just in time to see Jack leave in his truck. She continued to watch as Ashcroft and another uniformed officer helped Bennet stand upright. The pair then helped him into his own car and he left.

While she freely admitted feeling Bennett's balls crunch under her knee was satisfying, she also knew it wasn't going to go over well with Captain Rodgers when he filed a complaint. A com - plaint she knew was forthcoming as there was no way his ego would be able to handle that she had now both rejected him and made him look foolish. She expected a call from Captain Rodgers would be forthcoming.

Nonetheless, happy Bennet left, she leaned back against the countertop and sipped her coffee, contemplating what had transpired, wondering how else she honestly should have handled it. She told herself she should have just let Bennet confront Jack and watched the show. She guessed Bennet would prefer the smashed gonads to whatever pain Jack would have inflicted on him. While she knew Bennet also practiced martial arts, she knew instinctually he wasn't in Jack's class when it came to fighting, having seen what he did to officer Poles in the restaurant. Not to mention the obvious differences in physique. The mental image made her smile until the thought was interrupted "Damn Greene, you always smile like that after you smash a man's manhood?"

Looking up she saw Ashcroft standing in the doorway clearly amused by his own quib. "He has had it coming," was all she could say.

"Yeah I heard y'all had history but that ain't none of my business. Did you and your new friend get done already? Learn anything?"

"We saw four of the five locations. Was afraid we were going to run out of daylight so we cut it short, though he said if I needed him to he could look at the Audra scene with me later. I will tell you though it was fascinating to see how his mind processed the scenes. He put things together so quickly when it came to the logistics of it all."

"But did you learn anything?"

"I wouldn't say, 'learned' per se," she said using air quotes with her fingers "but he did confirm a few things. For one our killer is a smaller guy. He also pretty much confirmed the place out next to Johnstown couldn't have been a drive by like some in the task force suggested. He even found the way into the thicket and the likely pathway the shooter took. Not to mention he also probably found the place where the shooter had laid in ambush up in Tucker County. On top of the damn well tank, further up the hill side than was ever searched."

"That is good," Ashcroft said sounding genuinely impressed. "Anything else?"

"Nothing really definitive but he did say the way that the scenes looked to him he doesn't think the shooter is working alone. He suggested we look back at the gas well connection again. I told him that was a dead end but after seeing all that had been missed, I think I may just take another look anyhow. I mean what do we have to lose right?"

Ashcroft nodded in response to which CB added "Did you learn anything from your CI?"

"No, not really, my guy said the rumors say the pill trade is controlled via one group or person around here but that it is one of the best kept secrets around. My guy also said the guy who controls the trade must also be a very scary dude for him to have kept his identity a secret for so long."

"We know that whoever it is, certainly isn't afraid to kill or have people killed. We know that for sure," CB concluded emphatically.

Again Ashcroft nodded grimly before asking, "Are you going to tell the Captain all this when he asks for his update?"

"I am going to send him an email here in a minute to tell him I went back to view all the crime scenes today. I'll summarize what I saw, send him a few of the photos and tell him I plan to fol-lowup. I am going to try to keep Jack out of it though."

Ashcroft nodded in understanding and added, "I don't blame you. I don't trust that asshole Rodgers as far as I can throw him."

CHAPTER 46

The big man was bent over a laptop at a desk, when his phone buzzed indicating a text mes-sage. He opened the phone and checked the message, which simply read, "They are back in the office and done for the day. Checking Audra out another time."

The man pondered the text a moment before sending his own text to the man at the last site, "No one is coming. Get some rest. See you tonight."

CHAPTER 47

Jack awoke Wednesday morning at 5 am after sleeping soundly for solid seven hours. Feeling good, he thought the previous day's field trip with CB had been therapeutic for him, though he was unsure why. It was something to consider he thought to himself.

Walking into the kitchen, he made coffee trying to be quiet as possible, while his parents still slept. He lingered over his second cup realizing he was without any plans for the day. It was an uncommon experience for him and he wasn't really sure how to react to it, as he wasn't a big fan of idle time. He told himself he would have to get a workout in and maybe go back out to talk to Gary again or call Dr. Hartman, maybe both.

His thoughts were interrupted when his mom walked into the kitchen, "How'd you sleep?" she asked.

"Good" Jack said, relieved it was a true statement and not simply lip service for his mom's piece of mind.

"Oh good I was worried since you're up so early"

"Mom I am always up this early. The last few days have been the oddity. I never sleep late like I have been."

"Its probably just your body telling you that you need to slow down some. Everyone has to relax once in a while."

"I guess" Jack said.

After pouring her own cup and adding creamer she sat down at the bar next to Jack and asked, "Are you going to go over and see your brother today?"

The question surprised Jack who had forgotten today was when Bob would be back in town for a few days. Having something to do made him feel better. "What time will he be home?" Jack asked.

"They probably actually got back last night. But your brother loves the night shift at work and sleeps during the day. He usually gets up around 2. When I go over there, I usually go around 3 when he has been up a bit. He's never really been a morning person you know."

Jack laughed, knowing the truth of the statement. He recalled fondly how when they were kids Bob would often not shower before school because he had refused to get out of bed until the last possible moment; then rushing to get dressed, brush his teeth and get out the door, barley in time to catch the bus.

It was a reminder to Jack of just how much he and Bob were nearly opposites in so many facets of their lives. Jack had always been the early to bed, early to rise type, who had always been driven and stayed out of trouble. Bob, on the other hand, had always been the more laid back of the two, more of the go with the flow type, who was also a bit of a hell raiser though generally a good guy.

Bob had gone to work for the rigs right out of high school. Since the he had worked for nearly all the drilling companies in the area, on nearly every kind of drilling rig there was. The diversity of his work history was because he was known to get upset with people and quit. But once his money dried up, he'd go back to another rig and start all over again. Nonetheless, his services were always in demand as he was known as a top hand within the industry.

Ironically enough it was the connections he'd made by bouncing back and forth between jobs that saved him during the lull in drilling. During the depressed cycle, people who were putting crews together knew Bob, having either worked with him previously or by reputation, making it easier for him to get a job than some of the other guys on the unemployment line who had only worked one or two rigs in their lives with a very limited amount of connections or experience with other types of equipment.

Despite their differences, Jack always enjoyed seeing his brother and was looking forward to that afternoon.

CHAPTER 48

CB arrived to the office early the next morning. After getting a cup of coffee from the break room she sat down at her makeshift workstation and checked her emails. She ignored most of them but spend the one from Captain Rodgers in response to her summary of her tour of the previous crime scenes. She was surprised by his response: "Good job Detectives. Sounds like the two of you had a productive day keep up the good work and let's get this thing solved."

She realized Rodgers must have thought Ashcroft had been with her. She considered correcting him but then thought twice about it, not wanting to open that can of worms. That decided, she pulled out the hard copies of the files she had carried with her the day prior. She preferred the paper files to the computerized files. With paper she could lay a file out in front of her, arranging and rearranging as the saw fit; seeing the picture all at once, which was more effective in her mind than switching back and forth between the windows on the computer. She also felt the paper files with actual photos she could hold and feel made the cases feel more real as op-posed to the sanitized images on the screen. She suspected that was subconsciously another reason she took so many of her own photographs, to reinforce the crimes and victims were very much real and justice, whatever that meant, was indeed needed.

She printed the photos she had taken the day before with Jack and added them to the files along with notes describing the observations Jack had made. The notes made her think of the man again. She admitted she was attracted to the guy. Not only was he very physically attrac-tive, but having spent time with him, she realized he was also smart and personable. She even liked he was a bit mysterious, though she couldn't quite place a finger on why she felt that way other than he seemed somewhat guarded in some of their conversations. She considered tex-ting him and asking if he was still willing to go to the park the next day to look at the last crime scene, but talked herself out of it — unsure if she was more afraid he would see through the pretext or he wouldn't at all.

Shaking off the thoughts for fear of where they could take her, she decided to start reexamining the files. She had been over the files so much she could literally quote sections of them from memory. Yet she knew she was missing something; she had to be, she told herself. Because of the feeling, she wanted to try to look at the files again; as if she did not already know anything about anything and eliminate her own preconceived notions and biases.

CB began by reviewing the profiles of the men again. They were all oil field workers. They were all addicted to pain medication, and they all were either found with opioids on them or in their systems at their times of death. The review of their backgrounds by first the task force and then herself and Ashcroft had found no known associations outside of those two facts. It was known there were a large number of oil field workers who had substance abuse problems. It was just as well known the men on the rigs had access to all kinds of drugs including pills, and had for a long time. However, it wasn't until the couple of years later the murders started to happen. The assumption was the murders were connected to the drug trade but no one had ever really fig-ured out what changed to trigger the sudden onset of killings. Some hoped the capture and subsequent death of Tony Kincaid would end it, but that hope had quickly been dashed with the most recent killing of Roberts.

Having finished reviewing the men's profiles she moved on to the ambush locations. She re-minded herself not to take anything for granted here because of Jack's feeling this was where the connection had to be. While he wasn't an investigator, she had been impressed about his ability to deduce the information at the scenes and come up with plausible outcomes.

The five gas wells were operated by four different companies, three large corporations whom she had heard of and a smaller company called Hawker. Hawker, though the smallest entity, controlled two of the wells.

She once again crossed referenced the 4 gas companies to the 5 victims. Only one of the men, Rodriquez was actually killed on a site where he was working. He was also the only one who worked for one of the 4 listed companies, Hawker. The other men had all worked for various other drilling companies but none of those companies were related to the ambush points. Not to mention, she thought to herself the other 4 were actually ambushed on properties unrelated to the wells themselves. The connections were loose, the men had all worked for the gas compa-nies and the shooter had set his ambushes near gas well roads. It had to mean something, 'but what?' she asked herself.

Continuing on, she opened the file for Dennis Roberts, the most recent victim. His killer had set up on one of the Hawker properties, however he had worked for Marshall's Drilling. As she wrote she was suddenly struck with an epiphany. Marshall drilling was only a contractor, mean-ing his company didn't actually own any wells, but simply drilled and service wells for other companies. And she knew he was one of many companies who did work for the big holding companies. She quickly went back to the previous searches. Though there were still missing notes, what she had indicated that both she and the task force had only investigated the holding companies, confirming they still held the properties. She kicked herself for only going through the motions previously overconfident the task force had done a thorough back ground check. Realizing none of the holding companies had been asked if they drilled and serviced their own wells. Excited for the break through she went through the files and got the contact numbers for the four companies again.

She was about to call when she looked at the clock. 8:20 am. Still to early call she realized, knowing from her previous endeavors it was unlikely to get ahold of he people she needed to before 9. She further assumed whomever she talked to would want to clear it with their legal departments before they provided her with any information. She detested people were always so guarded about what they were willing to reveal to the police. While she understood the need for privacy, she also valued the safety of the general public and helping her fellow man; even if a majority of the lawyers she dealt with seemingly didn't.

To kill some time CB grabbed her phone and before she could talk herself out of it again, she sent a text to Jack asking if he was still willing to help the next day. After hitting send she laid the phone on the table and tried to shake off the apprehension she still felt in the pit of her stomach the man would figure her out. However, the feeling was quickly quashed when Ashcroft walked in and asked her how long she had been there.

She considered telling him about the misunderstanding with Rodgers but decided not to. Instead explaining that she hadn't been there long and she was taking a fresh look at everything again. She then emphasized the new line on the oil companies she wanted to explore.

Much to her surprise and disappointment, Ashcroft acted dismissive of the plan. Asking her if she really thought exploring who serviced the wells would be helpful. "Honestly CB, the entire state is full of gas well roads and everybody knows it. I don't see how you're going to get any-thing from the information. It just seems a waste of time."

CB was about to argue when her phone chimed with a text message. Glancing down, her screen showed Jack had responded to her earlier inquiry. Excited, and arguing with Ashcroft forgotten, she picked up the phone to read the message. "Sure thing. 9 am again? Want to grab lunch after?"

The last sentence caught her slightly off guard and she felt her face begin to flush having read it. Looking up she saw Ashcroft still standing there staring.

"Everything ok?" he asked.

"Oh. Yeah it's good. Just got confirmation about something," she said just as Ashcroft's own phone buzzed.

"Oh ok," Ashcroft answered, staring at his phone while pulling out his own chair at the desk. Yet he never sat down seemingly lost in the phone. After a moment, he said without ever looking at CB "I am going to go talk to a guy here in a bit about the pills. He doesn't like people much, es-pecially cops. I am going to have to go alone but I shouldn't be gone long. You run down the old well things ok."

"Uh sure sounds good," CB responded, somewhat curious about the change in attitude. Watch-ing the man leave the room, CB got up and walked to the window, for a reason she couldn't quite explain. She watched as Ashcroft walked to his car and got in. But he didn't go anywhere, instead he made a phone call. It turned out to be a short conversation. From her prospective it appeared Ashcroft spoke into the phone a few moments, paused as if he were listening to someone, then abruptly stare at the phone as is he lost signal before dropping the phone in a manner suggesting frustration.

A moment later he drove away. The oddity of the whole thing made CB feel something was astir, though she admitted to herself she did not know the man well and narcotics officers were notoriously finicky everywhere.

Shaking it off she returned to the files intent on looking at the gas companies closer. While she thought it as still to early she began calling the individual gas companies to ask about their drilling and service companies. The first company she called was the largest corporation, who controlled the well where the first victim, Micah Lowe had died near Fairmont, West Virginia in a parking lot while sitting in his car. Because it was such a large corporate structure she imagined it would also be the most difficult to access the information she wanted without a warrant. Much to her surprise however it only took her about three transfers and 40 minutes to find out the cor-poration itself serviced their own wells but back when it was drilled they subcontracted the actual drilling to a local company: Marshall's Drilling and Troubleshooting Services - Jeremy Mar-shall's company.

The second company she called leased the well from the parents of Gumm, the youngest victim who had died in his parents yard, near Philippi. Similar to the first company, they were very helpful and reported they used subcontractors for both the drilling and servicing of the well. They used a company called Hyre's Servicing Corporation to do the servicing of the well but they had hired Marshall's Drilling and Troubleshooting Services to actually drill the cite. The factboth companies used Marshall's had CB's interest piqued and made her feel like she was onto something; though she triedto temper her excitement by reminding herself Kincaid worked for Marshall as well.

She then call the third company where victim number three, Charles Harp, who had been shot from ambush from atop the holding tank. It took nearly an hour to get the information she want-ed because the man on the other end of the line liked to talk. But after much banter he ex-plained according the record he had the well had been a real pain in the ass to drill and they subcontracted the job out three times before they made any progress. But finally Marshall's Drilling and Troubleshooting Services made the well successful, though they also used Hyre's Servicing Corporation to maintain the well. Three for three, she thought to herself, sensing she was onto something. Hoping she may finally have found something concrete on Jeremy Mar-shall himself.

Finally, she called Hawker, who was listed as the controlling company for both the last well she had visited the day before near Audra Park and where victim number 4, Rodriquez was killed in Harrison County West Virginia near a small village known as Johnstown. Again much to her surprise, the person on the other end was more than willing to help. He assured her they serviced all their own wells and only used local people to do it like Rodriquez. As to the well where Rodriquez was killed, he explained they too had to subcontract the job because of the hard rock in the area. Liking the sound of his own voice he told CB how it was actually cheaper for them to subcontract the job than the price it would have been for them to do it themselves because of the specialized equipment it involved. The subcontractor they used: none other than Mar-shall's Drilling and Troubleshooting Services, who specialized in difficult jobs. CB was really ex-cited at the news, feeling as if the last piece along the outer edge of the large jigsaw puzzled had just fell into place; making the remaining task more manageable.

However, her euphoria was quickly doused when the man told her about the well road she had stumbled upon at the most recent killing. The man was unable to tell her who actually drilled the well explaining Hawker had acquired the well 15 years prior when they purchased a smaller gas company. He added it was likely the former company had drilled it though because they didn't generally outsource. He finished by telling CB the well was nearly tapped out after 40 years and they would soon cap it off and remove their equipment.

The statement threw CB off. If the well had been 40 years old then she knew Marshall couldn't have drilled it, as he had really only been in the drilling business the past handful of years. Fur-thermore, since Hawker serviced its own wells it eliminated Marshall's connection to the well. Disappointed she thanked the man for his time and hung up.

CHAPTER 49

Bob lived about 15 minutes, from his parents' house just off of Route 119. Like many in the re-gion Bob lived in a single wide trailer. And like many in the area it appeared Bob's truck cost more than his house did, a phenomenon Jack never understood personally. Bob always ex-plained he was in his truck everyday and only at home every couple of weeks and if he got lucky a few nights he wouldn't even be sleeping there then. The answer was perfect Bob logic.

Jack pulled into Bob's driveway at about 3:15, in time to see Bob, wearing a dirty set of green overalls, cigarette dangling from the corner of his mouth, walking towards his Chevy carrying a big hammer. A closer inspection revealed Bob had the rear end jacked up with both wheels and tires off the big 3/4 ton truck. Bob didn't even acknowledge Jack's arrival, instead sat down on the tire he had taken off the driver side of the vehicle and began looking underneath.

Jack shifted into park and climbed out. No sooner had his door closed then he heard, "Mom said you were coming. You're just in time to help me replace this damn rear end."

"What's wrong with the one that's in it, I mean other than being a Chevy?" Jack joked.

"Fuck you and the Ford you drove in on," Bob chided right back. "The damn thing has been slip-ping for a while, so I bought a new 14 bolt to put under her. Ain't nuttin going to stop this bitch onc't we get this thing in her."

"Shit then lets do it. You got another set of coverall's I can borrow?"

"Yeah there's a set hanging on the hook just inside the door on the porch. Probably a pair of boots there too if you don't wanna get yours all fucked up" Bob replied then quickly added "grab us a few beers from the fridge while your in there too". He then proceeded to start pounding on something under the truck with the hammer Jack couldn't see.

Jack walked to the house. He hadn't been in here in a few years but could tell Bob had done some work to the place. The tin underpinning was gone, replaced by brick all the way around. Bob had also built a new roof over the existing one by anchoring 4 posts on either side of the house and then framing in a roof to cover the structure. The roof structure over hung the trailer by four feet on the back side, where Bob had laid a stone walk way, and eight feet on the front, which he had closed in, forming a sunroom / porch with windows running the length of it and a big storm door on the front. The framed in structure was then sided disguising that the home had started as a trailer.

Jack opened the door and walked in to see the space was filled with a variety of boxes and buckets filled with all kinds of odds and ends. Jack didn't know exactly what most of them were but he knew his brother, like his father, was a bit of a pack rat and the piles probably contained various parts used on the oil rigs, parts for his truck, or his Harley, which was housed in the shed behind the house. While to Jack it looked like a complete mess, he knew his brother could walk in and find anything in a matter of seconds.

Along the wall of what used to be the exterior of the trailer, was a long board full of hooks which held a variety of clothing items, most looking incredibly dirty and oil covered. Jack knew Bob wouldn't take his nasty work clothes inside the house and thus used this space to keep them.

Amongst them he saw a couple pair of coveralls and selected the least dirty of them. Jack knew the coveralls would fit because he and Bob were the exact same size and always had been. Sit-ting on an old metal porch glider that had been their grandparents, which sat in front of the living room window, he took off his boots and donned the coveralls.

He then walked into the house which was a complete contrast to the porch. It was very tidy and orderly, much like Jack's own apartment. There was a large sectional dominating the small living space and a large flat screen television mounted on the wall. Between the two sat a large cof-fee table on top of which sat a pack of rolling papers, a 3 foot glass bong and a large bag of weed, which Jack knew Bob had probably just picked up since coming back to town, again clas-sic Bob.

The kitchen was also clean. Jack noted the only dirty dishes was a coffee mug sitting on the counter next to the half full coffee pot and a bowl in the sink. Opening the fridge Jack was re-minded Bob too was a lifelong bachelor finding only a few condiments, a half gallon of milk, a 12 pack of Pepsi, and a case of beer - Natural Light. Although he though it was a little early, he grabbed 4 cans of the beer, walked back to the porch, put his own boots on before returning outside.

"Do you ever splurge on good beer?" he asked handing Bob two of the beers.

"Shit it's the same thing as Bud Light, just a different can," Bob said, dead serious.

"I was meaning more like Guinness or something a little darker," Jack said.

"Fuck that man. That shit is too heavy. You cant drink but a few before your full. How the fuck am I supposed to get drunk if my belly is to full to drink another beer?" Bob asked rhetorically.

Jack laughed, "Yeah, yeah. So what do you need me to do?"

*****

The two men worked steadily for the next few hours and had a relatively smooth time of it, though there were a few occasions Jack had to talk Bob out of getting his torches out to loosen bolts. Despite those few happenstances they were able to get the rear end off and the new one in place. Job accomplished, Bob also put new brakes on. Once complete, Bob told Jack to jump in and they would take the rig for a quick test run right up the road.

Bob drove a couple miles south on 119, going through all the gears and braking hard a few times, giving the new brakes and reared a real workout. Seemingly satisfied he turned left off the main road towards an old mining community called Century number 2.

"Where are we going?" Jack asked.

"Just up this little trail up here. Gotta make sure this thing is as good off the road as it is on it?"

"Uh huh" Jack replied sardonically.

"What man? With my job I'm legitimately off road as much as on them going into well sites. And more often than not those things are all tore up. The companies will gravel them to get the drilling equipment in there. But then the damn gravel settles and gets tore up by weather and trucks. Hell most of my sites you can't even get to without four wheel peel.

They don't fix the damn things up again until the rigs are getting ready to pull out."

A brief moment later, Bob found the trail he was looking for though to Jack it appeared as noth-ing more than a pair of ruts off the side of the road. Bob took the turn at a faster speed than Jack would have liked causing both men to lean against the g-forces. Both men then bounced as the big tires left the pavement and hit the rutted trail. Smiling, Bob downshifted and gave his best Dukes of Hazard "YeeHaw".

Bob drove the trail aggressively and Jack could tell he had been on it multiple times by how his brother was anticipating the turns and avoiding the nastiest of the bumps. After what Jack esti-mated to have been less than a 1/2 mile they came to the bottom of a very steep and tall hill with ruts going up its face.

"Now its time to see what the 4 wheel can do" Bob said shifting the truck's transfer case into gear. "It hasn't rained in a bit. Good thing too cause when it's wet you can't get up this place but we should be ok today."

"Thats comforting," Jack said.

"Whats the matter big brother, you used to love this shit back in the day," Bob replied smashing the gas rocketing the big truck forward.

As the front tires found the hill, the truck shot up in the air but quickly landed and began spin-ning furiously trying to ascend the embankment. Jack, white knuckled the handle in the corner between the windshield and the door, known in the four wheeling community as the "shit handle" for support while Bob ran the truck through its gears.

The roar of the big V8 motor and the sound of the wheels spinning up the dirt as the truck dug for traction really did take Jack back to his high school days when he and his friends used to go four wheeling on the weekends. His heart was pounding with the adrenaline created by both the hillclimb and the nostalgia of it all. For the first time in a long time, Jack was able to appre-ciate the feeling of the rush without having a gun in his hand. The feeling was short-lived how-ever, as near the very top of the climb, the grade became even steeper still and Jack felt as if they were about to roll over backwards. Gritting his teeth Jack tightened his grip even more on the handle with his right hand while he braced himself against the floor boards with his feet by extending his legs fully pushing himself back into the seat, until finally they leveled out on the top of the hill where Bob stopped on another graveled lane.

"What's this?" Jack asked.

"Just an old service road for the old mine that used to run up to the old conveyor. Its just like the one at the top of the Holler climb if you remember it?" Bob said turning left on the road.

At mention of the Holler, Jack told Bob about his recent visit there shooting with Jeremy a few days prior.

"I worked for him for a while, when he was first starting up his drilling stuff," Bob said.

"Yeah what did you think of it?" Jack asked.

"Not much really, like I said it was when he first started and he really didn't know what the hell he was doing. He was drilling wells in the worst damn places you ever saw but we gotter done. Broke a bunch of shit though until he figured out he needed better equipment."

"So what happened. Why did you quit working for him?" Jack asked though he figured he knew the answer.

"The pay sucked, though I reckon he paid me more than some of the others because of my ex-perience. But mostly I didn't like the other guys he had on the crews I worked on. When your on a drilling site like that you have to be able to trust the other guys on the rig with you and I never felt comfortable with a lot of the guys he brings on"

"Because they have records?" Jack finished the statement

"Shit man lots of guys have been to jail. Hell I been in the drunk tank a time or two my damn self. But those guys he had working then always seemed to be doped up on something. Now you know me. I like my weed and a few to many beers from time to time, but not at work. That shit is to dangerous. You cant be stoned and react quick if a damn drive chain breaks or a bit busts or you need to run another pipe. Fucking around out there will get your ass hurt" Bob replied.

"So they were all drugged out huh?" Jack said.

"Not all of them, but enough. They were mostly pill poppers. I know I was asked a few times if I wanted any but I always said no. Then one day I was sitting at home and a guy called me from a different company asking if I'd be interested in running one of his crews and I left. Better pay and better crew."

"Was Jeremy upset you left. Hell you spent as much time with him in school as I did".

"No, not really, to him it was just business. He's cool like that. People are always talking bad about him because of how successful he's been and how he handles business, but to me he just plays the game better than most. They are simply jealous of the guy. I don't begrudge him his success."

"Really? But what about the people he hires you don't think it's for anything else?"

"No, I mean, I know he knows that's what people think and he is willing to look the other way at things others aren't. He knows his guys aren't all good guys but he also knows they will work cheap, because they don't really have anywhere else to go."

"Yeah but doesn't that make them more of a problem on those sites? I mean from what I hear he is only doing the trouble shooting stuff now. Wouldn't that be even more dangerous?" Jack asked curious.

"Yes and no. From what I hear through the grape vine, his actual skilled guys are really good now. The guys actually running the rigs he has and the crews he has that consult are top notch hands. Plus from what I hear he has 3 or 4 guys that run things with an iron fist on the sites and the crews know not to fuck with them. Its cleaned it up a lot from what I gather."

"Yeah I think I met one of them. Thomas Greene, big dude, seemed nice enough, but not someone I would pick a fight with I don't think"

"Yeah he is one of them for sure. Good driller, knows his shit too. They all call Jeremy 'Boss' as an ego thing but from what I gather Thomas is the real 'Boss' over there."

"You ever work with him?"

"No, I've met him a few times here and there but never worked with him. Wouldn't want to now anyway, not with Wren being one of his right hand men. That dude ain't been right since he got out of the big house man and I just don't like his vibe if you know what I mean? Like a damn ra-bid dog that needs put down. Especially when Troy is always there to back his play, which is most of the time."

"And Jaime?" Jack added.

"Not so much on that one, Jaimie is his own man still. He hasn't been back in town for too long really. Jeremy hired him and he is out and around with Wren or Troy some but not like the old days. He works that crew because those two were willing to work with him even though he didn't have any experience. But I've also heard Jaimie and Wren don't always see eye to eye, ya know."

It was something to ponder for sure Jack thought as they emerged back onto the main road. As soon as Bob hit the smooth pavement he tore through the gears again like a Nascar driver, the sound of the big truck drowning out any further conversation. Pulling into his driveway, Bob asked if Jack wanted to come in and have a beer or hit his bong. Jack declined telling him he had to something to do the next morning. But asked when Bob was going back to the rigs. Bob told him Saturday night but said he would swing by the parent's house Saturday for breakfast first, promising to see Jack then, probably Jill too.

CHAPTER 50

The next morning, Jack awoke to a dark room. He laid in bed a few moments before he got up and looked at the clock. 4:45. A little early but not bad, he thought. Walking into the kitchen, Jack turned on the coffee maker and considered what to do before meeting up with CB who had confirmed they'd go look around the Audra site at 9 am. She had told him they would just meet up in the lower parking lot as it was closer for him than the drive to town would have been. He was also excited when he referenced lunch afterwards she had simply responded, "it's a date".

The problem he currently faced was Jack knew he had to do something or he'd go stir crazy awaiting the appointed hour, 4 hours away. As he continued to wait for the coffee to brew, he went back into his room and found an old notebook and pencil. He decided he would finally take Dr. Hartman's advise and try to write down some things going on in his head and heart.

Returning to the kitchen, he poured a large mug of the freshly brewed coffee, went to the table and proceeded to write. He began much as he had when he and CB had talked; writing about how he had always wanted to be a soldier and his time in the army. He even smiled at the memory of the Ghost moniker and SFC Bates. From there he went on to write of his times overseas and the soldier's / survivor's guilt he had spoken about with Gary about and how the Bible had talked about the plight of soldiers and how it wasn't a new phenomenon. Then he changed again to his times with Dr. Hartman herself and how he felt recently in Nebraska and the question of "what if". Then he started to write of his fear, anxiety and anger of the event thereafter, his guilt for killing a man, who by all accounts was truly evil. While the writing began slow and forced it quickly gained momentum and flowed out. So focused was he on his work that when he finally noticed his coffee cup was empty and he got up to refill it the pot itself only had one cup left in it. It was then he realized his parents were both awake and sitting at the bar reading; his dad the paper, his mom a book.

"How long have you guys been up?" Jack asked.

"Oh about 30 minutes or so," his dad answered.

"You looked busy," his mom added, "we didn't want to bother you."

That they were able to walk right by him without his even realizing it was a weird anomaly for Jack. He had been so hyper vigilant for seemingly his entire adulthood that his parents unex-pected presence was both unnerving and relaxing to him. He made a note quickly adding the sensation to his list for Dr. Hartman. He then wrote of his experience with CB the day before and how much he enjoyed the experience, both because of her and the fun it was analyzing the crime scenes. When he was finally done the notebook was half full and he realized he was go-ing to be late if he didn't get ready to go.

*****

Jack pulled into the lower lot at the park at ten minutes till 9. He knew he was early and expect-ed he would have to wait for CB, but was pleasantly surprised to see her Jeep already there. He backed his truck into the spot next to hers and got out to meet her.

"Good morning," she said in greeting as his feet hit the ground.

"Good morning to you," Jack responded walking to her, "you ready?"

"Yeah lets go. The site is a decent little hike down the trail. But you don't seem the type to mind a little exercise" she joked.

"No, I don't. It keeps me sane, or as sane as I can be I guess" he said retuning the quib.

She smiled at his self deprecating humor and led off towards the trail. A few hundred yards into the woods, the trail went from being wide enough for the two to walk side-by-side to a narrow path forcing them to walk single file. Unlike there previous encounter, Jack did not feel as guilty for admiring her back side in another pair of flatteringly snug khakis as they walked in the crisp morning air.

As they walked CB told Jack of how she and her friends in high school used to come out to the park in the summers to walk the same trail and to go swimming in the deeper pools of the river.

Smiling, Jack told her of how he and his friends did the same thing, though he consciously de-cided not to mention those friends were Jeremy, Troy, Wren and Jaimie. He did, however, share how he and his unnamed friends had unsuccessfully tried to get numerous girls to come out here with them; but the girls in his class weren't outdoorsy types.

To which CB said, they just didn't ask the right girls telling him in high school most of the fresh-man girls had a crush on either him or Wren.

"Really?" Jack asked somewhat taken back.

"Really" she said. "You were the star athlete and by all accounts a nice guy. And Wren was the bad boy type but also a really cute little guy who wasn't as intimidating size wise to the girls my age, unlike you and Jermey and the other football players."

The statement caused Jack to laugh again easily, something he admitted to himself he didn't do enough of.

"Whats so funny?" CB asked.

"Nothing really, but would you believe me if I told you in high school I was scared to death of girls? I couldn't figure out what y'all actually wanted and every time I tried to talk to a female I got all tongue tied which made it worse."

"You? No way, all the girls I knew just assumed you could have had any girl you wanted. Though obviously you guys didn't exactly hang out with us or invite us to your parties."

Jack laughed again. "Yeah we didn't really have a lot of parties you needed an invitation for. More often than not it was just finding someone to buy us some beer and drive out to a field somewhere or the holler. We'd build a fire and stand around talking about what we were going to do as soon as we could leave the place. Not to many girls seemed interested in joining us very often."

Unable to see her reaction to his statement but wanting to keep the conversation going Jack added, "Hell, while I'm in confession mode, I asked out Alison Simms to homecoming freshman year and she said no. And then asked Amy Johnson my sophomore year who also declined. I honestly gave up after that. I went to the movies a few times with a few girls but never anything serious and I never even bothered with prom either as a Junior or Senior. I remember my Ju-nior year me and Jeremy went to some movie. Then our senior year, Jeremy, Wren, Troy, Jaime and I somehow decided we were going to be the official after party hosts and went to an old cabin way back in the woods north of town and got everything set up after."

The memory caused him to laugh again as told CB the night turned out to be a disaster. The cabin was built in the middle of a field in a valley. The week before prom it had rained heavily.

When their friends and classmates arrived, most driving cars instead of trucks, got stuck in muddy field. Jack and some of the other football players spent half the night pushing the cars out of the ruts. Then everyone who came still wearing their prom dresses and tuxedos were having to stomp through the mud to the cabin, ruining their outfits. On top of that, the cabin turned out to be to small to hold everyone so they were jammed tight into the little space drink-ing and smoking pot. But they ran out of both, the beer to early and pot to late. So most every-one was drunk and or stoned with no food or anything else to drink. At some point in the night, it got cold and someone decided to start a fire in the old fire place but whoever did it didn't check the flu and soon thereafter the entire cabin was filled with smoke forcing everyone back outside in the mud.

The next morning the cops showed up and found Wren and Troy still there, passed out in the cabin. They were arrested for destruction of property and trespassing. They both ended up spending the rest of the weekend in jail. To get released the two had agreed to repair the dam-age to the field caused by the cars coming in and out; and to the cabin, which had some broken furniture and smoke damage as restitution. A few weeks later Jack, Jeremy and a few others went back to help the pair with the repairs. Wren never did forgive most of the others who were there that night; angered they were the ones who had caused most of the damages but never bothered to help clean up. A few weeks after the owners had said they were satisfied with the work they had done Jack had left for the Army. He hadn't seen any of them again until recently.

At the conclusion of the story Jack noticed CB had stopped and turned towards him smiling.

"What?" he asked.

"I actually remember hearing about prom night at school the next week," she said. "I was friends with most of the varsity cheerleaders and they had all gone up there with their dates. I remem-ber them saying how it was a sloppy mess but once they got there they had fun even though their dresses were ruined. I also remember hearing about how one of the girls was all excited because she thought she was going to lose her virginity that night but the guy she went with got to drunk and passed out on her instead. She was so mad she broke up with the guy. It was pretty funny hearing the story."

Jack laughed again "That's awesome. If nothing else, I would say it is an adventure most of us will never forget, that's for sure."

"I bet," CB agreed as Jack realized the two had arrived to the stone steps leading to the narrow passage way through the boulders where Roberts had been killed.

"Here it is," she said, handing Jack the crime scene folder and the pictures of the scene.

Jack took his time looking at the photos. He then climbed the stairs and turned around very similarly to how CB had when she had first came to the scene. "So across the river?" Jack asked rhetorically. "Impressive. That shot is a little tricky since the wind off the water could effect the trajectory of the bullet. I am guessing the guy had his car up on the old Ferguson well road?" Jack added.

"On the what?" CB asked.

"The gas well road across the river," Jack replied pointing to the other hillside.

"How did you know that was there?" She asked, truly curious of how he knew of it.

"I told you, growing up I used to spend a lot of time down here. Me and Jeremy Marshall proba-bly know this area as well as anyone, or at least we used to. Shit we even tried to throw a party back up there one night once we had been ran out of the Holler by the cops to many times. But turned out no-one else could find the place." He answered laughing at his own memory before recognizing a strange look on CB's face. "What?" he asked again afraid he had said something wrong.

"So you're saying Marshall would have known of that road?" she asked seriously.

"Of course he would have.   But a lot of people know about that road. Why?"

"Look, Jack. I am going to share something with you. I know he is your friend, but these five murders, Jack have one thing in common. Jeremy Marshall. His company drilled all four of the other wells and Roberts, the guy who died here worked for him too. But we never could connect him here or show he knew of its existence. But you, you just confirmed he knew it was there."

"So what? You're seriously saying, Jeremy is your killer?" Jack asked incredulously.

"I think it's a possibility," CB stated calmly

"You're crazy and I can prove it." Jack responded icily.

"Oh really, how is that?"

"It's easy. He doesn't fit your own profile. Jeremy is a big ass dude. He wouldn't've made the marks under the bushes in the road at the second place we visited Tuesday. He also wouldn't have been able to get into the position to make the shot in the laurel over next to Johnstown. Both those places, would've had to have been a much smaller man. Shit Wren is more likely than Jeremy." As soon as he said it they both froze in place; a look of shock on their faces.

"Oh my god!" was all CB could say. It all fit. He worked for Marshall and had for years. He was a really good shot, and shot regularly at the range Marshall had set up.

"Damn it" Jack said interrupting her thought.

"What?" she asked.

"Wren had a .270 at the range Saturday when we were up there."

"Are you sure"

"Positive, rifles are kinda my thing, and I made it a point to look to see what everyone was using just out of curiosity. Wren had a .270, Jeremy was using a 30-06, Troy had a 7 mm and your dad had an old M1. Lots of AR-15s too and Jaimie even had a 30-30."

"Crap. We have to find him and get that gun to run a ballistics match on it."

"OK so how do we do that?"

"We call Ashcroft and get an APB out and a warrant" she responded, pulling out her phone. "Shit, no service. We need to get back to the parking lot. I have bars there"

The duo fast footed back to the parking lot covering the distance in a little under 12 minutes. Once there CB checked her phone for service and dialed Ashcroft. As quickly as she could she told Ashcroft they needed to get an APB out on Wren as he was now the prime suspect in the killings. She went on to explain what they had discovered and how Wren fit with the profiler: from working with Marshall, being a small man and being known to own a .270 rifle.

Ashcroft listened to her information and case theory. Afterwards, he told CB he thought the APB was unwarranted and the case she had built was purely circumstantial. He also warned it was a bad idea to announce Wren's name in relation to the case after what had happened to Kincaid. Sensing CB was about to protest he tried to pacify her by saying he would write out a search warrant and see if he could find a judge or magistrate willing to sign it to see if they could get the rifle "Jack thinks he saw" for testing. He also warned they needed to be careful with it because even the friendliest of judges may find the evidence lacking probable cause after the taint the case still had on it after Kincaid's death.

CB argued regardless Wren was still in violation of the law as a felon in possession of a firearm, which again Ashcroft threw water on, stating she or Jack should have arrested him when they saw him with the weapon if that were the case. Infuriating her even more, he told her conde-scendingly, if they got the warrant then they would be able to arrest the man, if there were in fact weapons in the home, if he were home when they executed the warrant. By the time she had gotten off the phone with Ashcroft, CB was so mad she was ready to scream.

Jack had watched and listened to CB's side of the conversation. He noted how her voice went from one of excitement, to one of even tone, to one of frustration speaking. When he asked what the problem was CB recapped the entirety of the situation; explaining Ashcroft felt the case was strictly circumstantial and currently all they had was possibly probable cause to get a search warrant. At the moment he didn't want to broadcast Wren's name out there so no one was going to be actively searching for him. She also told him it wasn't going to look good that two officers of the law had seen a known felon in possession of a firearm and had done nothing about it.

The two stood silently for a few moments. Watching CB, Jack could see the disappointment on her face and he wanted to reach out to comfort her but he resisted the urge for fear she would view it as inappropriate. Instead he began to consider options to solve the problem. Suddenly it occurred to him. "Wait a minute. We know where Wren is. Or at least, we know how to find him."

"What are you talking about?" CB asked.

"Wren works on your dad's crew.   Call your dad and ask where their site is and lets go get him."

CB looked at him for a moment and Jack could tell she was thinking about it. "Dad, doesn't of-ten answer his phone when he is on site but I can text him for sure and hope he answers." Tak-ing out her phone she began to send a text but stopped and looked back up at Jack.

"What?" Jack asked.

"I don't know what to say. I am afraid to ask to much and either tip Wren off or worse yet have dad do something crazy and get hurt you know?"

Jack thought about it and agreed and then said, "I could ask Jeremy, where they are."

"No, we can't do that either. You said it yourself, Wren has an accomplice and Jeremy Marshall is still a linchpin to this case. I definitely don't want to tip him off because he has the resources to disappear for real". She said.

"Shit" Jack said seeing her point and also not wanting to argue with her as he still didn't believe his friend could have anything to do with it.

After a few more moments of contemplative silence, CB looked up again and asked Jack if he had plans the rest of the day.

Confused, Jack told her he didn't.

"Want to go with me to Dad's house" she asked. "He used to make notes about his job sites and plans for how he planned on doing things. Maybe he left something that'll give us a clue to where to look. The problem is Marshall literally has his crews working all over the place. Dad and them have been everywhere from upstate New York to North Carolina drilling wells. So if they are out of state somewhere we are screwed".

"Lets go," Jack said simply.

CHAPTER 51

The route to CB's father's home took the pair past the state police barracks where they left CB's Jeep. Jack drove the rest of the way, while CB provided the direction.

It had been years since Jack had driven beyond the police barracks. He drove cautiously on the windy road as a result. As he drove, CB went into detail about many of the landmarks they passed including, the Sago Mine disaster that killed 12 miners in 2006. Further along, at a long straightaway, she told him how she and her friends would drag race after school; she told him of her recent breakfast with her father at Maggie's Diner and even how she had read over the win-ter the Game Farm had three new Elk, as a few of the cows had babies. Jack thought the con-versation was cute, though he could tell she was talking because she was nervous.

No sooner had the thought crossed his mind when CB began to give him a hard time about dri-ving like her grandma, adding he had just turned a 20 minute drive into a half hour and they still weren't there yet.   Looking down at the gauges on his truck, Jack confirmed he was driving less than the speed limit. Laughing, he pressed the accelerator, pushing them both back in the seat and causing CB to exclaim, "That's more like it boy."

Finally, as they approached an intersection she told him to turn right. A mile and a half later, she told him to slow and turn left into a long gravel drive, flanked on either side by trees, creating a wooded cavern to drive through. Though the leaves had fallen from he canopy, Jack was sure the lane was even prettier in the summer.

Studying the property as he went, Jack noted to his left there was a decent sized stand of trees, which appeared to be a few acres in size. To his right the trees had been planted in a single row to act as wind break from the large field beyond. It made Jack wonder how big the property ac-tually was. As if reading his mind, CB explained the farm was 80 acres in size and had been in her family since before the Civil War. Her father had inherited from her great-grandfather before she had been born.

Emerging from the trees, Jack saw a big well maintained yard, and a brick, rectangular, ranch style home with a full front porch. There was also a large metal garage with two full sized garage doors that looked as if it would hold 8 cars easily.

Jack was surprised to see no evidence of the original homestead or barn and said so. CB told him how she, her father and mother had actually lived in the old farm house when she was a little girl. She remembered having her own room at the top of the steep stairs and how her mom was always worried she would fall down them. She told him how she had never been afraid of the stairs, but she never liked the old stone basement, with its dank smells and scary noises. But after her mom had left, her dad had tore the old house and barn down and built the new house and shop on the property.

Climbing the 4 concrete stairs to the front door, Jack laughed as CB ran into the door when she tried to walk right in, only to find it locked. Obviously embarrassed, she told Jack how as a youth the doors had never been locked and it still wasn't something she was accustomed to. Digging out her keys, she let them in.

Inside, they stepped into a large open living space, which was simply decorated and neat. In the living room sat a leather sofa and matching recliner in front of a large flatscreen television mounted to the wall to the left. To the right was a kitchen with a bar, large island and black shiny appliances. As Jack looked around, CB headed through the living room and down a hall beckoning Jack to follow.

In the hall, Jack watched as CB turned into the first door to the left. He also couldn't help but notice the walls on either side of him were adorned with numerous pictures of CB; from birth, throughout school and even a picture of her in her State Police uniform. One photograph in par - ticular caught his attention, a young CB and a pair of girls were smiling in the stands of the high school football game, the field in the background. But visible in the background Jack saw his own number 11 along with Marshall's number 69 chasing an opposing ball carrier towards, the nearest sideline. Jack removed the frame from the wall and carried into the room where CB was.

The room turned out to be an office. Unlike the rest of the house, this room looked much less tidy. There were multiple filing cabinets along the wall to the immediate left and 2 folding tables set up along the walls to form an L at the opposite corner of the room. On the tables was a mess of papers appearing anything but organized. On the walls were pinned various maps and other graphs Jack guessed, given his rudimentary understanding of drilling, were some kind of geolo-gy profiles. CB was sitting in a desk chair and staring at the papers on the table looking lost.

"What's the matter?" Jack asked.

Looking up she looked to be on the verge of tears. "This is a fucking mess. It looks like he has notes from four or five wells he has worked on here. I know he has a system he's explained to me before, but I never really paid attention. He has all these notes on the wells he has done previously and what they needed, his plans and strategy from there. He also has a list of names and random numbers on a ledger. The only problem is there is no rhyme nor reason to this stuff. No addresses or numbers or anything that I can use to figure out where they are currently."

"Are you sure you don't want me to ask Jeremy?" Jack inquired again. "I am sure I can ask it in such a manner to not tip him off."

"NO!" CB said emphatically. "I can't risk it. We are so close. We can't have any missteps now."

Jack understood, though it still rankled him. He was trying to think of another way to find Wren when CB interrupted his thoughts by asking "What's in your hand."

Jacked looked down seeing he still held the framed photograph from the wall. "It's a picture your dad had out there," He said holding it up. "I was wondering when it was taken?"

CB rolled towards him and took the picture from his hand. She studied it and said, "It would have been my freshman year right after I had my braces taken off. Me and the other freshman cheerleaders went to the games to make a good impression on the varsity cheer coach. Why?"

Jack smirked, "Ahhh. So your dad has had picture of me and his boss hanging in his house all these years"

"What are you talking about?" CB asked.

Jack kneeled down to be more level with the photograph, leaning in, and pointed to the back-ground. "See there. Number 11 and 69. That's me and Jeremy, you were a freshman when we were seniors."

CB leaned in to see what he was pointing at but in doing so bumped foreheads with Jack caus-ing them both to jump back a little. They stared at one another a second before they both laughed. A little harder than was probably appropriate for the moment but both were glad to ease the tension in the room. Finally, CB got up and said, "Ok lets go back to the office. This was a waste of time."

Before they left Jack asked, "Do you think you should leave a note or something? I mean don't you think he will recognize someone was there."

After a moment of thought CB agreed and asked Jack if he had a pen and paper which he gave her. She scribbled a note.

'Dad,

I came out to see if you. I need to ask you a question. Call me.

Love, CB.'

Jack watched her run back to the house, fold to the paper and stick it in the door where Thomas should see it. Retiring to the vehicle she told Jack to take her back to her office.

CHAPTER 52

It after noon when the big man finally took time to check his phone. There were multiple text messages, most of which he didn't rate worthy of a reply. However one message caught his eye. "She knows about your man and will get his name and picture out to all the agencies soon. I will delay as much as I can but it wont be long. You may consider getting rid of him because if they get him it wont take long to figure out the rest"

The big man checked when the message had been sent. "Shit" he muttered seeing it was nearly 3 hours prior. Sitting down, he considered what to do. He thought to call Wren and telling him to run, but dismissed the idea quickly knowing Wren would refuse. The big man couldn't count the number of times he had heard Wren say he would never go back to prison and if he were caught he would fight it out, taking as many cops with him as he could.

The big man then tried to think of ways to set Wren up on a collision course with the police but quickly dismissed the idea, knowing there were to many variables, too many ways it could go wrong. Finally, he reasoned he was simply going to have to do it himself and made a plan to make it happen.

CHAPTER 53

Jack and CB made it to the office where CB observed three officers walking into the building carrying fast food bags. Looking at her watch, she saw it was lunch time. "Oh shit, Jack I promised we'd go out for lunch!"

"Oh no, it's ok, I understand your busy today," Jack replied.

"No, its fine Jack. Until we get a Judge to sign off on a search warrant there isn't anything to do right now anyway but sit around and wait. Just let me run in real quick and make sure nothing has happened and then we can go grab something ok?"

Jack nodded in agreement and watched as she ran into the office. While he was glad they were going to have their "date" he knew it was a less than ideal time for it to occur given the circum-stances. He felt bad she was taking the time to have lunch with him. He decided he would take her to a nearby restaurant, T&L Hotdog, a local chain Jack always made it a point to eat at while he was in town. As a child, Jack's dad had always brought he and Bob there. Jack recalled fondly the contests the three of them had to determine who could eat the most. He remembered his personal best was six but afterwards he was so sick he refused to eat there again for months. Jack figured the two of them could grab a quick bite and then he would bring her back so she could return to work.

He was hoping if lunch went well maybe he would ask her out on a real date before he went back to Kansas. However his thoughts were interrupted by a car pulling into the lot driving so fast the tires were screaming turning in. His curiosity piqued, he watched the car, seeing Ashcroft get out and trot briskly to the office door before going in. The hurriedness of the man's actions made Jack think there must be some kind of break in the case. Jack anticipated CB either coming out or sending him a message he could go but it never came. In fact, Jack remained in the truck until he began to think CB had forgotten him. He started the truck and was reaching for his phone when he saw the station door open and CB come marching out. He rolled down his window to talk to her but she instead walked to the passenger side of the truck and got in, surprising him.

"Drive" she said angrily.

Jack put the truck in the gear and asked her what was wrong.

"That asshole Ashcroft. That son of a bitch didn't do one thing while we were gone. He didn't write the search warrant request. He didn't even find Wren's address for Christ's sake," she exclaimed.

"So what was he doing? I mean I watched him come flying back into the office while I was sitting in the parking lot"

"He said he had an informant call him and he had to run out and see him. I asked him what an informant could possibly have to say that was more important than apprehending a murderer but he couldn't tell me. Goddammit, it pisses me off. Anyway I got the warrant written up and he is now working on finding a judge to sign it."

"Oh man, I'm sorry. Are you sure you can be away? I understand if you can't."

"Yeah its good, they know to call me if anything happens. But honestly I have to get out of there because I can't look at Ashcroft right now. I am so pissed off I need a drink for lunch."

Jack wasn't sure if she was joking or not but was saved as they made it to their destination, T&L hotdog. Jack turned into the parking lot and saw it was packed, far busier than he had ever seen it.

His first thought was to pull straight through the parking lot and to go somewhere else until he heard CB say, "Oh I love this place. Go through the drive through and we will take it over to my apartment, it's not far from here." She then quickly added "If that's ok?"

Jack tried not to sound overly happy at the invitation responding "Yeah, that's cool" though he was unsure if he pulled it off. Nonetheless, he got in the drive through line.

Pulling up to the speaker Jack was about to ask CB what she wanted. Before he could ask however, CB unbuckled her seat belt, leaned over the center console held his shoulder for support and spoke loudly into the speaker she wanted 3 hotdogs with hot chili, coleslaw, onions and mustard and a large order of chili cheese fries.

Jack looked at her somewhat taken back when she told him not to judge her because she was stress eating and she hadn't been here in a few years, so she was going to get her money's worth. Jack grinned and then ordered three dogs of his own with chili and cheese, and a bag of chips. The lady on the other end asked about drinks and as Jack turned to CB, she shook her head no telling him she was serious and she was going to have a beer at home once they got there.

After receiving their order, CB provided Jack directions to her apartment. The building was new and hadn't existed when

Jack had lived in the area. She led him up to the second floor where she opened the door marked 2C. The apartment was eerily similar to Jack's own, a small one bedroom unit. There was a galley kitchen to the left of the entry with a small eating bar overlook-ing a small living space which was to the doors right with the bedroom and bathroom to the rear.

It was immaculately clean. However, unlike his own home, the place was very much decorated and color coordinated. While no expert, Jack guessed her bright red couch with golden rivets and gold inlaid wood trim, likely cost as much as all of his furniture combined, though he admit-ted that wasn't a very high bar to exceed. Flanking the couch on either side were two wooden end tables that matched the wooden trim and gold inlay perfectly that would taken the cost up even more.

The couch and tables looked out a large bay window which had blinds though they were pulled up revealing a wooded area. The sight made him pause in the doorway, which CB noticed.

"What's wrong?" she asked.

Jack hesitated momentarily before explaining he didn't like windows, especially ones people could see through from the outside. He was happy when she accepted his simple answer and seemingly didn't judge him at all about it. Instead going to the window, she released the blinds and closed them. For good measure she also closed the curtains though in reality they were made of a sheer red material that would not have been any kind of real deterrent if not for the closed blinds.

"Better?" she asked.

It was Jack told her, though when he closed the door the room became overly dark until CB turned on the lights in the kitchen as she went to the fridge and grabbed two beers. Jack joined her at the bar.

As they sat down Jack said, "I like your furniture," in an attempt to lighten the mood.

CB smiled and replied, "You can thank Dad then. He bought it for me as a housewarming gift after I moved back. I think it looks like it came straight out of a whore house but I could never tell him that. I feel like I have to keep it though."

Unsure how to respond Jack opened the food bag and handed out their meals. He had only taken a few bites of the first hotdog when CB asked him, "Have you ever felt like you're com-pletely ill-equipped to do your job?"

Confused by the question Jack asked her to clarify what she meant.

"Its just this case. I have never been so frustrated about a case in my life. I mean even cases that have gone into the unsolved files have never bothered me like this," she said on the verge of tears, her lips quivering.

Unsure of what to do but wanting to comfort her he said, "I do"

She looked up at him oddly with eyes glossed over by the nearness of tears, "You do what?"

"I know what its like to be unsure if I can do my job," he answered.

She sat back looking even more hurt. "C'mon Jack you are just trying to make me feel better. Your damn jacket says your one of the damn best in the world. I've seen you shoot and you picked stuff up out there on those sights an entire team of forensics experts missed."

Afraid he offended her Jack quickly confessed the reason he was on this particular visit home was because he had been put on a psyche hold by Dr. Hartman. He then explained what had happened in Nebraska; how since, all he could think about was all he had done in Iraq and Af-ghanistan and all the other missions, feelings of guilt, not understanding his place in the uni-verse, his fear of being judged by his unit and worse yet himself. His confession took almost 30 minutes to complete and included little things he had never told Dr. Miller or Pastor Gary.

During the entirety of his confession, CB remained silent looking Jack in the eye, even when Jack arose to continue the rant. Her facial expression evolved for the one of aggravation when she thought he had been mocking her; to a look of surprise; to one of sorrow by the time he was done.

After Jack stopped talking, CB stood, stepped to him and gave him a big hug. Unsure of what do Jack hugged her back, a feeling of relief washed over him. "Confession is truly good for the soul" he muttered to himself.

Hearing his words, CB stepped back from their embrace and looked at him once again. "Jack I am not the most unbiased person on this subject but seriously society needs men like you to protect it from guys like Deen and Wren. You told me about Sergeant Bates and the lessons he passed onto you. My Sergeant Bates, was a man named Lieutenant Walter Murphy, the special agent in command the summer I interned at the ATF. L-T used to say for centuries farmers have used dogs to protect their herds from the wolves and thieves who would like to do their flocks harm. Jack, I think both Sgt. Bates and Lt. Murphy would agree the sheep continue to need protection."

Jack couldn't help but grin and stretch out his arms as an invitation for another hug.

CB stepped forward to embrace him again. "Jack, you were put here to be a protector. You car-ing so much is exactly what makes you so good at what you do. As long as you have that, you have all that you need."

Jack pulled her tighter and responded "You know I think thats true for you too, it what makes you a good investigator and always will"

She looked up at him again, only this time she stretched her face upward to his. He met her halfway and the two shared a kiss. The kiss started tender and sweet but quickly evolved into one of passion and need, aggressive even. Soon thereafter they were each tugging at the oth-er's clothes as each pursued to fulfill long repressed physical needs. They ended near the ex-pensive couch in a tangle of arms, legs and clothes each breathing heavily. Unable to control himself, Jack turned CB forcefully around and ran his hands across her entire body as she backed into him grinding up and down on him breathing heavily. Feeling him she then broke free of hands bent over the back of the red couch, looked over her shoulder at him and bit her bottom lip. The pose was the sexiest Jack had ever seen and he stepped to her where they joined and shared their lusty needs with one another.

CHAPTER 54

Wren had only been asleep a few hours when he was awoken by a frantic pounding on the door of his trailer. He tried to ignore it but the knocking refused to stop and seemed to be shaking the entire structure. Finally, getting out of bed, Wren grabbed a pistol he kept at the bedside and walked towards the front door shouting, "Whoever the fuck you are better have a good goddamn reason for waking me up." Jerking the door open, the man standing there was one of the last people on earth he ever expected to see.

"Ashcroft, what the fuck are you doing here?" Wren exclaimed, looking over the drug agent, the gun still by his side.

"I am here to warn you. You need to fucking disappear and you need to do it now. Greene and that Fed she is running around with know it's you and they are going to have the entire state and more on you in the next few hours. I am trying to give you a head start." Ashcroft spouted out, his entire attention on the gun in Wren's hand, knowing the smaller man's finicky nature.

Wren remained silent, obviously thinking and then raised the weapon to Ashcroft's face. "So why the warning?" he asked. "I mean your a cop too."

"Look man, I felt I owed you that much. We have scratched each other's backs quite a bit over the years and have both made some money off this deal. I just didn't want you to get taken unawares is all." Ashcroft explained shakily.

"What's the matter, you afraid I would tell them of our little arrangement? You afraid I am a rat, you bald bastard?" Wren asked pulling the hammer back on the gun.

Ashcroft swallowed hard before answering in a way he hoped the deranged little killer might understand, "No man. I told you out of respect. Like I said. Shit I haven't even said anything to the boss because I figured you needed to hear it from me. If I thought there was any chance you would turn on me, I would have come up here with a gun and shot you in your bed as you sleep through the fucking window."

Wren continued to look at the man across the barrel of the gun. Though it was really only a moment, to Ashcroft it seemed an eternity, before the man put the gun down. "Fuck!" Wren shouted, "Alright man thanks for the warning. And let me give you one too. From here on I see a cop, I shoot a cop. That includes you. I ain't goin back to prison."

"Fair enough," Ashcroft said before adding, "Wren, you can't shoot em all. Seriously man. If I were you I'd get the hell outta Dodge and go somewhere with a warmer climate."

"Yeah, I will, but not before I take care of something first," Wren said sadistically before turning on his heel, slamming the door in Ashcroft's face.

Ashcroft exhaled loudly, unaware he had been holding his breath. Then remembering Wren's warning he ran back to his car. As he started the engine his hands were shaking.

*****

Two hours after Ashcroft left, Wren stood in his bedroom staring at the items on his bed. A bag of clothes; a bag of cash, more than $40,000; a shoe box full of pills, 3 guns and 8 boxes of ammunition. Not a lot to restart on, but it was enough he decided. He had less when he had been released from prison and he had survived. Hell in his mind he even thrived.

He was sent to prison for talking to the wrong girl and shooting a few deer. But the punishment he received was far beyond any crime he may have committed. Inside, he had been raped and beaten repeatedly, mostly by his cellmate and his friends, who seemingly took great pleasure in his torment. Yet never a rat, he never told a soul of what was happening to him, though he knew the guards knew. If the bruises on his face weren't proof enough, the knowing looks on the guards faces certainly confirmed it.

When he was first released, he was a broken man. Returning to his hometown, the first few months he kept completely to himself. He struggled to find a job finding, with so few willing to hire a convicted felon even though he had plenty of experience work experience. While he picked up some odd jobs here and there working for local farmers and made a minimal subsistence he continued to feel slighted by his circumstances.

Then everything changed. He had just completed work one evening, stretching fence for a local farmer, who had dropped him off at a local store on the edge of town. No sooner had he said goodbye to the farmer when to his surprise he saw his former cellmate walk into the store. At the sight of the man, Wren instinctively hid behind a nearby car. The reflexive action angered him. Fueled by the emotion, he walked to where he had seen the man come into the parking lot and waited for the man to emerge from the store, intent on confronting the man. However, when his former cellmate emerged from the store, carrying a small brown bag, he turned and walked in the opposite direction than he had come in from, away from Wren. Wren followed, still intent on facing the man.

As he followed, Wren watched the man fiddle with the bag and then periodically bring it to his lips as he walked the sidewalk along the main road. After about a half mile, the man turned down a small alley. Afraid of losing him, Wren increased his own pace causing the distance be-tween himself and his former cellmate to close.

Finally sensing someone behind him, the man turned just in time to catch a blow from a pair of fence pliers in the face Wren still carried from the day's work. Fence pliers are used by farmers to string barbed wire fence. One side features a hammer head used for driving staples; the other a clawed hook for pulling fence staples. Wren used the hammer end, striking the man just above the left eyebrow, dropping him to the ground instantly, screaming as he fell. Afraid some-one would hear the screams, Wren bent over and struck the man in the head again, and again, and again, and again until the man stopped making any noise or moving at all. After realizing the man was no longer moving Wren looked closely enough to see his entire head and face were caved in. Understanding the man was obviously dead, Wren ran from the alley to his own home where he remained for the next week.

After the week, he determined the police weren't looking for him. He walked back the same store he had encountered his former cellmate. As he walked a two different police cars rolled by him on the street, neither bothered to give him a second look. Arriving at his detention, the per-son at the counter greeted him as usual and Wren preceded to pick up a few items for his home. As he shopped he grew more and more confident no one was paying him any mind. By the time he got home he was feeling completely empowered. He had gotten away with it! And he didn't feel bad about it at all.

A month later, he ran into Jeremy Marshall, who offered him a job. He was assigned to work for Tony Kincaid's crew. At first, he remained quiet and kept his head down, just happy to be work-ing again but the feeling faded quickly when he had overheard some of the other crews they worked with discussing what they were making. Realizing his old friend was undercutting them on pay, Wren could hep but complain one night when his crew went out for drinks.

Fueled by alcohol and hate, he was on the verge of quitting until Kincaid suggested he could help him earn some more money on the side. Curious, Wren asked how to which Tony explained he had a nice little side business supplying pills to the workers they encountered. Wren joined in becoming a mule for product. Then one day on a site Wren noticed Tony looking very distracted on the rigs, which was very unlike him. When he asked him about it Tony revealed there was a man named Micah Lowe threatening to narc out the operation if Tony didn't give him a cut. Wren said he could take care of it. Three days later, the problem was no more and a new tool was available to Tony Kincaid and his side business. From that point forward Wren became one of Tony's top lieutenants.

It had been a good run, Wren told himself, but all good things must end. He was still trying to figure out exactly what he was going to do when he received a text message from the big man. The message told Wren him to meet the man at his house at 4.

Wren thought he knew what he was going to say, "Leave those cops alone and get the hell out of town". The little man however didn't agree. 'Fuck you and fuck the cops', the little man thought to himself. 'The only good pig was bacon and cops don't qualify' was his moniker. Be-sides the big man didn't have as much to lose as the did. After all it was him pulling the trigger on all those guys. If he was caught, Wren knew it was a straight line to the needle for him. Worse yet he knew death wouldn't come quickly. Death he imagined he could handle, but being stuck in a cage for 20 plus years awaiting his fate, he thought was the real punishment. He would not let that happen. Slowly a plan formed in his head, but to make it work Wren knew he would need to get to the big man's property first.

CHAPTER 55

Wren had been to the larger man's home multiple times. Having walked around the property with the big man, he was very familiar with the terrain. Thus, as he approached the property via the main road instead of turning into the main driveway he drove by it; instead, about a quarter mile past the driveway he turned his truck into another small gravel lane leading to a gate.

While the gate itself was locked preventing him from driving any further, the scrub brush and high grasses on either side of the lane were sufficient to hide the truck. It helped it was fall and the truck's red paint blended in with the foliage, unlike it would have against the vibrant greens of summer. Satisfied the truck was sufficiently hidden, he got out and folded the bench seat for-ward. Behind the seat on a pair of hooks the little man had installed for the purpose sat his pride and joy, the semiautomatic .270 rifle with Nikon scope, which until recently he thought was the nicest shooting rig available. Along with the rifle he grabbed two loaded 15-round magazines and another full box of ammunition.

He did not like leaving his truck here unattended. Momentarily he wished Troy were there to watch his back and be his get away driver again. But knowing there wasn't time and Troy feared the big man thus would be unlikely to go along with the plan anyway, Wren proceeded alone.

Carrying the weapon, he climbed over the gate and made his way across a large open field. He moved hurriedly for while the grass was high along the fence line near the gate the rest of the field had been recently mowed for one last cutting of hay for the winter leaving him exposed. He felt naked and afraid as he covered the open space and it was a feeling he didn't like, making him all the more determined to put the big man down.

Finally he covered the distance to his preferred destination, an area just below the crest of the small ridge line where 3 large boulders protruded from the ground. Amongst the rocks, Wren turned to look the farm over. From his vantage point the little man could see part of the long driveway, the large garage and the house easily. Crawling into a crack between the rocks, he leaned his rifle against the right hand wall of rock before laying down to check the line of sight to the position to where he anticipated his target would be at the house. He judged the distance from where he laid to the steps of the house to be roughly 350 yards. Beyond the house he could view roughly 20 yards of driveway; enough to give him ample warning of the man's approach. Confident in his position and the distance to his target, Wren settled down to wait for the arrival of the big man.

His plan was similar to those he had used previously. Once the big man arrived home, Wren would take him down as he walked from his truck to his front porch. He knew the space from the end of the drive to the steps was roughly 30 feet. He hoped as he had done previously he would catch him unsuspecting halfway between the truck and the house without cover — giving him a margin of error should he miss. While he didn't plan on missing he wasn't so dumb as to not plan for the possibility either. As he waited the little man considered other possibilities but couldn't see any holes in the plan. One thing he had figured out in life, the simpler the plan, the better.

He hadn't been waiting long when from out of the trees along the driveway he saw the big man's truck emerge. As the truck approached, he settled in behind his rifle and took up a comfortable firing position awaiting the man to step from the truck. Through his scope, he took his aim across the line of travel along the sidewalk leading from the end of the drive to the house. Waiting for his prey to walk from the truck to his home and into the cross hairs.

This was always his favorite part, playing the role of God and choosing when his victim was going to die. The power was like no drug he had ever tried and he could feel the adrenaline course through his veins. A smile formed at the corners of his mouth as waited for the big man to enter his crosshairs as he whispered "you ain't gonna be nobody's boss no more."

However, nothing happened. After a quick internal debate about whether or not to break his position and sight picture, the small man removed his cheek from the stock of the rifle and looked towards the truck where he saw the big man just sitting inside unmoving. "What the fuck!" Wren muttered having never considered the big man wouldn't go into his house.

As the adrenaline rush left him he began to consider the development. Thinking on it he became angered; realizing the big man had no intention of inviting him into his home, though he had been inside previously. Frustrated and upset Wren took aim at the truck watching as the big man briefly began fidgeting around inside. Unable to figure out what the big man was doing; Wren continued to watch mesmerized by the strange movements, until finally he saw the man produce an old flip phone. "Cheap bastard," he whispered as he continued watching the man play with the keys for a moment before flipping it closed and placing it on the dash.

No sooner had his target leaned back in his seat than Wren's phone chimed in his pocket, sounding loud in the enclosed space echoing off the rocks around him. "Goddamnit!" Wren cursed, rolling over to retrieve the phone. Removing his phone from his pocket, he saw the big man had sent him a text, "Where u at?" With a wry smile, the little man thought, 'you'll never know you fat bastard'.

Phone off and angry, Wren took aim at the man through the windshield. Growing up hunting deer along the hills of the area and from tree stands Wren knew because he was above his tar-get he needed to aim low to compensate, which he did. As he did he was reminded how the through a windshield it had not gone well. He still did not understand why, but knew the rounds were not hitting where he aimed though he had checked his rifle again a few days later at the range and found it was still zeroed in. Since he had simply avoided shooting through glass — the simpler, the better. Nonetheless Wren took aim now. His first inclination was to try for a head shot but decided against it; again flashing back to his previous failure shooting through glass. Lowering the crosshairs to align with the center of the man's chest Wren angrily jerked the trigger.

CHAPTER 56

After sending the text, the big man continued to sit in his truck awaiting the little man's arrival. In his lap was a big .357 revolver. He left the truck running and the music playing on the radio trying to not think about what he was about to do, though he had decided it was necessary. While he was a man who would regularly sing along to the radio while alone, today his mind was fixed upon other issues. Primarily how he had gotten into this mess. He knew the walls were closing in on him. He also knew he had to fix it and the first step was taking down Wren. The two had never been friendly but tolerated each other when Kincaid was in charge each appreciating the other was needed. The big man for the logistics, the small man for keeping people in line.

As he contemplated all that had occurred in the last few years the windshield in front of him suddenly spider veined. As his brain registered the broken glass he felt a stabbing, burning pain in his abdomen. Instinctually he bent over, clutching his stomach with his hands, feeling a warm stickiness. Looking down and seeing the blood, he felt another burn across his massive left shoulder and down his back.

This time he leaned right and fell headlong into the truck's center console. Looking up, more holes suddenly appeared in the windshield above him. "Son-of-a-bitch, that little mother fucker is going to kill me" he thought. With the realization he determined he had only one choice.

CHAPTER 57

CB and Jack were sitting together on the couch still out of breath, sweaty and in various stages of undress, neither speaking. Both to nervous to discuss what they had just shared, yet neither wanting to part and acknowledge the moment was likely as fleeting as two ships passing in the night. The uncomfortable silence was broken by the buzz of a phone vibrating on the floor. Both jumped and quickly dug through the clothes on the floor to find their phones, thankful for the re-prieve. Finally tossing aside Jack's shirt CB found her phone and snatched it up. Staring at the screen she saw it was her father.

"Hello," she answered.

"Baby girl," Thomas half groaned / half whispered.

Immediately sensing something wasn't right CB asked, "Dad what's wrong?"

As Thomas was answering the sound of his voice was interrupted by the sound of popping and what sounding like glass cracking. "Fuck!" Thomas yelled into the phone.

"Dad!" CB screamed sensing the angst in his voice.

"Baby girl. I done bad and right now I'm gettin shot at".

"Oh my God, Dad where are you? Are you hit?"

"I… I'm in the driveway in front of the house and yes I am hit. Wren is out there somewhere shooting the shit out of my truck" he said sounding weaker than he had seconds ago.

"Ok, ok. Sit tight we are on our way. Just stay with me" CB pleaded.

"No baby girl. He's a killer. He's the man you are looking for. Always has been."

"What? Dad you aren't making any sense. Just hold on we will be there" CB said hitting Jack in the chest while grabbing the remainder of her clothes from the floor; doing her best to put them on while keeping the phone to her ear. Hearing the pain in her voice and seeing her reaction Jack followed suit, dressing hurriedly.

While the pair were dressing Thomas responded softly "Catherine. No, it's to dangerous. He has his gun and is still shooting. He isn't going to let you get in here without shooting. You need to call in the swat team to ferret him out."

"No Dad, we are coming. Just hold on," she pleaded.

But the only response was the sound of more shots and an indistinguishable thunk.

*****

As Thomas was pleading with his daughter to not come the shooting stopped, which he assumed meant Wren was reloading. In the reprieve he sat up with the intent to flee. However no sooner had he gotten his hand on the selector lever on the steering column the shots began anew. Instinctively he dove back down into the floor, dropping the phone but in doing slammed the truck into drive. Because of his size, when diving into the floor board, seeking protection from the hail of bullets his left knee pushed into the gas pedal causing the large V-10 motor to roar. The truck blasted forward, spinning gravel from the driveway. From the floor board Thomas felt the truck surge forward, giving him hope, thinking that moving was better than sit-ting still.

But the feeling was short-lived when the truck hit something hard. The jolt had further shifted him within the cab, taking his weight from the gas pedal and onto the brake bringing the big truck to a full halt. The stopping place so precarious the truck's passenger side was left elected to such a degree, Thomas was sure the truck was about to roll over on the driver's side.

******

With the first shot, Wren knew he hadn't made a kill shot. Seeing Thomas's big body jump but continue to move within the cab to of the truck confirmed it. Wren consciously thought it sure as hell wasn't like the movies, bullets didn't go through glass and stay on a true line. With the realization, he put the full effect of having a semiautomatic rifle to use, pulling the trigger as fast as he could without truly aiming, but systematically sending bullets into the windshield until the rifle was empty. His magazine empty, he took a moment to look through the scope and saw Thomas still moving!

As quickly as he could, he reloaded, knowing his time was limited. Reloaded, he immediately took aim and began pulling the trigger.

However, as soon as he fired the truck shot forward. Wren watched as the truck plowed forward into the concrete stairs tilting the truck so severely it was near rolling over but miraculously stopped, both its roll and its forward momentum.

Taking a moment to peer through the scope Wren studied the cab of the truck but was unable to see anything inside. He knew Thomas was ducked down again, but this time he wasn't going to let him try to drive away and thus began firing into the big truck's hood and grill with the intent on disabling it.

CHAPTER 58

Jack drove, realizing CB was to hysterical. Driving as fast as he could without crashing, the tires squealing around each turn in the road as they fought to stay attached to the ground, Jack made it to the driveway in just over ten minutes. Despite the bleating of the tires, CB had plead for Jack to go faster as she white knuckled the door handle and center console, until finally Jack took the left hand turn into driveway of the property.

The driveway remained long, along the side of the rolling hill, with a grove of trees to the left and field to the right. Clearing the final bend in the drive Jack looked up the small hill to see the house. Jack's senses immediately went on edge as he saw Thomas's big truck sitting haphazardly in front of the house. Stopping to study the situation closer he saw, the large truck was parked at a nearly impossible angle with the passenger side front and rear tire sitting on the concrete stairs of the home's porch, with the other rear tire on the side walk leading to the stairs and drivers side front tire in the grass. The elevation of the passenger side made the truck look as if it were on the cusp of rolling over. The degree of the angle was reinforced by the open dri-ver's door which looked to have been half buried in the soft earth of the home's lawn.

Studying closer still, he saw the trucks windows were full of holes. Holes Jack instinctively knew were from bullets. Upon recognizing the holes, Jack threw his truck into park so they could come up with a plan of rescue. However, before he could complete the shift, CB was out and running towards the white truck.

******

At the site of the truck with its windows shattered CB could no longer control her emotions. Without thinking as soon as she felt the truck drawing to a stop, she was out the door and sprinting up the slight grade of the hill towards the house. Taking a straight line towards the open door she called out "Dad!" She was running so singularly focused on the truck she tripped on the side walk. As she went down she heard a loud explosion.

*****

Jack finished putting the truck in park and watched after CB as she ran towards the open truck door. He heard her scream "Dad!" when the sound of a rifle cracked. To his horror Jack watched her fall into a heap behind the truck. However, he didn't have much time to dwell as immediately the sound of a second, third and fourth shot shattered the air as more glass flew from the truck's windows.

On the ground, CB was stunned by what had happened, though the sound of another explosion of glass made it clear. Wren was up on the hill and still shooting. Lying there, she understood tripping on the sidewalk had likely saved her life or at least from a serious injury knowing one of those rounds was likely meant for her. She also recognized she was still exposed and needed to find cover. Looking she saw the closest cover was behind the truck. Staying low, CB crawled closer to the truck as more gun fire erupted.

Climbing from his truck, Jack saw CB moving along the ground towards her dad's truck as more gun fire sounded. 'Good Girl, now stay there' Jack thought to himself, relieved she was still alive, though still unsure if she was wounded but comforted somewhat that she appeared to be moving okay.

While his instinct was to go and drag her out of there, his training took over. Jack knew until the danger was removed from the field either by death or retreat, CB, her father, and himself remained at risk. The thought made Jack angry. Using the anger as motivation he decided it was time to give the hidden shooter a taste of his own medicine.

Carefully, opening the rear door of his truck Jack pushed the rear seat skyward, revealing the box beneath. Quickly he popped the latch, opened the lid and removed the sniper rifle. Rifle in hand, Jack attached the weapon's tactical optics, bi-pod and sling. After a quick double check to ensure all was secured properly, Jack slung the rifle on his back; grabbed two magazines, a box of ammunition and stalked into the tree line.

In the tree line, Jack began feeding bullets into the two magazines. Instinctively, he utilized the cover of the trees to move towards the edge of the small wood where he hoped to find a better position to see what was happening in the yard to CB and her father and where the shooter was hidden. As he moved toward's the edge of the wood he was trying to form a mental image of the scene from his previous visit. He couldn't remember much beyond the house, garage, yard and the mowed fields beyond the house.

Taking the little he remembered about the place he cross referenced in his mind what he knew about Wren's modus operandi. The man liked to work from ambush; preferably from a safe distance. He also knew the man always left himself an easy means of escape. Knowing a leopard didn't change his spots Jack quickly formed a theory of where Wren could be.

Finally, arriving at the small wood's edge, with his magazines loaded he confirmed the mental images from his memory: house, garage, yard and field. He saw CB had remained in the rela-tive safety under Thomas's big truck, with the house to her right providing even more cover. Jack could also see Thomas's big feet hanging from the open door of the truck. They appeared to be slightly pistoning back and forth, which Jack knew from the battlefield people did while they are in pain. Yet, it also meant the man was still alive and relatively protected from further attack unless the shooter had moved. Satisfied with their safety, Jack began to search for the shooter.

Based upon his theory Wren would continue to work in the same manner he had previously and the trajectory of the bullets Jack had seen from the driver's seat of his truck he could see but two possibilities of where Wren could be hidden: along the ridge line, hidden in the grass or a little closer in the rock outcropping further down the hill. All Jack needed was for the man to move and show himself or shoot again and give his position away.

CHAPTER 59

"Damn it" Wren cussed himself for not killing Thomas "Why hadn't the man gotten out of his truck and walked to his house," he muttered briefly, "this would all be done and I'd already be in Pennsylvania on the way to Canada." Angrier still and frustrated he began to load another magazine, intent on finishing the job, refusing to leave the man alive.

What was worse was now Wren thought was Thomas's bitch cop daughter was down there. And though he vowed to kill every cop he saw before he would go to jail again he knew killing a cop, would up the stakes greatly. Killing a cop meant every cop alive would be hunting him. More importantly, her presence meant more cops were likely to be on the way and he needed to act fast if he was going to get out of there. Once again he wished he had called Troy and had him ready to drive the getaway car again. "Shit," he cursed.

Refocusing, Wren knew Thomas was hit, but he didn't think badly the way the man had driven the truck had forward moments ago. He also knew CB had fallen behind the truck. He felt sure he had at least wounded her, having seen her fall under his last burst of firing, but he wasn't sure if she were dead because his line of sight was blocked by the truck.

To finish the job, Wren knew he would have to move to get to them. He knew he needed to do so quickly, sure more cops were on their way.

Having reloaded the gun he looked and saw he had but a few rounds left in the box. He decided to be sure he would need get closer. Arising from his resting place he moved forward to the opening of the crevice ensuring he kept himself along the side wall. Keeping his head down he peered out looking for another nest where he could get to the two he had pinned down behind the truck. Seeing nothing between himself and his prey but freshly cut field and fence posts he decided he needed to make his way along the ridge then to the bottom of the hill into the trees that went all the way down the driveway and flank the pair. Destination decided Wren slinked back into the crack and took a deep breath, ready to make his move.

He was just about to stand when he was suddenly struck with the realization, 'if CB was down there that also meant Jack probably would be too'. "Shit" he cursed aloud remembering how the man could shoot. He wondered if the man had the fancy rifle with him and if he was already down there aiming for the position, the thought paralyzing him.

******

The shooting having momentarily ceased, CB was trying to figure out how to get to her father without exposing herself to more gun fire. In the silence she heard the faint sound of sirens in the back ground. The sound was a huge relief and she yelled "Hold on dad, help's coming!"

******

In some dark recess of his mind, Thomas heard his daughter's voice and it brought him to a higher level of consciousness, though he wasn't quite sure if he actually heard it or if it was his imagination. He wanted to call back to her and warn her to get away but before he could he suddenly heard another sound, the distinct shrill of sirens. "Shit," he muttered, thinking his daughter never did listen to him. Nonetheless, the corners of his mouth turned upward in a small grin.

******

Jack was in the prone, scanning the rocks and hill side through his scope for a target when the sounds of the sirens came to him. The sound sent an icy chill through him. He couldn't let them ride into a damn ambush he thought, before changing the thought to he wouldn't let them ride into an ambush. Refocused he began his search anew.

******

The sound of sirens hit Wren last and woke him from his frozen state. "Fuck" he cursed aloud, reminding himself he wasn't going to go back to jail. Steeling himself for what was about to hap-pen, he checked the rifle one last time, ensuring it was fully loaded and crept forward to take aim on the driveway.

******

CB was watching the drive as the first car, with its light bar flashing and its sirens blaring came into view around Jack's truck. The sight made her momentarily forget what was going on around her and she rose from her hiding spot behind the truck and race to her dad's side.

******

Wren got forward and was aiming towards the driveway when he suddenly saw the girl arise from behind the big truck and start forward. "Oh no you don't bitch," he yelled as he adjusted his aim from the car entering the drive to her as he quickly began taking up the slack on the trigger.

******

Scanning for his target Jack could hear the sirens getting closer, sounding damn near on top of him. Finally he saw a flicker of movement in the rocks. Adjusting slightly he peered through the scope of his rifle. There in the rocks he saw his former friend aiming a rifle. In that moment, Jack closed everything out; no more sirens, no wayward thoughts about CB or Thomas, only the target. His vision tunneled and all he saw was the cross hairs and the target. Forced his breathing and his heartbeat to slow, he took another half breath and slowly let it out relaxing his mind and body as his padded finger found the trigger.

Even over the sound of the sirens, the sound of the gunshot was clear to all.

******

The sound of the gunshot took CB by complete surprise and she dove for cover once again. On the ground she looked and patted herself all over trying to feel or see anywhere she could have been hit. Nothing!

******

Wren was sure he was finally about to get her when his entire world went black as his body fell back into the crevice in the rocks, the rifle falling from his hand.

CHAPTER 60

The sound of the first round had yet to fully dissipate and Jack had already worked the bolt chambering another round. Just as quickly he attempted to require the target but saw nothing through the scope. Scanning the area, Jack located the rifle Wren had been holding laying on the ground beyond the crack, though he was not able to see Wren. While he was fairly certain he had made the shot, he didn't like being unable to confirm the man was indeed neutralized, thus he continued to hold his position. He also couldn't help but wonder if Troy was lurking around.

He would have held the position longer but for hearing the commotion going on above him, including someone calling his name. Though it irked him in every bone of his body as a professional, he finally relented and made his way back up to his truck. At the edge of the woods, from behind a tree, he called out to the officers standing along the driveway, fearing they may be on edge and shoot him. Having their attention, he identified himself and told them he was armed. At their direction, he laid down both his rifle and his pistol before emerging from the woods. One officer retrieved the weapons while the other guided him to where a small group of officers were gathered. Jack did not see CB among them, though he recognized Ashcroft and a few other officers from the times he had been at the station.

He explained to the group who he was and after a moment of hesitation Ashcroft acknowledged he knew of him. Jack then told his account of how he and CB had driven here after her father had called her in distress and how they had taken fire upon arrival. He then explained he had made his way into the trees and had just fired a single round at the man with a rifle who was in the rocks on the hill above them as the first responders arrived. He reported he believed the man disabled while his rifle on the ground below the rocks.

When asked what took him so long to reveal himself, Jack told them that he was trying to continue to hold over-watch for the group. He also told them he was unsure if there was another bogey in the area but had seen no further movement from the rocks.

The man who appeared to be in charge then dispatched a group of officers to check it out. Jack offered to take up over-watch for them again but the commander declined the invitation, which Jack understood given the circumstances. Nonetheless, Jack was permitted to stay with the commander; thus he was able to monitor the communications of the group as they investigated the rifle and rock pile. Jack heard the team confirm there was a man down in the rocks from what appeared to be a bullet to the head. He further learned Thomas was in transit to the local hospital and CB was in the ambulance with him. The early report said while there was a lot of blood in the truck, Thomas Green was still alive and the paramedics were hopeful he would still pull through. By happenstance as the report came over the radio Jack was standing near Ashcroft, whom he thought he had saw mumble something under his breath. Jack wasn't sure what exactly the man said — he hoped a prayer.

Sometime later as the command group awaited the coroner to collect the body from the rocks, Jack heard another car approaching on the gravel drive. Turning to see who was coming he was surprised to see a big black Tahoe approaching. The big SUV was eerily similar to the one his team drove and screamed Feds. Watching the truck come to a stop and all four doors opened. Climbing from the vehicle were 4 men wearing DEA jackets, two of whom were carrying weapons at the ready, looking as if they were more than ready to use them. Looking closer, Jack noted three of the men were complete strangers, the fourth however was someone Jack knew: Jaime. Catching Jack's eye, Jaime nodded as way of acknowledgement.

The four men marched straight into the command circle of county and state officers where Jack had been standing. The eldest appearing of the four men flashed his credentials and asked who was in charge. The same trooper who had allowed Jack to stay nearby stated he was in charge, though the quiver in his voice undermined any presence of authority he may have had previously. The DEA agent informed the officer in charge, the DEA was now taking control of the scene and asked the officer to please continue to secure the area until a field team from their agency could arrive to process the evidence.

Then unexpectedly the DEA man told the two men carrying their weapons to take Ashcroft into custody. The two armed officers moved quickly to secure Ashcroft who didn't even say anything. Though many of the others did.

As the officers continued their protest Jaime caught Jack's attention and motioned subtly to with his head asking him to follow. Jack followed Jaime to his own truck where Jaime put down the tailgate, hopped up and took a seat. Jack followed suit.

"Been a long time Jack. I wished we'd have met again under different circumstances," Jaime said as his feet dangled.

Still unsure of what was occurring Jack shook his head before finally asking, "You wanna do me a favor and actually tell me what is going on and where you fit in into all of this?"

Jaime spent the next 30 minutes catching Jack up. He told Jack after high school he had joined the Air Force becoming a member of their para rescue group, the Air Force's Special

Force's branch. It is the job of the para rescue to jump into hostile and hazardous environments to res-cue those in harms way. Similar to Jack, as he was getting out he had been recruited by the DEA and had been an agent with them since he was discharged from the military.

He went on to explain the local area had popped up on the radar as part of a huge pharmaceutical investigation. Recently, the DEA had deployed agents to the area as part of a task force that coordinated with state and local officials to break the ring. The task force's work had paid off fairly quickly and within months of being on the ground they had been able to identify Tony Kincaid as a person of interest and had taken him into custody. What the task force hadn't anticipated however, was Kincaid's immediate execution once in custody.

The killing appeared to have been a well coordinated hit even though the task force had been ordered to protect Kincaid's identity. That was particularly concerning to his bosses because there wasn't but a handful of people inside the task force to know Kincaid was even in custody or where he was housed. Shortly after Kincaid was killed, the original task force disbanded, their key capture now gone.

However, the DEA wasn't so willing to give up its investigation into either the drug ring or how Kincaid had died. It was then Jaimie explained his superiors asked him if he had stayed in con-tact with anyone from the area. He told them no, he had lost touch with everyone since his father passed away and his mother had moved to Florida with her sister; explaining he had no reason to come back to the area otherwise; never being overly social to begin with. Satisfied with his answer, his superiors asked if Jaimie would be willing to go in undercover leveraging the connections he already had in the area from growing up in the region. Though he had never worked under cover operations before he had agreed to do so and had been conducting the investigation since.

As part of the investigation, the DEA had been running wire taps on Ashcroft's phone for the last few months. They had gathered enough details from the overheard conversations to know Ashcroft was dirty but had been unable to ascertain who the new drug boss was because the person was smart; using burner phones that he used but rarely, changing them out often. How-ever, that morning they had finally caught a break. After CB called Ashcroft, he subsequently called a number he never called previously but then sent a text and made a phone call to a number already on one of their watch lists from the task force days: Wren. Afterwards Jaimie went to Wren's trailer, where he witnessed the interaction amongst the two men. He asked his handler if he should detain Wren but was told to stick with Ashcroft until they were able to get the arrest warrant together, which he just saw them execute.

Jack nodded at the explanation and then asked about Troy and Jeremy's roles in the operation. Jaimie apologized and told Jack he wasn't really permitted to divulge anything else because the investigation was on going. However he did say Troy was already in custody as a team had picked him up before they made it out here, apparently waking him from a deep sleep and detaining him without incident. He added he didn't think Jeremy would have much to worry about beyond needing to bring on new foremen and crews. Jack nodded in understanding and told Jaimie he would be in town a few more days if he wanted to get a beer and catch up for real. Jaimie told him it sounded good and they exchanged numbers.

Jack remained at the scene a while longer until he was finally directed to drive back to the State Police Barracks where he would need to be debriefed. He spent the better part of the night answering the same questions about what happened over and over again from the State Police, DEA and FBI who were now in on the investigation. He was surprised by the fact the feelings he had after Nebraska were not present. Instead he felt secure in his actions, knowing if not for him it was likely CB, Thomas and other responding officers would have been killed.

Near midnight, Jack received a call from Captain Dickson. After a long discussion, much of which was Dickson complaining about Jack being the only person he had ever heard of who could be on suspension and be involved in such a mess. Yet Captain Dickson conceded from all he had been told it sounded like Jack had done the right thing and he looked forward to working with him again soon after Dr. Hartman cleared him. Finally, at almost 4 am he was told he could go home. In the parking lot before he left he sent CB a text message and asked for her to get a hold of him when she could.

When he finally got to his parents house he went straight to his room and fell into the bed with-out bothering to get undressed. He slept the sleep of the of the dead. If he dreamt he did not remember it.

CHAPTER 61

He was finally awoken at 11:45 am by his ringing phone. He answered without checking anticipating it was CB. He was surprised however, when he heard the voice of Dr. Hartman. "Good morning Jack, Captain Dickson informed me of what happened and I just wanted to check in and see how you were managing" she said.

Jack told her he was doing fine through the fog of sleep. She then asked if he could explain to her what happened though she said she would understand if he were not yet ready. He told her he didn't mind and walked her through the events. He explained the situation as he saw it be-fore concluding his actions were more than justified, stating matter-of-factly there was no alter-native or else others would have been hurt or killed.

She then asked him if it mattered the person he had killed was his former friend.

He paused before he answered. "Doc that wasn't the same person I knew back then. He may have been in the same body but he wasn't the same person. And even if it were, the minute he took up a weapon and was actively firing upon others he was just another bad guy." He said dryly.

Dr. Hartman was silent on the other end of the phone for a moment but Jack allowed the silence hang in the air. Finally, she responded. "Jack I think that is about as good a perspective as you can have in your position. I will see you in a couple of weeks with your list. We will discuss it and get you back to work. I have already heard there are some guys on your team complaining you're not there."

The comment made Jack feel appreciated and it was just another reinforcement for what he did.

He thanked Dr. Hartman for checking in and told her he would see her soon.

Sunday morning Jack went to church with his parents again. They arrived about 15 minutes early and walking in Jack was surprised to see Jeremy Marshall near the front congregating with a number of the church elders like it was any other Sunday. It was also obvious to Jack that Mar-shall had seen him. His suspicions were confirmed as the big man excused himself from the conversation he was in and walked the aisle towards Jack, his hand outstretched.

Skeptically Jack shook the bigger man's hand as Marshall said, "Glad you could join us today."

"Of course" Jack said, unsure of what else to say to the man.

After a moment, Marshall continued somewhat awkwardly, "Jack, I just want you to know your my oldest friend and even though my attorney says I shouldn't talk about anything I want you to know I truly had nothing to do with what those guys were doing. I don't really care what a lot of people think of me, but your one of the few I do."

Jack contemplated before responding "I appreciate that Jeremy. I really do but I don't live here man, and likely never will again. But your in a position to make a true difference in the community and I just hope you learned something from all this and can use your influence to make a difference."

Jeremy seemed to think over what Jack had said for a minute and then stuck his hand out once more "I just wanted to let you know. Take care of yourself" he said before returning to the front of the auditorium and taking his seat.

The service was good once again. As usual, Jack felt Gary was speaking directly to him. He prefaced the sermon with a brief discussion of what had occurred in the community in the months prior and then pleaded with the congregation to look after one another as he quoted: "Be sober-minded; be watchful. Your adversary the devil prowls around like a roaring lion, seeking someone to devour." 1 Peter 5:8."

Gary then led a sermon about the shepherd and his flock based in the book of First Peter, be-fore coming full-circle and finishing the sermon by telling the congregation to not forsake the officers in the community who try to serve even when they all know that there are a few bad apples. He concluded the morning's lesson quoting Romans 13:4 "For he [the soldier] is God's servant for your good. But if you do wrong, be afraid, for he does not bear the sword in vain. For he is the servant of God, an avenger who carries out God's wrath on the wrongdoer".

As he was making his way to the door to leave Jack was thanked by a number of the parishioners, some whom he knew but many he did not, for his service and all he had done and continued to do to keep them safe. When at last he made it to the door, Gary was there. Shaking Jack's hand firmly, Gary reminded Jack should he ever need to talk his door was always open. Gary even handed Jack a card telling him his cell number was on it and he was more than happy to speak with him even after he returned to Kansas City. Jack thanked him sincerely and made his way out the door towards the parking lot.

CHAPTER 62

As he was making his way across the lot he pulled out his phone and turned it back on. It immediately chimed and buzzed multiple times informing him he had messages. Looking it showed he had 4 messages, all from CB. The first was an apology for not having contacted him sooner. The second was asking if he would like to meet up later that day. The third was a qualifying statement that she understood if he didn't. And finally the fourth was thanking him for saving her and her father.

He quickly text her back saying he had been in church and he would like to see her when she was available. She responded immediately asking if he could come and meet her at the hospital. He agreed and told her he would be there shortly.

In the hospital parking lot he text her letting her know of his arrival and asking what room she was in. She replied she would meet him in the lobby at the coffee shop, saying she needed one.

He went to the stand and ordered two large coffees, black. The barista was just handing him the cardboard cups when CB appeared at his side. He handed her one of the cups and she thanked him.

Though she looked tired, he still thought she was one of the prettiest women he had ever met. He gladly followed as she beckoned him to come with her. She led them outside into a small garden area with benches where she sat. He took a seat next to her.

Without looking up she thanked him once again.

Jack ignored the statement and asked, "How's your dad?"

"The doctors say he will likely be able to be discharged in a few more days. He lost a lot of blood and had multiple wounds in the belly so they ended up taking out some of his intestines and putting him back together. They were afraid of infection for a while but it appears he avoid-ed it".

"That's good," Jack said. "What's going to happen to him?"

"That's kinda what I wanted to talk to you about. The DEA has offered him a deal that if he will testify against his suppliers they will place him in witness protection. They didn't say it but I think part of the reason is because I was the lead investigator on the case and the evidence can all arguably be tainted and it could be hard to get a conviction. Jaime told me he only has 48 hours to take the offer or they will pass it on to Troy, though they know Troy doesn't know as much nor are they sure if he will even talk."

"What's your dad saying?"

"I don't know. He feels bad about all that happened."

"I'm sure," Jack said though it came out more skeptically than he attended.

CB though didn't get defensive about it saying, "I know. He says it's not quite how it appears. He said that when Tony Kincaid first got him the gig with Jeremy Marshall he was in debt up to his eye balls with the house and legal costs and Marshall wasn't paying him enough to cover everything. Then Kincaid offered to bring him in on another thing he had going. Turns out he was operating a huge drug distribution ring throughout the oil fields. Because Marshall's company dealt with all kinds of companies, they made a ton of contacts and their ability to get in and out of the rigs all over made for the perfect cover. At first dad was just a distributor for Tony but by the time Tony was arrested he was his right hand man and in charge of the logistics for the ring; making good money at it. When Tony got arrested and killed, the people Tony was working with asked dad to take over, or else. He did, which left Wren as the enforcer. Dad swears it was the bosses who began ordering the hit on Roberts. Saying Dad needed to send a message that just because someone new was in charge they weren't going to be able to get over on old debts.

He also said all the guys who died were in deep, real deep. To make matters worse, Wren en-joyed being the enforcer and the taking of lives. Said he was like a wolf who had gotten the taste of blood and that the only way he would have ever been stopped was by being killed. But that is his tale. Now I don't know if he is going to take the amnesty offer or not but I know either way it's unlikely I will ever see him again, whether he goes into witness protection or prison."

"I am truly sorry," Jack said unsure of what else to say.

"Thank you," she replied.

The two sat in silence for a bit more before CB asked Jack how he was doing. He told her honestly better than her. She nodded, then bent in and kissed him on the cheek. She then thanked him again and asked if maybe she could get a hold of him sometime after all the stuff with her dad was cleared up. Jack told her he would like that. They sat on the bench and finished their coffees before she told him she had to get back up to her dad. Before they parted ways CB hugged Jack and kissed him on the cheek again. Jack left the hospital and returned to his parents house where he stayed for another few days.

Three weeks later, Jack found himself in a conference room in Kansas City Missouri, sitting in his regular chair in the corner away from the windows as Captain Dickson opened a team meeting by welcoming Jack back to full duty status. Jack's team gave a friendly round of applause and Jack sat back in his chair happy to be where he was, back to doing the thing he was best at.